Y0-BXV-157

3 1833 05381 2613

Getting in is easy.

Into the ruins, into the enemy camp, into trouble . . .

"So what are you hunting in these ruins with Toram's god-sight goat?" Archlis repeated the odd phrase, gesturing with the tip of his metal crutch at Kid, who cringed away as though he expected it to spit fire at him.

"What do you think we seek?" Sanval answered question with question, his voice very steady and low, even as he took a half-step in front of Kid, sheltering the little thief behind his well-armored back.

"I am the magelord Archlis, the terror of Fottergrim's army," snapped the wizard. "Do not play games with me, little captain from Procampur."

"I am Sanval Nerias Moealim Hugerand Filao-Trious Semmenio Illuskia Hyacinth Neme Auniomaro Valorous, a captain of Procampur's army." Sanval drew a deep breath after that recital. "I can say with complete honesty that I did not enter these ruins to capture you." Sanval's expression showed no more emotion on his handsome face than he had when confronted with Mumchance's leaping pack of mutts at the camp. His Procampur training in courtesy still held, even as the long-nosed Archlis sneered at him. "And I never play games with wizards."

It's getting out again that's hard.

JAN 1 1 2008

SCIENCE FICTION
FANTASY

FORGOTTEN REALMS

THE DUNGEONS

DEPTHS OF MADNESS
Erik Scott de Bie

THE HOWLING DELVE
Jaleigh Johnson

STARDEEP
Bruce R. Cordell

CRYPT OF THE MOANING DIAMOND
Rosemary Jones

THE DUNGEONS

CRYPT OF THE MOANING DIAMOND

Rosemary Jones

The Dungeons
CRYPT OF THE MOANING DIAMOND

©2007 Wizards of the Coast, Inc.

All characters in this book are fictitious. Any resemblance to actual persons, living or dead, is purely coincidental.

This book is protected under the copyright laws of the United States of America. Any reproduction or unauthorized use of the material or artwork contained herein is prohibited without the express written permission of Wizards of the Coast, Inc.

Published by Wizards of the Coast, Inc. FORGOTTEN REALMS, WIZARDS OF THE COAST, and their respective logos are trademarks of Wizards of the Coast, Inc., in the U.S.A. and other countries.

All Wizards of the Coast characters, character names, and the distinctive likenesses thereof are property of Wizards of the Coast, Inc.

Printed in the U.S.A.

The sale of this book without its cover has not been authorized by the publisher. If you purchased this book without a cover, you should be aware that neither the author nor the publisher has received payment for this "stripped book."

Cover art by Erik Gist and Meadow Gist
First Printing: December 2007

9 8 7 6 5 4 3 2 1

ISBN: 978-0-7869-4714-0
620- 21533740-001-EN

U.S., CANADA,
ASIA, PACIFIC, & LATIN AMERICA
Wizards of the Coast, Inc.
P.O. Box 707
Renton, WA 98057-0707
+1-800-324-6496

EUROPEAN HEADQUARTERS
Hasbro UK Ltd
Caswell Way
Newport, Gwent NP9 0YH
GREAT BRITAIN
Save this address for your records.

Visit our web site at www.wizards.com

Dedicated with grateful thanks to:

Diane McClure Jones, for always patient editing,
wonderful action ideas, and working on the *other* book
without me.

Michael Hacker, for a diamond, a corpse, Realmslore,
and chats about writing.

And, with great sorrow that he did not see this one,
Robert Eugene Jones.

CHAPTER ONE

Ivy punched the camel. It backed out of her tent and stood with its big, shaggy brown head still sticking through the opening. Its large half-closed eyes stared at her, and it opened its mouth and rolled its lips back over huge yellowed teeth. Ivy hit the creature again, square on the nose, and the camel sidestepped—wide-bottomed feet on skinny legs—onto the equally wide feet of its screaming owner.

The camel's driver took a swipe at Ivy as she emerged from her tent, swinging his open palm to slap the impudent female abusing his camel. He shouted something that Ivy decided was uncivil even if she did not know the dialect. She sighed—a sound only slightly less annoyed than the camel's snorts. After all, she had not hurt the idiot's mount (and the man's bruised toes were not her fault). Ivy lacked the time for a really good fight, a beat-his-head-into-the-dung brawl, especially after spending most of the morning clearing lost dromedaries and their droppings out of her crew's tents. One of Mumchance's strays slipped between her legs. The mangy dog snapped at the man. The camel's owner snarled and threatened the mutt, flipping a small dagger out of his belt to brandish at it.

Maybe there is enough time for a little fight, thought Ivy, as she moved between the stray and the Shaar mercenary foolish enough to swing a knife under her nose.

One kick from Ivy knocked the dagger into the dirt. A swing of her mailed fist caught the man under his jaw, rocking him back. A second kick landed him flat on his back in a less-than-fragrant pile left behind by his frightened camel. Gasping, his breath knocked out of him, the camel driver lay there, glaring up at her.

"Go away," said Ivy, one booted foot resting on his dagger. "Take the camel with you."

The camel driver glanced at the sword that Ivy had not bothered to unsheathe. Ivy cocked her hip slightly and grinned. She did not need the blade to keep him down, and—as they were fighters of the same siege force—serious maiming made little sense. The man apparently took her point of view. Rolling up in one fluid and slightly squelchy move, he picked up his dagger, grabbed his camel's halter, and led the beast in the direction of his people's tents. The cur just plopped its bottom in the dust and started scratching for fleas.

"You're welcome," said Ivy to the unconcerned mutt. "No problem at all defending your scruffy hide."

The camels had slipped out during the night and rampaged through the camp—at least as much as a dromedary could rampage, which was more like a blundering through the tents. It was, Ivy considered, exactly what the Thultyrl deserved for hiring Shaar mercenaries to fill out his siege forces. Except, of course, the camels knew better than to shamble their way through Procampur's neatly ordered pavilions. Instead, mercenaries like Ivy had to spend their morning shifting the smelly, spitting, four-legged, one-humped fleabags out of their gear while the Shaar drivers wailed and moaned and threatened terrible retribution to anyone who harmed their precious mounts.

Unless, of course, somebody taught them a well-deserved lesson in manners and kindness to small mongrels.

Cursing the loss of time, but not regretting the brief tussle, Ivy swatted the last stray camel out of the camp area. She almost chased off a few of the dogs panting at her heels as she searched the camp for something to eat. But a quick survey of wagging tails, moist noses, and panting tongues led her to the conclusion that every mutt was one of Mumchance's strays, and the dwarf would never forgive her if the whole pack was not there to greet him on his return from the dig. Ivy decided that she should be just thankful that Mumchance and the other Siegebreakers had set off earlier to the dig, leaving the camels to her. If they had stayed, she was certain that the day would have ended with a camel added to the odd menagerie that the Siegebreakers seemed to augment every time they went out on a job.

As she continued to search for a breakfast that had not been trampled or tasted by camels, Ivy tripped over Kid's pile of odds and ends. Since he almost always stole food as well as any shiny object that attracted his attention, she did a quick shuffle through his little bags and boxes. One leather pouch yielded up a quantity of stale—but still quite chewable—campaign biscuits.

Even as she crammed the first bite into her mouth, a soft cough interrupted her. Just from the tone of the cough, she knew who it was, who it had to be. Nobody coughed that decorously except Captain Sanval, the officer who escorted her every day to the Thultyrl's tent. In the courteous tone he always used, the captain said, "The Thultyrl requires an audience with you, lady. I am to accompany you."

Ivy took another bite of the sour biscuit and wondered if he had arrived just in time to see her stealing from Kid's gear, or if he had been standing there long enough to see her roll the

Shaar through the camel dung. While contemplating that last thought and avoiding Sanval's patient gaze, she stirred Kid's cache with a toe. Most of it looked worthless: odd scraps, lengths of rope, the purple leather pouch (containing the biscuits she had purloined), and a number of small utensils. There was nothing in Kid's trove that could not be explained or would attract an angry owner seeking to reclaim his property, decided Ivy, but she resolved to remind Kid again that this was a Procampur-controlled camp, and Procampur's officers took a very dim view of thieves.

Sanval coughed again. As usual, no emotion showed on his handsome face. He never had any expression, other than polite and attentive interest. The captain looked almost exactly like his fellow officers, so much so that Ivy wondered if the Thultyrl had some clay mold that he used to stamp out row after row of stalwart, polite young men. Like all the other Procampur officials, Sanval wore the cleanest gear that Ivy had ever seen: every cord matched, every buckle gleamed. Even his boot heels were polished. The dust and the stink of the siege camp never seemed to touch him.

Today, although the sun was beating down hard enough to make even a Shaar sweat, Sanval wore his complete armor: from the shining greaves on his long legs to a brilliantly polished breastplate beneath his square shoulders, right up to a well-buffed helmet sitting absolutely straight on the top of his head. Once, and only once, Ivy had seen Sanval pull off his perfectly shined helmet. Then one little black curl had stood straight up on the back of his head, defiantly out of place from the rest of his clipped and well-brushed wavy black locks. Ivy had rather liked that freestanding curl.

When they had first met, Ivy guessed that Sanval was one of those that Procampur citizens would call "born under the silver roof"—a nobleman in service to his Thultyrl as a matter of duty rather than financial necessity. Besides all the wonderfully well-polished and obviously expensive armor, the full list of his names was much too long for anyone except a noble. Common people made do with one or two names. But Sanval had recited a dozen sonorous sobriquets including, unless she had misunderstood, the rather unlikely name of Hyacinth. After a tongue-twisting moment of trying to repeat back all his names, Ivy had suggested that she just call him Sanval. He had mentioned that "Captain Sanval" would be more proper.

Other than the long list of personal names and the fact that he had brought three horses to the siege, Ivy had been unable to pry any personal information out of the discreet captain, despite her best and most congenial efforts at quizzing him. It wasn't easy asking questions of a man who insisted on walking either three paces in front of you (if you were going to the Thultyrl's tent) or three paces behind you (if you were going away from the Thultyrl's tent), but Ivy tried. After a short time (the duration of one walk up the hill to the Thultyrl's tent), Ivy gave up on being congenial and switched to the more familiar and comfortable tactic of being annoying. After all, just because none of her armor matched—or had ever been shined until it reflected sunlight like a silver mirror—did not mean that she lacked pride.

"I am eating my breakfast," she said to the silent captain. "It took some time this morning to clear the camels out of here."

Sanval's smooth brown brow creased, very slightly. Ivy waited. She kept waiting. In silence. Two could play that game.

"The animals," said Sanval finally, when it became evident that Ivy was not going to say anything else or even move until he responded, "did not come into our area."

"Of course not," drawled Ivy in a perfect imitation of his even tones. She had been a gifted mimic since childhood and matching the clipped, even cadences of the Procampur accent was a simple trick for her. "That would have been rude. Even camels have manners around Procampur."

One corner of Sanval's perfect lips almost quirked upward. The possible smile disappeared too quickly for her to be certain, and Ivy decided that it was just a trick of light and shadow playing across those finely chiseled features. The gods only knew what it would take to make the man bend, even for a moment, and indulge in a little camp gossip.

Sanval apologized again for interrupting her breakfast but insisted courteously that she make herself ready to meet with the Thultyrl.

"I can wait while you wash, but we must not take too long," said Sanval, with a slight bow. Ivy knew that his quick glance had not missed a single spot of dust on her face, the grime on the mismatched armor that she wore, or the new patch on her unpolished boots. Ivy knew she looked every inch a grubby, uncouth mercenary, and—if she were forced to admit it—she rather enjoyed the dirt. It was certainly easier to maintain than the well-scrubbed look favored by the Procampur officers, especially when living in the middle of a siege camp in the last and hottest month of summer.

If Sanval had been an aristocrat out of Waterdeep, he might have sneered at her obvious lack of fortune and armor polish. But Sanval was from Procampur. Courteous Procampur officers never sneered. He just stood there, making no fuss at all, while she twisted up her sweat-soaked blonde braid and jammed it under her favorite leather cap.

Ivy located her armored gloves and thrust them through her belt. With her bare hands, she dug through Kid's leather pouch and removed as many biscuits as she could. Ivy stuffed them into the top of her tunic, securing them behind her breastplate. Satisfied that she could eat some breakfast later, she rubbed the crumbs off her mouth with her grimy sleeve.

"All done, and I'm as ready and as clean as I am going to be," she said, figuring that this time she would get a response from him. Although she had not been certain about the smile earlier, she had definitely seen him wince when she deliberately smeared extra biscuit crumbs down her front. The crumbs, Ivy reasoned, would shake off in the walk up the hill, or she could brush herself down before she entered the Thultyrl's tent. Annoying Sanval was one thing; revolting the ruler who was going to pay her a lot of gold to end an unprofitable siege was another.

Sanval turned to lead her to the Thultyrl's tent, starting out at the regulation three paces in front of her. Ivy quickened her step so she was even with him. They were almost the same height, and her legs were as long as his. She could easily match him stride for stride. He quickened his pace so that he was again three steps in front of her. She wondered if she should push him into a jog this morning, just to see him sweat.

Mumchance's mutts decided that Ivy and Sanval were playing a new game. A little brown-and-white shaggy one barked and leaped for Sanval's ankles, apparently intent on slowing him down for Ivy. Sanval neatly sidestepped the dog without even looking. Not even a spot of drool from its lolling tongue touched his highly polished toes. Ivy was impressed. The rest of the mutts came boiling out of whatever patch of shadow they had been panting in and ran toward them. Sanval came to a complete and rock-solid halt. He and the entire pack of dogs looked back at Ivy. She shrugged. This time, Sanval waited until she did what he wanted.

Ivy snapped a Dwarvish command at the dogs. The motley troop dropped to the ground with drooping tails. A yellow cur, a three-legged dog Mumchance had brought back yesterday, whined piteously. Ivy dug a biscuit out of her tunic. She broke off a piece and threw it to the yellow dog. The rest of the mongrels whined too. She pulled out the rest of the biscuits and tossed them to the dogs. So much for breakfast—she hoped that the rest of her company had thought to bring food to the dig site.

"Your dogs seem . . . hmm . . . better behaved today," said Sanval. He was right. None of them had jumped up on him today. Ivy knew that the dogs appalled him, but she could never get the polite captain to yell at them, swear, or even grumble. So she had stopped saying "jump" in the Dwarvish dialect that Mumchance used for training his mutts and that Sanval didn't speak.

So the dogs had failed to annoy him today. He had not reacted to her usual grimy state, no matter how much it contrasted with his own shiny image. And it really was too hot to try to make him trot through the Procampur tents—probably the only person who would end up sweating would be her. Ivy considered other options to tease some human response out of Sanval. Restraint like his, in Ivy's experience of war camps, was not only uncommon, it was positively uncanny. She suspected that it might even be unhealthy.

But it was typical of a citizen of Procampur, a city so regimented by manners and so enamored of its laws that they had banned the thieves' guild and, even more surprisingly, made the ban stick, keeping the guild permanently out of the city. Like the highly polished officer now leading her through the camp, Procampans made civility seem ordinary and the picking of pockets the height of bad manners.

Such things weren't natural. Take this war, thought Ivy, which had started because Procampur's ruler decided to honor his treaties. Now, most kingdoms and city-states had treaties with one another, but rarely bothered to read them, let alone act upon them. But Procampur had a treaty with Tsurlagol that they would protect the city from outside invasion or, if invaders managed to take control of Tsurlagol, free the city. When the inevitable happened, and Fottergrim's ramshackle army of orcs and hobgoblins (and a few humans and half-breeds who should have known better) captured Tsurlagol, Procampur's ruler decided to go to war. Unfortunately, the orderly city had only an orderly army—just enough to serve its own needs, but not nearly enough to defeat the forces encamped in Tsurlagol.

To free Tsurlagol, Procampur needed more than its own citizens. It needed, as its senior nobles and officers had most reluctantly admitted, to hire mercenaries. After a long hot summer of paying the untidy and decidedly disorderly mercenaries, Procampur's Thultyrl desired a quick end to the siege. The Thultyrl was a king who could afford to pay to have the siege broken, and the Siegebreakers had all the technical, practical, and magical expertise needed to make that happen—or so Ivy had spent the last tenday assuring the Thultyrl. The Siegebreakers also badly needed the payment promised by the Thultyrl, but Ivy felt that Procampur's ruler did not need to know that. It might make him inclined to haggle, and she preferred to be the only haggler in a transaction.

Now, all Mumchance and the rest of her Siegebreakers needed to do was collapse a section of Tsurlagol's sturdy walls. All Ivy had to do, and she considered her job the harder of the two, was persuade the impatient Thultyrl to give her friends enough time to complete the task. For the last tenday, she had trudged far too many times up the hill to the Thultyrl's tent to explain once again why the walls could not fall instantly. She wondered if the Thultyrl would believe her this time.

◆━━━◆◆◆━━━◆

Ivy skipped over the ditch that separated Procampur's section of the camp from the mercenaries' tents. Shallow and narrow, the ditch served no defensive purpose. It existed to warn mercenaries returning from the latrines in the dark to head down the hill rather than up the hill.

As they climbed the hill to the Thultyrl's pavilion, located squarely in the center of Procampur's tents, Ivy paused and turned to the north. From here, she had the clearest view of the city on the opposite hill. As usual, a few mounted troops were trotting back and forth in the valley, well out of range of Fottergrim's archers. The horsemen raised a fine cloud of dust, as the grass and any other vegetation had long ago been trampled. The sun caught a glint of armor along the tops of the walls. Ivy squinted. Tall shadows and bright helmets were clustered thickest along the southern wall. Fottergrim had stationed the bulk of his troops there to watch the horsemen in the fields below. According to reports from the Thultyrl's scouts, another array of orcs and hobgoblins, well mixed with a few bugbears, kept watch along the eastern wall, ready to raise the alarm if any charge came up the harbor road. Looking south and looking east was exactly what Ivy wanted. Let Fottergrim keep his attention fixed in those directions. She had no intention of entering the city through the eastern gates or by a charge up the steep southern hill. Ivy preferred Fottergrim's army to mass their largest numbers where she was not going.

"Any sign of Fottergrim today?" she asked Sanval.

He did not pause in his steady march up the hill, but answered over his shoulder. "Earlier. Shouting insults as usual and daring us to try the gates."

"Then he's got hot oil, hidden archers, or a good spell set there," said Ivy. "Your Thultyrl's restraint is spoiling all his fun."

"*The* Thultyrl," said Sanval in the faintest rebuke of her casual tone, "cannot wait forever."

"Your officers are pressing him to go home again?" It was less of a question than a statement. It was an unpopular war, and costly, and Procampur's nobles and merchants liked to see a profit in their ventures. Since Sanval was apparently willing to talk politics, if nothing else, Ivy wanted to obtain as much information as possible. The more the officers pressed the Thultyrl to end the war quickly, the faster the Siegebreakers had to dig. If the walls of Tsurlagol did not fall soon, the Thultyrl was going to try some other tactic to draw out Fottergrim and engage him in a decisive battle. And that, in Ivy's opinion, would be a disaster. Nobody was going to pay the Siegebreakers for failing to make a wall fall down.

"Another petition has come from the merchants. They protest the loss of the Thultyrl's leadership and demand that he return to his duties in the city. There are a number of civil cases that need his judgment," Sanval said.

"And none of your green-roof merchants can settle their own disputes?"

Sanval started to say something and then thought better of it. Obviously it went against his personal code of conduct to criticize his fellow citizens. Ivy sighed and wished the gentlemen of Procampur were more like the humans of Waterdeep or the gnomes of Thesk: ready to slander anyone of low or high station. If Ivy knew what the various factions in the camp wanted, she could always bargain in such a manner that made it seem like everyone was going to be satisfied (even if the only ones who really benefited were her Siegebreakers).

"It is impossible to explain to an outsider," began Sanval, apparently responding to the deep sighs that she heaved behind him. "Our customs and our laws are very ancient and must seem strange to someone like you." He stopped and looked over his shoulder at her. Obviously he felt unable to describe what he thought "someone like you" meant, but Ivy had a good idea, and she was more than a bit annoyed by his judgment. Looking messy did not mean that she lacked understanding of the way that silver-roof nobles lived. She understood all too well—she just chose to live differently.

Ivy began to sing in her crow's voice. Daughter of a bard, she couldn't carry a tune to save her life. But she had the same wicked memory for lyrics that she had for accents. Also, only last night, she had found a minstrel with a goodly collection of bawdy songs favored in the worst parts of Procampur. "I'm quite the red-roof girl, in fact, all the warriors declare . . ."

Now Sanval sighed, turned around, and quickened his pace through Procampur's tents. The Procampur pavilions followed the same straight lines of their city's famous Great Way, not at all like the mercenary section of the camp where the canvas coverings randomly clustered. There, mercenaries pitched their tents in whatever order they liked. Far from the latrine pits was considered a prime location for most mercenaries; other than that, they didn't pay much attention to their surroundings. But in this section of the camp, tents were planted in perfect formations, with the rustling banners and ribbon tent edgings matching the colors of Procampur's famous roof tiles: gold for the Thultyrl's personal enclave, silver for the nobles, yellow for their servants, black for the priests, and so on. The only color not showing was red. That was the symbol for adventurers as well as the areas that housed those adventurers passing through Procampur. That element, as far as the Procampur army was concerned, was already too thoroughly represented by the mercenary camp.

Ivy marched behind Sanval, doing her best to uphold the mercenaries' low reputation. She continued the song that was worth every drink that she had bought for the harper's parched throat. By the time she reached the second verse, with the rousing line of "Once the men lived for my sighs, but now they want a peek of . . ." the back of Sanval's neck shone pink beneath the rim of his helmet.

The Thultyrl's pavilion dominated the center of Procampur's section, much as his palace reigned in the center of the city. One enormous tent, with silk walls dividing the interior into multiple rooms, housed the Thultyrl and his many retainers.

Only their arrival at the Thultyrl's tent prevented Ivy from completing the ballad. Even she didn't have quite enough nerve to sing the last three lines of *I'm Quite the Red-Roof Girl* in front of the Thultyrl's stone-faced bodyguards, members of the famous Forty who followed him in every pursuit.

The two on guard today were standing rigidly at attention and staring into space. The one on the left was very young, and Ivy noticed his cheeks were very flushed under the flanges of his helmet. Her voice may not have had the quality of her mother's, but she could pitch it to be heard over long distances. She must have been singing even louder than she had intended. She glanced at the other bodyguard. He was older, and he was not blushing, but he did wink at her as she passed him.

During the day, the canvas outer walls of the Thultyrl's pavilion were rolled up to allow the breezes to blow through the tent; but the gold silk walls were down—probably in a vain attempt to keep the dust from covering the scrolls belonging to the scribes busy working inside the pavilion. The dozen scribes assigned to the Thultyrl's Great Codex fought a constant battle with the grit of the camp, which clogged their inkpots and stained their fine parchments. Still, as far as they were from their cool halls, they continued their mission to copy Procampur's many laws into one great law book. Behind them paced the legal scholars, already debating the exact wording of each law, consulting the original crumbling texts that were being copied, and occasionally leaning over a scribe's shoulder to correct a comma there, a dash here.

As Ivy stood there, brushing biscuit crumbs onto the canvas floor, she reflected that she had known commanders who went to battle with their entire families, often dragging whole harems of lovers and children to a siege camp. But the Thultyrl was the first that she had known who brought his secretaries and lawyers to the edge of a battle. When she had first heard of the Thultyrl's personal passion—the Great Codex to be placed in a library to eclipse all libraries—she had expected to meet an old man, white-haired and wrinkled, determined to build a monument that would outlast his death.

Instead, this Thultyrl was her own age, an energetic young man who adored hunting so much that he had also brought his hounds, his hawks, and his master huntsman with him. It was the hunting that had led to his present incarceration in bed. While coursing a stag in the hills above Tsurlagol, his party had surprised a troop of mountain orcs coming to reinforce their kin inside the city's walls. During the ensuing dust-up, the Thultyrl had been speared in his leg, breaking the thighbone.

Now the Thultyrl commanded from his camp bed with all the sweetness of temper of a lion tied to a stake. Ivy could hear him roaring as they paused beside the scribes scratching at their scrolls. Sanval conferred with two more members of the Forty, sitting on stools in front of a silk curtain embroidered with flying griffins—the personal symbol of this Thultyrl. A scribe's apprentice pushed past Ivy to pull last night's guttered beeswax stubs from the silver candlesticks. The Thultyrl was rich enough to keep his pavilion lighted all night long for his scribes, but not wasteful enough to allow them to throw away good beeswax. The incense pots were already lit, in a vain attempt to stifle the usual morning stink wafting through a war camp. No one was smiling, and everyone was working in absolute silence, which meant the Thultyrl was in worse humor than usual. After a long whispered conference, Sanval gestured for Ivy to follow him. He lifted aside the gold silk curtain to let them pass into the inner room of the Thultyrl's tent.

The Thultyrl was clutching a snow white towel to his freshly shaved chin. The barber was crouched on the floor, his bowl clutched to his chest and his forehead pressed against the purple wool rug hiding the canvas floor of the pavilion. The barber appeared frozen in the traditional bow signifying absolute obedience (and terror) that former Thultyrls had instituted in their courts.

"Oh, for the sweet suffering of every black-roof priest," swore this Thultyrl, "get up, man! You will not be beheaded for nicking the Thultyrl's royal chin. Beriall, pay the poor fellow something extra for his fright."

Beriall, the Thultyrl's personal secretary and the camp steward, swept forward with a swish of perfumed robes and whispered to the barber. The man nodded and tentatively smiled, bobbing his head as he retreated backward out of the tent.

"A man should be able to curse when his chin bleeds without his barber collapsing on the carpet," grumbled the Thultyrl, still dabbing at the nick with the towel.

"If he is a commoner, the barber will swear back at him. If he is a king, the barber will grovel. It is the way of the world," answered the Pearl in her deep voice. Behind every Thultyrl stood a Hamayarch, the highest rank of wizard in the court. The Hamayarch ruled the magic users of Procampur as the Thultyrl ruled other citizens. But the Hamayarch always bowed to the Thultyrl and ruled under the Thultyrl's blessing. The Pearl had held the title of Hamayarch for at least three generations. Her true name, her age, and even her race were unknown. Tall and slender, with hair the color of snow and the face of girl barely in her teens, some whispered that the Pearl had elven blood. Others claimed demon ancestors for her.

Having met many strange inhabitants of the North in a tumultuous childhood spent wandering behind either her bard mother or her druid father (but rarely the two together), Ivy doubted the Pearl of Procampur was either elf or demon. There was something very human about the Pearl's eyes, even though they were a strange aquamarine color and slanted slightly down at the corners.

According to camp gossip, the Thultyrl had left the Pearl behind to govern Procampur. But the day that he was speared in the thigh, she had appeared inside his tent and had overseen his physicians as they dressed his wound. Since then, the Pearl remained always close at hand. She seemed to have arrived without servants of her own, coach, horse, or baggage, but she appeared each day in clean linen and silk. Today, the Pearl's white hair was looped up in an elaborate coronet of braids, baring her ears, which were pierced and studded with three diamonds on the left lobe and two rubies on the right. Her hands were covered with rings of both silver and gold, many set with gems. The Pearl favored linen as her undertunic, topped with a layer of embroidered silk displaying white peacocks on a dark blue background. She rustled when she moved, a sound like dead leaves stirred by a cold wind.

If the Pearl was winter in her dress, then the Thultyrl was all warm summer. A thin silk tunic lay open across his smooth brown shoulders, baring a chest already gleaming with sweat. A light blanket was draped across his lower body, hiding the wounded thigh and preserving the Thultyrl's modesty.

When he saw Ivy, the Thultyrl called for his campaign desk. Pressing a hidden spring on the brass-and-wood box, the Thultyrl watched with the satisfaction more typical of a young boy than a king as the campaign desk sprouted shelves and drawers and a long flat surface on top. Beriall rushed forward to pull out a map scroll from one polished drawer; from another drawer, the man unearthed bronze map weights in the shape of rearing griffins with their wings outstretched. With the fluttering of his plump fingers, Beriall unrolled the map and positioned the weights carefully. With a growl of impatience at Beriall's usual fussiness, the Thultyrl beckoned Ivy forward. Beriall stepped back to allow Ivy a clear view of the map, sniffing loudly as Ivy passed him and whisking his silken robes close to his ankles as if he were afraid that her mere presence would stain his beautiful peach-colored skirts. Used to Beriall's sniffs and occasional muttered comments about barbarians in the tent, Ivy examined the map as the Thultyrl had indicated.

Ivy loathed the map. She had peered at it at least once a day for the past eight days, always conscious of the Thultyrl watching her. The map showed the walls of Tsurlagol in exquisite detail: every gate, every tower, every turn.

"Well?" asked the Thultyrl. "Do you remain satisfied with your choice?"

"Very satisfied, sire. As we expected, the ground is soft and unstable at the base of the western wall," said Ivy, who had walked that section of Tsurlagol's walls two nights ago, skulking in shadows, and praying that she didn't twist an ankle in one of the ruts and holes. She had not told the rest of the Siegebreakers that she was checking the walls again (she knew how much they would protest), and it would have been incredibly embarrassing if the sun had come up and caught her lying in full view of Fottergrim's archers, just because she'd put her foot in a rabbit hole.

"The weakest section is here, the southwest corner, where they joined a new wall to an old wall." She tapped that turn on the map with one grimy finger, noting the smudge that she had left yesterday from the same gesture. "We're already shifting ground water toward that spot, and it is running deep enough that Fottergrim's watchers won't see anything. But water alone won't be enough. We need to tunnel, as we discussed earlier, and crack the foundations from underneath. Then the water can do its work and bring the wall down."

While Ivy was talking, one of the Thultyrl's officers approached him. Beriall tried to block his way, but the Thultyrl waved the officer closer. The man carried papers for the Thultyrl to stamp with his personal signet. Once that was done, Beriall hustled the man away. No conversation with the Thultyrl went uninterrupted, but the man had a ruler's ability to focus on three things at the same time. Ivy stayed where she was. When the Thultyrl wanted to, he would start asking her questions again. It wasn't as if he didn't already know the answers.

"Another draft on the treasury," the Thultyrl said to the Pearl. "These mercenaries will drain us dry if we don't end this soon." Beriall returned to his position at the Thultyrl's right shoulder, nodding at the last comment and staring directly at Ivy. One of the codex scholars appeared at the Thultyrl's side with a stack of rolled scrolls. The Thultyrl nodded his thanks and dropped the scrolls into an already overflowing basket by his side.

"Once inside the walls," said the Pearl, "we can recover our expenses from Tsurlagol's treasury. The treaty does allow for that."

"It does," sighed the Thultyrl. He popped open a drawer in the campaign table and pulled out an ivory message chit, which he handed over his shoulder to Beriall. The secretary beckoned one of the Forty to him and handed off the chit. That man bowed and rushed away to fetch whomever the chit signified. The Thultyrl ignored the passing of the chit and concentrated on his conversation with the Pearl. "But we can't bankrupt Tsurlagol—we are supposed to be saving the city after all."

"Once inside the walls," repeated the Pearl in her deep voice, "we can make some equitable arrangement with all concerned. After all, we were not the fools who let Fottergrim dance his army through an open gate, all the way to Tsurlagol's main square."

Ivy suspected that the fools who had let Fottergrim into the city were long dead. That was the problem with thick walls and high towers: people forgot that such defenses were only as strong as an underpaid gatekeeper's resistance to bribery. Unfortunately, Fottergrim's troops were all that was left of the Black Horde. Having avoided the debacle at Waterdeep, they'd been moving steadily north for the last ten years. Years of constant attacks had made them extremely suspicious of strangers and fanatically loyal to the big orc who had kept them from being slaughtered.

In their first attempt at breaking the siege, Ivy and Mumchance had disguised themselves as a Gray Forest goblin and orc, as these creatures had been flocking to Fottergrim's banner since the orc commander had arrived back in the North.

"Won't they notice that I am barely the height of a goblin?" the dwarf had asked her.

"And I am no orc," Ivy admitted. She was a tall, hard-muscled woman, but still. The orcs were huge. Ivy had added padding and oversized armor until she could barely bend her knees and elbows. "I'm hoping that when they look down from the wall to identify us, the perspective will confuse them."

The dwarf merely grunted in reply.

"Also, I am counting on bribery," she added.

But they had been driven back by a hail of arrows before they could even start jingling coins at Fottergrim's sentries.

The next morning, at her first meeting with the Thultyrl, Ivy recommended undermining the walls as the most the logical way to enter the city. As she told the rest of the Siegebreakers that night, a rain of arrows tended to make her cranky, and there was no point letting the Thultyrl know that one of their favorite tricks had already failed.

So far, the Thultyrl of Procampur had agreed with her suggestion, but now he seemed inclined to argue.

"You have been digging for how many days?" said the Thultyrl, startling Ivy with the swift change of his attention from the Pearl to her.

"Only two days, sire," she answered, trying to meet his gaze calmly. "And I need three more days at least. We had to start the tunnel well back from the walls, behind some scrub trees, to avoid Fottergrim's sentries spotting us."

"But you are still aiming for that corner?" Without looking down, the Thultyrl tapped the map in the exact spot where Ivy had pointed. She wished she knew how he did that trick. It was impressive, she had to admit.

"Yes, sire," said Ivy, risking a quick peek at the map to make sure that she had not suddenly chosen a new corner of Tsurlagol's walls before tapping that section herself. "The walls are always weakest where there is a turn, especially in this case. It is better than trying to go under a straight section or one of the gates. Besides, it is the southwest corner, and Fottergrim keeps his strongest watch on the eastern wall. He expects you to come up the harbor road."

"Of course," said the Thultyrl. "Just as we would like him to come charging straight down that road." Procampur's navy had sailed into the harbor at the beginning of the summer siege. Fottergrim had no sailors in his horde and had retreated quickly up the harbor road, shutting himself safely behind Tsurlagol's high walls and well-fortified gates.

Another officer entered the chamber, led by a member of the Forty. The gray-bearded man carried the Thultyrl's ivory chit in one hand. He was short and heavy, and his armor gleamed more brightly than Sanval's breastplate. He also had the distinctive bowed legs of a horseman. The man bowed and handed his chit to Beriall. Ivy almost missed the Thultyrl's next question, so distracted was she by the entry of what was obviously a very senior officer of Procampur. "Can you dig faster?"

"We might be able to reach that corner faster, but we still need adequate time to prepare the wall," said Ivy, concentrating on the Thultyrl and ignoring the officer so obviously impatient to be noticed by his ruler. "Making walls fall down is easy, sire. Making them fall down where and when you want is a little harder. Myself, I prefer not to be standing directly underneath when the walls start to fall."

The Thultyrl smiled. "We understand your point of view," he said. "But we need you to excavate more rapidly. In two days time, Enguerrand will begin the charge that he has been so eager to lead."

The graybeard bowed at the mention of his name. "Sire," he said, "I promise you that our assault will free the city."

"And you are certain that Archlis is gone again?" asked the Pearl.

Enguerrand nodded. "He's not been seen since yesterday."

"So," said the Thultyrl to Ivy, "you understand the need for haste." It was a statement and it was obvious that the Thultyrl was not going to listen to any arguments. "Archlis only disappears for four or five days at the most. We cannot be certain of even that amount of time. We need to strike while he is off the walls."

Ivy could sympathize with the Thultyrl's desire to rush the walls when the wizard Archlis was gone. According to camp gossip, Fottergrim's personal spellcaster had engineered most of the orc's recent victories, including the successful occupation of Tsurlagol. Most annoyingly for the Procampur troops, Archlis was an expert at throwing fireballs and appeared to own a nearly inexhaustible supply of fire spells.

Unless Archlis was standing on the section that collapsed, and Ivy rather doubted that they would get that lucky, his fireballs would still be a formidable problem. Luckily the wizard had a tendency to disappear for several days at a time. In fact, that was how they'd learned his name, by hearing Fottergrim screaming for him to come up on the walls and attack Procampur's troops.

She stared at the map and considered the route of Enguerrand's charge. North and south was where the hill was steepest, and it was clearly marked so on the Thultyrl's map. East was the well-watched harbor road.

"The west is the only approach," said the Thultyrl. Keen-eyed as a griffin, the Thultyrl had spotted what she had seen: the faint dotted line that marked an old route leading to Tsurlagol's west gate. "There's a good road leading north from Procampur, well west of Tsurlagol and out of range of Fottergrim's patrols. We will move our people, south out of the camp, angling toward the road, then turn and come north fast."

"And turn again and come at the wall at sundown, when any sentry looking west might be dazzled by the sun." Ivy knew that trick. "And mercenaries, with their stinking camels, roaring up the harbor road to distract Fottergrim and split his strength." Old tricks and half-forgotten tactics—the kind of information that a Thultyrl's scholars might find in the histories of war and ancient maps tucked in the baskets with the legal scrolls. But they were clever tricks and it took a clever man to think of them—a man who went hunting deer on the western side of the city just to see if the ground matched what his maps had shown. No wonder the Thultryl had been so furious to be surprised on his hunt by mountain orcs and so intent on riding them all down before they got to Fottergrim.

"I walked the length of the western wall," said Ivy, "the day my company came here and two nights ago. There is a gate there."

"We know," said Enguerrand. "It is on the map."

"The map doesn't show the size," said Ivy, looking at him with pity. "It's a nightsoil gate. One horse wide, and barely that. If you breach it, you still need to go in one by one. A big orc with a large axe could hold that gate forever. He will just pile your dead in the doorway."

"Then we will use ladders to scale the walls," said Enguerrand.

Ivy shook her head. "There are old holdings on the top of that wall." Seeing everyone but the Thultyrl and the Pearl giving her puzzled stares, she sketched in the air the shape of the wooden-roofed balconies that overhung the western wall. "There will be arrow slits in the floors," she explained. "They shoot straight down on your ladders. It will be bloody fighting to climb over that wall."

"Then what do you suggest, lady?" asked the Thultyrl, who obviously had considered this drawback. His face was too calm in Ivy's judgment for this setback to be a surprise.

"Burn the holdings if you can."

"Fire arrows," suggested the Pearl.

"No spells?" asked the Thultyrl. The Pearl shook her head and spread her hands wide, displaying them as empty. Ivy wondered why so powerful a mage (by reputation if not demonstration) could not throw a little fire here and there. Certainly Archlis had been almost careless with his power over the past few weeks.

"They may have thought of that and laid some protection into the wood. Then again, they are orcs, never the cleverest at defensive warfare," advised Ivy. "But expect to lose half your force right there. The holdings may burn, but the wall is stone, and it will hold. Also, such a fire will bring everyone running from the other towers. Best to follow the plan we gave you: wait for the wall to fall down and make your charge into Tsurlagol across the fallen broken bodies of your enemies." It was a stirring speech, and with luck none of the Procampans would recognize that the last few words came straight from the chorus of one of her mother's favorite ballads.

"Then bring that wall down," said the Thultyrl, sitting straighter and wincing as the movement pulled on his unhealed wound. "At sunset, in two days time. We have decided."

———◆·◆·◆———

The Thultyrl has decided. The Thultyrl has decided. The refrain echoed through Ivy's head as she marched back down the hill, trailed by a silent Sanval.

"The Thultyrl may have decided," said Ivy, "but we're the ones who have to dig! Can't be done. Not that fast. Not safely. But maybe. If Gunderal can speed up the underground water. Mumchance would know. There might be old tunnels on that side. We could use those. If Zuzzara ever finds them. Can't be done. Could be done. The Thultyrl has decided! Oh, blast!"

She was arguing with herself because Sanval was not saying a word. In fact, he seemed stunned into even deeper silence than before. He had stayed completely rigid in his burnished armor the whole time they had been in the Thultyrl's tent. Then the Thultyrl had addressed him directly.

"We regret," the Thultyrl had said to him, "that we must refuse your request to rejoin Enguerrand's regiment. We need your services as assigned for two more days. To bring us word,

you understand, of the success or failure of this lady's work."
The Thultyrl nodded at Ivy.

Sanval had bowed, very deeply, to his ruler. Ivy thought
that she had heard him sigh, but it had been a very, very soft
sigh.

But it was the Pearl who apparently had mystified Sanval.
She waited until they had left the Thultyrl's presence and then
stopped them.

"You will find your glory easier underground than in
Enguerrand's company," the Pearl said to Sanval. "If you
remember who you are and forget your vanity." Sanval stared
at the white-haired woman and did not seem to know what to
say to her.

The Pearl turned to Ivy next. She picked up one of Ivy's
gauntlets. The armored glove had slipped from where Ivy had
tucked it into her belt and had fallen to the ground. The Pearl
handed the gauntlet back to her, fingering the little silver token
sewn onto the leather cuff. The token felt surprisingly warm to
Ivy when she slid the glove back under her belt.

"You need no prophecy from me. You have always known
your way and are wise enough to trust your luck. Continue
to believe in your luck when you make your plans," said the
Hamayarch of Procampur. Then the Pearl glanced down and
smiled faintly. "But I would suggest that you clean your boots."
The Pearl rustled back inside the silk-draped pavilion.

Now, marching down the hill, Ivy muttered to herself,
which meant she was loud enough for only Sanval to hear
clearly. "If she can see the future, I wouldn't mind knowing it.
I can take a prophecy as well as the next woman. It's not like
my mother or my father wasn't always meddling in some great
magic. There were long prophecies, short prophecies, incredibly cryptic prophecies all naming one or the other at some
time. But do I get some prediction of glory? Of course not!

The woman just tells me to clean my boots. What is wrong with my boots?"

"They have camel dung on them," said Sanval from behind her. "On the back."

Ivy ground to a halt. She pulled up one foot and twisted it to look at the back of her boot. She put her foot down slowly. She pulled up the other leg and looked at the back of that boot. Both of them were liberally splashed with dung. She had walked through the Thultyrl's silk-lined, wool-carpeted, incense-scented pavilion with dung-mired boots. Even for her, that was a bit much. No wonder Beriall had been sniffing so loudly today.

"I would have told you," said Sanval, "but you kept singing that song."

Ivy thought about hitting him. But they were still in the Procampur section of the camp, and somebody was sure to make a fuss if she knocked down a Procampur officer and ground his face in the dust.

"Come on," she said. "I need to tell the others that they have two days to do a tenday job. The Thultyrl has decided."

But even as she hurried toward the tunnel, she wondered if she could make good on her promise. No matter how fast the Siegebreakers dug, she was not at all sure that they could bring down the wall in time to save the Thultyrl's troops from disaster.

CHAPTER TWO

O nce Ivy arrived at the site of the tunnel, she considered that meeting the Thultryl's deadline might be easier if anyone were actually digging. Instead, the Siegebreakers were resting in the shade of a small grove of trees. Out of the corner of her eye, Ivy caught a glimpse of a slight disturbance on Sanval's handsome features before his face smoothed into its usual stoic expression.

"So what do you think is wrong?" huffed Ivy at Sanval, because it was easier to be mad at him than start yelling at her friends.

"Pardon?" said Sanval, startled enough to turn his head so she could see his face clearly under the brim of his shining helmet.

"You disapprove of something. I'm an excellent judge of those non-expressions of yours," Ivy replied.

"Really?" His tone was as even and bland as his face.

"Quarter turn down of the left corner of the lips: deep disapproval from Captain Sanval."

Sanval choked slightly at her retort, and the recently criticized left corner of his lips quirked up for moment. "They are not in armor," he observed. "This far from camp, that is not well advised."

"They are digging a hole in the ground, which is a little hard to do in full kit," said Ivy, ignoring the fact that she had been shouting only last night that they were too close to the walls to fully ignore all precautions. Of course, she never felt comfortable in a war camp without armor. Besides, her gear hid the stains on her shirt and breeches. Sanval was fully armored too, but then he seemed to live in halfplate (and live in it without sweating or feeling the weight, which was most unfair). Ivy suspected that even the shirt underneath the plate was gleaming white.

Still, Sanval was right. So close to the walls, the Siegebreakers should not be lazing about in the shade like they were taking a break on the farm. There was a siege going on only half a field away—even though, like most sieges, it was more often than not an exercise in yelling insults at your opponents from a safe distance, out of range of their weapons and spells.

Stripped down to her shirt sleeves and leather waistcoat, sitting on a rock with her legs dangling before her, Zuzzara appeared to have no cares at all. At her feet, the wizard Gunderal was lying on her back, watching the clouds float by, weaving strands of water between her pale fingertips. She was lazily nodding along to Zuzzara's reading of a letter that had arrived yesterday with the latest shipment of supplies from Procampur.

Ivy stared at the two women, hoping they would see her wink her right eye toward the Procampur officer standing politely and silently beside her. Gunderal gave her a languid little wave.

Zuzzara was squinting too closely at the parchment to notice Ivy's approach. "Mimeri says that the sundial and the water clock no longer agree."

"Then Mimeri needs to shift the sundial," said the dwarf Mumchance. At least he was wearing his helmet and chain mail vest. But, Ivy knew, that was only half-armored for the old dwarf—his big war axe, his full plate, and other more vicious weapons were currently buried under a pile of panting dogs back at the camp. "I told Mimeri to adjust the clock as soon as the solstice had passed. What about the shingles for the barn roof?"

"I think we have more pressing concerns right now," said Ivy, sidestepping around Zuzzara's shovel, carelessly propped against a large rock. Sanval sidestepped right with her, saying nothing. She smiled, a friendly showing of teeth directly at the others, in the hope that they would get the message.

With a vague smile back at Ivy, Zuzzara continued to puzzle over Mimeri's cramped scrawl. "She says that the carpenter will bring the shingles when we have the payment," Zuzzara said.

"You'd think that man would give us credit by now," Mumchance grumbled. Ivy tried a gentle cough to attract his attention, but the dwarf ignored her and Sanval. "We have replaced that roof often enough."

"Only twice," murmured Gunderal. "And this time was not my fault." The wizard rolled over on her stomach with a swish of silken skirts and caused a tiny rain cloud to shower on a nearby weed with a waggle of her right hand.

"Never said that it was your fault," Mumchance stated. "But it is a good thing that we have got this payment coming."

"Not if the walls of Tsurlagol are still standing," interrupted Ivy very loudly. Enough of winks, smiles, and discreet coughs. Subtlety around her friends rarely worked. Very aware of Sanval watching the whole group over her shoulder, Ivy continued, "Are we not supposed to be digging a tunnel today? Mumchance, I'm surprised at you. Where's that fabled dwarf work ethic?"

"Ground is too soft," replied the one-eyed dwarf, squinting up at Ivy. The shadows dappling the little glade barely softened the heavy scars on his face. "Told you yesterday that we needed to shift the entrance."

"We don't have enough time to move it if we want to earn our fee," said Ivy, with a quick glance at Sanval and a frown at Mumchance. She did not want the silver-roof noble from Procampur legging it back to the Thultryl's tent with the message, "Send these foolish farmers home and let us charge the walls like true warriors." Of course he would probably be more elegant in his wording as he lost them their payment.

When they had first broken ground, the Siegebreakers had been lucky enough to hook into an older passageway that ran under the ruined remains of a former city's wall, probably dug hastily and long ago for the same reason that the Siegebreakers were digging their tunnel. That older siege tunnel had led into a city that had long since vanished. Tsurlagol had been invaded, burned to the ground, and then shifted to a new location so many times that one jester suggested the city's best defense would be to build all the houses as boats on wheels and run them into the sea every time a new invasion force came into view.

"We need to slow down, not dig faster," argued Mumchance. "We're moving away from the first tunnel, and the ground doesn't feel right."

"Did the roof collapse again?" asked Ivy.

"No," said Zuzzara. "Just the usual bits of dirt down the back of my neck. But Mumchance pulled me out and sent Kid in."

"He's smaller than Zuzzara and lighter too," explained the dwarf. "And he has a good feel for the dirt under those hard little hooves of his. It is the ground below, Ivy, not above, that I don't like. Nothing feels right. I wanted Kid's opinion. I left Wiggles with him. She'll bark if anything starts to go wrong."

"Wiggles to the rescue," drawled Ivy, who did not have nearly the same faith in Mumchance's favorite mutt. He had picked up the yippy little horror two years ago when they had been in the south. Mumchance always claimed Wiggles had a dwarflike nose for trouble underground.

"You have never appreciated Wiggles's talents, not even when she saved us under that sorcerer's tower," muttered the dwarf.

"I gave her a bone afterwards," said Ivy. "A lovely bit of ham hock." In Ivy's opinion, it was just luck that Wiggles had sounded the warning in time. Wiggles barked almost continuously, so the dog was bound to yap at a strategic moment some day.

"Which you picked out of the rubble," Mumchance reminded her in a sour tone. As if a little dust on a bone had ever stopped Wiggles's enjoyment. The dog loved bones, with meat on them, or without. It did not matter to Wiggles as long she got something to chew.

Zuzzara ignored the argument about Wiggles, as the dog never woke her at dawn with her insane barking (Zuzzara snored too loudly to hear it). Instead, she was busy telling Sanval that she always did most of the digging for the Siegebreakers, and even a half-orc of her size could only dig so fast and so far in a day.

"I could bring more men from the camp," offered Sanval. "And some guards. We must not let this position be overrun."

Ivy gestured at the scraggly trees surrounding them. "We have enough cover to hide us from Fottergrim. They are not paying much attention to this side of the wall—that's why we picked this spot!"

"Just what we need, more humans!" huffed Mumchance. "Doesn't matter how many dig, or how fast. The ground is rotten, Ivy. I know it is."

Ivy stared at the dwarf. He gave her that one-eyed stare back that said most clearly that he was a dwarf and she was a human, and everyone knew who knew the most about soil conditions and digging. But if the tower did not fall, then there would be no gold for their purses, and that meant a long winter with no roof over the animals sheltering in the barn. Which, Ivy knew, meant every single dog, cat, goat, chicken, pig, mule, and stray bear cub currently sleeping in the barn would end up in the farmhouse's kitchen or, much worse, her room.

"We have two days or we don't receive a clipped coin from the Thultryl," Ivy explained more bluntly than she had intended, her voice rising to a bellow. Her crew knew that voice. Zuzzara stood up and grabbed her shovel, swinging it up to her shoulder. She reached a hand down to Gunderal. The wizard floated daintily to her feet, fluffing her skirts around her. After a couple of quick twists with her fingers, Gunderal's hair obligingly arranged itself into long blue-black ringlets, perfectly framing her pale oval face.

"Oh, Ivy," said Gunderal, her violet eyes widening in disapproval. "You are wearing that cap again."

Ivy put up her bare hand and tugged the brim of her leather cap lower on her brow. Just because she had plucked it off that dead man's head—and he certainly did not need it at the time or since—Gunderal had taken the most unreasonable dislike to her current cap. Well, Gunderal said that it was the stains and the reek of the leather when the cap got wet in the rain that she disliked. When Ivy had responded that it did not smell any different from the rest of her gear, Gunderal had given one of her huge sighs and said, "That is part of the problem."

Ivy frowned at Gunderal. She was not going to start a discussion about her cap in front of Sanval. After all, she doubted that officers of Procampur wasted time discussing the quality of their leather goods when they could be doing something else. Or, glancing over at the brilliantly polished boots that Sanval wore, maybe they did. But she knew that the Siegebreakers had better things to do. "It won't rain today," Ivy said as firmly as she could.

"I know, but really that cap! I swear there are teeth marks on the brim."

"Well, if you hadn't thrown it at the dogs and encouraged them to play tug-of-war with it . . . Took me forever to get it back!"

"I was just trying to discourage you from wearing it."

"Thought you wanted to see what Kid found in the tunnel," said Zuzzara, placidly stepping between the two of them. Since she was digging today, Zuzzara's braids were bound back from her face in a neat array, and she was wearing a sturdy leather waistcoat rather than one of the more ornate brocade ones that she favored in peaceful times. Heavily influenced by Gunderal's nagging, Zuzzara's style did not match the many other half-orcs roaming the North—the kind who typically wore rough untreated pelts with the occasional bone jewelry decoration.

Ivy, however, refused to heed Gunderal's criticisms. Ivy was a mercenary. Mercenaries wore what they could loot. That was tradition and certainly easier than commissioning matching sets of armor (and cheaper too). When something got too dirty or battered to wear, you grabbed something new or traded with the guy in the next tent over for what you needed. Ivy did not see the point of Gunderal's constant little lectures that inevitably started with "you would look so nice if only . . ."

"Maybe there is a way around the rotten spot?" the half-orc suggested, gently steering Gunderal away from Ivy. The wizard followed her with a sad little comment on how nobody really cared about beauty but her.

Grumbling under his breath about how nobody but him

really cared about dirt, Mumchance hooked his dark lantern carefully to his belt and checked that his pick was securely fastened. "Tinderboxes?" he asked the Siegebreakers.

"I have mine," said Ivy. "Old fusspot, it's not that deep yet." She handed the old dwarf his short sword. As usual, he had taken it off and left it leaning against a tree trunk. He did not like fighting with it, preferring to use pick and hammer when he needed to.

"Hey, Zuzzara, where's your broadsword?" Ivy asked the half-orc. If Gunderal was obsessed with clean clothing, Ivy was equally obsessed with weaponry, or the defensive and offensive capabilities of it.

"Ivy, it's too heavy to lug all the way down here. Don't need it and don't want it today."

"Mumchance is fully armored. I'm fully armored. Captain Sanval"—she glanced over at the officer whose plate shone like a dozen mirrors in the sun—"is even wearing his helmet."

"Of course," he said, seemingly a little surprised that she had noticed him and said something that could be construed as a compliment. "It is a requirement that all officers be fully dressed in their armor if they leave the boundary of the camp."

"It's a good rule," said Ivy. "From now on, I want everyone to show up in full gear. We are close enough to the walls that we might be overrun by a raiding party or orc scouts."

"You are just saying that because you don't like to wear anything but your ratty old gear. And Mumchance is always more comfortable in chain mail than anything else," muttered Gunderal, who avoided armor whenever she could. Helmets, claimed the wizard, did unattractive things to her hair.

"Ivy is right," said the dwarf to Ivy's surprise. He usually argued with her on the general principle that any right-minded three-hundred-thirty-year-old dwarf knew more than a twenty-five-year-old human. "And you should all be carrying tinderboxes and extra candles for underground work. It is not like Gunderal could light a candle if we needed it."

"No, but I can use your flint and stone; you always have some with you," Gunderal said to the dwarf, unruffled by his comment. Her genasi heritage made all water spells fantastically easy for her—but it also caused fire spells to fail in a puff of damp smoke whenever she tried even the simplest flame tricks. "And there are other ways to light the dark, that don't need fire."

"Magic," grumbled the dwarf, as he led them to the entrance. "It's not wise to rely too much on magic. I keep telling you girls that, but you never listen to me."

"Yes, Mumchance," said Zuzzara and Gunderal together. "We know."

At the tunnel's entrance, Mumchance cocked his head and listened, then he whistled. A faint shout came back from Kid and a shrill yap from Wiggles.

"Probably safe," Mumchance decided. He jerked a thumb toward the officer from Procampur. "Is he coming?"

Ivy turned to Sanval. "Are you coming?"

"Perhaps I should stay here," said Sanval, looking at the dark entrance to the tunnel. Ivy was sure that he was calculating how long it would take his servant to clean his armor after squeezing through the dirty hole. "And guard the entrance."

"There's no danger," said Ivy, squeezing around Mumchance so she could go first. "None of Fottergrim's patrols have left the walls for days. And, besides, Gunderal has a potion to hide the entrance."

Once everyone had entered the tunnel, Gunderal extracted a crystal flask from her heavily embroidered belt pouch. She pulled the glass stopper out and carefully let three drops of the flask's contents fall on the ground. A pale smoke rose, darkening as it filled the entrance. "From the outside, it just looks like a shadow cast by one of the trees," Gunderal explained. "You have to step in it before you can see this hole."

Ivy shifted her sword from her side to her back and tightened the straps to keep it close to her body. The last thing she needed was to go tripping over her own blade when trying to show the tunnel to Sanval. She wanted to impress him with her explanations of the intricacies involved in undermining walls (and why those intricacies needed more than two days), not stumble about looking like an idiot. After a few awkward paces in she was able to stand upright.

As they advanced farther into the tunnel, Ivy explained to Sanval how they had used their own timbers to stabilize the roof.

"So it is safe now?" Sanval asked, as dirt continued to dribble down the walls, little clods landing behind them with soft puffs.

"For a rabbit," muttered Mumchance. "Anything heavier . . ."

"Is just fine," finished Ivy. "See, here's Kid and Wiggles."

Kid greeted her with a fleeting smile and a ducked head. Small and compact, with features almost as pretty as Gunderal, most people thought Kid was "sweet" until he dipped his long fingers into their pockets.

"Well?" said Ivy as soon as she reached him.

Kid stamped one hoof against the dirt and then moved two paces over and stamped again. Both stamps sounded the same to Ivy, and she said so.

"Little different, my dear," explained Kid. "Like Mumchance, I hear something wrong here." His pointed catlike ears were good; he often heard things that the others missed, and that was saying a lot in a group that included a half-orc, a half-genasi, and a full-blooded dwarf.

"Told you," said Mumchance, coming up to them. The others all clustered closely around to hear the discussion.

"All right," said Ivy. "The ground is a little soft." She stamped too. Her foot sank down into the dirt, and a little more dry earth trickled off a tree root above her head and dropped on her nose. Ivy sneezed.

"Ivy, can you move a little farther down the tunnel?" asked Gunderal, with a wrinkle of her delicate nose. "All I can smell is your boots."

Ivy obediently shifted behind Zuzzara, farther away from Gunderal.

"Phew!" said Zuzzara, waving a hand in front of her sensitive orc nose.

"It's not that bad," said Ivy, scraping her boots against a tree root. She had done the same thing earlier when she was leaving the camp, using a rock to rub off the worst of the muck. She guessed she must have missed a spot or two.

"Hush!" said Mumchance. A worried look wrinkled his scarred face. The dwarf relied more on his hearing underground than any other sense. He claimed that he could usually hear danger before he saw it. Wiggles whined at his feet, and the dwarf picked up the little dog and popped her into his pocket. It was an old habit, but it startled most people to see the dog's sharp white nose and large pink ears suddenly emerge from the pocket of a stout, gray-bearded dwarf.

"Phhstt," said Ivy, brushing the dirt off her face and trying to stifle a second sneeze. It came out as a loud snort.

Mumchance dropped to one knee to get his head closer to the ground and patted the earth with one gnarled hand. "There's something here."

"Yes, I smell something below us," said Gunderal.

"What?" asked Ivy.

"Water," said Gunderal. Another gift from her genasi

ancestors, Gunderal's sensitivity to water's proximity was as strong, or stronger than, her ability to detect magic.

"Water, running fast, and the earth moving with it, unable to hold it, breaking away as old rocks shift," Kid's voice echoed eerily in the tunnel. Like Gunderal, Kid often sensed things that the others couldn't see or hear or smell, especially changes created by magic. No one knew what ancestor had given Kid that ability—probably the same one who had left him both the little ivory horns hidden under his dark curls and the fine pair of hooves at his other end.

Ivy shuffled her feet. Mumchance was right: the ground did feel soft under her feet, almost like stepping on something rotten. She looked back to the entrance. They could go out, maybe probe for another way into the tunnel. This spot was too soft. Look at Sanval, she thought. The weight of his armor was causing him to sink into the dirt; it was almost to the level of his ankles. The same thing was happening to Zuzzara, trying to sidestep cracks growing in the tunnel's floor. Ivy realized what she was seeing. "Oh no!" she yelled. "Get back! Get back!"

She tried to pull Mumchance back from a suddenly appearing crack, and pulled too hard. He stumbled into Gunderal, who grabbed at Zuzzara, who swung around and got her shovel entangled in Sanval's sword, who fell heavily forward, almost crushing Kid beneath him. They all swayed together and began to fall. They kept falling as the tunnel floor collapsed beneath them.

Ivy grabbed for all of them, trying to save everyone and failing to get a grip on anyone.

The ground crumbled below her feet. She plunged into darkness, into the swift, cold water below. She fell fast and hit the water hard. The icy current shocked her silent as the river pulled her under.

CHAPTER THREE

Ivy surfaced, coughing and spitting out water that tasted of mud and ice. The strong current surged around her hips. The water was cold, pulled–out-of-the-mountain cold, pulled-out-of-the-heart-of-the-earth cold. It felt cold. It smelled cold. It even sounded cold, the river's hissing whisper running swiftly around her.

She could barely keep her balance. The sodden leather breeches and damp padded tunic that she wore under her mismatched pieces of armor added to her misery. The weight of her sword on her back was her only comfort. The crisscross of leather straps keeping the scabbard high on her back still held the blade safe. She checked the side of her belt. Her dagger was still secure in its sheath. She thought about loosening the ties on her belt dagger so she could use the knife quickly. But in the water, with her footing so unstable, she decided that she might drop any weapon that she drew.

Her braid lay sodden across the back of her neck. With bare hands she reached up and confirmed that she had lost her leather cap. She swore a little. She liked that cap. Being secondhand, it was nicely softened for the most comfortable fit possible. Now it was gone, and Ivy would have to find another one. Maybe she would get lucky and fall over another dead body wearing a cap.

Luckily, her gauntlets, armored and lined with sheepskin, had survived the fall and were still stuck in her weapons belt. She pulled them on to protect her hands from the cold water. Besides, the scaled armor on the knuckles of her gloves made a formidable weapon if something jumped her before she could draw her blade.

Ivy stood in the darkness, with water hissing past her, and blinked. She blinked again. It was still pitch black, and she couldn't see anything. She patted her pouch. She had her tinder and flint but no candles. The icy current hissed past her hips and she heard a faint splashing sound farther down. She tried a hesitant step forward. It felt like she were moving downhill. Ivy lost her footing, slipped, and slid under the water again.

When she surfaced, cursing steadily, the water sloshed off her. The sound of her splashing progress made it impossible to judge what direction she was heading. The river was not deep, just bitter cold as if it ran underground from a mountaintop glacier. Freezing to death seemed more likely than drowning. Ivy started moving, deciding it made no sense to stay still and shudder herself into pieces. If she ran into any sort of enemy—a hobgoblin or an orc seemed likely with a city full of them nearby—she wasn't sure how well she could swing her sword while shivering.

With no light, she relied on her less-than-perfect human hearing to get her bearing. She listened for her friends but could hear nothing save the increasing howl of the river rushing past her. Moving against the current pulled her further off balance, so she decided to wade downstream, hoping to hit some type of bank. She yelled and waited to hear some answer, but her own yells boomed in echoes and confused her sense of direction more. Low ceiling, Ivy guessed, and rock all around her.

Her boots slipped on the rocky bottom, and she half-fell, half-floated. Getting her feet under her, Ivy realized that the water was creeping up her chest. She needed to find dry land fast. Surging forward, she clanged against a metal grate. The shock jarred her through her armor.

With another curse, Ivy began to feel along the grate. Her armored gloves scraped across the grate with a piercing screech of metal on metal that made her wince. The metal grid rose higher than her head. Knowing that she could not get any wetter, Ivy drew a deep breath and dived. Feeling under the water, she found the grate extended down to the river bottom, leaving only a hand's width of space between it and the stone.

Resurfacing, she felt along the grate, all the time whistling as loud as she could past chattering teeth, being half-winded and steadily more chilled by the water. She might not be able to hear her friends, but she knew that if they were in range, they should be able to hear her. Being right-handed, Ivy groped toward the right along the cold metal.

Out of the corner of her left eye, she saw a faint glimmer of light. The light jerked and weaved toward her. Flattening her back against the grate, Ivy drew her sword from her dripping scabbard. She waited where she was, to see if it were friend or foe that advanced upon her.

A high *yip-yap-yap* sounded from the source of the light. Ivy sighed and one-handedly, over the shoulder, sheathed her sword and sneezed. The bouncing light resolved itself into Mumchance, running clumsily along the bank of the underground river, while Wiggles weaved around his ankles. When he saw her, he stopped running and bent over, breathing heavily. He was an old dwarf, and running in full chain mail and leather, also sodden with water, had left him out of breath.

"I thought we'd be in the sea before you stopped swimming," Mumchance panted. "Didn't you hear us yelling for you?"

"By the time I got my ears out of the river, all I could hear was water," grumbled Ivy as she sloshed to the bank, guided by Mumchance's lantern. "Where were you? Is everyone safe?"

"We were directly behind you. You kept swimming downriver, away from us as fast as you could go." Mumchance twisted his head up to get a clear look at her with his one good eye. He was trying to look fierce, but the smile pulling his scars askew undercut the attempt to scold her. "Daft human!" It was his worst epithet at such times.

"Wasn't swimming. I was busy trying not to drown." Ivy heaved herself inelegantly out of the water, the bank being almost shoulder-high; so she more rolled and flopped than lifted herself out of the river. The hilt of the sword on her back poked into her neck. She lay on the bank, nose to nose with Wiggles, who pranced back from her. The dog obviously considered one unexpected bath enough of a wetting for one day and did not want Ivy dripping on her. Ivy sneezed again and heard, far in the distance, an answering sneeze.

"Zuzzara," said Mumchance. "She sounds like a trumpet down here, doesn't she. What are you waiting for? Don't expect me to carry you, do you?"

"Just getting my breath back," sighed Ivy as she shifted into a sitting position. Out of the river, she felt even wetter and colder than she had in the water. To think that only this morning, she had cursed every layer of armor worn in the summer heat. Cold, wet, and surrounded by darkness, she wondered why dwarves liked living underground. Give her the dust, stink, and sweet summer heat of the siege camp over this!

"Hope Gunderal brought along one of her warming potions," the shivering Ivy said as she swung to her feet.

Mumchance and Ivy trudged back to the group, leaving a trail of wet footprints behind them.

"Gunderal's the only one who didn't fall in the river," said Mumchance. Ivy looked down at him. It was impossible to see the dwarf's face underneath his helmet from this angle, but his voice sounded worried, which worried her further. "Hit the rocks hard instead."

"Of course, the one who can breathe underwater and has webbed toes never goes in the water!" said Ivy, trying to coax a smile out of the old dwarf. Usually misfortune drew a bitter chuckle out of Mumchance, who took the admirable view that if you could not laugh at bad luck, then you would spend your life crying. But the dwarf did not respond to her feeble joke—another bad sign. "What makes you more sour than an old pickle?"

"My belt came loose in the fall. My best hammer and my pick are underwater somewhere down here." Mumchance's gloom was blacker than the hole they were in. He adored his tools and took excellent care of all of them. The pick was only a hundred years old or so, but it was a favorite of his. Ivy glanced at him. The dwarf still had his short sword fastened securely to his weapons belt as well as a small spare hammer, but that wouldn't help them dig their way out of the tunnel.

"Well, I have my sword and dagger," said Ivy, doing a mental inventory of what weapons they might have.

"And I've got my eye." In the lantern's light, the diamond under his left eyebrow flashed. When he was young, Mumchance had been caught in a mine fire. The flames scarred his face and ruined his left eye. When he had enough gold, he paid another dwarf to carve him an eye out of a black sapphire. That was the first of his gem eyes, and he had sold it two hundred years ago to join an expedition to the Great Rift. Since then, he had owned several gem eyes—some magical, some not. Keeping a gem in an empty eye socket was as good a place as any to hide his wealth, he once told Ivy. After all, even the most ruthless of tax collectors or the most skillful of thieves did not want to plunge their fingers into the eye socket of an elderly dwarf.

His current hidden treasure was a gem bomb made from a polished diamond. Although his right eye was a dark green, many people did not realize that the left one was a fake. The advantage of having extremely bushy eyebrows and equally bushy eyelashes, claimed Mumchance.

"This stayed stuck," said the dwarf, popping the fake eye out and then tapping it back into the socket—a gesture that always made Ivy a bit nauseated, "even when I fell tail over head into the water."

"At least you landed on the hardest part of your anatomy," Ivy said. The dwarf snorted. "No, it's good to see that diamond sparkle. We want you staying pretty." It was a running joke between them: that his current fake eye could keep them all pretty in a bad situation. Gem bombs cost a terrific amount, but Ivy had been happy to pay her share of the expense for this particular diamond.

"Not losing the gem bomb is the only bit of good luck that we have had. You'll see," the dwarf pronounced in despondent tones. Mumchance's expression could have won him a prize for the champion pessimist of the Vast.

When Ivy reached Zuzzara and Gunderal, she found the wizard looking paler than ever. She was clutching one arm and turning blue-white around the mouth from pain. Ivy knelt by Gunderal's side. In the dim light of Mumchance's lantern, even Ivy could clearly see that the wizard's arm was dappled with bruises. Pulling off her gloves and thrusting them through her belt, Ivy felt along Gunderal's arm with as gentle a touch as she could manage. The wizard bit her lip and didn't say anything while Zuzzara grumbled, "Don't pull so hard. She's already fainted once."

"At least you smell better," joked Gunderal with white-lipped gallantry as Ivy poked and prodded her arm. "More like cold water than camel."

"I've had a bath since we last talked," Ivy quipped. To a worried Zuzzara, she said, "No breaks."

"Are you sure?"

"Yes," said Ivy with more conviction in her voice than truth. She was no healer, able to sense what lay beneath the skin. She hadn't felt any movement in the bones, but that didn't mean the arm wasn't broken. "Strap it tight, Zuzzara, so she can't jostle it. Do you have any of your healing potions with you, Gunderal?"

Gunderal nodded her chin toward a smoldering mass of leather and broken glass. Puffs of noxious purple steam rose from it. "My potions bag is useless. Everything broke and mixed together."

Ivy hid her dismay with a shrug and a wave of her hand. "When did you ever need potions for your spells? Can you dry us off a little? Once Zuzzara has your arm tight?"

"I can't even make a light," sighed Gunderal. "I'm sorry, Ivy, I tried earlier when we were looking for you. It hurts, and I can't move my hand, and the words run together . . ."

"Just stop trying," growled Zuzzara. "You always try too hard."

"You don't understand," Gunderal snapped back, a slight flush of anger warming her wan features. "Magic is not just waving your hands and shouting some words. It takes concentration. I certainly can't concentrate with you fussing at me."

"Not to worry," said Ivy, hoping to avoid an argument between the two. Zuzzara would throw her body between any danger and Gunderal, but then she always turned around and fussed at the little wizard, which always set off Gunderal. This could lead to some odd results when she was spellcasting, like that flood when all they wanted was a little gentle rain. "Who needs magic?" Ivy added. "We can get out of here without your spells. Just rest now."

Mumchance shook his head at Ivy. "It's not new spells that should worry you. It's what she started before we fell in here."

"What?"

"Look at the water." The dwarf swung his lantern over the river. The river flowed along the very top edge of the bank. "She's been pulling all the water toward Tsurlagol for the last few days."

"To undermine the wall."

"Well, it's working very nicely," said Mumchance. "It undercut our tunnel and now it's rising higher."

"Can we get out the way that we fell in?"

Mumchance grunted. It was not a happy sound. "I sent Kid and that Procampur fellow to look. But I doubt it. The ceiling of the tunnel has probably collapsed between here and the entrance. We're buried alive and in danger of drowning."

Ivy stared into the darkness, listening to the water hissing below her. "That is a pleasant way to put it," she said at last. "Any bad news?"

Mumchance shook his head. "It could be worse. I can smell fresh air—well, not too stale air—and so could Kid."

"So another way out?"

The dwarf shrugged. "Hope so."

A clatter of hooves against stone announced the return of Kid and Sanval. They shared the party's other light between them, one of Kid's candles stuck in an earthenware bowl. Kid always had candles, bits of string, and a few odd dishes tucked in his clothing. Apparently some of his treasures had survived the fall.

"Blow it out," said Ivy, gesturing at the candle. Kid did as she asked, but Sanval looked like he wanted to protest at the sudden lack of light. With only Mumchance's lantern to hold back the darkness, the humans were at a distinct disadvantage.

"Why do that?" Sanval asked. He kept his voice low and polite, just as if they were sitting in the camp. He hadn't shouted, yelled, or screamed, although Ivy would have done all those things, and a bit more, if she had been dropped through somebody else's tunnel into this mess. Since she was the one who had started this tunnel, she was just managing to swallow her temper. After all, it would do her no good to scream at herself and it would worry the others.

For Sanval, she gave a fuller explanation than usual, mostly because she knew Procampur's forces were predominately human, and he'd probably never fought beside dwarves, half-orcs, half-genasi, and whatever Kid was (one of these days, Ivy meant to figure that out, but she wasn't too sure that she'd like the answer). "Because we may need that candle later," she explained to Sanval. "And by we, I mean you and me. The others can see in the dark."

"It's not so much seeing," explained Zuzzara, as she worked with a quick gentleness to bind Gunderal's arm into a comfortable position. For now, the half-orc seemed content to play nurse rather than nag.

"It's more like using the other senses. Sometimes a scent can have color and texture," said Gunderal.

"Smell, and sound, and touch, my dear," said Kid, with a tilt of his head.

"Even with one eye, I can see farther in the dark than any human." Mumchance snorted.

"So we can't afford to waste a candle while the lantern still has fuel," Ivy concluded. "We save the light and trust the others—by which I mean everyone who isn't human—to keep watch."

"It is your company, Captain," said Sanval, giving Ivy a title that she rarely used. But he was right; she held the high rank in their group, if only because nobody else wanted the title, and it sounded good when negotiating with someone like the Thultyrl. Ivy stared at Sanval. He gave her that straight-ahead, honest gaze that went with the square chin and rigidly straight helmet (she wondered if it had stayed straight during his fall, or if he had shifted the helmet back into its perfect alignment the first chance he got). Still, the level, honest stare was better than that nobleman's down-the-nose look that he wore sometimes when she was being truly obnoxious. Ivy chose to interpret this as meaning he would not openly disagree with her orders—after all, it was her company, not his.

"Thank all the gods little and small, or heavy and tall, that Procampur is too polite to fight," she hummed under her breath. It was another one of the camp songs, a ditty that the mercenaries favored as an explanation as to why Procampur's soldiers rarely got into the kind of camp squabbles that kept life in the mercenary section so interesting on a daily basis.

The Procampur gentleman acted as though he had not heard her and mused in his usual mild tone, "Fighting by candlelight or lamplight poses some interesting challenges."

"We will have no need of swords," Ivy said. "There is probably nothing down here but mud and a few rats." Or at least she hoped that was the case. They had a job to do, and one of the worst parts of tunneling under other people's walls was the nasty little surprises that you found underground. There were days when Ivy could swear that there was more wildlife below the earth than above it.

Mumchance muscled between the two of them.

"So now where?" said the dwarf. "If it would please you, Captain"—and his emphasis on the title was as dry as his beard was dripping wet—"to make up your mind while our boots are still out of the water." Like all the Siegebreakers, Mumchance took Ivy's title for what it was—a sham meant to fool other people—but he generally listened to her orders before criticizing. "Humans are never half as clever with their hands as the silliest dwarf child," Mumchance once told her. "But your race is good at the obvious when it comes to survival. Given half a chance, you can wiggle your way out of a bad situation faster than a rat can gnaw through cheese."

"River isn't over our heads yet," said Ivy, "but we're still all soaked and freezing. I want to be dry and I want to be warm before I start any march out of here. Can't use Gunderal's potions. How about that ring of yours, Zuzzara?"

The half-orc held up her bare hand, displaying a heavy gold ring with a crystal set within the band. "There's only one spell left." She sneezed. "Shouldn't we save it?"

Ivy looked them over. Gunderal looked like a carving made of bone, her complexion more yellow-white than its usual pale pearl. The tip of Zuzzara's nose was turning a nice shade of purple to match the deep gray shadows under her eyes. Mumchance huddled down into the collar of his armor like an old turtle trying to disappear into his shell, while Wiggles shivered at his feet, a miserable bundle of soggy fur. Only Sanval and Kid weren't shivering. In Kid's case, the heat of his ruddy skin was causing the water to literally steam off with a smell like wet goat and sulfur combined. Sanval, of course, stood like a carved post, apparently oblivious to the water dripping off his shiny helmet, streaming across his bright breastplate, and pooling around his well-polished bootheels.

"We need to be dry," said Ivy. "If only to get rid of that stink that Kid is giving off." With a little pointed grin, Kid clattered his hooves and flapped his arms to encourage the cloud around him to drift over the others. Zuzzara sneezed again.

"Zuzzara should save that spell, especially since I can't do anything," argued Gunderal, but she shivered as soon as she spoke. "We may need her ring later."

Zuzzara shook her head. With a worried glance at Gunderal, she replied, "No, we'd better use it now. Your magic will come back quick enough." The half-orc twisted the ring around on her finger and muttered the words needed to set off the spell.

The spell smelled like roses and felt like a desert wind, a long warm breath that blew across them. Heat, dry heat, surrounded them. The whole group was caught in a mini-tornado of hot, whirling air.

The warmth of the spell slid right down into Ivy's bones. She sighed with pleasure. Dry and warm was the best feeling in the world, Ivy decided. And the cleaning that went with the spell was rather nice too. At least one or two layers of grime had disappeared from her armor, not that magic could ever give it a polish to compare with Sanval's breastplate.

The rest of the group looked as happy as Ivy felt. Kid's curls tightened around his horns, Gunderal looked more pink than white, Zuzzara stopped sneezing, Sanval's armor practically dazzled the eye in the lamplight, and even Mumchance's scanty beard had curled back up around his chin, instead of dripping down his chest. Wiggles danced on her back legs, obviously delighted to be a white fluffy dog again instead of resembling a drowned white rat.

"Love that spell," Ivy said to Zuzzara.

"Good," said Zuzzara, "you can pay to recharge the ring next time. You know how much fire and air spells mixed together cost?"

"What was that?" asked Sanval, holding up one arm to examine with bemusement the regained brilliance of his armor.

"Couple of spells, combined, and caught in the gem,"

explained Gunderal. "One spell dispels the water and dries you off. Another warms you up. And your clothes are cleaned in the process." She gazed with satisfaction at her silk skirts, once again swirling like flower petals around her dainty ankles.

"You only stay warm for a bit," said Zuzzara, "but you stay dry until you fall into another river or snow bank. Gunderal thought it up for a winter campaign."

"It was the most horrible, miserable time of my life," murmured the wizard with an exaggerated shudder. "I was not just wet and cold all the time. My clothes were muddy and stayed dirty. There was no place to take a hot bath or clean your things."

"That wasn't so bad." Ivy shrugged. "But having your feet wet and cold all day and all night is never fun."

"So I thought of a way that we could combine a few spells to clean us all up," said Gunderal with a shake of her head at Ivy's usual dismissal of the importance of baths. "But since I can't cast fire spells, we have to hire someone else to cast them and store them in the ring. Of course, I can't wear the ring either. Something about the fire spell turns my finger bright red!"

"So I wear the ring," explained Zuzzara.

" 'Dry Boots' is what we ended up calling that combination of spells. Although the wizard who charged the ring used fancier words," recalled Ivy.

"Dry Boots is what it is. Dry boots is what it does," said Zuzzara. "Wizards can be too fancy at times."

"Not me," whispered Gunderal. She was still pale from the pain of having her arm strapped, but she used the fingers of her good hand to twist her curls back into their perfect, blue-black ringlets. Her potions were smashed, but her enameled hairpins and shell combs had survived the fall. She made two more twists of her hair, achieving a fetching topknot. "I just like to be warm, and clean, and well dressed."

"An excellent preference," Sanval agreed with a nod of approval at Gunderal. Ivy sighed and shook her head at the pair's mad obsession with cleanliness.

"Zuzzara was talking about magic," said Mumchance with a roll of his good eye at Gunderal's grooming. "And even you, lovely Gunderal, can get carried away. You can't just make it rain. When you call the rain, it has to rain with black clouds and lightning strikes, and a cold wind rising up from the earth. Has to rain until it floods, and we're all floating away on the barn roof."

"Just that one time," said Zuzzara, stepping in front of Gunderal. She might fuss at Gunderal all day and night, but she always defended her when others did the same thing. "Don't be so hard on her."

Ivy let them chatter when they should have been moving because she knew the wizard needed time to regain some strength. But the delay still worried her. The water was definitely lapping over the edge of the riverbank.

"All I'm saying . . ." said Mumchance.

"Is that we had a magnificent rainmaking business until we had too much rain. You humans and demi-humans never learn to control your magic—not like dwarves," said Ivy and Zuzzara and Kid all together. Gunderal giggled, a faint flush of color coming back to her cheeks. Mumchance rolled his eyes.

"It's an old argument," said Ivy, "and it never quite goes away." Zuzzara snorted.

"Well, Gunderal, my lovely wizard," said Mumchance, "you've done even better this time. The river is rising, Ivy."

"I know, I know," said Ivy, "and it's my fault, not Gunderal's, that we're sitting so low underground. If Gunderal feels well enough to move now, we need to find a way out. Mumchance? Kid?"

The dwarf nodded at Kid, who nodded back. The dwarf's

sense of direction underground was superb, but Kid came a close second. Sanval started to say something, but Ivy laid a finger against her lips. Silence was needed now.

The dwarf closed his eye and cocked his head. He stomped his feet a bit, his boot heels ringing on the ground; and Kid stomped back, making the high sharp clicks of hooves against stone. Kid's ears swiveled under his glossy curls, forward, back, and then flat to his head. Mumchance nodded left and then nodded right, and clucked his tongue. Kid whistled. The two opened their eyes at the same time and turned in the same direction.

"That way," said Mumchance pointing off to the right. "There's a tunnel entrance down there."

"Maybe two, my dear," said Kid, sniffing the air. "Big hole and little hole, running close together."

Ivy nodded. Underground, Mumchance had the best sense of direction, but Kid often surprised them with his unerring instinct for the safest route or the quickest way to the surface.

Zuzzara bent down to pick up Gunderal. "I can walk," whispered the wizard. "It's not my legs that are broken."

"What if you faint again?"

"Don't argue," said Ivy, "or argue later. We need to move." Even with her human eyes, she could see the water was higher now, almost to the lip of the ledge where they rested. "No more Dry Boots, remember?"

Gunderal made a face and stood up, following the others away from the river water. Although she was descended from the water genasi on her mother's side and could, with a simple spell, breathe perfectly well underwater, she was not dressed for swimming and was rather relieved that nobody had asked her to try to find a way out through the river. Normally, when Gunderal went swimming, she had a special, magical scaled outfit to wear—one that looked stunning both wet and dry.

The Siegebreakers felt along the ledge, walking cautiously in the direction that the dwarf had indicated.

Unlike the ledge, which appeared to have been made by men or dwarves, and was part of some ancient canal running into one of the earlier incarnations of Tsurlagol, the new tunnel appeared to have been dug out by some huge animal. Letting Kid lead, Ivy gestured for the others to follow. They fell into their usual pattern for a cramped space, a single file line. Kid clicked away first, Mumchance following with the lantern, and then Gunderal behind him. Ivy swung into her usual place behind Gunderal and felt uneasy. She glanced back to encounter Sanval's cool gaze rather than Zuzzara's "hurry up" stare. Zuzzara's bulk loomed behind Sanval. It was the usual order, but with one added. At her back was someone unknown. Would he know the right way to duck if she needed to swing in a cramped space? She would never hit Zuzzara by accident in a fight; the half-orc was used to Ivy, and Ivy was used to her. They knew which way the other would move. Ivy hoped that Sanval could stay out of the way in a fight. She suspected that cutting off one or two of Sanval's limbs might not help her win payment from the Thultyrl.

More importantly, now that she was not in immediate danger of drowning or freezing to death, Ivy considered the Thultyrl's request. They had to be reasonably close to the city walls, and that meant they still could undercut the foundation. They had water, lots of water, running swiftly behind them. They had magic. Well, they would have magic if Gunderal could ignore the pain of a possibly broken arm and call up a spell or two. In all probability, they could still collapse the southwest corner of Tsurlagol's walls in time. And that meant they could collect their payment. Maybe even pad the bill a little for additional hardship—after all, they would need to pay some wizard to create a new Dry Boots ring, and then there were all those potions that Gunderal had lost. Most likely, the potions could be added under miscellaneous expenses. That sounded fair to Ivy.

Things were not so bad, Ivy thought, but she was too wary to say it out loud. Luck had a way of turning on you, she had found, especially when you believed the worst was over.

CHAPTER FOUR

The tunnel branch smelled bad—like something had dragged carrion through it. It was a tight squeeze for Zuzzara. The half-orc bent low, pulled in her shoulders, and used her shovel to dig herself a wider opening at one point. Mumchance kept muttering at them to hurry, that he could smell the water rising behind them.

"Move then." Ivy pitched her voice loud enough for the dwarf to hear her. "Get those short legs stepping." A sharp bark sounded from Mumchance's pocket. "And stifle that dog. You can hear her for miles."

Mumchance scratched Wiggles's head. "Don't mind her, sweetie. Don't mind the bad-tempered lady who didn't listen to us when she should have . . ."

"Just march," snapped Ivy. She might not have a dwarf's keen sense of smell, but the rank odor of damp earth surrounded them, evident to even her very human nose. Years of tunneling behind Mumchance had taught her to be wary of such places. Wet earth tended to be unstable, and a collapsing wall or ceiling in this place could leave them buried forever. "Gods, grant me cremation and not burial in wet earth," muttered Ivy as she burrowed like a half-mad rabbit after the others.

Behind her, silence reigned. Sanval, true to his silver-roof dignity, had not uttered one complaint, not even when Zuzzara's digging had cascaded dirt down his back. Ivy wished the half-orc was as restrained. Louder than Wiggles's barks, a steady stream of muttering came from Zuzzara as she tried to squirm through the narrowing hole.

The tunnel angled steeply upward, and the scent in the air changed. It was no longer quite so rank, but still musty. But a big musty, like a large space, Ivy thought.

The light from Mumchance's lantern bobbed up and down and then disappeared with a sudden drop.

"Cave ahead," said Gunderal, repeating Mumchance's instructions down the line. "Small drop."

Ivy hissed that description back to Sanval and heard him tell Zuzzara.

"Good, good," the half-orc replied in a booming voice that brought down another trickle of dirt from the ceiling, "my back is aching. Just let me stand up straight, that's all I ask."

What Ivy dropped into was not a cave, but a huge hall buried completely underground. The walls were too far away to be lit by Mumchance's little lantern. Great columns rose from the floor to support a ceiling lost in the black shadows above. They looked like strong support columns, which was good; but there was no way to see the condition of the high ceiling, which was bad. The air still smelled stale, but there was an older smell, harsh beneath the damp.

"Ash," said Mumchance, stirring up a cloud with his booted foot. "Floor was burned long ago."

"Bones, too," reported Kid, skipping back into the circle of light. "Old bones, my dears, scorched skulls and blackened ribs."

"Kid, stay away from those," Ivy snapped. He ignored her, continuing to poke among the piles.

Gunderal walked up to one of the black columns and rubbed her good hand across it. She left a white streak shining in the lamplight. "Soot," she said, displaying the black marks on the ends of her delicate fingers. She frowned at the mess on her fingers and pulled a lace handkerchief out of her pocket to clean off the grime. "A fire storm inside. It smells like magic, Ivy."

"How long ago? Is it gone now?" Ivy wondered if it could be a lingering spell or curse, something that could collapse the place on top of them if they touched some forbidden object.

Gunderal whispered a few words and tilted her head and gave the slightest of sniffs, as if she were trying to smell a faded perfume in a room long abandoned. "Before we were born—before our mothers or our grandmothers," she said, shrugging and wincing as the gesture pulled at her arm sling.

"Speak for your own grandparents," said Mumchance. "Mine probably carved these pillars. Look at the fluting on the base, Ivy, that's good clean stonework. Dwarves carved that; humans wouldn't have the patience for it."

"Men can build and carve well, if they desire it," said Sanval, coming up to them with a solid rap of hard boot heels against stone. Ivy thought about pointing out that his firm tread was stirring up more ash, which was settling back down on his beautifully polished boots. But she decided not to comment, not until his boots looked exceptionally bad.

"There were great temples and palaces in Tsurlagol once, before it fell," continued Sanval. "Not all were built by dwarves."

"I still say it is quality work, and that generally means dwarves," said Mumchance. "Tsurlagol was always a steady source of income for those inclined to work with humans. The city's name became another word for 'job available' among dwarves. After all, the humans needed it rebuilt so many times."

Ignoring the arguments, Ivy asked the important question. "So we're in Tsurlagol?"

"In the ruins of some earlier Tsurlagol, I think," said Sanval slowly, as if he were dredging up an old story from his memory. "This city has been destroyed and rebuilt so often, it can be hard to know one level from the next. There are tales of fire once destroying Tsurlagol, sweeping through the city. A fire begun by wizards. It burned so wildly and so free that they finally buried the city under the earth to stifle it."

"Earth magic and fire magic," said Gunderal. "I can smell traces of it in this place. But both extinguished now. And something else too, something even older. Something strange, that pulls on the Weave in a way that I do not recognize."

"So how far are we from present day Tsurlagol?" asked Ivy, whose interest in history had never been strong and tended to be even less when she was trapped underground and had missed her breakfast and had little hope of lunch.

"Outside the walls still," said Mumchance. "We've been traveling too far to the north to be under the current city. That's what I think, and I'm usually right."

"Yes, and a disgusting habit that is too," replied Ivy. She rubbed her eyes—the old ash kicked up by her passage made her itchy—and peered into the gloom. "Best way out?"

"Many ways, my dear," said Kid, trotting back and forth like a restless racehorse. "East, west, south, north. Lots of tunnels going out of here. Bigger than the way we came. Men and dwarves have been down here since this burned and been busy, busy, busy digging away. Others have come since. Animals slithering on bellies, four-foot and two-foot and no-foot, hunting behind the humans and dwarves. Old tracks overlaying older tracks, all hunting one another." Kid's tongue flickered in and out of his mouth, as if he tasted all those passages in the air itself.

"At least there are not any rats," said Zuzzara, who had a strong dislike of rodents. It was Gunderal who always had to clean out the rattraps in the barn, unless she could talk somebody else into doing it.

"Too many reptiles, my dear," said Kid, bending over to examine a small pile of bones.

"Reptiles?" said Gunderal, who had a bigger dislike of snakes than Zuzzara had of rats. Ivy could not stand either rats or snakes, and so she killed them whenever she met any. Slicing off their little heads always made her feel better.

"Snakes, lizards, something else, my dear," said Kid, still stirring through the skeletons on the floor. "But these bones are men and halflings and dwarves."

"Treasure hunters," explained Sanval. "The ruins were rumored to be laden with ancient treasures, magical artifacts, and so on. Men came, and dwarves too, and others as well, to dig through the buried cities. Tsurlagol has been many cities—each one destroyed in a siege and then rebuilt."

"And wherever the treasure hunters go, predators follow close behind," grumbled Mumchance.

Sanval nodded. "The ruins gained an evil reputation, and most of the entrances were sealed. Then Tsurlagol fell in another battle, and another."

"Until they lost track of their own ruins," Mumchance said.

"Sort of place that my mother would have loved, if it were stacked with treasure," observed Ivy. "She probably could have sung you the city's entire history right back to when the first stone was laid for the first wall. When she wasn't saving the world or singing for some king, she was the most avid treasure hunter, always going underground after some artifact or other. That was one of the things that my father could never understand. He thought all jewels and gems were just worthless sparkly rocks compared to a nice flowering bush or a flourishing oak tree."

As they talked, they all circled slowly around the enormous hall, careful to stay within the small circle of light cast by Mumchance's lantern. Kid ventured the farthest into the dark, reaching into the shadows to feel the walls and better assess their condition.

"Your parents sound . . ." Sanval hesitated. He obviously could not find a polite way to inquire about her ancestry, but he tried. "They don't seem to have been quite the same as you."

"Not hardly," said Ivy with a snort. "They were heroes. When your Thultyrl finishes his great library, you can find their exploits in a dozen story scrolls. Saved the world from incredible evil a dozen times." She always found her parents hard to explain, especially to romantic fools like Sanval who believed in honor, great deeds, and noble acts of sacrifice as much as keeping their boots shined and their armor polished. Nor would he understand that the legacy of their heroics could be a greater burden than a boon to their daughter.

Mumchance pulled Wiggles out of his pocket and dropped the dog upon the floor, letting her run loose as he continued to examine the carvings at the bases of the pillars. She pawed at one pile of ash, turning up one of the scorched skulls that Kid had mentioned. Mumchance bent down to look closer at the dog's treasure. Several teeth had been broken out of the jaw. He shooed the dog away from the bones. He never allowed any of his dogs to chew on anything that resembled people, whether it was human, dwarf, or even orc. It made for bad feelings in a mercenary camp and, he believed, was bad for the dogs' teeth.

"Something came down here and pried the gold teeth out of the jaws," he speculated as he held the skull out of Wiggles's whining reach. "This area has been pretty well looted. There's no treasure left down here. Just ash and bones."

Kid made a little grunt in agreement as he brushed away the ash covering a headless and armless skeleton. Unlike the other bones scattered nearby, this skeleton glowed an odd phosphorescent green.

"Blast," said Ivy, catching sight of the shimmering green light surrounding the bones. "Kid, I told you to leave that stuff alone."

The odd skeleton moved, a very slow tentative movement, wiggling through the ash like a worm. Kid skipped neatly out of its way, not particularly frightened but not fool enough to let the skeleton touch him.

"What is it?" asked an amazed Sanval. In Procampur, bones did not go crawling around on their own.

"Skeleton warrior or what is left of one." Gunderal sniffed. "Badly made too. It should have a head, hands, and weapons." The thing staggered upright and wobbled on unsteady feet toward them. The Siegebreakers circled out of its way. It tottered after Kid, as if it were playing some grotesque child's game of hide-and-tag.

Wiggles spotted the moving skeleton and with a joyous bark started chasing after it. The little white dog wove in and around the skeleton's ankles with little yips, obviously regarding the whole thing as one giant snack. She rose up on her hind legs, dancing like a beggar before the green glowing bones.

"Oh blast," said Ivy seeing Mumchance's frown at Wiggles's actions.

Mumchance whistled one high sharp note. With drooping tail, the dog came back to his side. "It's your fault, Ivy, that she chases after such things," scolded the dwarf.

Ivy had taught Wiggles to catch bones when she threw them to her. "Well, she started doing that little dance for bones all on her own," Ivy said, defending her earlier actions to Mumchance.

"She did not. You encouraged her to do that. And it's just not dignified!"

Ivy considered that any dog bearing the unfortunate moniker of "Wiggles" already lacked dignity, but she knew better than to say it out loud. Instead, to soothe the dwarf's feelings, she asked him if he thought the skeleton warrior could be of any use to them.

"Lead us out of here, you mean? No, those things are brainless, and this one is more so than most," observed Mumchance as he circled left to avoid the headless skeleton. "Somebody looted whatever armor and weapons these poor sods had. They just left the bones behind because they're worthless." The skeleton seemed to sense that Mumchance was talking about it, because it began its mad lurch toward the dwarf.

"Let's leave before it bumps into anyone. It looks a bit moldy under that glow," said Gunderal, pulling her skirts close with one hand to avoid any contact with the thing. "Or before it kicks up more dust!"

"Shouldn't we kill it?" asked Sanval, still eyeing the lurching green bones with an uneasy look.

"Gunderal can knock it over with a spell," declared Zuzzara. "Go on, show him."

"It's a waste of magic," answered the wizard with a small frown of her pink lips. "Why should I do anything to it?" The skeleton was now reeling back and forth, obviously both attracted and distracted by the sound of their voices.

"It is harmless," agreed Ivy. "And it is already dead."

"I think we need to go east," said Mumchance, still walking in circles to avoid the skeleton. The dwarf ducked around the columns.

"Hey," yelled Ivy, "don't leave us in the dark."

Mumchance popped around the column that Gunderal had marked earlier, holding his lantern above his head to cast the widest possible circle of light. "Kid was right. Several ways out of here. I think we have gone west of the city, so we need to find a tunnel leading east."

"And that will lead us under the walls and then out," Ivy concurred. "Let's start moving. Come on!"

But Gunderal and Zuzzara were paying no attention to Ivy. They were still arguing about Gunderal's reluctance to cast a spell.

"I am not disanimating that skeleton," said the wizard, with the suggestion of a pout starting to form on her lower lip.

"Why not?" Zuzzara wanted to know. The half-orc's teeth were beginning to show under her upper lip—a sure sign of annoyance.

"Just because I don't feel like doing it," Gunderal replied. The headless skeleton started its weaving wander toward them.

"You always put down bones when you can. You have lost your magic!" The last was shrieked by the half-orc. The skeleton made an abrupt about-turn and lurched away from them.

"Don't be foolish! I can't lose my magic. I'm just tired, and my arm hurts, and you keep screaming at me!" Gunderal stamped her foot, raising up a cloud of ash. "Look what you made me do. It will take me forever to clean these skirts."

"You're still in pain. I told you that I should carry you out of those tunnels. You have exhausted yourself," said Zuzzara, modulating her voice into something less than an orc shout but still loud enough to make everyone else in the room wince. The skeleton picked up speed away from the half-orc, lurching rapidly toward the nearest tunnel entrance. Ivy watched it go with a mild expression of envy. Once Zuzzara and Gunderal got to the screaming stage, it was difficult to shut their mouths with anything less than an avalanche.

"I'm not a child," Gunderal answered back, her voice going higher, like a stubborn little girl. "Besides, that tunnel was so narrow, you could barely get yourself through it."

"But you're all white and dizzy."

"Because I'm wasting breath arguing with you. Leave it be, Zuzzara, I'm fine. The arm just aches. I'm not going to die from a sprained arm."

"So why can't you do any spells? You can always do spells."

"Not when I'm in pain and somebody is shouting in my ear!"

The skeleton was just a faint green glow, disappearing into the black tunnel.

"Shut up!" shouted Ivy, cutting across their words with a parade ground bellow. "They can hear you all the way back to the Thultyrl's tent. Zuzzara, if Gunderal faints or even starts to faint, sling her over your shoulder. Until then, leave her be!"

"Sorry, Ivy," muttered Zuzzara.

"Sorry, Ivy," echoed Gunderal.

Ivy shook her head at them, a little startled that they had actually paid attention to her. They must both be feeling exceptionally bad. "You should be sorry. Disgraceful, Zuzzara spending so much time worrying about you, Gunderal. And Gunderal, you should stand up to her more. Just because you're such a shrimp . . ."

Gunderal squealed an indignant reply. Zuzzara frowned at Ivy. "She's not a shrimp. That's not a nice thing to say, Ivy. She can't help being short."

"I am not short!" yelled Gunderal. "I'm just not oversized!"

"Yes, yes," said Zuzzara, patting Gunderal on her head.

"Zuzzara!" Gunderal ducked out of reach of the half-orc's friendly pats and checked her topknot with her good hand to make sure that it was still straight. Her hair had slid a little to the side. Gunderal pulled a small round silver mirror out of her pouch with a sigh. The mirror, unlike her potions, had survived the fall. She handed it to Zuzzara with a sharp command of "make yourself useful, hold this for me."

Ivy rolled her eyes. The world could be ending and Gunderal would still be combing her curls or arguing with Zuzzara. "Never, ever, go campaigning with a pair of sisters," Ivy said to Sanval. "Just because they are related, they will drive each other crazy as well as everyone else around them."

"They are *sisters?*" He nodded toward them, his eyes wide. The half-orc, with her gray-streaked braids caught in iron beads, her sharp-toothed grin, and her large-boned frame, towered above the delicate Gunderal, with her fine features, rose petal skin, violet eyes, and a cloud of blue-black hair sliding out of its enameled pins and shell combs. Ivy could see why he had not caught the family resemblance.

There were never two women more physically different than Gunderal and Zuzzara, and most of the mercenaries in the camp never even guessed that they were half-sisters—unless they came flirting after Gunderal only to meet the point of Zuzzara's sword. Or picked a fight with the half-orc and suddenly found themselves entangled in one of Gunderal's spells.

After a decade of living with them, Ivy sometimes forgot about the physical differences. It was something about the tone of their voices, the quickness in which they could dissolve each other into tears or laughter, or the way that they would both nag her simultaneously. She had a hard time seeing them as anything but sisters.

"How can they be so different and still be sisters?" Sanval asked.

Ivy shook her head at the Procampur's stodginess.

"Same human father, very different mothers," she said.

"They each take after the maternal side of their family. Look, we don't have time to discuss their family history, because it is extraordinarily complicated. Ask Mumchance some time; he knew their father." To everyone else, she shouted, "Let's get moving!"

"Ivy, I hear something," Mumchance said. "Listen. Something is coming. From there."

The dwarf pointed toward the far side of the huge hall in the direction they would have to travel. Ivy shifted her sword off her back, clipping the scabbard on to the side of her weapons belt, so it would be easier to draw. She saw that Sanval already had his blade out. It, of course, gleamed in the light of Mumchance's lantern.

Kid pricked up his pointed little ears, swiveling them in the direction that Mumchance was pointing. "Feet. Many little feet." Kid licked his lips with his purple tongue. "Many little scaly reptile feet running toward us."

CHAPTER FIVE

Z uzzara pushed her sister behind her, then stood with her shovel raised over her head, obviously listening. She peered through the darkness in the direction that Kid had pointed out. "He's right, Ivy," she said. "Something is coming—something small and fast!"

Mumchance tapped the remaining hammer in his tool belt to be sure it was in easy reach, then lifted his lantern higher, to light the hall to its fullest extent. Ivy hissed to the dwarf, "Your sword, don't forget your sword." She did not have to remind Sanval or Kid about the importance of edged weapons. Sanval shifted to a position closer to the front, facing where Mumchance had pointed earlier. Two slender stilettos appeared in Kid's hands. In a few moments, even the humans could hear the sounds of hard, scaled little feet pattering quickly toward them.

"Kobolds," groaned Mumchance, a dwarf with far too many centuries of memories of the little lizardfolk that plagued the underground routes of the world. "Those rotten little pests."

Kobolds burst through two entrances, attracted by the noise that Zuzzara and Gunderal had been making earlier. A few carried glowing green bones to light their way. Others were bearing flaming torches. Still more were heavily armed with pointed sticks, wooden clubs, and looted weapons. They flowed like a river through the cave—a tumbling, angry river of small, scaly brown creatures. From their horned heads and reptilian snouts to their nasty ratlike tails and long-clawed toes, they shook with the fury of their barking. The Siegebreakers could barely hear one another's warning shouts over the racket.

Ivy realized that their ragged line formation was about to be overrun. She bellowed, "Tight in! Tight in! Form a knot!" Sanval and Zuzzara shifted closer to her, forming the classic square position taught by military tacticians from Tethyr to Narfell. The smaller members of the party gathered close behind them, to be better shielded from the onslaught. Of course, long shields were normally used in this tactic. Any shield would have helped, but none of them had bothered to carry campaign shields to a tunnel dig. Ivy saw Sanval shift his left arm to the classic shield lock position, grimace when he realized that he was presenting just his forearm and elbow armor to the kobolds, and then use that same armored elbow to deliver a devastating blow to a kobold's vulnerable throat.

"Back-to-back?" asked Sanval. It was another classic, especially if fighters lacked shields.

"Too many," said Zuzzara, her half-orc vision allowing her to quickly assess the size of the threat about to overrun them.

The kobolds swirled out toward the walls of the pillared great hall, then rushed inward, under and over one another. They wore ragged clothing and bits of stolen armor—armbands from humans now wrapped around kobold thighs, a human-sized elbow guard used as a knee guard—and they waved their spears above their heads. It was hard for human sight to separate them; they looked like one big scaly mass of prickly arms and knobby legs. Ivy found that when she swung her sword at the kobolds, she was apt to bring it down on a sudden gap between them and then lift it with several kobolds clinging to the blade. They flew upward from her raised thrust, flying over one another and slamming into Ivy's head and shoulders on the way down.

Ivy stumbled and dropped to one knee. The kobolds swept over her in a ceiling of lizard underbellies, tattered shirts, and flashing red eyes. With a death grip on her sword's hilt, Ivy pushed herself upright, jabbing with her elbows and kicking out with her boot heels. The kobolds scrabbled to cling to her. She reached out with her free hand and grabbed a kobold by his ragged collar, swung him around to gain momentum, then tossed him back against the others. That created a momentary gap in the mass of bodies and gave her room to settle into a fighting stance. Once she regained her balance, she pivoted rapidly, her sword circling in a wide arc. The flat of its blade smacked into scaly bodies, clearing her path.

Another mass of kobold fighters flew toward her. She beat them back with her sword.

Sanval fought as Ivy had expected he would—with the absolutely correct posture of a man who had been trained by the very best tutors and then practiced every day as they recommended. The swift strokes of his sword cleaved a clear path through the kobolds. Unlike Zuzzara, Mumchance, or—it must be admitted—herself, Sanval did not scream or yell or curse as the little scaly pests swarmed around them. He just moved in perfect time with Ivy's attacks—backing up a step when she backed up, lunging forward with her when she lunged, his dagger in one hand, his sword in the other, in a perfect fighting stance. The kobolds tried to take advantage of his upright position, ducking beneath his weapons and wrapping their arms around his leather boots. They scratched and clung and tried to climb, curling their fingers around his belt to pull themselves up. He raised his arm, tapped his dagger on the top of his helmet to straighten it, then dropped into a lower position—all the better to hit vulnerable parts of the kobold anatomy with his shining sword and dagger.

The creatures parted before him, obviously intimidated by the fighter in brilliant armor. Sanval just smiled and dived after them. He seemed much happier now that he was confronting living things. He had lost the consternation evident during the earlier encounter with the glowing skeleton, but he did pause to say over his shoulder, very politely, "Is it acceptable to kill these creatures?"

"Not even their mother will miss them!" yelled Ivy, slicing a hand off a kobold that was making a grab for Sanval's brightly polished elbow guard.

The beast fell down with a gurgle of blood gushing over its companions. The other kobolds seemed distracted, obviously trying to decide between looting their injured companion and attacking the warm-blooded humans before them. Two kobolds looked down at the easy prey at their feet and up again at the warrior woman with her sharp sword and stolen spear and the man in the impossibly bright armor. The half-orc was still bashing right and left with her shovel and getting nearer. The two kobolds looked at each other again and broke off from the fight, dragging their screaming former companion to a shadowy corner and snarling at anyone trying to take their prize from them.

With the kobolds distracted by the scuffle over the wounded member of their tribe, Ivy took advantage of the lull in the fight to glance over her shoulder.

Everyone was knee deep in the short reptilian fighters (except Mumchance, who was nose deep). Like Ivy, the dwarf turned in circles, to protect himself on all sides, keeping the metal lantern as high as possible to give the fighters the most light. He kept jerking his head from side to side to see out of his one good eye.

Zuzzara—a mountain in the sea of kobolds—beat down from her height, her neat braids and big gold earrings swinging around her head, her finely tailored leather waistcoat stretched tight. The shovel became a no-nonsense club in Zuzzara's big hands, perfect for smacking heads, breaking spears in half, and sending kobolds flying.

But for every little brute that they knocked down, more appeared.

Ivy screamed at her friends to beat a strategic retreat up the nearest tunnel that was kobold free. "Knot hold, small fall back," she shouted.

Mumchance, whose responsibility in such formations was to lead the rear retreat, yelled that he had a tunnel. It was a narrow hole, only two or three kobolds wide and barely tall enough for Zuzzara to stand without bending.

Zuzzara was the last to leave the hall. She stopped in the shallow cave in front of the opening and tried to make a door of herself, closing the entry to the kobolds with her width and her slamming shovel. The majority of kobolds, still hungry, tried to rush around Zuzzara to follow them. Zuzzara gave a shout when one of the creatures trying to circle around her attempted to ram its spear into her backside. The spear caught on the long tails of the half-orc's leather waistcoat, proving Gunderal right in her argument that the style was not only fashionable but good protection too. Then Zuzzara swung around and brained the kobold with her shovel.

Ivy shoved little Gunderal in front of her as Sanval defended her back. The dainty wizard turned, obviously worried about her sister. Facing the pack of reptilian human-oids, Gunderal brought her uninjured hand up to her face and blew hard, making a high whistling noise. A blue light streaked across a startled kobold's face, and a fine icicle suddenly appeared hanging off the end of its nose. But the creature took no harm from the spell, shaking off the ice and wading back into the attack. "Go on, go on. Zuzzara is doing fine," Ivy shouted at the obviously dismayed wizard. "Keep up with Kid."

Mumchance swung flat against the tunnel wall, letting Kid and Gunderal scamper past. A kobold snuck past him as well, and Sanval made as if to follow, but Ivy caught his arm. Kid would keep Gunderal safe. He kicked back with his hooves, catching the kobold smartly on its scaly snout and giving it a flowing bloody nose. Another kick caught the kobold lower down, right below the stomach, and the creature folded into a small ball of whimpers.

Mumchance knocked it into its fellows with a hard blow from his fist. Wiggles gave the creature a nip on the tail in passing and then bit the ankle of another kobold trying to sneak up on the dwarf.

"Good dog!" said Mumchance, pulling the remaining hammer from his belt and braining the kobold with it.

"Use your sword!" Ivy shouted at him. The dwarf always forgot his sword.

Mumchance shoved his hammer back in his broad belt and pulled out his sword, waving it wildly. A number of kobolds ended up with sliced ears and nicked toes. The dwarf delayed following Kid. He still carried the Siegebreakers' only lantern, and he knew the humans needed him to light their exit from the tunnel.

Ivy whipped around, checking behind her and cutting off a kobold sliding along the tunnel wall. She rammed her sword through the belly of the scaly attacker and grabbed its spear with her other hand. She jabbed back with the spear, just under Sanval's arm, to catch another kobold in the throat.

Mumchance's energetic, if less effective, fighting sent the beams of the lantern swinging wildly. To avoid being blinded by the sudden light shining in her eyes, Ivy glanced up. Above them, she saw that one of the old wooden beams holding up the tunnel was clearly cracked.

"Zuzzara!" yelled Ivy, and she gestured with her thumb at the beam. The big half-orc glanced in the direction of the beam and then swept her shovel through the kobolds as though she were sweeping dust out the door. The creatures squealed as they went rolling down the tunnel.

"See it!" shouted Zuzzara.

"Come on, Procampur," Ivy said, dropping the kobold spear that she still clutched and grabbing Sanval's shiny steel-clad shoulder. She shoved him in front of her, almost ramming his nose into the side of the tunnel as she swung him around. "Time to run!"

"Your friend—" Sanval sounded a little muffled as he tried to keep his face out of the dirt wall in front of him.

"Can take care of herself," interrupted Ivy. "Follow the dwarf and stop fighting the kobolds. Zuzzara will get them!"

Falling farther behind her fleeing friends, the half-orc continued bowling kobolds into their kin using her shovel. The kobolds retreated, a bit intimidated by the tall, scream-ing half-orc woman with pointed teeth who was swinging an iron-headed shovel.

Zuzzara waded right into the group of kobolds. Now she swung the shovel like a scythe, a long, low sweeping motion that mowed through them. The little brown creatures ricocheted off the shovel's flat end, bouncing head over tail onto their fellows. *Thunk, whack, thunk.* The shovel rang against their scaly hides and horned heads. The kobold's leader—a little taller and greener than the rest of the crew—barked something high and sharp that sounded like Draconic commands, and his guards lowered their spears and tried to overrun Zuzzara. Most of the spear points simply bounced off her thigh guards and her wide leather belt with its big brass buckle. She was far too tall for the kobolds to reach any vulnerable points.

"Come on," said Ivy, still propelling the rest of the group in front of her. "Run!"

Once again, Sanval swung around Ivy, obviously intent on backtracking down the tunnel to join Zuzzara. Ivy grabbed him by his sword arm, disregarding the danger of being skewered by his blade, and pulled him completely around by shifting her weight and digging her feet in.

"We must help her. What are you doing?" yelled the captain.

"No. Keep going," Ivy shouted the order, and the tone got through to him. He blinked in confusion at her. "She'll bring the ceiling down. She knows what she's doing. Run, you idiot hero, run!"

Zuzzara flipped another kobold off the end of her shovel and plunged the blade straight up, catching it against the timber holding up that section of the ceiling. The half-orc bulged her muscles as she levered the shovel against the cracked beam. One brass button pinged off her waistcoat, and the kobold leader screamed as he caught it squarely in the eye.

The crack widened, and dirt rained down upon the squeaking kobolds. They raced away from the terrible giant who had wreaked such destruction upon them. With a loud splintering sound, the beam split in two. The beam's loose end bounced upon the head of the kobold's leader, cracking his skull.

Zuzzara spun around and raced back to her group, scooping up Sanval and Ivy as she ran. She tucked one under each arm, as if they were small children. Her shovel crashed against Ivy's knees as she tightened her grip around Ivy's waist. Ivy hoped that her armor would hold and tried not to think about breathing. "Let's go," Zuzzara cried.

With a crash, the rest of the ceiling collapsed, sending clouds of dirt through the tunnel. Coughing, choking, and with streaming eyes, the group stumbled out into a large, hollow space. Zuzzara gently set Sanval and Ivy down.

"Thank you, Zuzzara," said Ivy, once she had spat some of the dust out of her throat.

The gentleman from Procampur lowered his head in a quick bow toward the half-orc. "I also thank you, Lady Zuzzara, but I am sorry that I was not allowed to aid in your defense."

"Sanval, there was no need to play the hero. Zuzzara can take care of herself. Take care of the rest of us too," Ivy said, once she had figured out that he was courteously criticizing her order to retreat.

"But the thought was sweet," said Zuzzara, smiling wide enough to show off her long white canines.

"Maybe we all need a short rest," Ivy said and sat down on the ground with her legs straight out in front of her, her hands on knees, and her back bent. She tried not to gasp too loudly as she endeavored to catch her breath.

Sanval stood beside her, but from somewhere under his armor, he had retrieved a cloth and, to no one's surprise, began polishing his sword. "What are your plans now, Captain?"

Ivy looked up at him, trying not to look too discomposed. She was fairly certain that there were still bits of kobold stuck to parts of her gear. She pulled off her gauntlets and shoved them through her belt. "We will bring the western wall down for your Thultyrl, just as we discussed. This is just a little detour; but we will end up under the wall, and do a little strategic digging with Zuzzara's shovel. Let the river do its work. And then, plop goes the wall. We just need to be out of the way when the whole thing topples down."

"At least today is still better than that time with the hogs," muttered Zuzzara.

"Oh, definitely better than the hogs," Gunderal agreed. The little wizard motioned Zuzzara to sit down and immediately began readjusting her sister's braids—a good sign that their latest spat was over.

"Hogs?" Sanval said, watching them with a puzzled frown. Ivy wasn't sure if he were confused by the reference to pork or still trying to figure out how the pair could be sisters.

"If we had had more time to work on the fuse and to pack those pigs correctly, we would never have had any problem," said Mumchance.

"What pigs?" said Sanval glancing at the dwarf. So it was definitely the pork that had aroused Sanval's curiosity. Ivy stifled a grin at this evidence of his humanity. Only dead men could keep silent around her friends, once they started one of their rambling tales; and, as she suddenly recalled, even that lich had not been able to resist joining in the conversation once. Oh, that had been a strange campaign!

As usual, each of the Siegebreakers began talking as fast as they could, trying to beat one another to the end of the pig story.

"Dead hogs, actually," said Mumchance and was immediately interrupted by Zuzzara.

"Very dead hogs," said the half-orc, who had complained unceasingly during that campaign that she had to carry most of the pigs.

"Absolutely rotten hogs. Bloating," added Gunderal, blowing her cheeks out to illustrate. Anyone else who did that would have looked hideous, but Gunderal just appeared even lovelier, if slightly fishlike, with her bloated cheeks.

Sanval looked baffled, and then enlightenment dawned. At that point, he looked mildly nauseated.

"Exactly," said Ivy with a chuckle, getting into the conversational game. "We packed a bunch of these dead hogs under a tower."

"The smell was awful," shuddered Gunderal, who had stayed as far away from the dead pigs as she could and kept a perfumed handkerchief over her nose whenever she could not maintain her distance.

"Then we lit a fire under them, dear sir," said Kid, who was wandering in and out of the group as he usually did, too restless to sit still for more than a moment.

"Nice long fuse, right into dry tinder packed under the hogs," said Mumchance. "Only it burned a little faster than we expected."

"And the tunnel that we were in was a disused part of the dungeons," explained Ivy. "Typical place. Scraps of this and that, stacks of dried-out bones from old prisoners, old spell books that the wizard who owned the place had tossed away."

"Everything caught on fire," said Gunderal. "And Wiggles did warn us, Ivy, when all that smoke started pouring up the tunnel toward us."

"The dog was a hero," said Ivy with a roll of her eyes.

"But the pigs? The dead hogs?" said Sanval. Ivy liked that about the officer from Procampur—he could stick to a point. Which is more than any of her friends could do.

"The hogs did exactly what they were supposed to do," said Ivy with a grin.

"The pigs went boom!" said Zuzzara, with a lot of satisfaction, flinging her hands up in the air and giving a very orclike chuckle.

"And the tower fell down," concluded Mumchance.

"Served that wizard right for trying to steal that land from those pig farmers," pronounced Ivy.

"An interesting method of destruction," Sanval said. "Why did you not try to do the same here?"

"Not enough hogs," sighed Mumchance. "What you've got, you eat. Pity. With a little refinement, more containment of the blast, it could be a very effective technique. But there is water here, so we decided to use that instead."

"At least three underground rivers in the area. I just joined them together to form one large river," explained Gunderal. "Then I sped up the current a little and persuaded that river to change course to run under the western wall. It won't last forever; eventually the rivers will split back into their true courses."

"But it should give us an enormous amount of water to wash out the foundations with. Better than pigs really," said Mumchance.

"If we are not in these tunnels when the river goes through," said Ivy and then wished she had kept her mouth shut.

"My dears," said Kid, whose wandering led him to poke his nose down another tunnel, "there is another buried building here."

"All burned out like the last one?" asked Ivy, pulling herself upright and walking over to the entrance.

"No, my dear," said Kid. "Just dusty and smelling of blood."

CHAPTER SIX

Mumchance swung his lantern around. The tunnel opened into a room from another long-buried level of the city. Everyone moved cautiously into the dark new space, listening for the sound of kobolds barking or the patter of little skeleton feet. But only silence filled the shadows. None of them feared a fight; but, as Ivy reminded them in her fierce whispers, each battle cost them time. They needed to find a way out so they could complete their mission and collapse the wall before Enguerrand's charge.

Although they only had Mumchance's lantern to light the gloom, the ceiling was low enough that they could see a delicate mosaic of shells and blue waves.

"How pretty," said Gunderal. She loved shell patterns and had painted similar waves all around her room at the farm. Then she coughed. "What is that smell?" A sharp metallic odor surrounded them like an evil fog. "It smells like a butcher's shop," she said. "Please tell me it is very old blood."

"Fresh blood," said Kid, his nostrils quivering. "I wonder what died here?"

There were no signs of fire, just the awful smell of blood, underlaid by a moist smell of moss and mire. Wiggles whined and then whimpered. Mumchance patted the little dog on the head, trying to quiet her, but finally scooped her out of his pocket and set her down on the tiled floor. Yipping high enough to make Ivy wonder if her ears would start bleeding, Wiggles raced away into the darkness, with Kid trotting quickly behind her.

"Come quick, come quick, my dears," cried Kid. "Here's a fresh kill."

"More kobolds?" grumbled Mumchance, swinging the lantern toward the sound of Kid's voice and Wiggles's barking.

"Bigger. Much bigger," said Kid, sounding pleased.

A freshly killed bugbear lay at Kid's feet. The bugbear's head had been chewed off, and one arm was missing. When it had walked upright and had had a head, it had been taller than Zuzzara. Scraps of black leather armor bound together with heavy chains decorated the bugbear's body, but its hairy legs were bare, and rope sandals covered the sole of each hairy foot. The stench rising from the corpse was nauseating.

"Look at that blood trail," Zuzzara said, pointing at a mixture of slime and blood that led into another dark tunnel entrance. "Something took the missing arm that way!"

"Well, they can keep it," said Ivy. "Let's see what else that he's got."

"It's a she, not a he," said Zuzzara, looking more closely at the curved leather breastplate and studded leather skirt.

"Well, whatever it is, it is dead," said Ivy, leaning down to search the body. She tried breathing through her mouth to lessen the impact of the mildewed smell. Ivy ran quick hands down the bugbear's bulky body, liberating a leather pouch tied to the creature's weapons belt. She opened it and saw with satisfaction that it held a number of cheap tallow candles, well wrapped against damp. "More lights," she said, and she tied the pouch to her own belt. She fished out a handful of candles, shoving them at Sanval.

"There's a torch under the body too," said Mumchance, pushing at the bugbear. "Here, Zuzzara, roll it over and let's get that." Zuzzara leaned down and flipped the bugbear over.

"You are looting the dead," said Sanval. He sounded troubled and a little disgusted, and was still holding the candles in one armored hand.

"Of course," said Ivy. "Stow those candles somewhere. If you get separated from us, you'll need them." Reluctantly, Sanval tucked the candles behind his breastplate, while Ivy questioned the half-orc. "Zuzzara, what have you got?"

"Torch dropped over here, and two more fastened to its back."

"Excellent. Any food?"

"Just a water bottle, and that's almost dry," said Mumchance.

"So the bugbear came down here from the city, do you think?"

"It came with others," said Kid. "There are more tracks here, back and forth: human or two-foot at least, my dears."

"Bugbears? Orcs? Humans?"

"They all wear boots," said Kid. "But big. No little feet like Gunderal."

"I am not little," squeaked Gunderal. "Ivy, somebody has been casting spells in here."

"Whatever killed the bugbear?"

"No." Gunderal sounded puzzled. "It feels more like light or fire. Not my sort of spell. Complicated, arcane, sort of a seeking spell."

Sanval looked doubtful. "Can she tell that?"

Ivy nodded. "It comes from her mother's side of the family. She's got a good sense for magic. When it has been used, how it has been used. She can usually tell if something has been warded or laid with magic traps, which is useful when you're sneaking into places that you don't know."

Gunderal sighed. "I can't tell you more than that, Ivy. But whatever it was, it happened not long ago. Not even a day. It is very strong, much stronger than that room that we just left. That was old magic. This is new."

"Wonderful," said Ivy. "That means that there is someone else down here." She passed out the candles and the torches, spreading the lights around so that Mumchance could wander off with his lantern and not leave the rest of them stranded in the dark. Zuzzara relit the bugbear's torch and held the light over the blood trail leading off toward the dark entrance of the tunnel.

"Funny marks in the dirt," she said.

"Footprints," speculated Kid. "Big four-foot with round, flat fleet."

"Hope whatever it was is off enjoying lunch," said Ivy, "and will take a little nap afterwards."

"Just so long as it doesn't wake up hungry for a snack," said Mumchance.

"Lovely thought! Anything else worth taking?" said Ivy, poking the bugbear's recumbent body with her toe.

"Nice rope," said Zuzzara, unwinding the coil of rope from the bugbear's shoulder.

"The weapons are trash," replied Mumchance with a dwarf's contempt for shoddy metalwork. "Worse than ours. The sword is blunt, and the knife has a notched blade. The scabbard's not bad—it's better work than the rest, gilt on leather and some nice stitching."

"Loot then, picked up here and there," said Ivy, knowing the signs. "Making do with what the others don't want. Fancy scabbard kept after someone else has taken the good blade."

"Fottergrim's raiders were so armored," said Sanval. "Carrion crows, picking what they can out of other's misery." Ivy wondered if he was still describing Fottergrim's troops or delivering a bit of a rebuke. She decided to take his comments as referring to the former.

"There might be more of Fottergrim's people in the ruins," he added.

"Must be more," answered Ivy. "A bugbear like this wouldn't come down on its own."

"Maybe they were countermining us," said Mumchance.

"Countermining?" asked Sanval.

"Digging under where they think we are digging," Ivy explained, "to collapse our tunnel. Except we did such a very good job of collapsing it ourselves and saved them the trouble. Mumchance, they are pretty far off the line if they were looking for our tunnel. And the bugbear doesn't have any shovel or pick."

"Maybe the others took the tools with them," suggested the dwarf.

"And left the weapons and the torches?"

"No, my dears, they did not stop to take anything. When this one was killed, the others kept their distance," said Kid, who was circling back and forth, peering at the tracks on the tiled floor. "They started forward, *stamp, stamp, stamp,* not running, just walking, but then they stopped very quick, *shuffle, shuffle* back and to the side. Two of the big ones tried to turn back again, but the other one, the one with man-sized feet, drove them away."

Silence fell on the group, as they realized what Kid meant.

"They moved out of range and let whatever it was chew on the poor bastard. Or their officer ordered them not to attempt a rescue," said Zuzzara, voicing all their thoughts. "Remind me not to fight for Fottergrim's pay, if that's the way that they treat their mercenaries."

"A wise decision," said Sanval with that little quirk of the lips that indicated he was amused.

"Especially since we're fighting for Procampur," emphasized Ivy with a quick kick at Zuzzara's ankles. She missed her target; Zuzzara could move fast when she chose.

"Why are they here then, Ivy?" said Gunderal to cover up her sister's mistake and Ivy's embarrassment.

"A little quick treasure hunting?" guessed Mumchance.

"In the middle of a siege?" said Ivy. "Well, it can be boring sitting on the walls waiting for someone to attack."

"Because of this," said Mumchance, who had moved from the bugbear's looted corpse. Before him gaped a black square. He swung the lantern forward to reveal an ancient city bath, with marvelous mosaic pictures covering the bottom of what was once a large pool.

With the use of Mumchance's lantern, they could make out footprints trailing through the dry and dust-filled bath. Kid jumped in the pool and began tracking the tracks, his nose almost brushing the floor.

"Here a big two-foot knelt," sang out Kid. "Here his four companions waited, *jog, jog, jog* from one foot to the other. They were impatient. Scared too, most certainly frightened. They kept turning to peer behind them. Why, my dears, why?"

"They heard a noise, or thought they heard one," speculated Ivy. "They were expecting an attack. Then they came out of there and were attacked."

"Five at the bottom of the pool?" asked Sanval.

"Oh, five, definitely five," said Kid. "Five walked down here, and five went out. But only four ran away from this room."

"Leaving one dead companion behind them," said Ivy. "They were right to be nervous. Something was hunting around here."

"Then why wait for someone to look at pictures in the bottom of a dried out pool?" asked Gunderal.

"There are armor scrapes against these tiles. From where the one with man-sized feet knelt," said Kid, peering even closer. "Here's a line a little ways back. Sword, scabbard maybe, brushed the dust behind him?"

"Officer then. They had to wait for him," said Ivy, sitting down cross-legged on the edge of the bath. When Kid went tracking, he could grow a bit obsessed. From past experience, she had learned to make herself comfortable until he was done. Sanval remained standing, straight as always, shifting slightly from one foot to the other. Ivy reached up with her fist curled and rapped his armored knee. "Rest now and stand at attention later," she said.

Sanval nodded and knelt on one knee beside her to watch Kid. Well, sometimes the man displayed sense, thought Ivy.

"Look at the picture, Ivy, that's a wizard in the center of that picture," said Gunderal. "Zuzzara, can you bring the light closer?"

Zuzzara nodded and jumped down into the bath. She swung her lit torch over the pattern that Gunderal had pointed out.

The dust had been carefully swept away from the center of the bath, displaying a series of mosaic pictures. The first picture showed a wizard, with runes woven in his azure cloak, standing before a tall tower with flames sprouting from it. More flames played along the walls behind the tower, and behind the walls a hint of rooftops, also engulfed in flames. Men and women ran along the tops of the walls, arms outstretched as if pleading with the wizard to save them. A great jewel, portrayed in tiny crystal tiles, glittered in the wizard's hand.

A trail of more runes, picked out in silver and gold tiles, circled away from the picture and led to a second one. The burning tower was leaning forward, and men fell from its crenellated top to lie on the ground before the wizard. Black lines zigzagged away from the wizard's feet and led to a final picture, which showed men carrying the supine wizard away on a bier, the gleaming gem resting on the center of his chest and portrayed as twice the size of any man's head.

"And down go the walls of Tsurlagol," said Ivy, waving a hand at the center picture. "Which siege do you suppose that was?"

"Long ago," guessed Gunderal. "Look at the runes on his cloak."

"Two or three generations before they built this bath, and the tile work is old to begin with," guessed Mumchance. The dwarf dropped over the rim of the bath and stalked toward the picture to examine it more closely.

"What do you mean? Why two or three?" asked Sanval.

"Takes that long for humans to turn something horrible into art," said Mumchance with all the authority of a dwarf who had already celebrated his three hundredth birthday. "Mighty big shock for the folk like me—leave a town with all the humans swearing that they will never forget this or that, come back in ninety years, and it's all a fairy tale to those humans' grandchildren. Or a decoration for their city bath. Why if half the heroes in the world were as tall as their statues . . ."

"They'd all be giants," chorused Zuzzara and Gunderal. This was an old, old complaint of Mumchance, and they'd heard it almost as often as his tale of having to earn his first mining tools by shoveling away snow higher than his ears from the mountain entrances of his family's diggings.

"And dwarves don't do that?" asked Sanval, and Zuzzara and Gunderal groaned.

"You shouldn't encourage him," translated Ivy when Sanval glanced at the sisters. "Let's hope this is one of his shorter lectures."

"It takes dwarves longer to lie to themselves," admitted Mumchance, ignoring Ivy's comment. "And we don't do pretty just for pretty's sake. Well, not in pictures. Armor and jewelry—that's metalwork and another story. Elves, now, they have the longest memories. When they make a picture like this, it's to remind other folk, and they hate it when you question what's real and what's not. Everything is real to an elf."

"Some of them just have a finer sense of humor about it than others," added Ivy, who got along better with elves than the rest of the Siegebreakers. She appreciated their efforts to seek out her father in Ardeep when he disappeared during his last journey into the forest. It wasn't the elves' fault that he had not wanted to be found after her mother's death. Ivy suspected that he was probably one of the murmuring oaks shading the path there. He had always talked about the simplicity of life as a tree—trees, after all, did not have hearts that could break, or even crack a little.

"So, is this a real event or not?" asked Zuzzara, who never could stand much philosophizing and disliked talk about elves because of some bad experiences with one of her stepmothers.

"Well, it's not an elf-made picture, which makes it a bit tricky to tell," started Mumchance.

"Somebody came down here in the dust and gloom, not to mention risking kobolds and whatever chewed that bugbear, and stopped to look at it," said Ivy.

"Maybe we should discover who that person was," suggested Sanval.

"Or maybe we should look for a way out that keeps us out of their path," Ivy said loudly.

Nobody was listening to her. They were all carefully puzzling over the picture on the floor. There were times when kobolds were more sensible than her friends. At least kobolds concentrated on the basics like finding food and left mystical patterns written in the floor tiles alone.

"I don't think that they were just looking at the pictures. I think they stopped to read the runes," added Gunderal. "Look how the dust is cleaned away so carefully."

"Can you read them?" asked Ivy, because it was obvious that nobody was going to do anything until they had solved this little mystery.

Gunderal shook her head. "Too old. Four hundred years or more, if I had to guess. And it's only a guess." She looked at Mumchance where he was bent over the runes, tracing the edges of each shape with a stubby finger.

"I'm old," snorted the dwarf. "But I'm not that old. Runes change, meanings change. But these . . . These might be corruptions of old Netherese symbols."

"That is not possible," said Sanval.

"Even I know that empire was dust long before the first Tsurlagol was built," added Ivy, just to stay in the conversation.

"The empire disappeared long before Tsurlagol was built," agreed Mumchance. "But that doesn't mean all their magic disappeared overnight. Dig deep enough and you run into strange things in the Vast—artifacts, toys, bits of spellbooks that those mad sorcerers left behind. They were human, after all—that meant they bred like rabbits and ran like deer when the disaster finally overtook them."

"Mumchance," said Ivy in gentle reproof. "Both Sanval and I would like to think our race has a few redeeming qualities."

"Many and many," said the dwarf. "You humans are usually nice to dogs and other small furry creatures. But the best of all is that you know when to run to survive. Dwarves can be too stubborn sometimes." He fingered the old scars on his face and shook his head at memories of the mine fire that had destroyed his family. He shrugged and continued the discussion of Netheril, because ancient history was always more pleasant than his own memories. "When the shining cities fell, not everyone died. Some carried mighty magic into exile. There have always been rumors about a fantastic treasure buried beneath Tsurlagol. The story goes that the first time Tsurlagol fell into dust and ruin, it was because of a great magic that men could not control. That sounds like Netheril to me. Then later they started that mad fire that they had to bury under the earth. That was fairly recent history for a dwarf, not much before my grandfather's father's time. And they used some fancy artifact to bury the city, something like what would have come out of Netheril."

"But is there information here that can help us?" said Ivy, glancing around the shadowed bath.

"The dwarf is right, my dears. These symbols are not well made, but they do bear great resemblance to those used by Netheril and its sorcerers," said Kid, circling back to peer over Mumchance's shoulder. He pursed his lips. "These are copies of copies, made by men who could only draw what they saw, but could not read."

"And how do you know that, young thief?" asked Mumchance.

"Because I had a master once," said Kid, very softly. Ivy, who had only paid mild attention to Mumchance's lecture on ancient history, was caught by Kid's depressed tone. He never spoke of his past, and this was the first time that she had heard him mention a master. "He was not a good man. But he was fond of old things, very old magic. Spellbooks with runes like these and worse."

"Worse?" asked Ivy. Kid ignored her and trotted away, his nose down to examine the footprints in the dust.

"So when fire consumed the city, they used a magic jewel to bury it," said Gunderal, still discussing the mosaic with

Mumchance, pointing at the burning walls before the cloaked wizard.

"Just one wizard with a fancy gem? Doesn't seem likely," said Ivy.

Sanval wrinkled his brow. "I was never that fond of history lessons, but I always heard that it was an earthquake sent by the gods in answer to the people's prayers."

"I doubt it was the gods. That wizard must have caused the earthquake with a spell, maybe something stored in that jewel that he is holding, like we store Dry Boots in our ring," said Gunderal, on her knees at the edge of the bath, still staring at the mosaic. "Why show a spellcaster with a gem if you don't have a gem in the tale? It must have been a wonderful spell. I told you that I could still feel echoes of weird old magic in that hall."

"Fascinating, all of it, but we are not here to go treasure hunting. In fact, if someone is looking for that magic rock, I would rather avoid them," said Ivy. "Kid, which way did they go? Our party of five less one?"

"They came from the east, my dear," said Kid, trotting to the edge of the bath and flipping himself easily to a handstand on the rim, giving a quick click of his hooves at the top of his handstand, and then somersaulting to a dark archway across the room. "And they left to the north, through that wide arch there."

"Is he always like this?" asked Sanval.

"No," said Ivy. "He's tired, or he would have done a couple of extra cartwheels. We've thought about selling him to a faire once or twice." But Kid's actions disturbed her. In more recent years, Kid only did such extravagant show-off gestures when he was in one of his black moods.

"But we've never found a faire," grunted Mumchance. "Come on, girl, give the short guy a hand up." The last was said over his shoulder to Zuzzara, who grabbed his belt with one hand and easily lifted him over the edge. Zuzzara followed with a little hop. She wandered back over to where the bugbear lay, to pick up the extra torch left by the body.

"So we go east," Ivy decided. "That group came from Tsurlagol. I'm sure of it."

"If we go north, we will learn why they came here," said Sanval in polite disagreement, obviously deciding that now was not the time to defer to her status as Captain of the Siegebreakers.

Ivy sighed. She knew being in charge without opposition would not last that long—it never did with her friends, and why should Sanval be any different—but she was willing to try. "Do we care why they are here? They're deserters or treasure hunters or lost fools," said Ivy.

"What if they are planning an ambush?" Sanval asked.

"Well, jolly good luck to the Thultyrl, then," said Ivy, "but I'm not his bodyguard. I'm here to bring down a wall, and to do that we need to go east, not north." Sanval still looked troubled. "That sounded a bit crude. Most assuredly, we wish the Thultyrl a long life and much happiness," Ivy added.

"Until we get paid," muttered Mumchance and winced when Ivy's elbow connected with his ear.

Zuzzara gave a shout. She'd been poking around the bugbear's body, muttering about the smell of moss getting stronger. Suddenly, the half-orc yelped with pain. She spun around, flailing at the air. "Something is here," she screamed. "It bit me!"

CHAPTER SEVEN

Zuzzara stumbled back toward them, one leg angled oddly out in the air, shouting that she could not shake her attacker off her leg. The only problem was that nobody could see anything.

Gunderal told Zuzzara to stop playing stupid jokes.

Zuzzara screamed, "Half-orcs never play practical jokes!"

She slammed her shovel down on the space near her leg. The shovel hit something with a sickening thud. The smell of rotting mushrooms filled the room. Zuzzara and her invisible attacker tumbled into the empty bath.

"Look at that!" said Mumchance, pointing at the dusty tiles of the bath.

The group could clearly see the signs of four big round feet being dragged after Zuzzara as the half-orc stumbled in circles and continued to beat down with her shovel. Each stroke of the shovel thwacked into something solid that stopped it at the level of Zuzzara's knee. Each stroke also released more fungal stench into the air, so that even Kid was choking a little and covering his nose with one ruddy hand. But Zuzzara's efforts seemed to have no effect on her attacker.

Ivy and Sanval leaped into the bath. Both swung their swords at the same time, cutting through the air near Zuzzara.

Ivy felt her blade hit something solid and sticky. When she pulled back on the stroke, she could see a gelatinous shimmer drip down her blade.

Closer to Zuzzara, the stench was overpowering and reminiscent of the strange mossy smell that had clung to the dead bugbear's corpse. Ivy gagged and staggered back. She concentrated on breathing through her mouth and sawing away at whatever was attacking Zuzzara.

Kid's two stilettos went whistling past Ivy, and thankfully missed Zuzzara. One struck and seemed to stick in whatever was attached to the half-orc's leg. The little stiletto bobbing in the air gave them another reference point for their attacks.

Beside Ivy, Sanval swallowed grimly against the stink and slashed at the invisible creature. Like Ivy, he had trouble with his sword sticking in whatever he struck. His blade was almost wrenched out of his hand, and he overbalanced, dragged to one knee as he wrested the sword free. Sanval rolled to one side to avoid Ivy's next awkward stroke and jumped straight into the air. As he launched himself forward, he brought his blade point down with a two-handed stroke into the space nearest to Zuzzara's ankle, trying to skewer whatever was attacking her. He missed. The sword buried itself into the mosaic floor with a sickening thud. Even Mumchance winced as the big fighter's shoulders and arms took the shock of the misdirected stroke. Sanval simply grimaced, pulled his sword free, and immediately swung around to assault the invisible foe again.

Zuzzara's attacker dragged her in a circle. She was pivoting on her right leg with her left leg almost straight out in the air. Ivy danced around her, trying to figure out from the angle of Zuzzara's leg where her attacker was. She slashed down just as Zuzzara pivoted farther right. Ivy stopped the stroke in midair, nearly knocking herself off balance, but she managed to avoid slicing into Zuzzara's knee.

"Watch her leg! Watch her leg!" screamed Gunderal, as both Ivy and Sanval continued to swing their swords blindly at the area near her sister's left boot. "Be careful!"

"Get it off me," cried Zuzzara, the leather in her boot now starting to visibly shred around the calf. "Gunderal, do something! It's magic!"

With an elegant swirl of silk skirts, Gunderal leaped into the bath. She landed gracefully but with a wince of pain as the movement jarred her sprained arm. With her uninjured hand, Gunderal fumbled loose the canteen at her belt, worked its cap open, and tucked it into her sling. She sprinkled drops of water into her good hand. Her canteen slipped out of the sling and fell onto the floor a thud. Stepping over the canteen, Gunderal muttered the words of a spell as she walked toward her half-sister.

"Get back!" screamed Zuzzara, terrified Gunderal would walk into the blades of the fighters or fall victim to whatever was trying to chew off her leg.

Gunderal ignored her. She continued to chant, cupping her hand in front of her face, and blowing out her breath.

Gunderal's breath sparkled in the air, glittering like crystals. A frost formed on the invisible creature revealing four stumpy legs and a square body, with a cluster of round nodules covering its sides.

Now able to see the creature, Ivy and Sanval hit it on each side with their swords.

"Go for the head, go for the head," cried Gunderal.

"Where is the head?" screamed Ivy.

"Where it is attached to my boot!" yelled back Zuzzara, giving a mighty kick. The creature hung on. Sanval swiftly spun and sliced away the cluster of nodules on the top of the creature's head, barely missing Zuzzara's foot. The creature gave off an even more noxious puff of stink and collapsed.

A mottled green and brown hide became visible underneath the glittering frost that coated it. Although it was not easy to tell head from tail, what appeared to be the attacker's mouth remained locked around the calf of the half-orc's boot.

Using Zuzzara's shovel as a crowbar, Sanval broke open the creature's jaw and released Zuzzara's leg.

Gunderal observed with satisfaction that the creature had not been able to completely bite through Zuzzara's double-dragonhide boots. "I told her that the expense was worth it," she explained to Sanval, who was still looking a little dazed from the stench of the creature. "Besides looking fantastic, those boots can survive the worst attack. It never pays to wear cheap footwear."

"Certainly," Sanval replied courteously. He flicked out a clean cloth from his belt pouch to wipe disemboweled fungus off his sword and the front of his own fine leather boots.

"But look at that tear," said Zuzzara, leaning down to finger the long rent in the top layer of leather.

"We will just take them back and get them exchanged for a new pair. Probably something in green, that would be nice."

"Do you think that cobbler will do that?"

"He gave us a lifetime guarantee," said Gunderal with the assurance of a wizard who was always willing to make merchants live up to their promises.

Ivy poked the creature with the tip of her sword, just to verify that it was dead. It let out another puff of stink.

"Ivy, leave it alone," said Gunderal, pulling up one of her long silk neck scarves to cover her nose.

"Poor baby," said Mumchance, looking down at the four-legged creature. He snapped at Wiggles. "Don't touch. Don't roll in it! Bad dog! Wiggles, stay!" He lunged for the little white dog and scooped Wiggles up into his pocket before she could roll over the corpse.

"Poor baby!" said Zuzzara. "It nearly chewed my leg off."

"Oh, stop making a fuss," said her unsympathetic sister. "I told you that we can get you new boots."

"What is it?" said Ivy. "Besides smelly."

"Phantom fungus—you get them in old tunnels and caves. It's a little one though. Full grown, it would have been chewing off Zuzzara's hip, not biting her ankles," said Mumchance. "Good thing you used that frost spell, Gunderal. It is the only thing that could have made it visible. Their invisibility talent is immune to most magical counterspells."

"It should have frozen in place," said Gunderal. She sighed from deep in her chest and shook her head. "Not just sparkled."

"Hey," said Zuzzara, "last time that you did that freeze spell, you turned me into a snow orc. That spell can sting!"

"The spell did not work anyway," said Gunderal, ignoring her sister's criticisms as she usually did. "I just can't seem to concentrate long enough."

"The frost was fine," consoled Ivy, "all we needed to do was see it to kill it."

"It was an excellent use of magic," agreed Sanval with a slight bow. "In Procampur, we say that subtlety always takes more talent than brutality."

"Oh, do we say that?" said Ivy, remembering some of her wilder strokes as she tried to bash Zuzzara's attacker. "How very refined of us."

Sanval simply looked puzzled at her tone.

"So, if this is the baby," said Kid, poking at the dead pile of fungus with one shiny hoof, "where is the mother, dear ones?"

Everyone glanced around the room.

"I think it is time to start moving again," said Ivy.

For once, nobody argued with her.

CHAPTER EIGHT

"Three possible exits from the city bath," Ivy pointed out to her friends, ticking them off on her fingers. "There's the lovely, dank, animal-dug tunnel which that baby phantom fungus came from."

"Where that bugbear's arm has gone, my dear. I'm sure that the mother fungus has it," said Kid, sniffing the air in that direction as he retrieved his stilettos.

"Which may have body parts and bigger phantom fungi," agreed Ivy. "Thank you for reminding us."

The whole group decided against exploring that tunnel.

"Then there's the northern way," said Ivy, gesturing at the line of footprints that indicated where the rest of the unfortunate bugbear's party had apparently fled.

"That is the way that we should go," said Sanval. "If the bugbear was one of Fottergrim's raiders, then they may be setting up an ambush. They may be aiming for the Thultyrl's camp."

"We don't know that," said Ivy. "All we know is that they were down here, and they are probably not friendly."

As an officer of Procampur, Sanval pointed out that it was his duty to find out what the raiders were doing in these ruins and, if possible, capture or kill them. He was very courteous about it and obviously expected everyone to agree with him.

Ivy looked at her friends, and they all rolled their eyes.

"We were not going that way," she told Sanval. "We need to get under the walls of Tsurlagol and bring the western wall down. As the Thultyrl decided."

Sanval looked unconvinced. But before he could voice another argument or strike out on his own, following that mysterious trail of footprints, Zuzzara grabbed him from behind in a friendly headlock. He squirmed, but the half-orc was stronger and quite a bit taller than the officer from Procampur. She leaned over his shoulder to look into his face and show him her grin, full of pointy teeth.

"I owe you my life for being so quick with your blade," said Zuzzara, "so I definitely cannot let you run off and get yourself killed."

To avoid getting his windpipe crushed by Zuzzara's concern, Sanval agreed to stay with the group, but he kept casting glances back at the line of footprints leading away from the bath.

"I should follow them," he said.

"Sweet," said Zuzzara, giving him another hug against her brass-buttoned waistcoat that caused all the breath to leave him with a giant whoosh.

"She's more dangerous friendly than angry," said Ivy, pulling Sanval away. "But she's right too. Sweet of you to want to do your duty. But not proper behavior for an officer."

Sanval's dark eyes widened. "I would never do anything that was inappropriate."

Ivy gave him her most innocent smile. "Then you will want to follow the Thultyrl's orders. He ordered you to go with us and stay with us and help us bring down the wall, didn't he?"

Sanval looked as if he had just swallowed something very bitter. The logic of Ivy's argument was inescapable. Yet, she could see a certain doubt crawled across his handsome features. Would it be more fitting to chase after a possible threat to the Thultyrl or to carry out the Thultyrl's orders and stay with the Siegebreakers?

"It would be best to stay with us," Ivy answered his unspoken question. He looked even more troubled that she had guessed what he was thinking.

Kid trotted back and forth at the entrance to the eastern tunnel.

"Are we going or staying, my dear?" he said to Ivy, clip-clopping a little ways into the darkened entrance.

"Give me your torch," Ivy called to Zuzzara, putting her hand out for it. She took the lit torch from the half-orc and thrust it into the entrance of the tunnel. A long, smooth way ran straight ahead. Strong stone walls and ceiling were clearly visible. It was a tunnel built by humans (or more likely dwarves, added Mumchance). Best of all, it did not look as though it would easily collapse on them.

"It looks like a passage to Tsurlagol," decided Mumchance. "But it might take us farther east than we want, toward the harbor gate rather than the southwest corner of the wall."

"We'll worry about that when we see where we come out," decided Ivy. "We do not have time to try every tunnel. This one looks the most promising to get us close to the wall."

The tunnel ran in a long curve, at times so narrow that they had to go in single file and at other times so wide that four could walk abreast. Kid led, so he could backtrack on the trail of the bugbear's party.

"Quick step, quick step," he chortled as he followed the faint trace of the footsteps in the dust. "They march straight, no pause, no doubt. They are hurrying away from where they came."

"Were they pursued?" asked Ivy.

"Yes, but much later; other feet have passed through here," said Kid. "But the followers miss the arch where we entered and go farther that way." Kid pointed to another tunnel, slanting west and north as far as they could tell.

Bending down to examine the floor, Kid seemed puzzled by some of the marks. "Footprints, here and here, but older tracks too. Tracks of rats on four little feet, tracks of kobolds chasing after the rats, tracks of something with no feet chasing after the kobolds."

"I do not like the sound of that," said Gunderal with a delicate shudder.

"Oh, my dear, these are old, old tracks," said Kid, one ear twitching back and forth in thought.

Ivy wondered if this tunnel had been a good choice. Still it was better than wandering after whatever party that bugbear came from, no matter how much a certain shiny gentleman kept making longing glances over his shoulder.

"What are the freshest tracks in this tunnel?" asked Ivy, convinced that she would not like the answer.

"Those we also saw in the room behind us, big feet and man-sized feet." Kid scratched his nose, obviously mulling over his answer. "And then there were those tracks that hugged the walls and never went to the center of the room."

"You didn't tell us about those!"

"You were in a hurry to leave, my dear. Another group of big feet went tiptoe through the room. The tracks were a little fresher than the dead bugbear that Zuzzara found. Another party of orcs or bugbears perhaps, following the first group. Big hobnailed boots, all of them wore, and there were many treading over the other footsteps."

"Blast." Just what they needed: entire troop movements underground. Could Fottergrim be considering an ambush, using these tunnels to sneak some of his horde outside the walls for a quick attack on the camp? Or was it someone else, with their own secret mission in this rotten, mixed-up, tangled ruin of a dead city with its long buried secrets? "Blast, blast, and blast!" muttered Ivy as she considered their options. Well, there was no way to go back, and whatever way that the bugbears or other creatures had entered, that had to lead to the outside. Get her above ground and in the open air, and she could work out a strategy. Or let her find the foundation of Tsurlagol's current western wall and she would topple it with great pleasure.

"Is there a problem?" As usual, Sanval's tone was courteous and pitched low enough to be discreet.

"Problem?" Ivy gave an exaggerated roll of her shoulders. "No problem at all! Just thinking about the best way to bring down that wall. A good spell blast, maybe."

"Ivy, we found something!" Zuzzara's bellow echoed through the long, narrow tunnel. An open doorway was carved into the wall. To enter the dark room beyond, they had to step up over a broad stone threshold. From the other side, the Siegebreakers could see the lintel of the door was carved with a procession of men and horses, dragging wagons full of jars behind them. The flare of Zuzzara's torch and the light of Mumchance's lantern revealed a long, narrow room with niches carved into the walls, filling the space from floor to ceiling. Neatly piled bones, three or four skulls resting on the top of each pile, occupied each niche.

"Funeral procession," said Mumchance, glancing up at the carving on the lintel. The carved parade continued across the ceiling, and small flecks of old paint brightened the ribbons carved around the spokes of the cartwheels and in the horses' manes.

"We are in an ossuary," said Sanval. "We have these in Procampur too. The dead are taken below the streets once their bodies are burned."

"That is what I love about being underground," said Ivy, "the wonderful things that you get to see, like other people's graveyards."

"Look at all the names on the wall," said Gunderal, going from niche to niche. "I can read them; this writing is not that old. There are whole families in some of these niches: mother, father, children."

"Not here," said Zuzzara, pausing before another niche. This one had a smaller pile of bones than the others, and only one skull rested on top. The skull looked a little lonely, Ivy thought. Gunderal leaned against her sister's shoulder and recited the epitaph inscribed upon the wall, her voice growing softer and sadder with each line.

> "As for the name of this warrior, I do not know it,
> Nor do I know from what place he came.
> But he rode to our walls,
> With his banner displayed and flying in the wind.
> At his boasting, the defenders drew their blades.
> We could not resist from beginning the battle.
> Four fellows caught him and beat upon him,
> Each stroke like a hammer upon an anvil.
> His armor split to reveal the treasure beneath.
> The wizards stole his gem, as they steal all.
> When he died, the ground was hard with hoar-frost.
> So we burned his body to keep him warm,
> And stored his bones among our dead.
> But his name we never learned,
> And his family mourns unknowing."

When Gunderal finished, even Zuzzara gave a little sniff and knuckled her eyes. Mumchance cleared his throat and rubbed Wiggles's ears. The little dog licked his hand.

Ivy just shrugged. She would not let such a memorial affect her. "So died a mercenary. Unknown, unnamed," she said.

Sanval gave her a peculiar look, almost sympathetic. Ivy ignored him. "I wonder what his treasure was."

"Probably meant that they cut out his heart," said Mumchance.

"I do not think it was his heart," said Gunderal. "Wizards would not have much use for that." She brushed an errant curl back behind her ear, tilting her head to one side in puzzlement. "There's something else here. Some runes below the bones, like the ones back in the mosaic. See that one"—she tapped the symbol with one shell pink nail—"is almost the same as the one written near the big jewel carried by that wizard toppling towers in the picture."

Distracted by a clattering sound, Ivy whipped around to see Kid poking through another pile of bones. She snapped an order at him. "Get away from that!"

Kid just gave her one of his pointed smiles and said, "No magic here, my dear. No spells. Just dead, cold dead, in their little pots and niches." He trotted back to where they stood. He leaned very close to the wall to study the peculiar runes pointed out by Gunderal. "Beautiful Gunderal is right. These are the same as the ones written in the mosaic. Jewels—these marks may mean jewels. And there are footprints below the niche that are the five that we tracked before. Looking for something, but finding nothing, I think." Something about the lone pile of bones discovered by the sisters intrigued him. Kid stuck his long, black-nailed fingers into the pile of bones before them, shifting the skull out of his way as he felt around the niche.

"I swear if you stir up another pathetic skeleton to attack us, I'm leaving you behind," exclaimed Ivy.

"Do skeletons attack him often?" asked Sanval, remembering the lurching collection of bones in the hall of ash.

"With depressing regularity," Ivy replied. "Skeletons, animated corpses, crawling hands of the undead. There's something about him. Like honey to bears. Get away from those bones! We don't have time, and there is nothing there for you to steal!" Ivy suddenly could not bear to see the lonely mercenary disturbed again. Eventually, everyone should be allowed some peace and rest. She reached out and smacked Kid not too gently across his bottom.

"I go, I go," bleated Kid in mock terror, skipping out of her reach. "See how swift I run. Can you catch me, my dears?"

Rounding a corner at a quick trot, Kid almost smashed his nose on the stone wall that blocked the tunnel ahead. Ivy swore. They had reached a dead end.

"Just need to find the handle," said Mumchance, running his hands over the smooth marble wall. "It must open. They did not walk through solid stone."

Gunderal nodded and passed her hands over the wall as well, making ladylike sniffs, as she tried to divine what type of lock might hold the door closed.

"So who do you think is down here?" Sanval asked Ivy as the pair in front of them tried to open the secret door.

"Treasure hunters, most likely, and not from Procampur's side of the wall," Ivy admitted with as much candor as she could spare. She was not going to mention her worries about possible stray troops from Fottergrim's horde. That would be enough to send Sanval dashing off in the darkness to save the day and probably get himself killed. "You have camels but no bugbears among your mercenaries. It could be deserters, which would be an encouraging sign, but you would think that they would be carrying more gear with them."

"Why are deserters a good sign?"

"Now you want to chat? When we are in a hole in the ground with no clear way out?"

"Do you have something else to do? Just now?" And the man even made his comments sound reasonable, much to Ivy's disgust.

Mumchance muttered something about missing his good pick and gestured Zuzzara to come forward. He took her shovel and tried to wedge the blade under the secret door. Ivy and Sanval moved farther back down the tunnel to give them room to work.

"Why are deserters a good sign?" When Sanval wanted to talk, he evidently wanted to talk.

"Because you don't desert if you think you're going to win. You leave when the food starts running low, or the water runs out, or the guy in charge turns out to be a raving lunatic with delusions of immortality and world conquest. Which happens far more frequently than you would think sensible. Look at Fottergrim."

"World conquest?"

"Well, no, not since the Black Horde was destroyed. But why be such an idiot orc and seize a city? Especially such a city with such a history of bad luck. No one has ever managed to hold onto Tsurlagol. Wandering here and there in the hills, he could survive. Raid a town for a day, carry away the chickens and children, that I can understand." Sanval gave her one of those straight down the nose looks that were a specialty of his. "Not approve, mind you, but understand."

"About the chickens?" His tone was exceptionally dry.

"And the children. An orc has to eat, and he has to have somebody to wash out his laundry. A moving horde like Fottergrim's needs slaves to do all the tasks that fighters think are so far beneath them."

"Laundry."

"Cooking, digging latrines, washing socks. Even if you only change your socks once a year, it is nice to have a clean, dry pair."

"So why not take a city and enslave its citizens?"

"Because it is too big. Somebody is sure to object, like Procampur, and knock the walls down and take it back. It is strange. Fottergrim has been unusually clever for an orc these past ten years. It is almost as if someone talked him into taking the city. Or he was seized by divine madness. And I will bet you my nonexistent lunch and unlikely dinner, he is up on the walls right now, regretting that he ever invaded Tsurlagol."

"So you think we can win the siege," persisted Sanval.

"Certainly hope so," replied Ivy, trying for a nonchalant tone to impress him. "Because we don't get paid unless Procampur wins. So I would like to bring a wall down before I leave for better places. And nothing is getting done by standing here!"

The last was pitched much louder and Mumchance responded with, "We're trying, Ivy." The dwarf dropped to his hands and knees, sniffing along the floor like a hunting hound, obviously trying to scent some stray draft blowing under the door that might reveal an opening. Wiggles ran around him, occasionally giving the dwarf's red nose a big lick. "Get away, sweetheart," muttered Mumchance at the dog. "Let me do my work."

"Perhaps Enguerrand can succeed without your help," suggested Sanval. He probably meant his words as a kindness, but that statement pricked Ivy's pride.

"Give me pike dwarfs and gnome archers, and I can topple any cavalry charge," said Ivy. "And Fottergrim has much more than that."

"Pikes and arrows would not work against such trained cavalry as Enguerrand leads," stated Sanval with calm conviction.

"Does. Did. That's how I met Mumchance," said Ivy.

Sanval cocked an eyebrow.

"In the mud, pinned under a horse, having been on the wrong end of the charge," explained Ivy. "Terrible day, rain pouring down, fresh plowed field all gone to muck. But there were these dwarves and gnomes. Just standing there. Waiting for us. They looked so very short from where we were sitting on top of our great big chargers. So the trumpets sound, the drums beat, and we go racing up hill in full armor in the stupidest charge in the history of horse-mounted warfare. I was one of the lucky ones. The arrows got my horse, and it rolled over on me. That horse's death saved me from being spit on the pikes. Also I fell face up, rather than face down, so I didn't drown in the mud."

"How old were you?" said Sanval.

"Fifteen and foolish at that age, like all young humans," said Mumchance standing up and brushing off his knees. He hooked his little hammer out of his belt and began tapping on the door, pressing one ear against the stone to listen for echoes. With a roll of his good eye toward Ivy, he added, "But she was politer than most."

"Keep working," said Ivy. "You don't have time to gossip." To Sanval, she said, "My mother taught me court courtesy."

"Really?" said Sanval, clearly remembering the song about the red-roof girls and a few other comments.

"Oh, I can speak like a lady when I need to," said Ivy with a blush. She remembered the song too. It lacked elegance. Any Procampur court lady would swoon at the first verse alone, and it was probably just as well that she'd stopped before she'd gotten to the last lyric, because that might have caused a few of the more squeamish Procampur gentlemen to faint too. That boy in the Forty had been extremely pink in the face when she had passed him in front of the Thultyrl's tent. "And my father was a druid who taught me how to keep my mouth shut. The elves used to call him the Silent Walker. For example, he would never interrupt a good story halfway through. It was one of the things my mother liked best about him whenever his silence wasn't driving her crazy."

Sanval did not say anything.

"My manners saved my life," Ivy continued. "There I was, pinned under a dead horse, with this dwarf sitting on top and asking me what I thought I was doing there. I told him the truth. I absolutely didn't know why I was fighting that war, but I would appreciate a little help."

"So I dug her out and dried her off. By then the girls' father had disappeared, and their mothers were gone, and I thought I could use a little extra help at the farm." Mumchance pushed Zuzzara's shovel's edge against the bottom of the stone door. Scraping sounds, the high-pitched kind that made the back of Ivy's teeth hurt, filled the tunnel and caused the others to retreat a few steps. With a grunt, Mumchance pulled the shovel out from under the door and returned it to Zuzzara. "Well, that didn't work. Gunderal, any luck?"

Gunderal muttered something that sounded terribly close to a swear word. Zuzzara looked slightly shocked; Zuzzara's mother had never let her use language like that! But, being a water genasi, Gunderal's mother had possessed a very salty tongue when she was angry. Gunderal's vocabulary was far less delicate than her looks.

"There is a lock, a magical lock," muttered Gunderal. "I am sure of it. But it is on the other side of the door, and I can't tell you anything more."

"It was the most miserable little war. Neither of us could see any reason to stay," Ivy continued talking to Sanval. She never had any luck with magic doors. If Gunderal and Mumchance could not open it, they would have to go back. She kept chattering to distract herself from screaming in frustration. "So we deserted, Mumchance and I. It was the sensible thing to do."

"And this war?" asked Sanval with more than polite curiosity.

"Oh, as miserable as the rest," said Mumchance, still staring at the door. The dwarf frowned, the lines crossing his forehead deepening, and the scars across his face more pronounced than ever. With the iron clad toe of his boot, he softly kicked the obstacle facing him—a straight line across the bottom of the door, *clang, clang, clang*—but nothing rattled or echoed in the stone door. "But war pays our bills. That is why mercenaries fight, boy. For the money. Not honor, not glory, not history. For loot. Well, except for the odd bad one. . . ."

"The ones that fight because they like it," said Ivy. "And before you ask, we are the good kind of mercenary. The ones who care most for gold."

Sanval did not look reassured.

"So why do you fight?" she asked.

"Because I am a noble of Procampur, pledged to the service of the Thultyrl. And he is a good king, the wisest we have had for some time. But even if he were the worst of tyrants, I would still answer his call. My family has always served the Thultyrl."

"What sort of family do you have?"

Sanval frowned. "None now, but I come from people who do their duty. My parents did as their families asked. They were betrothed in their cradles and married at the most auspicious time determined by their parents."

"And were they happy?"

"I do not know," admitted Sanval. "I never saw them except at formal gatherings. We send our children to the schools for those of our district, to be raised together by approved tutors. Like most boys, I seldom left my dormitory until I came of age, and by then my parents had perished from the same fever that killed the old Thultyrl."

Ivy grinned at him. "Bet you never thought your path would drop you underground with a bunch of mercenaries unsuccessfully trying to break through a door." The last sentence was made directly to the dwarf still kicking the door in front of her.

"Maybe a counterweight, above the door," speculated Mumchance, ignoring Ivy. "Hey, Zuzzara, give me a boost up."

Zuzzara grabbed the dwarf around the waist and lifted him to her shoulders. His head rapped smartly on the stone ceiling. "Sorry," said Zuzzara with a grunt as she adjusted the dwarf's feet on her shoulders.

"No," said Mumchance feeling along the lintel. "Nothing here. Let me down. Gently! Gently!"

Zuzzara caught him as he flipped off her shoulders and just prevented him from landing headfirst on the floor. Kid snickered, and even Gunderal looked a little less depressed.

After several more attempts to get the door to open, they declared themselves defeated. Mumchance admitted that without the exact knowledge of how the door locked and unlocked, they could not open it.

Gunderal, in particular, was very upset by her failure after having such recent improvement with the phantom fungus. Zuzzara told her sister not to worry, that her spells would come back soon.

"Like you would know anything about magic," said Gunderal with a tearful sniff. She fumbled a handkerchief out of her pocket and dabbed her eyes.

"I know nothing about magic," admitted Zuzzara with one of her deep chuckles and a pat on the back that caused Gunderal to stumble. Ever since Gunderal had managed at least the frost spell against the animated fungus, Zuzzara had cheered up. She no longer suggested carrying her little sister or whispered to Ivy about the possibilities of blood poisoning developing from a sprained arm. "But I know you, little sister. You may be pretty, but you are not dumb."

It was the start of an old family joke, and Gunderal giggled. "And big and ugly doesn't mean you're stupid."

"Unless you fall down on the way to the outhouse." Zuzzara added the obscure punchline that Ivy had never understood.

Gunderal started laughing so hard that she had to stop to mop the streaming tears out of her eyes.

"Sisters," moaned Ivy. "I will never, ever, campaign with sisters again!"

"You say that every time," said Mumchance. "Hurry up, you two. No point standing around here now."

As he turned, he bumped into Ivy, who stumbled and thrust out her left hand to catch herself. As she fell against the wall, she felt a stone shift beneath her gloved hand. A grating sound came from the floor beneath them, and the entire room shook.

"Earthquake?" asked Sanval in a calm but resigned tone, as he kept his balance on the shifting stone.

"Wizard work," shouted Mumchance over the crunch of rock sliding over rock. The whole room lurched to the left and bumped to a stop. A new door opened in front of them, with a black corridor running before them. The stone door behind them and the entrance to the ossuary before them had disappeared.

"Shifting passage," grumbled Mumchance. "Sort of stupid thing that wizards put in for short cuts."

"Well," said Ivy, still determined to be optimistic, "perhaps this leads straight outside."

"Did you suspect such a possibility?" Sanval asked Mumchance.

"I suspect everything, but that never finds the key to a shifting passage. Only a truly lucky or miserably unlucky accident does that," the dwarf complained and stamped ahead of them through the opening.

"And which kind of accident is this, my dear?" speculated Kid with a soft laugh at the dwarf's grumbling.

"Won't know until we get there," said Mumchance over his shoulder. "Come on, Wiggles, hurry up." The little dog was lagging behind and seemed reluctant to enter the room. The dwarf whistled. Wiggles tucked her tail firmly between her legs and slunk into the passage behind him.

In the darkness far ahead of the Siegebreakers, the magelord hissed and stopped. He had felt something, like a cold draft across his spell-laden shoulders. The charms attached to his robe murmured to him, giving him advance warning of a new danger. Magic . . . Somebody or something had woken up an old magic in these tunnels.

"Fools." He peered back into the blackness outside the yellow light cast by the torches. Fottergrim had set trackers on his trail. He had known that the big orc would do that. Who knew what those idiots had stirred up? If only that foolish orc had done what he had told him to and stayed outside the walls of Tsurlagol, letting him explore these tunnels in peace. No, no, the big stupid oaf had to smash his way into the city and start a war!

The bugbears surrounding him shuffled their broad feet and voiced their complaints. They had been growing more obnoxious in their objections since they had had to abandon that one female bugbear. As if such a creature mattered to him! A quick snap of the fingers, and a quicker flash of fire lit up the tunnel, turning the bugbears' complaints to sullen but subdued snarls.

"We are being followed," he informed them. After all, it was the bugbears' job to guard him while he went about his business. He had already paid them a half-horse worth of nearly fresh meat that morning. And promised them more in the evening. "Be alert!"

But he decided not to rely on the bugbears alone—they were stupid creatures whose big muscles gave them their only worth in his estimation. Something else slithered through the ruins of buried Tsurlagol, something large and scaled and hungry.

With a few muttered words, and at the cost of only one charm, the magelord called the creature to him. At his feet was the big hole that they had just climbed out of. It was another dead end for his treasure hunt, but a perfect trap for anyone foolish enough to follow him.

The new tunnel led the Siegebreakers into another broad room, wider than the first. Like the ossuary, it contained bones—only these were strewn across the floor as well as piled into niches. At the sight and smell of the bones, Wiggles's ears went up. The little dog tentatively wagged her tail. Mumchance snatched at her collar to keep her from grabbing the nearest bone. While hauling Wiggles away, the dwarf noticed that there was one peculiarity about all the skeletons scattered across the floor.

"There are no heads," Mumchance said. "Where have all the skulls gone?"

"Burial rite?" guessed Ivy.

Kid advanced into the center of the room. He glanced at Ivy, waiting for her to tell him not to touch. When she said nothing, he stretched out one little hoof and stirred the bones. An odd grin of amusement spread across his face. "Perhaps someone took away the skulls for a collection, my dears, or to roll them through the ruins for their pleasure."

"There's something evil here," said Gunderal with a shiver at the little thief's suggestions. "I can feel it." She passed Kid, going into the center of the room and looking right and left. "There's something hiding here. I know it."

Gunderal peered into the shadowy niches lining the walls, with Zuzzara following directly behind her.

"Let's just get out of here," suggested Ivy.

"No," Gunderal almost snapped at her. "We have to find it first. If we try to pass before we find it, we'll end up like those skeletons."

"How can you be certain?"

"Because I am a wizard," said Gunderal with more force than normal. "Evil was done here."

"Come on, Gunderal," said her sister. "You are just nervous. It has been a bad day."

The wizard heaved a sigh. "Don't tell me what I'm feeling. This is what I am good at, sensing magic, just as you are good at hitting things." Gunderal moved back to the center of the room. Rather than skipping lightly around the bones on the floor, as she would normally do, she kicked her way through a rib cage, sending bits rolling off to one side. "Show yourself. I know you are there," she said.

Everyone looked at Gunderal, then looked around the room, not asking to whom she spoke. She was a wizard, and they respected that. Still, they had never seen her talk to a pile of bones before. When a thin, strange voice answered her, they all became motionless. Ivy liked to think that standing frozen like a statue in the marketplace was a sign of alertness on her part, never fear. She glanced at Sanval. As always when faced with danger, his face was as frozen as the farm pond in mid-winter. But he did give the tiniest shrug of inquiry. Ivy raised her eyebrows and shook her head when he started to move forward. She trusted Gunderal's instincts. The little genasi had gotten them out of more than one magical trap. Besides, from the way that Kid's ears were swiveling back and forth in nervous agitation, she was sure that he felt something peculiar in the room too.

A voice said, "The wizard is clever. Very clever. But is the wizard clever enough to best me?"

In an unnoticed niche, a soft green glow began to brighten. As it floated out into the room, they saw the light was a human skull surrounded by a jagged green flame that ringed it much like a lion's head is ringed by its mane. Its eyes glittered, points of green fire. The light increased and reflected off the walls, turning the room into a flickering green grotto.

"All heads belong to me," said the flameskull, apparently untroubled by its lack of a body. The thing had no lips, no flesh at all, just clean jawbones clacking away. Unfortunately, it did have a few teeth—brown and half-rotted—that wobbled in a disgusting manner when it spoke. "They told me that when they left me here."

"And who would they be?" Gunderal sounded as if she were making pleasant conversation in her own parlor, but she waved her uninjured hand frantically behind her back, gesturing to the others to gather closer to her.

"My two friends, my two fond friends, my two cherished *dead* friends," said the flameskull, floating effortlessly in front of Gunderal. "We had heard that Tsurlagol had fallen and all its treasures were buried in its ruins. So we came to dig them out again. We were wizards too—not insignificant spellcasters or mountebanks, but masters of magnificent magic. We came looking for the glittering gems and the great diamond buried with them."

"Any luck?" Ivy could not resist asking even as Gunderal made shushing motions.

For a creature with no face, it was amazingly clear that the flameskull had settled into a sulk. Ivy guessed it had something to do with how the flames writhed in the eyesockets and the tone of voice issuing from its mouth. "They left me behind," it said with a distinct snarl. "They left me behind and told me to take the skulls of any who followed us. But I cursed them both even as they chopped off my head and arms and hid my body in the ruins."

"There's nothing worse than an argument among thieves, my dear," said Kid in a tone laden with bitter experience. "Especially when they are magical thieves."

"They left me behind," the skull repeated. The flames around the bony head died down a little, as if depression dampened the creature's fire.

"Obviously not the best of friends," said Ivy, hoping to keep the skull talking, because she could see that Gunderal was about to cast some type of spell. "I wouldn't do what they told me to do. Especially if they cut off my head before they told me."

"Huh! As if I have a choice," snapped the skull with a click of its rotted teeth. His flames brightened to a wide halo of green fire around his head. "They have been dead and gone for a generation or more! I am still here! And all have to pay toll to me. Pay me in skulls! Or rot as they rotted!" The creature's voice rose in anger, its fiery halo brightened, and two bolts of flame shot from its eyesockets.

Before the fire could touch anyone, Gunderal raised a wall of water between the Siegebreakers and the flameskull. The flames licked out in pointed flickers, tossing a spray of green sparks. They hit the water wall and hissed, spat, and sizzled. The wall shimmered green, and then the flames extinguished themselves in the water.

"Well done, wizard," said the flameskull. "Quite well done. But what will you do now? Remember, whoever collects the most heads wins. And that is always me, me, me!"

"Cheeky thing for a dead head," said Mumchance.

"Does your game have rules?" Ivy shouted at the flameskull, hoping to keep it talking and distract it from flinging more flame spells at them. Gunderal's wall of water looked very wobbly, and Ivy suspected the spell was not too stable.

"You've got to smash it," Gunderal muttered to Ivy, confirming her worst fears. "Quickly. The wall won't hold."

"It moves pretty fast," Ivy said. The flameskull was zipping back and forth, trying to find a way around the wall, but it was also keeping away from the water. It appeared to not want to get wet.

"I can hit it," said Sanval, sliding his sword out of his scabbard. "Should I jump through the wall?"

"No!" they all yelled. "That will just make the wall disappear!" All the Siegebreakers knew the basic mechanics of Gunderal's spell. They had used the wall of water many times before to shelter from some flame or other, even from fires that they had started themselves.

"I can make you faster," said Gunderal to Sanval, "but I need to drop the water wall. I can't do two spells at the same time." Already the wall was becoming misty around the edges as the water started to fade away. The flameskull bobbed closer, obviously trying to listen to their conversation. It tilted its bony head, and odd sparks shot from its eye sockets.

Zuzzara shifted so she was nearer to her sister. "I'll protect you while you're casting your spell," she said to Gunderal, "but be quick, little sister, be quick."

"Drop the wall, Gunderal," commanded Ivy. "We'll scatter and try to divert its attack. Sanval, you'd better crush that thing on the first try!"

The wall vanished, and Ivy flung herself directly under the

skull, sliding on her stomach through the bones on the floor. As she had intended, the flameskull spun in place, turning itself upside down as it tried to track her movements. A bolt of energy from the skull's mouth whizzed by her ear and extinguished itself in the floor beside her.

Zuzzara swung with her shovel at the back of the flameskull at the same time that Ivy flung herself under the floating flaming head. The half-orc missed, the flameskull shooting up toward the ceiling too quickly for her to connect with. The flameskull twisted around, trying to hit her with blasts of energy. The mane of flame whipped around the skull, long green tendrils hissing through the air. Again, with a howl of frustration, the skull's energy bolt undershot its target as Zuzzara grabbed her sister around the waist and leaped out of the way.

Gunderal let out a little squeak as the two of them rolled across the floor, outside the flameskull's range. "Let me down. Sanval, get over here," the wizard called.

"Missed, missed, missed with your missile," yelled Kid, cartwheeling around the skull, which had zipped lower again in an attempt to hit Ivy with a whip of fire. His hooves clicked on the floor, then spun in the air close to the skull as he went into a handstand. The flameskull blasted upward with a whistling screech, dived in a wide arc over Kid's flailing hooves, and aimed itself again at Ivy. In desperation, Ivy grabbed an old shinbone off the floor and lobbed it with her left hand at the skull. One end knocked against the flameskull's bony pate. The skull hit the floor with a thud and rolled to a dazed stop, then slowly drifted upward. Ivy heard a sharp bark and a "No!" from Mumchance. Wiggles raced past her, barking wildly and dancing on her back paws, trying to catch the skull floating above her.

"Crazy dog!" yelled Ivy, grabbing for Wiggles's collar.

"That's a bad, old bone. You don't want that." She scooped the little dog up and tossed Wiggles to Mumchance. The dwarf caught Wiggles and dropped her behind him.

"*Stay!*" said Mumchance sternly in Dwarvish. Wiggles folded her ears back and dropped to a crouch. She kept giving out eager little whines as she watched the flameskull bounce and dip around the room. The little dog started to crawl forward on her front legs, rump high in the air and fluffy tail wagging madly.

"*No!*" said Mumchance again in Dwarvish. "*Bad dog! Settle!*" He picked up a collarbone from the floor and chucked it with a big overhand throw at the flameskull. The undead head bounced out of the way with a jeer.

"Can't hit me!" yelled the flameskull and spat another ball of sparks at the dwarf. Mumchance skipped to one side with the lightness of a dwarf half his age, Wiggles dancing at his heels.

Kid spun around the flameskull, flipping and cartwheeling to confuse the creature. With one big spin, he managed to clip it with the edge of one hoof, shoving it back against the stone wall. "You cannot catch us. We are too quick for an old cracked head like you!" he said.

A spray of green sparks zoomed past Kid. Several settled on the toe of one of Sanval's boots. The smell of burnt polish and leather filled the air. Glaring at the boot, Sanval rubbed the damaged toe against the back of the opposite shin, then glared again as he stamped down his foot. A large scorch mark marred the shiny polished surface of the toe.

"That does it," he muttered. "Get me there, wizard!"

Sanval slid into place next to Gunderal. With a quickly whispered spell, she slapped Sanval hard between the shoulders, shouting, "Go, go!"

Screaming, the skull dived after Kid, spreading a trail of

green fire and ignoring Sanval, who charged after it. With magically enhanced speed, Sanval swung his sword down on the skull. The brittle bone shattered, scattering pieces around the room.

It had only taken a few moments. As quickly as the threat had appeared, it was gone. Ivy sat at the edge of the room, shaking her head. "Well, that was fun, I think. Good work, Gunderal."

"Oh dear," said Gunderal, pointing at the shattered bits of skull scattered through the other bones. Tendrils of green flame were sprouting from each separate piece of the skull. As they all watched, the pale green flames twisted across the room, reaching for each other. "We should leave now."

"Isn't it dead?" asked Sanval, straightening his helmet after he sheathed his sword.

"It was always dead," explained Gunderal, pushing them toward the archway at the opposite end of the room. "But it is one of those dead things that can put itself back together again."

"I hate those types of dead things," grumbled Mumchance.

"Dead should stay dead," added Zuzzara, picking up the torch and shovel that she had dropped when she grabbed Gunderal. She thrust the shovel, handle straight down, through her belt and raised the still-lit torch high to illuminate the exit.

"I could not agree more," said Kid, skipping back and forth and watching how the green flames tended to bend toward him whenever he passed too close. "But perhaps we can break this spell." He reached down and scooped up one rotten molar that had been knocked out of the flameskull's jaw. Kid tucked it into one of the many pouches dangling from his belt.

"Ugh, that is one terrible souvenir," commented Zuzzara as they left the room. "Kid, you should leave it be."

"No, he should take it," said Gunderal. "Such guardians can rarely reassemble themselves if you take away a piece."

"Hope you're right, little sister," said Zuzzara. "That thing nearly burned my britches."

"Of course, I'm right. I told you. Trust me, I know magic."

<hr />

Beyond the room containing the flameskull was a swift, hidden passage back to the place where they fought the phantom fungus. Once they reached that room, the Siegebreakers would have no choice but to follow the northern passageway that Sanval had wanted to take in the first place—the one that sent them on the trail of the other party in the ruins and, possibly, a troop of Fottergrim's raiders. Ivy thought that Sanval looked smug, but when he caught her staring his face smoothed into that irritating bland look that he was so very good at.

"Gunderal seems pleased," said Ivy to Mumchance, watching the little wizard walking in front of them. Although she still cradled her injured arm, the wizard held her head straight, and her long black hair bounced on her shoulders, free at last from its confining top-knot.

"Yes," said Mumchance, but there was no elation in his voice.

"What is wrong?"

"Not all her spells worked," Mumchance replied with a frown. "She couldn't throw a decent frost, that wall of water nearly collapsed, and she should have been quicker with slapping that last spell on Sanval. That trick should have been easier for her. And, Ivy, we may need more from her before we are out of here. The river is going to worm its way into these tunnels. I just know it. And the only one of us that has any control over water is Gunderal. But if she has no control over her magic, then we are sunk—way down in the mud sunk."

"You worry too much," said Ivy. Gunderal had been slow in the fight—Ivy had never seen her more unsure when casting a spell—but she was not going to give the dwarf the satisfaction of agreeing with his gloomy prognostication. After all, she was the captain of this little company, and a captain should be optimistic even when she was stuck up to her hips in a mucky situation with only one shovel to dig herself out. She tried to cheer the dwarf up. "After we got away from the river bank, it's been bone dry, even in the ossuary!"

"Make jokes if you want. But it doesn't feel dry to me. Just you wait and see."

As they entered the baths, the smell of the dead phantom fungus assaulted their noses. Mumchance glanced down into the dry pool with the mosaic bottom, shifting his head so he was staring straight down with his good eye. He cursed—quiet little curses that made Wiggles whine—and waved his lantern over the edge of the pool. Dry dust had become slimy mud, and water clearly shone in the light of the torch.

"The river is rising," Mumchance said, "and the water is running through the old pipes that fed the bath."

"Well, that's something less than wonderful," observed Ivy before Mumchance could say anything more and upset everyone. Nobody needed to hear "I told you so" right now, most especially her.

But Ivy was more worried than she let her friends see. The water was rising, and they still had no idea how to get out of the ruins of Tsurlagol. Ivy feared they might have to swim to make it out.

CHAPTER NINE

When they passed out of the chamber still stinking of dead bugbear and fungus, the Siegebreakers entered into a network of much broader tunnels. Looking at the ledges running high above them, Mumchance suggested that they were traveling down an ancient and dried-out storm sewer.

"And," he pointed out glumly, "if it was a storm drain, it means that it had pipes feeding into it—the type of pipes that will carry the rising river water into it."

"We'll worry about that when our feet get wet," countered Ivy.

Kid picked up new sets of tracks in the tunnel. The four who had fled from the phantom fungus and a larger group following them. "Wide feet, short legs, iron nails striking sparks on the stone as they march along," said Kid, clicking beside the group, still watching for tracks in the dirt. "And that other thing behind, dragging over their footsteps and wiping some away." At one point, he stopped and stooped, tracing the peculiar track with one hand. "One very large snake moving very fast." Satisfied once the mysterious track was identified, Kid wandered out of the circle of lights cast by their torches and lantern, sniffing the air for more tunnel entrances.

"Fottergrim had hobgoblins and mountain orcs moving in and out of the city until we bottled up the western woods," observed Sanval. "We never could find their tunnel. Maybe this is it." He sounded excited and pleased by the prospect of running into an unknown number of adversaries.

"Maybe these are old tracks," said Ivy, with very little hope.

"New," said Kid, rejoining the group. "A day, not more, perhaps less, my dear."

Upon hearing that, Ivy shifted her position to the front, grabbing a torch from Zuzzara in passing. In her opinion, she was the best fighter among them, even if she did not have the shiniest armor.

"Who is playing hero now?" whispered Mumchance to her.

"Hey," said Ivy in sharp if not coherent rebuke.

The dwarf jerked his head back toward Sanval. "You are mad that he killed the fungus."

"Not at all," hissed Ivy. "Did you smell that thing?"

"And smashed that skull."

"He needed Gunderal's help to do that."

"And Zuzzara stopped the kobolds."

"Zuzzara is good with kobolds. I am more than happy to let her bat them around."

"So why are you shoving to the front?"

"Because I don't know if it is kobolds, fungus, or more talking skulls around the corner. And you know the rule. It's only a good day . . ."

". . .When everybody gets to go home."

"So far, it has been a very bad day. I want it to be a good one," said Ivy. "Besides, right now, if we run into anything that is not an ally, I would prefer to hit it hard and keep hitting it until I feel better."

"Fair enough," agreed Mumchance. The dwarf put Wiggles down to run. She raced past Ivy, *yip-yap-yip*, except the last yap cut off abruptly.

"Wiggles!" yelled Mumchance. The dark way before them was filled with silence and shadows. "Wiggles!" The dwarf whistled and whistled again.

Kid's sharp ears caught the answering bark. "Ahead, dear sir, ahead," he said. "And down."

Around the next corner, the floor just disappeared. Ivy spotted the darkness half a step short of the edge, her foot raised. She stopped and leaned back, slapping her hand against the wall to balance herself. She raised the torch that she was carrying as high as possible to illuminate the hallway. The hole stretched halfway across the corridor. There was no sign of Wiggles.

"Stupid, stupid mutt," murmured Ivy as she hung over the edge and waved her torch in an attempt to see Wiggles. Ivy's torch barely lit the wall for several feet down, and then the hole went black. "Dumb, dumb dog." But she muttered softly, so Mumchance could not hear. He was too busy whistling and calling to the little dog to pay any attention.

"Stay, Wiggles, stay!" the dwarf yelled into the black hole.

"Truly, truly wonderful," said Ivy.

"I'll go, Ivy," said Mumchance. "I can grab her and get back here fast."

Ivy stared at the dwarf, who was at least three centuries older than her and never a good climber, and sighed. "No, I will go down. I will get Wiggles. I will bring her back. You will all stay here and do nothing foolish, like come after me."

She did not hear a chorus of agreement.

"That was an order," she said.

There was still silence.

"I am an officer of Procampur—" Sanval began.

Ivy interrupted him. "Which means that small white dogs are not your responsibility. Protecting my friends, however . . ."

"They will be safe. I will protect them," he stated in his quiet manner. Ivy believed him. It had to be, she decided later, the way that he just gleamed in the torchlight. Shiny armor. It just made a man look like a hero, Ivy thought. Something about the way that he stood too. Absolutely straight. Sword drawn and clasped in both hands, point down. She had tried that stance a couple of times when she was younger. It had never worked for her. But Sanval, he made it look natural—like one of those guardian statues in the better class of temple. Although most guardian statues did not have a huge scorch mark running across one shiny boot and a worried frown wrinkling a normally smooth forehead.

"It will be all right," she said, just to make that line disappear. It certainly did not suit Sanval's usual noble and serene demeanor. Ivy handed her torch to Kid, who just stood there looking at her with an eerily similar crease in the middle of his forehead that made the outer edges of his eyebrows tip up even more dramatically. "Don't worry. Whatever went down there is long gone. Just look after my friends."

"Ivy, I got a rope off that dead bugbear," said Zuzzara, uncoiling it from around her waist.

"See why we loot the dead when we can?" Ivy said to Sanval. He made no reply.

Ivy pulled her gloves off her belt and put them on to protect her hands from the rope. She shifted her sword on her back again, making sure the ties were tight

"Now, remember, everyone is going to stay right here," she said. Zuzzara found a protruding rock and tied off the rope, dropping it down into the black hole. Ivy grabbed the line and slowly descended into the darkness below.

A torch dropped past her. It lit the bottom of the hole with a faint pool of light. Ivy glanced down. She could not see Wiggles, but she could hear the dog whining below her.

She hit the sandy bottom of the hole and began to call the dog. "Come on, Wiggles, come here," she cajoled. "Come on, darling."

A sharp bark sounded ahead of her. Ivy picked up the torch and advanced farther into the hole. She spotted the shine of white fur. Wiggles was backed into a crack in the wall, tail between her legs, ears flat back against her head.

"Come on, Wiggles," said Ivy, "you know me. Nothing to be worried about. Come out, there's a good girl."

The dog remained motionless, her eyes staring at Ivy, and she gave a soft whine.

Intent on the dog cowering away from her, Ivy tripped over the giant black snake slithering across the floor. The creature reared up with a hiss, its mouth open and its fangs gleaming. Its head swung slowly, dipped to the floor of the pit, and led the curve of its body in a circle around her feet. She grabbed for her sword, trying to pull it one-handed out of the scabbard tied on her back while keeping the torch between her and the serpent's bobbing head. The creature lashed out with unbelievable speed, uncoiling its length and circling upward around and around, over her ankles, around her knees, and up her thighs. Ivy lost her grip on the torch, which bounced harmlessly off the snake's back and rolled away.

The serpent twisted up Ivy's body faster and faster, like lighting striking up from the ground. It pinned her arms in place; her right hand was twisted awkwardly up by her shoulder, still fumbling for her sword hilt. But her armor protected her arm, and, as painful as her pinned arm was, the position also kept the snake off of her throat.

Ivy screamed—outraged at the suddenness of the attack, furious at the pain of her twisted arm—and tried to lunge out of the snake's coils. She could not move! The creature's body lapped around her, pressing against her ribs, and little stars danced in front of her eyes as the breath was slowly squeezed out of her. Her pulse beat frantically in her throat, and she knew that soon her heart would be crushed to a stop. The serpent's terrible head brushed against her face. She twisted her face clear, drawing shallow breaths against the overwhelming pressure, desperately trying to think of a way to escape from the crushing grip.

Fangs, fangs, the thing had enormous fangs. She remembered the ivory flash in the torch light. Poisonous? Did crushing serpents need poison? Something snagged at the edge of her thick blonde braid and pulled it forward around her neck so that it hung over the front of her shoulder. For a terrible moment, her own hair felt almost like a second serpent around her throat. She could not draw a deep enough breath to scream again, but in her mind she was shrieking.

When Ivy screamed, Sanval raced past Mumchance. He leaped straight out and, as gravity grabbed him, disappeared straight down.

"Sanval, stop! That is the most unbelievably *stupid*," the dwarf yelled as Sanval's brilliantly shined helmet disappeared below the lip of the hole, "and *brave*. . . . Zuzzara, follow him! Ivy is in trouble!"

The Siegebreakers rushed to the edge of the hole. Zuzzara grabbed the rope and swung after the Procampur officer.

Wiggles barked hysterically.

Landing on the sandy floor with a thud, Sanval scooped Ivy's still burning torch from the floor. He thrust it toward the serpent's eyes, less than a hand's width from Ivy's face, momentarily blinding the beast. The heat of the torch flared against Ivy's cheek, but the serpent's grip was so tight that she could not even wince. The giant snake hissed and wavered, obviously confused as to whether to bite Sanval or crush Ivy. Sanval ground the torch into one of the serpent's eyes. It popped and sizzled with a sickening smell right under Ivy's offended nose. She gagged. The giant snake tried to twist around and face this new threat with its one remaining eye.

With a prolonged hiss, the creature struck at Sanval. Its ivory fangs gleamed more brightly than the Procampur captain's sword.

Faster than one of Ivy's thundering heartbeats, Sanval thrust up with his blade, skewering the serpent through the jaw and piercing straight into its brain. The creature collapsed, its coils tightening in one last spasm of cruel strength, then going slack around Ivy's body.

Ivy could clearly see her open-mouthed expression in the polished gloss of Sanval's breastplate as he tried to catch her with his free hand. She slid down in front of him until she was kneeling on the floor.

"That was . . . That was . . ." She could not think what to say. She remained on her knees, gasping for breath.

A worried Zuzzara dropped from the rope, arriving on the pit's floor with an audible thump of haste. Her shovel was held high, ready to brain any attacker. "Ivy? Sanval? Are you all right?"

Wiggles crept out of the hole where she was hiding and rushed to Ivy, collapsing by her side with a doggy sigh of relief.

Ivy swallowed and tried to speak again. She could feel her ribs creaking when she took a deep breath, but nothing felt broken. She shook herself free of the coils of the dead serpent, as Sanval pulled the weight of it away from her.

Sanval caught her elbows and helped her to her feet. Ivy nearly swatted his hands away. After all, she wasn't some weak court lady who needed a hand up every time she tripped over her silk shoes or a giant snake. Then she took a deep breath to clear her mind as well as her lungs, and decided that Sanval would reach down to anyone who needed help, not because that person was weak but just because that was what you did when you lived by the rigid rules of Procampur courtesy. Why not let him be polite for once—it would make the man happy—especially when her knees were wobbling and she was still seeing little stars dancing in front of her eyes.

Sanval did not even look winded. Just concerned.

"Ivy?" asked Sanval. "Are you bleeding? Your face, your hair?"

It was a trick of the torchlight. Ivy felt the dampness in her hair and a trickle down her face. It was wet, it was cold, and it was water, showering in rapidly increasing drops from the ceiling.

"Ivy!" Mumchance leaned far over the edge, head tilted to one side as he strained to see her. "We need to go! There's a lot of water coming down the tunnel."

"No, no, no!" Ivy could not prevent the childish sound of mutiny in her voice. The gods knew, she could take falling into a river, getting lost in a maze of dark tunnels, and fighting off kobolds, phantom fungus, and giant snakes. She could even take getting rescued by somebody who acted like he belonged in one of her mother's heroic ballads—though she meant to repay the favor as quickly as she could, because she did have her pride after all. Everything that had happened was just the sort of thing that could happen on the edges of a siege, when you were supposed to be doing a job and were getting lost instead in ruins that stretched on forever. She was serene about all of that. Most assuredly, she had handled anything that had come before. But she absolutely and completely refused to be sanguine about drowning in the dark. If she wanted to panic now, she would panic.

In the climb out of the hole, pulling herself up the rope slowly, each stretch of Ivy's right arm caused twinges all down her snake-bruised body. Wiggles rode triumphant on her shoulder, barking directly in her ear when she scented Mumchance above them. As soon as Ivy was level with the top of the hole, the dwarf reached out and snagged the little dog, hugging her tight to his chest.

As she clambered out of the hole, Ivy calmed down a little and decided to wait until they were above ground before she threw the mother of all fits. Right now, she was going to get them out of this dismal, damp disaster of a situation.

Water glimmered in the torchlight, dripping down the walls and flowing from the direction of the old city baths. Right now it was barely deep enough to cover the soles of their boots, and most was pouring down into the hole in the passageway.

Ivy glanced at Gunderal. The little wizard shook her head, looking close to tears. "I just can't stop it," she said. "Maybe slow it down a little."

"Do what you can," Ivy said to Gunderal. The moment that Zuzzara and Sanval cleared the hole, she shouted, "Let's move!"

Taking the lead, she set off at a fast jog into the black unknown as the river continued to worm its way into the tunnels, water rising fast behind them.

CHAPTER TEN

Intent on fleeing the water gushing into the underground ruins, the Siegebreakers trotted at increasing speed through the black tunnels. Once again, to Mumchance's distress, they were going down, not up, and the way was broadening before them. The underground road was now wide enough to run three or even four abreast, and the angry mutter of the river continued to follow them.

"We have to go higher!" cried Mumchance, gesturing with his lantern and sending the shadows wildly swinging across the wall.

"Wonderful idea," panted Ivy as she lengthened her stride. "But which way?"

"There," said Mumchance, pointing at the dark entrance to a tunnel that branched off the main way.

"More tracks!" squealed Kid, ears flicking nervously, nostrils wide as he tried to scent possible danger. He stamped his hooves against the dirt. "Many feet, running past, my dear, and hobnail boots. Smoke ahead too!"

"He's right, Ivy." Gunderal was breathing hard and looking even paler than before. "I smell fire and magic."

"Maybe I should go ahead, in case of danger," Sanval started to suggest.

"No! We stay together. It's safer. No more lone rescues—not even from me," decided Ivy, straining to smell whatever danger had spooked Kid and Gunderal. Her human nose just reported damp stone and the old sour scent of air trapped too long underground. She saw nothing but blackness beyond the light of their torches and Mumchance's faithfully burning lantern. "It's probably just another burned part of the ruins. More ash and old spells."

"Water's running fast, Ivy." This came from Zuzzara, staring over their heads, looking back along the way that they had come. Her half-orc vision clearly showed her the rising level of the water moving down the ancient sewers.

"Then we run faster." To Sanval, she said, "We are good at running. You should have seen us clear that tunnel when the hogs started to explode." That twitched his worried expression into a half smile. Pleased to have distracted him from any rash lone heroics, Ivy led them into the new tunnel, shouting at the others to turn and go in this new direction. "Regular formation, single file!" she yelled. "Sanval, fall in with Zuzzara, help Gunderal if she needs it! Kid to the back, watch our rear! Mumchance, keep up and don't forget your sword! Everyone stay alert!"

They scrambled up the slope. The tunnel turned sharply left. As they hustled around the bend, Ivy heard the clash of fighting—nothing else sounded quite like that. And then she heard shouting. She tried to turn back and warn the Siegebreakers to be quiet until they could assess the situation, but the momentum of the others behind her propelled her into the fight before she could shout a warning.

A man on fire, surrounded by hobgoblins and orcs, stood in the middle of the fight. Ivy slid to a halt, flipping her sword out even before she came to a complete stop. Startled by the sight of the burning man, she blinked and looked again, almost too dazzled by the flames to notice the orcs and hobgoblins yelling at the strangely calm gentleman.

Unperturbed by the flames licking around his body, the wizard (for what else could he be?) leaned on a smooth metal crutch and spat out some arcane command. Squealing hobgoblins and shouting orcs rushed the apparent cripple as a group, only to be deflected by the flames rising hotter and higher off the wizard's cloak. The smell of singed hides filled the air, but it was definitely the acrid stink of well-roasted monster. Flames might be sprouting from the wizard's body, but it was his enemies who burned!

The wizard's attackers wailed, throwing up their arms to protect their faces from the flames. When they turned aside, they fell afoul of a giant pair of bugbears—all snarls and big muscles and rusty chains holding together well-worn black leather armor. The bugbears fought with glaives, old-fashioned spears with oak shafts and leaf-shaped blades on one end and rough knobs of iron on the other. The bugbears swung the huge glaives around them as if they had no weight at all, slicing through the stomach armor of a hobgoblin or an orc with the sharp end and then braining the creature with the round end.

The howling hobgoblins and orcs backed away from the wizard and his bugbear guards. They rushed toward the tunnel, trying to escape out of the entrance that Ivy and the others had just stumbled through.

To avoid being trampled by the creatures, Ivy bent low into a defensive crouch, sword out in the right hand, torch still clutched in her left hand. Sanval settled naturally onto her left side while Zuzzara swung onto her right.

"I'll take the lead," shouted Ivy as she barreled forward, knocking hobgoblins and orcs back into the room, pushing them toward the flaming wizard who frightened them so. At least with a burning man in the center of the room, there was plenty of light. She could clearly see her opponents, and what she saw was trouble. Big, fat, well-seasoned fighters, with good armor and weapons, all bearing the black boar emblem of Fottergrim's horde.

"Oh blast and blast," said Ivy as she swung into the fight. They had stumbled into a dispute of Fottergrim's raiders. Didn't anyone stay above ground these days? Just what she did not need! And this was supposed to have been such an easy, quick job! Drop a wall, collect bags of gold, go home and fix the barn roof. She had a plan, and other people kept messing it up. Snarling louder than the bugbears, Ivy launched herself into the fight that she could not think how to avoid.

Her own torch made a lousy shield, and Ivy wished that she had her half-round buckler, that battered veteran of previous fights. But the buckler was propped up against the brassbound armor chest back at the camp, and wishes made even worse shields than torches. Copying Sanval's earlier trick with the snake, she thrust the torch toward the yellow eyes of a hobgoblin trying to sidle around her from the left. She set its shaggy red eyebrows on fire, and the thing ran screaming.

Once, several years ago, Ivy had studied swordplay. All the proper stances, the correct swings, the finesse of point versus edge, the elegant way to fight—the sort of thing that Sanval was doing at her side without even thinking about it. Her style in this fight was not like that. It was tavern basic—using the sword as much like a club to stun as like a pointed edged weapon. It was clumsy, it was nasty, and it was supremely satisfying to a woman warrior who was having an exceedingly bad day. Ivy charged into the fight, the heels of her boots banging on the floor, her long limbs swinging, her blonde braid whipping around her shoulders with every turn, her blue eyes glittering with fury and delight. Hobgoblins squeaked like baby pigs and tried to scramble out of her way. Orcs yelled even louder as they stumbled over their own big feet to avoid her. All were taller and much heavier than Ivy, but she was faster. She banged them on their round helmets and whacked them on their armored ankles. She cut high, she cut low, and she cut mean. She plowed into Fottergrim's troops like she meant to make each one personally pay for the absurdly horrible, rotten way that everything had turned out since that idiot camel had blundered into her tent and knocked her out of bed and made her miss breakfast.

Sanval and Zuzzara correctly settled into that important pace-and-a-half behind her that gave their rush into the room such nasty consequences to the enemy. What Ivy missed with sword and torch, Sanval skewered with style, or Zuzzara bashed with vigor.

As Ivy beat off one hobgoblin, only to see him brained by a bugbear coming up from behind him, she wondered just who that flaming wizard was. An enemy of Fottergrim? A good guy? A good guy with big, raggedy, nasty bugbear guards? Or were they all bad guys?

But there was too much happening all at once, and Ivy fell back on her training and experience. She stopped thinking and started hitting, and found the sound of her sword striking hobgoblins and orcs was a most soothing sound. She swung slightly to the left, and Sanval and Zuzzara adjusted their step to her. It was like dancing with two partners, she thought, as she stepped lightly over an orc rolling on the ground and Sanval hopped over the same beast, instantly taking the proper position to protect her back.

Some of the orcs, seeing the fight going so terribly against them, turned back to the flaming wizard, flinging down their weapons and dropping to their knees, crying for a truce; but a sphere of fire shot from the wizard's hand. Like some demonic toy, the flaming ball bounced twice against a hobgoblin commander trying to whip the orcs back to the fight, setting his fur on fire. The ball passed harmlessly over the bugbears stomping over their opponents with their heavy hobnail boots, before scorching half a dozen orcs across their snouts. The hobgoblin commander rolled on the floor, trying to escape the mysterious sphere. The two bugbears knocked him back and forth between them with their glaives, much like a pair of cats batting mice from one paw to another. The wizard twitched a finger to the left, and the flaming sphere bounced left to fry more orcs. He twitched a finger to the right, and the sphere flew to the right and set another hobgoblin blazing. Smoke filled the room, and that the wizard also controlled. With a small wind, the wizard whipped it into the faces of his attackers, so the creatures gasped and choked and dropped to the ground, smothered by the acrid fumes from their own burning comrades.

Fottergrim's raiders were routed. As a body, they rushed to escape the fate of their choking, frying fellows. They burst around Ivy, Sanval, and Zuzzara, streamed past the rest of the startled Siegebreakers, and disappeared down the dark tunnel that led down to the river—out of the fire and into the flood.

"Oh, blast," said Ivy when she saw how spell after spell burst from the wizard's hands in rapid succession. "This is not good."

She looked around, hoping to see a clear exit. There was no way out that was not clogged with dying or dead hobgoblins and orcs. More worrisome was the fact that the rest of her friends had followed her blindly into the room. Gunderal's violet eyes were round with shock at the easy burst of fire spells that came from the wizard.

"We need help," Zuzzara sputtered over her shoulder to her sister.

"You know I can't control fire!" Gunderal sobbed, her uninjured hand protectively crossed over the hand still resting in the sling.

"I don't mean to nag, sister," said Zuzzara as she punched an orc and then slung it over the heads of Gunderal and Mumchance to join its fellows, "but sometimes you can dampen down flames."

The black smoke still swirled around them. Zuzzara caught a lungful and coughed. At the sound of her sister's hacking distress, Gunderal's face turned even whiter. She muttered a spell, hissing out each word like an angry kitten. A swirl of damp but clean air, smelling pleasantly of evergreen trees and spring flowers, swept through the room. Zuzzara drew in a grateful breath of the healing mist, thumped the last standing orc over the head with her shovel, and gave her sister an enormous pointy-toothed grin.

"Knew you could do it," bellowed Zuzzara.

Gunderal acknowledged her with a weak smile and leaned more heavily against the wall. "That should have been stronger," she said, her voice rising barely above a whisper as she drew in her own deep breaths of the mist.

Noticing that the fighting had now completely stopped, Zuzzara added. "Hey, we did good, didn't we?"

Ivy almost agreed, but then she caught sight of Mumchance and Kid, both of whom still hugged the wall, flanking the more vulnerable Gunderal.

Mumchance looked as glum as a one-eyed dwarf could look—in other words well down the scale toward outright miserable—and all that could be seen of Wiggles was the tip of one quivering white ear poking out of Mumchance's pocket. But the expression on Kid's face worried Ivy even more. For the first time since she had plucked the little thief's hand off her purse and slung him over her shoulder to carry him home, Kid looked frightened. His head was pulled down into his shoulders, and his whole body was hunched over, as if he anticipated a blow or a beating.

Ivy glanced over her shoulder to see what terrified Kid so. She realized that Kid was staring at the flaming wizard still casually leaning on his big metal crutch. With an impatient snap of his fingers, the wizard plucked a scorched charm off his cloak and threw it to the floor. The flames springing from his clothes vanished.

The tall, thin man strode toward Ivy's group, confident and with no hesitation. The metal crutch under his left arm swung in perfect time with his legs and lent an odd and menacing thud to each step forward. Even slightly stooped, he still towered above all of them except Zuzzara. His face was young, but deeply lined; grooves of discontent ran from long nose to narrow lips.

He stared at them with absolute disdain and then smiled with the faintest upward tug of his closed lips. His yellow-green eyes narrowed with the type of pleasure usually seen in the face of a barnyard cat confronting a particularly plump baby bird.

"How interesting," the wizard said. "Toram's lost little pet goat and a pack of scruffy fighters, led by a fellow in such shiny armor that he has to come from Procampur. It is amazing what you find underground these days."

CHAPTER ELEVEN

In a soft whisper, Kid murmured, "Archlis."

"Oh, by all the gods great and small," swore Ivy. The last person she wanted to meet was Fottergrim's personal spell-caster, the master of Tsurlagol's walls throughout the siege.

The wizard focused on Sanval, obviously taking the Procampur captain as their leader. The others he had looked over with a disinterested eye and immediately dismissed as unimportant. Ivy kept quiet, wanting to observe without being too closely observed.

"So what are you hunting in these ruins with Toram's god-sight goat?" Archlis repeated the odd phrase, gesturing with the tip of his metal crutch at Kid, who cringed away as though he expected it to spit fire at him.

"What do you think we seek?" Sanval answered question with question, his voice very steady and low, even as he took a half-step in front of Kid, sheltering the little thief behind his well-armored back.

"I am the magelord Archlis, the terror of Fottergrim's army," snapped the wizard. "Do not play games with me, little captain from Procampur."

"I am Sanval Nerias Moealim Hugerand Filao-Trious

Semmenio Illuskia Hyacinth Neme Auniomaro Valorous, a captain of Procampur's army." Sanval drew a deep breath after that recital. "I can say with complete honesty that I did not enter these ruins to capture you." Sanval's expression showed no more emotion on his handsome face than he had when confronted with Mumchance's leaping pack of mutts at the camp. His Procampur training in courtesy still held, even as the long-nosed Archlis sneered at him. "And I never play games with wizards."

"Wizard! Do you think that is all that I am? I, Archlis, who know the ancient secrets of Netheril. A magelord of the arcane arts. I could turn you to ash with a single word." Archlis half-raised his Ankh, favoring Sanval with the same close-lipped smile he had given when he recognized Kid. Sanval's hand tightened on his sword hilt.

"So," said Ivy, stepping forward before Sanval could provoke him further, "noble magelord, how can we help you?"

The magelord looked her up and down. He did not seem impressed. "Mercenary," said Archlis as a definition and not a compliment.

Ivy nodded. "Definitely. We did a little detour from the siege and ended up falling down here."

"Do not lie to me. You think"—Archlis pointed at Kid, who was still half-hidden behind Sanval—"that will lead you to the crypt. But I still have the book, and without it, you could not hope to find the crypt, not even with the power of that trinket on your glove."

Ivy glanced down at her gauntlets. The left one bore a battered silver oak leaf, a gift from her long-lost mother. The tarnished token was so much a part of her gear that she rarely gave it any thought. Odd that Archlis should notice so small and insignificant a magical item—just as the Pearl had. On his tabard hung a multitude of charms. Some were forged from iron, others knotted from what looked like elf hair; still more were tarnished silver and yellowed bone. Below the shifting, clinking charms, Ivy saw arcane sigils and runes woven into the very cloth. His hands were studded with rings, and Ivy doubted that those trinkets were only charged with spells to dry out his boots. All in all, his charms and rings were a far more impressive display of magical protection and—most probably—magical destruction than her one lucky silver leaf. Still, Archlis had noticed the token, and he seemed thrown slightly off balance by Kid's presence in their group.

"Kid is very good at what he does. And I have my protections as well," said Ivy in the spirit of pure bluff. After all, if Archlis thought they were more powerful than they appeared, who was she to tell him that appearances were deceptive. And she would question Kid later about his supposed talents, just as soon as she was sure that Archlis was not going to sizzle their bones. "I could sell you his services. I could sell you mine. Cheap."

Kid gave an involuntary bleat and cringed farther away from Archlis. Sanval tried to say something, but Ivy stepped hard on his boot. When he started to protest, she gestured at Zuzzara, who clamped a large hand over his mouth.

Archlis looked amused at Sanval's angry eyes glaring at him over the big hand of the half-orc. "So, was this noble your prisoner, or is he your prisoner now?" Archlis asked Ivy.

"At the moment," Ivy explained, "he is our employer. But, as I said, for the right fee, and that fee does not have to be too high, we could terminate that contract. I would rather keep him alive. He is a powerful fighter and we have some . . . potions . . . that we can use to keep him under control. And, although from Procampur, his own character is none too noble, if you know what I mean." Zuzzara smiled her sharp-toothed smile and nodded vigorously in support of Ivy's story. The others were silent—Sanval because he had no choice, and the rest because they trusted her. As always in such moments, she wondered if this were the day that she would be unable to live up to their expectations of her ability to lie her way out of a bad situation.

Having begun her story of how they came to be wandering in Tsurlagol's ruins, Ivy added a few more details for verisimilitude. "We were scouting for the Thultyrl and, since we did not make it back to the camp by . . . now, we would be subject to discipline. As would this man, who is already under probation for his gambling in the red-roof district and patronage of undesirable, um, females. He won't want to go rushing back to camp, not if there is a chance of treasure."

Behind her, Sanval choked, and Zuzzara whispered a hoarse "hush" in his ear. Ivy paused to see if Archlis was going to balk at any of the lies she was ladling out as fast as she could. The magelord frowned at the word "treasure," his eyes narrowing as he scanned the group again. His glance lingered longest on Kid and Mumchance. "You know how it is," Ivy concluded hastily. "Better gold in the purse today than a promise for tomorrow."

Archlis did not immediately dismiss her offer. In fact, he seemed more amused then doubting after his second careful examination of the group. He even snickered a little—a grating nasal sound—at Sanval still clutched in Zuzzara's protective embrace. "Armor or no armor, that one is no threat to me. Your offer is interesting. I have fewer servants than I deserve." Archlis gestured toward the bugbears, one of which was picking his teeth with a looted hobgoblin sword. "These have proved to be more fragile than I assumed."

"And the hobgoblins and the orcs?" asked Ivy, waving one hand at the bodies littering the floor, still playing the role of one callous mercenary intent on negotiating a good settlement for herself.

"They had orders to return me to the defenses of Tsurlagol. Which was a waste of my time. Fottergrim never understood. I could have made him a king of the Vast, after I retrieved my treasure," said Archlis with no lack of self-confidence. The lines running between his nose and mouth became more pronounced as the magelord brooded. "I persuaded the fool to come to Tsurlagol. Fottergrim was supposed to have made my access to the ruins easier, not more difficult."

"Except he decided to take the city, rather than just hang around the edges," guessed Ivy.

"Gruumsh must have driven him mad," Archlis replied, still obviously peeved. When he named the orc's war god, both the bugbears straightened up and made some gesture, to either appease the angry god or, more likely, to avoid Gruumsh's notice. "The temptation was too great for Fottergrim. Once he seized the city, he had no idea what to do and refused to listen to my suggestions. Hobgoblins and orcs . . . Once they drink the taverns dry and eat all the meat in the butcher shops . . . Do they even pause to consider where the next meal is supposed to come from?"

Ivy asked in a sympathetic tone, "Down to eating the horses?"

"Yes. And what could be more foolish? How am I supposed to leave the city if they eat my carriage horses? I recommended that they eat their own mounts or, more practically, the citizens."

"And they refused? How surprising."

"Fottergrim muttered something about worgs tasting bad and wanting the citizens as hostages in case he needed to negotiate."

"Obviously, an unreasonable orc."

"A dim-witted buffoon, all stomach and no brains, like most orcs. He threw away my advice and power."

"And the treasure beneath Tsurlagol?" She wondered what a magelord of his power could want in these looted ruins.

"I tell you, not even that creature's powers can find the crypt," said Archlis. Again he gestured toward Kid.

"Actually, we have never heard of . . ." began Gunderal, but stopped when Mumchance tapped her on the knee.

"Let Ivy do the talking," whispered the dwarf.

Archlis switched his attention to Mumchance. "You are a dwarf," stated the magelord.

"Thought that would be obvious." Mumchance peered up at Archlis in his usual tilt-headed squint so he could see the magelord clearly out of his one good eye.

"Do not be insolent. What is that?" Wiggles had popped her head out of Mumchance's pocket.

"My dog." Mumchance could be very taciturn with humans he did not like.

"Ah, your familiar. You are a dwarf wizard, then?"

"Not a wizard." The dwarf put up one hand to rub his fake eye, as if he were tired or trying to clear some grit out of it. Ivy knew what he was doing—preparing to pop out the gem bomb. She shook her head slightly and got an even slighter nod back from Mumchance. The room was too small, and the chances too great that the rest of them might be hurt by the blast. Besides, given that the magelord could apparently set himself on fire and not be burned, she doubted a gem bomb would cause Archlis any serious damage.

"Then it changes shape? Becomes a creature of unparalleled size and ferocity?" Archlis was still fixated on Wiggles, who was snarling at him with as much ferociousness as she could manage.

"No," said Mumchance. "Wiggles stays a dog. A small dog. My dog."

"Wiggles?"

"That's her name."

Archlis was clearly baffled by someone wasting pocket space carrying anything as useless as Mumchance's fluffy white dog. It was an emotion that Ivy understood. Archlis abandoned his questions about Wiggles as profitless to himself. "Well, I may have a use for you—a dwarf in armor should be heavy enough." With that baffling remark, the magelord turned back to Ivy. "You will serve me. For now."

"All a matter of fee."

"I will decide the appropriate reward."

Ivy did not argue. Something about the way that Archlis kept fingering his Ankh and the bugbears kept backing up warned her that further discussion would not be beneficial. Pleased by her silence, Archlis continued. "A section of these ruins contains a simple trap in the floor, but it takes four at least to pass through safely. We made it through once, but we came upon a complication and were driven back. Then we ran into the hobgoblins."

"And there are only three of you now," pointed out Ivy, who knew that two bugbears and one magelord did not add up to four.

"There are only three," admitted Archlis, "due to the complication. Which I will explain after you take us through the trapped corridor. Four of you are all I need, but I will let the others live as part of your fee."

Archlis did not look like he was making idle threats. The stench of burned bodies still filled the chamber where they stood. Of course, they could refuse and fight. She knew the others were just waiting for a signal from her. Mumchance had even remembered to get a good grip on his sword instead of his second-best hammer. Zuzzara was swinging her shovel in idle little circles, drawing patterns in the dust as if she were paying

no attention at all to what was happening, and she had definitely loosened her grip on Sanval. Gunderal was looking pale
but more determined; her good hand had the fingers spread
wide to cast some water spell. But Kid was still cringing behind
her and pulling on her weapons belt. Three sharp tugs—the
little thief's signal for danger.

Ivy knew that they could take the bugbears. But she did not
know how fast Archlis could activate that Ankh. He looked
just crazy enough to set off a firestorm in a small room, and
who knew what protections he had for himself woven into that
coat of multiple charms.

"So," said Ivy, "how far is the corridor with the funny
floor?"

CHAPTER TWELVE

Archlis led them out of the room and into another tunnel that continued to run uphill, much to Mumchance's relief. The dwarf was still muttering about hearing water moving behind them. Personally, Ivy was just glad to be out of that small room littered with the burned reminders of the magelord's power.

After several twisting turns, the magelord called a halt. "I must consult my book," he declared. "The rest of you sit. Be quiet."

The bugbears slumped against the wall and began hauling out various supplies from their packs. As Ivy knew from past campaigns, if there was ever a creature whose first love was food, and who hated to share, it was a bugbear. And normally she would not annoy anything that big and furry and none too bright. But she was hungry, and so were the rest of her crew. She swaggered over to the biggest bugbear, stuck out her chin, and got her nose as close to his as possible. Like most males, this maneuver made him nervous. He tried to back up, but he had no place to go. She leaned a little closer. He growled, and she snarled back, "Give me bread! Give me water!" in the only orc dialect that she knew.

He answered back in Common, "Don't have to."

"Have to!" barked Ivy, relieved to be able to drop out of Orcish and into a language that didn't make her throat hurt. Still, she didn't know how much Common this creature knew. She kept it simple. "Archlis said!"

"Did not!"

"Ask him." Ivy jerked a thumb at the magelord, his long nose already buried deep in his spellbook and muttering to himself. "But he won't be happy if you disturb him."

The bugbear rumbled something at his companion, and the other bugbear grumbled back. "Females," the creature said, very pointedly in Common so Ivy would understand, "are nothing but trouble." He handed over a bag of supplies.

"I would never disagree," replied Ivy with a grin as she turned on her heel and headed back to her friends.

On the top of the bag was fresh bread, still warm, as if it came from Tsurlagol's bakeries only that morning. Under that was some dried meat. Everyone grabbed at the bread as soon as they smelled it. Ivy shrugged and snatched her share. It had been a very long time since breakfast; or, in Ivy's case, since a few bites of dried biscuit.

Mumchance offered some of the unidentified meat to Wiggles. The dog whined and turned up her nose at it. After seeing the dog's reaction, the rest of them set the meat aside.

While they ate, Archlis carefully turned the crumbling pages of his scorched spellbook. He bent so close to the book that the tip of his narrow nose looked in danger of smudging the ink. The expression on his face grew more sour, as if the spellbook did not yield exactly the answers that he desired. Yet he handled the decaying parchment with judicious care. The bugbears sat with their backs to Archlis and their attention on the group, but nobody did anything overtly hostile.

Released by Zuzzara with a friendly pat to the back that

staggered him, Sanval chose to sit down next to Ivy. She took it as a good sign that he had not minded her more colorful comments about his character when she had been dickering with Archlis. For the first time since he had come to her tent that morning, Sanval stripped off his gauntlets to accept some bread and fresh water from Ivy. She passed the food and drink over to him with a slightly apologetic smile. His own look lightened a little as he took the bread from her. When he took her peace offering, she noticed his big hands bore the usual scars across the knuckles and the backs of his fingers that came from sword practice. Even with wooden weapons, cuts were a common hazard; and no matter how good a cleric a house employed, not everything healed without a trace. Ivy's own hands had a similar pale network of white scars across her skin.

"Why was Archlis interested in that?" said Sanval, reaching out and touching the small silver oak leaf worked into the cuff of Ivy's left glove. Her gloves were stuffed, as usual, through her belt.

"Harper token. I told you my mother was a bard," she said with an affectionate glance at her mother's last gift. She still remembered the sting of the wind against her cheeks as she stood on the dock, watching her mother's ship sail away. Over the wind and the sailors' shouts, she had heard her mother's cries of, "Farewell, farewell, I will return." She remembered how warm the token had felt in her hand and how tightly her father's hands had grasped her shoulders as they watched her mother wave good-bye.

She tapped the little silver leaf. "This gets me free beer in an amazing number of places."

Sanval looked a little disappointed at her answer.

"No, unfortunately, it is not much of spell. Just a tiny bit of extra luck, my mother said. It does keep me from losing whatever it is attached to, which is why I sewed it onto the glove. I hate losing my gloves. Of course, it only keeps one glove with me at all times. So I replace the other one quite frequently. I should have sewn it on my cap. I miss that cap." She ran her hand across the top of her head, causing more short bits of blonde hair to escape her braid and trail across her face. She pushed them back with impatient, dusty fingers, ignoring Gunderal gesturing behind Sanval's back with one of her own delicate shell combs. They were in the middle of an underground ruin, surrounded by bugbears, and essentially held prisoner by an unfriendly magelord. Ivy was not about to let Gunderal rebraid her hair now, even if it did give her fussy friend fits to see her braid come undone. Ivy let Gunderal braid her hair once a tenday, after she had washed her hair and bathed, and that was enough as far as Ivy was concerned. If she listened to the vain little wizard's lectures on personal hygiene, she would be bathing every day and twice on holidays.

With a sigh, Sanval pulled off his metal helmet and ran his own hand across his hair. Ivy checked with a sideways glance. All his curls looked very washed and polished. He probably did bathe once a day, and then let his servants clip and comb his hair into that regulation cut that all of Procampur's officers favored for this particular war. Yet that one curl stood defiantly out of line with its fellows. Ivy smiled at the curl's crooked gallantry, and Sanval gave her an inquiring look. She did not enlighten him.

"I thought the charm on your glove was something that we could use against Archlis. He seemed disturbed by it," Sanval said.

Ivy shook her head. "It's not much of charm. Won't do anything spectacular. Besides, Archlis has a dozen or more charms sewn on that coat of his that are certainly more powerful than this. And look at his hands—a magic ring on each hand. Those are probably protections and spells too."

"But you must have more magic than that," said Sanval, tapping the token again.

"Zuzzara's ring, but we used that already. Gunderal's potions, which we lost in the fall."

"Armor? Weapons?"

"Mumchance has full plate with some extra protection hammered in, but he doesn't wear it in the summer. It is too hot, he says, and that's why he just has the chain mail today. All of us have charms against injury from falls, but as you can tell from Gunderal's arm, they are not too powerful." She thought about mentioning Mumchance's fake eye, but the secrets that Sanval did not know, he could not let slip to others. Archlis did not seem to be paying any attention to them, but wizards could have ears and eyes in the backs of their head, sometimes quite literally. Better to appear more harmless than they were, especially when they did not have that much magic to spare.

"But weapons. Magic swords? Spears?"

"Do you see any of those things on us? Zuzzara's shovel is most firmly unenchanted. My sword is just that—a sword. Good balance, keen edge, no spells. Mumchance's sword is the same. Better balance than mine, being forged by dwarves and all, but no spells of smiting. In fact, he usually forgets he is carrying it and uses one of his hammers instead. Gunderal never carries weapons, because she usually can cast spells or use her potions, when she hasn't broken all the potion bottles. Kid, do you have anything magical?"

"No, my dear. Two sharp little knives, but that is all." Kid had pitched his voice loud enough to carry to where Archlis was sitting. Good, thought Ivy, he has figured it out—do not give Archlis any reason to be nervous. Kid had flipped open the collar of his leather tunic to display the two needle-thin blades neatly sheathed there. Sanval seemed disappointed. Of course, he did not know that the stilettos were deadly in Kid's hands. The little thief could throw with frightening speed and accuracy when he wanted to. Kid's knives also had the excellent advantage of being able to double as lock picks on the cruder sort of lock. And, of course, being Kid, he had not shown all his knives. He carried another tucked in the back of his breeches. Gods only knew how he kept from slicing his furry little tail off. Of course, he kept that tucked away out of sight most of the time too.

"I thought you would have more magic," said Sanval.

"Why did you think that?"

"Because in the red-roof district . . ." Sanval stopped at Ivy's whistle of surprise and went a little pink across his cheeks. One of the bugbears glanced over at them, shrugged, and went back to eating something that dripped unpleasantly.

"So you do talk to the red-roof tavern girls. I wondered how you knew the end of that song."

"Everyone goes to a red-roof tavern," Sanval admitted, "when they are young. To hear the stories. You know, about the dragons, and the adventurers, and the great deeds done in the rest of the world. But in all the stories, people like you . . . They always own many items of magic that they use to defeat their foes. Great and terrible weapons of power are carried by all the mercenaries. That is what they say in the camp."

"You should never believe camp gossip," said Kid, reaching past Sanval to snag another piece of bread and stuff it into his cheek like a berrygobbler.

"Sound advice. What they always leave out in the ballads and the camp gossip is that magic costs, and red-roof adventurers like me rarely can afford much." Ivy looked at Sanval, a man who could afford to bring three horses to a siege camp, along with the necessary servants. He wore full half-plate armor, forged just for him, properly fitted and certainly kitted underneath with leather, silk, cotton padding, and whatever else was deemed necessary for his comfort. He probably even owned more than one shirt although she asked him just to make sure.

"I brought twelve shirts with me," he replied.

"I have two, one clean and one not," she said, but he did not look enlightened. She gave him a basic lesson in economics, the mercenary version of economics. "Magic costs. Gold. Coin. Gems. It takes wealth to buy the best spells and best enchanted items. We do all right, but we never make that much. And what we earn goes back to the farm. We made a promise to each other—that was what we would do."

"But he has magic," said Sanval, nodding toward Archlis.

"Because he is a wicked wizard!"

"Magelord, my dear," said Kid. "He stole that title from my master Toram, when he took Toram's book and Ankh."

"Magelord, magician, whatever he prefers to call himself, I would wager he's not trying to pay for a working farm, with vinestock that needs replacing, and a mule that deliberately goes lame when it doesn't want to haul the wagon (and nobody will let me turn into shoe leather), and more dogs and cats than you can count—or feed—because somebody is always dragging home some poor stray. I will not even try to account for the many expenses of an ill wyvern that ended up destroying our barn roof." Ivy subsided. There was no use trying to explain her problems to a man who could afford to bring twelve shirts to a siege camp and had probably never in his life had to sit up all night on a roof beam with a wyvern vomiting some type of acidic sludge.

"I would prefer your farm to any wizard's wonders," said Sanval, and he sounded sincere in his statement. "But I still wish that you had more magic, like that magelord's charms."

"Do not forget his Ankh," whispered Kid. "That is a weapon paid for by murder."

"Ankh?"

"That," said Kid, pointing at the metal pole that Archlis leaned against. It was topped by a smooth loop of metal and a crossbar of the same.

"I though it was a crutch," said Ivy.

Kid shook his head sadly. "No, it is the Ankh of Fire that he stole from my master."

"That is a rather large ankh," said Ivy, eyeballing the length of the thing. "I thought ankhs were little things that priests wore on their belts."

"This Ankh was forged for a giant and casts the most terrible and powerful spells. It took Toram years to find the tomb where it was hidden."

"What type of spells?"

"Fire spells."

"What sort of fire spell?" Her father had hated and feared fire as much as any tree in the forest.

"Many and many, my dear," said Kid, his ears drooping down and back, almost flat and hidden among his curls. "Enough to burn us all. He does not bluff when he claims such power."

"That settles it," Ivy said to Sanval. "You have to stifle any objections to an alliance with Archlis. You did notice how quickly he disposed of those hobgoblins and orcs," she continued when Sanval said nothing.

"But he is the sworn enemy of Procampur," protested Sanval.

"We are his enemies," agreed Ivy in soothing tones. What did it take to make one man in shiny armor to see reason? "And there are more of us, but does he look perturbed? That means he thinks he can beat us and, given the size and the number of fireballs that he was tossing off the walls of Tsurlagol over the last tenday, I think he can too."

"He won't dare try a fireball in here," said Gunderal,

catching the end of their discussion. "These tunnels are too narrow. He would burn himself."

When the others looked skeptical, Gunderal said with a huff, "Just because I can't do fire spells does not mean that I never studied them."

Zuzzara shook her head, setting her braids swinging and the iron beads on the ends clicking together. "What do you mean?"

"Flames spread, just like water! Simple enough for you, big sister?"

"Temper, temper," replied the half-orc. "You should eat something. You are getting cranky, *little* sister."

Gunderal started to reply and then obviously thought better of it. She tore off a small bit of bread and chewed dainty but deliberate bites. Zuzzara smiled to see her sister follow her advice.

"What about that sphere spell?" asked Mumchance. "That fire chased those hobgoblins and orcs precisely enough."

"For all those reasons, we are not going to get into a fight that we cannot win and will not gain us anything," Ivy emphasized to Sanval. "Don't play the hero."

"You always say that," said Sanval in a sharper tone than he usually used.

"Because I know what heroics can bring." A drowned mother, a father so torn by grief that he would rather be wood than human. But how could she explain that to a man raised in Procampur, who thought the world was built on straight, narrow, and well-ordered lines. One who believed you could define people by the color of their roof tiles?

"I will attack him alone," decided Sanval, apparently forgetting that she was supposed to be the captain and the one giving the orders. She had known that was going to happen— she had just known it. "Then you will have time to escape," the silver-roof noble concluded with a pleasant smile.

"And do you think that you would survive such an attack?"

"That does not matter." Sanval sounded happier than she had ever heard him, which was very bothersome to her peace of mind.

"What is the Procampur obsession with rushing in against all odds and getting yourself killed?" asked Ivy. She did not mean to sound harsh, but she did not want to fret about Sanval doing something suicidal. She had so many other things to worry about. "That is as idiotic as your city's ban of the Thieves Guild."

"What is wrong with our ban of the Thieves Guild?" said Sanval, distracted by the sudden criticism of the rules of his beloved city, which was exactly what Ivy had wanted.

"The ban on the Thieves Guild is unnatural, in my opinion," Ivy said, warming to her argument on why Procampur's citizens, especially the one sitting next to her, lacked basic good sense. "It is the same as expecting all the citizens in an entire city to come to an agreement to be honorable and deal fairly with others and not steal their goods."

"You would prefer to be robbed as you walked down the streets?"

"Of course not."

"Or to be allowed to rob others."

"Not me personally, at least not friends and family. But governments and rulers are somewhat stingy and should probably be encouraged to share the wealth at times."

"So you are willing to rob others as long as you do not know them."

"And they can afford it. Never steal from the poor, they don't have anything worth taking." She waited for some response. Sanval's features had settled back into the impassive, slightly stern expression that she knew so well. He did not speak. "That was a joke. But, honestly (or dishonestly if you prefer), thieves who are ruled by Thieves Guilds avoid stealing too much too close to home. City officials supplement their pay with some nice bribes, and the world rolls on. Procampur has to be the only city to take the quaint view that all its visitors, as well as its citizens, should be free to wander wherever they want in the city without having their purses cut or their pockets picked."

"And does that make our quaint view wrong, because it is not true in other cities?" A touch of acid stung beneath his words. And if Sanval's straight spine were any stiffer, Mumchance could have used it as a level. Worst of all, Sanval had gone from his impassive face to that straight-down-the-nose stare that he must have learned in the nursery beneath his mansion's silver roof. It was precisely the look of rebuke that his ancestors must have been giving red-roof adventurers like herself for generations.

Ivy could see a large philosophical hole opening before her—one that probably had a snake at the bottom of it. Which was confusing, because she knew that she had a winning argument when she had started out. A quick visual survey of her friends showed them all sitting there, resolutely silent, and waiting to see how she was going to finish the debate. She grimaced at the lack of verbal verification from those that she had expected to agree with her. Mumchance stared back with a very clear "you dig yourself out of this one" look. Zuzzara and Gunderal were leaning forward, Gunderal fluttering her eyelashes in some type of signal that puzzled Ivy. Even Kid, that hypocritical thief, looked disapproving of her argument. Wiggles just wagged her tail, obviously hoping that Ivy would shut up and somebody would feed the cute white dog sitting at their feet.

"Perhaps we could just agree that getting yourself killed is not going to help anyone, even if it is the most honorable thing to do," said Ivy, returning to the point that she had wanted to make.

"I will attempt no action that would endanger any of you," promised Sanval, replacing his helmet very slowly and very straight upon his head.

Only Ivy seemed to notice that he made no promises about his personal safety.

CHAPTER THIRTEEN

Once he was done with his book, Archlis neatly packed it away into a pouch dangling from his belt. Kid watched him from behind Ivy's back.

"So he still has it." Kid's voice was soft, just loud enough for her to hear.

"What?"

"Toram's book."

"And who was Toram?"

"A bad man. An evil man." Ivy had never heard Kid, whose own morality was rather questionable, state his disapproval so flatly. "But a learned one. He spent his life robbing the secrets of others."

"So are there maps in that book?" The tunnels were twisting round and round. As good as Mumchance's sense of direction was underground, Ivy would have loved to have a map that showed clearly where they were in Tsurlagol's ruins and, more importantly, where they could get out of Tsurlagol's ruins. "Could you steal it?'

Kid fingered the knives beneath his collar. "He has charms to protect him against theft," he reluctantly whispered. "He would have to be distracted and even then . . . I am sorry, my dear, I do not know if I can do it."

Ivy gave one of his horns a friendly pull. "Don't worry. There's bound to be some other way to get out of here. I have a plan or two in my back pocket."

"For just such an emergency," Kid said, looking more cheerful. "Well, I will watch and wait for my chance. For I do not like that man, my dear." And he continued to watch the magelord's back, fingering his knives in a thoughtful way.

Marching two by two through increasingly narrow tunnels, the group followed Archlis. The magelord strode in front, periodically lighting a finger the way another man would light a candle so he could better see some arcane symbol etched in the walls. He never hesitated, although they passed a myriad of tunnels branching away into the darkness. Of course, Archlis had come this way once before. Still Ivy had to admire a man who remembered directions after having dealt with and avoided some of the most devious traps of place.

One bugbear walked in front of them, and another walked behind them. So far there had been no opportunity for escape.

"We've turned east again," Mumchance said with the certainty of an elderly dwarf far underground. Wiggles once again rode in his pocket, sleeping off her late lunch. Everyone had slipped her part of their bread because she had looked so sad and hungry. Now the dog was so full, she could barely waddle.

"Back toward the city? The city wall that we want?" Ivy asked.

"Closer than we were." Mumchance fingered his fake eye. "We could still use our little treasure against them."

"And kill whom? The one in front or the one in back?" hissed Ivy. "You can't get them all." She turned back to her wizard, the one that couldn't light fires but could definitely feel water. "Where's the river?"

"Still running strong behind us," Gunderal whispered. "I can feel it flooding the tunnels."

"There is something else too. Something old and magical behind us," said Kid, one ear swiveling forward and one back.

"Oh, do you feel it too?" A relieved Gunderal bent down and gave him a quick hug. "I could not figure out what I was smelling, and it was giving me such a headache—I thought it might be a reaction to my own spell."

"What are you talking about, sister?" asked Zuzzara. "Are you ill?"

"I'm fine. But whatever the magic is, it is giving me such an itch in my nose. I feel like I'm going to sneeze, but I can't. It's driving me crazy."

Zuzzara pulled a large silk handkerchief out of her waistcoat pocket. "Blow."

Gunderal blew, delicately of course, and sighed. "Oh, that's better. I felt my ears pop."

Ivy chewed her lower lip and thought about a possible magical threat following them. Well, it was not treading on her heels like the bugbear, so she decided to ignore it for now.

"If we are heading back toward Tsurlagol," said Zuzzara, who was always the most optimistic of the Siegebreakers (as long as her sisters Mimeri and Gunderal were happy), "then maybe we can find our wall again. The one that we are supposed to knock down."

"The Thultyrl gave us two days," Ivy said. "And I don't think that we have even finished out half of the first day." She thought about the number of fights, wrong turns, and other disasters that had befallen them. "Well, maybe more than half."

Sanval answered softly, "The Thultyrl may not wait. I did not go back to the camp. They would have investigated and found your tunnel collapsed."

"And presume that we are dead?"

"Or unable to complete your task."

"What will they do then?" Ivy asked.

"Charge the wall without your help."

"Wonderful thought." Now she had to worry about an entire troop of Procampur's finest trying to scale the western wall and overrun Fottergrim's orcs in the holdings at the top. Even without Archlis opposing them with his fire spells, it would not take much to turn the charge into a rout.

"Well, this looks like trouble," said Ivy.

A pair of oaken doors blocked the way. The lock had been burned open, and the blasted doors hung half off their hinges.

"Waste of magic," Mumchance said when he saw the condition of the doors.

"He has magic to waste, dear sir," replied Kid with a significant wink toward Archlis. The magelord stood behind them, flanked by his bugbears, and was obviously waiting for them to survey the room beyond.

Peeking through the ruined doors, they could see a corridor with a checkered floor made from huge stone slabs. Some had a fine cross-hatch pattern cut into them. Others were marked with a spiral of stars, and still others with wavy lines. A few squares were polished smooth and blank.

"Earth, sky, ocean," said Mumchance. "And that which we find on the other side of death."

"Nothing," said Ivy, because this was an old lesson, one that her mother had taught when she had taken Ivy hunting for treasure in the wild. She had seen such patterns in ruins before. They invariably led to a tomb or crypt. "It's a path to the dead."

"A bit more dead than usual, my dears," pointed out Kid.

For the floor was littered with the bodies of hobgoblins and orcs, a ragged and rather squashed looking troop. Their lifeless, muscular bodies were limp, their blank yellow eyes staring at nothing, their hide and rough hair poking out from breaks in their once bright armor. Shields were as flat as plates, and swords smashed.

"More of Fottergrim's?" asked Ivy.

"They pursued us through this section," said Archlis, "but they did not know the secret of the squares. The ceiling crushed them as it does anyone who does not know the pattern."

At this pronouncement, they all glanced up. The ceiling was low and gleamed with a spectral light, clearly showing a lattice of iron suspended above the floor. A long pointed spike was welded to the corner of each tiny square formed by the ironwork. Some of the spikes were clearly blunted by repeated poundings on the stone floor below. Others still dripped with bits and pieces of the unfortunates who had passed below without the knowledge of the floor's pattern. Chains ran from the lattice into square holes cut into the stone ceiling above.

"The floor is constructed in such a way that if four people move across the squares in unison, the trap stays in the ceiling. Should one make a misstep, the trap comes crashing down. I have the pattern here," Archlis withdrew his spellbook from his pouch and unfolded a page twice as large as the book from its center. The parchment was blotched with terrible stains, but a series of gray-brown lines and rust red symbols could be seen on one side.

"You and you," said Archlis, pointing at Sanval and Zuzzara, "should go first, as you appear to be about the same weight. Then"—he nodded toward Ivy and Mumchance—"you will follow. You must step exactly as I say."

"And then what?" asked Ivy.

Archlis pointed with the head of his Ankh to the doors visible at the opposite end of the room. "There is a lever on the left-hand side. Turn it three times to the right. The lock handle must be turned delicately and correctly, but if done right, the trap will remain locked long enough for the rest of us to cross."

"Then it resets itself?" asked Mumchance.

"Yes. There is no way to lock it open permanently. But it takes some time for it to reset. After we had left this room, Fottergrim's trackers were able to cross it safely when they followed us. We eluded them in the maze that it is beyond those doors, but were forced back. We locked the trap from that side when we crossed the room again so more than half the trackers escaped with their lives and continued to hunt us into the room where you found us."

"So when the ceiling comes down, it comes down fast," said Mumchance with a speculative note in his voice. "And it probably goes up very slowly."

"Whether it is fast or slow does not matter. I hold the pattern here. We used it to cross once before. Once you have reached the other side, the dwarf will turn the lock and secure the room as I have instructed. That should be within his skills," said Archlis. Mumchance snorted. "Then we will follow you," continued Archlis. "Now take one step right, one step forward, and one step left, and repeat that pattern until you reach the other side."

"It sounds like a court dance," said Sanval, readying himself to cross by the usual straightening of his helmet and a quick check of his weapons.

Ivy looked across the room and at the corpses that littered many of the squares. She laid one hand on Sanval's arm to keep him from stepping out. "But there are extra bodies on the floor, and that will make it harder. Hate to trip over someone else's feet as we glide along."

"Or someone's severed head, more likely," said Mumchance, eyeing the carnage.

"Can we do it?" questioned Zuzzara. "If one is off count or stumbles . . ."

"All of us die," said Ivy, turning to Archlis. "I don't like this."

The magelord adjusted his grip on his Ankh, one rusty ring on his hand grating unpleasantly against its smooth metal surface. "If you refuse, you will die faster. Then the others can choose which danger is greater—the floor ahead or myself. I only need four to cross and turn the key."

"If he is so clever, why can't he break the trap's spell?" Gunderal whispered.

"It is not a spell," Kid whispered back. "Do you feel any magic here?"

Gunderal's pretty face smoothed into that look of perfect serenity that meant she was feeling along the Weave of magical forces. She slowly shook her head.

Mumchance nodded in agreement with Kid. "It's all mechanical."

Ivy backed away from Archlis, fingering the hilt of her sword. Sanval also had a firm grip on his weapon. Archlis did not look worried, which was worrisome. The bugbears were a bit too relaxed as well, just leaning on their glaives and watching with interest. They obviously felt no threat.

"Waste of time," said Mumchance, who had been studying the floor and then the ceiling while carrying on a whispered conversation with Kid. He squinted at the little thief, who nodded very firmly this time. "All that hopping back and forth. Kid, get ready. Come up here, Zuzzara."

"No," said Archlis, "it must be two of almost equal weight who start the pattern."

"Don't care about the pattern." Mumchance scratched

Wiggles's head as he contemplated the room. "Zuzzara, how far can you throw a dead hobgoblin?"

"Same as a live one," she said with grin. "Halfway across the room without much trouble."

"Should work. Let's get you a little help. Hey, you, big guy," Mumchance said, crooking a finger at the nearest bugbear. "Hook me a hobgoblin with that stick of yours. The little one near the door will work fine. He's almost intact."

The bugbear growled at Mumchance, but he went to the threshold of the room. The hairs on the back of the bugbear's neck were clearly visible just below the line of his battered helmet and just as clearly standing straight out. The bugbear muttered and grumbled, very softly in the back of his throat, as he looked beyond the room to the doors on the far side. Still, he obeyed Mumchance's orders, ignoring the scowling magelord. The bugbear leaned through the doors, carefully keeping his feet out of the room and off the carved pavement. He thrust his glaive into the nearest hobgoblin and dragged it back through the door.

"You get one end. Zuzzara, you grab the other," instructed Mumchance. "Kid, get ready to jump."

Kid crouched in the center of the door. Zuzzara and the bugbear swung the body twice and then sent it sailing over Kid's head and into the room. It fell heavily on the tiles. With a screeching of gears above the ceiling, then the clash of unwinding chains, the ironwork grid dropped from above them and crashed to the floor, again impaling the dead hobgoblins and orcs.

"Go! Go!" shouted Mumchance at Kid.

Kid leaped lightly on top of the ironwork and raced across the grid. A ponderous *tick-tick* of gears sounded in the ceiling. "It's starting up again," yelled Mumchance. Kid spurted ahead and dropped in front of the doors. He grasped the lever and twisted it savagely around to the right. There was a grinding noise that came from the ceiling and then a distinct *sproing* sounded through the room. The spiked grid remained where it had landed on the floor.

"See," said Mumchance, hoisting himself on top of the ironwork and strolling straight across. "Much easier to break it than to go dancing across the floor."

If the magelord was pleased, it did not show in his scowl. The bugbears looked on, expressionless, but then Ivy did not expect any sort of expression on a bugbear's squashed furry face.

When they reached the far side of the room, Ivy said to the dwarf, "That was just too easy. What terrible thing happens next, do you suppose?"

"Look, these old tomb builders weren't exactly mechanical geniuses," said Mumchance. "Well, one or two were good at it, and the others just copied them. I would bet you a good night's sleep that the gears are rusted out, the chains have weak links, and a couple more drops would have broken the whole thing. But the most delicate gears are always in the lock mechanism. The magelord was right. It's all about balance and counterbalance, the right pressure at the right time. Archlis had already forced it open twice today, so it was sure to be a bit bunged up."

"And if the ironwork went back into place while Kid was racing across?"

"Wouldn't move that fast. Archlis said there was enough time for a bunch of Fottergrim's raiders to follow him through and out once already, which meant some type of gear rotating in the lock and, most likely, the same sort of gear powering the resetting of the trap. Of course, if there had been any magic behind it, that would have been different, but Gunderal didn't smell anything. But, Ivy, that's all done and in the past. You should be worrying about something else."

"What?"

"Whatever chased them back into this room. You heard the magelord. They went through once, doing that hop-jump-hop across the floor. Fottergrim's hounds followed them and then something forced Archlis back across that room one more time. It wasn't those hobgoblins and orcs. He roasted them as soon as they caught up to him."

The dwarf had a point. Ivy just hated that. A magelord unhindered by hobgoblins and unflustered by stray warriors appearing in the middle of his battles (even if those warriors were a battered troupe like Ivy's) would only retreat from something very large and fairly fireproof. And deadly. She doubted that anything short of deadly would stop him. What came next must be far more dangerous than Fottergrim's fighters.

"I knew this was too easy," said a rueful Ivy. Staying next to Mumchance, she squeezed to one side to let Zuzzara, Gunderal, and Sanval pass into the corridor beyond. Archlis and his bugbears followed. "Well, at least we got through that trap with minimum fuss."

Kid sidled next to her, stamping from hoof to hoof.

"Those early tomb builders lacked sophistication." Mumchance poked at the broken mechanism that locked the trap into place, wiggling the long brass handle that disappeared into a square hole carved into the stone. Like any dwarf, he never could resist trying to pull something apart just to see how it worked. Ivy almost expected him to pry the mechanism out of the wall, just so he could examine it later. "Not like today. If I had built that bit back there, there would be some secondary trap or . . ."

Ivy never heard the rest of the sentence. The stone slab under her feet slid open with a sharp click and the rattle of chains running through a stone channel. She and Kid dropped into the darkness below. As she was falling, she caught a brief glimpse of Mumchance's surprised face, his mouth still open, before the stone trapdoor snapped shut above her.

CHAPTER FOURTEEN

The day after a fifteen-year-old Ivy had been dug out from under a dead horse by a kindly dwarf, she had wanted to stop at the nearest temple and make a few offerings.

Mumchance had dissuaded her.

"I wouldn't," he had said. "Over the last three hundred years, the one thing that I have learned is that it is best to ignore the gods. Take no notice of them, and they will take no notice of you."

It had seemed like good advice at the time. Now Ivy wondered if she had angered some god somewhere. Nothing else could account for her foul luck.

She sat up slowly in the darkness beneath the trapdoor, unsure which parts of her body still worked after her fall. Her ribs ached, her back hurt, and the rubble covering the floor was making itself felt through the leather of her breeches. But none of the pains felt fatal, just more bruises on top of the bruises collected in her earlier falls that day, not to mention the buffeting by kobolds, the squeezing of that snake, and—oh now she remembered—a few well-placed blows from the hobgoblins. Once she was free of this tangle of tunnels and traps, Ivy intended to march herself to the largest, most impressive healer's tent that she could find, lie down, and not get up again until every single cut, bruise, and kink in her muscles had been soothed away by some skilled healing hands. Some heroes might go to their temples to give thanks for salvation. Others might drink themselves blind in a victory party, and still others might pursue a new amorous alliance. From nauseous experience, Ivy had learned to avoid long drinking bouts, as they led to more physical misery. She did have a few ideas for possible lusty activities, and she most certainly planned to rethink her opposition to giving thanks in temples (although she supposed she would have to decide what god or goddess would be willing to overlook her long lapse in abstinence from worship). But at this moment, she needed to give herself some special promise to lure herself into standing up.

"I think I'll find the handsomest cleric, with the most delightfully smooth and strong healing hands," she muttered to herself. "And then add that bill to the long list of payments that I intend to collect from the Thultyrl."

A muffled snort of laughter reminded her that she was not alone in the dark. She heard the scratch of Kid's hooves as he climbed across the rubble toward her.

"Kid," Ivy called. "Are you all right? Where are you?"

"Here, my dear," his soft voice was right under her ear, causing her to startle like a young colt. Then she felt the exceptional warmth of his hard little hand as he patted her cheek in reassurance. "I apologize that I am not a handsome cleric."

His hearing was far too sharp at times. Ivy ignored his comment and asked, "Where are we, do you think?"

She could hear the rustling of clothing near her that meant he was searching through one of his many hidden pockets. "How can you manage to fit so many pockets into that tunic?" Ivy grumbled, impatient for him to find his candles.

"I once apprenticed to a tailor, before he objected to my stealing his needles. I do have the candles," Kid said, then added, "but my flint is missing."

"Some day, one of us is going to have to learn fire spells." Ivy sighed and handed over her own tinderbox before standing up. She could hear Kid's nails scratching against the lid.

Stretching her arms above her head, Ivy could feel the cool, smooth stone of the ceiling. She groped along the ceiling, trying to find some crack or seam that would indicate the location of the trapdoor. Her left hand bumped against something that moved—a handle or rope pull she hoped. She traced a long knobby object under her groping fingers, something that felt like an old tree branch or dried-out root. It kept shifting in her grasp and was attached in a smooth curve to another part, covered with stiff material that crackled like old linen. Ivy continued to walk her hands along the floating object until she felt an unmistakable triangular bump. She grasped it firmly between her left forefinger and thumb. It wiggled slightly with a ripping sound.

As she stood up, a familiar odor hit her—the type of moldering stench one found too often underground. Ivy screwed up her face and tried to keep her breathing shallow.

"Kid," said Ivy very calmly and slowly. "Could you hurry with that light?"

"Coming, my dear." There was a spark, and the sudden illumination of the candle made Ivy blink.

Ivy kept her left arm stretched up and her grasp firm on her captured prize as she stared into Kid's startled eyes. She was going to have to turn and look, but for now all the confirmation she needed was in the dumbfounded look on Kid's face. "So," she said pleasantly to him. "Am I holding a floating corpse by its nose?"

Kid nodded. His brown eyes were wide and round under

his curls, giving him the look of a startled deer. It took a lot to disconcert Kid, who would cheerfully loot through the newly dead and the decomposing dead alike.

"Rotting, is it?"

"I think it is past that, my dear. Some time ago."

"How do you think he got up there? And what is keeping him there?"

"I am not sure, my dear. Magic most certainly, and very old magic at that, as old as that flameskull that attacked us."

"Maybe it is one of that creature's friends."

"He did say that they were all dead," Kid mused.

Ivy tightened her grip and felt her gloved fingers slide through the rotted flesh of the nose into the open curve of the skull. She paused, tightened her jaw, and kept her gaze on Kid. She was in no hurry to look upward. Kid shrugged, then reached up also and caught hold of the decayed robe that hung loosely around the corpse. Together they pulled downward, Kid holding cloth, Ivy clutching bone.

The corpse resisted their efforts to drag it down to the ground. Every time they grabbed it and tugged, it drifted down, seemingly weightless, but then bobbed up again as soon as they let go. Ivy finally looked at the figure to better determine how to handle it. The man, whose flesh was so sunken and dried upon the skeletal frame that gender was not easy to determine, was dressed in some type of hooded linen robes. Thankfully, the hood had flopped forward and hidden the ruined features of his face. Ivy felt particularly bad about breaking off his long nose in her early attempts to pull him off the ceiling.

"Well, it is not his body that flies," Ivy decided. "The bits that fell off don't go floating away on their own."

Kid was standing directly under the body, his head tilted all the way back as he contemplated the corpse floating just out of his reach. "No amulets, no rings on his fingers," said

Kid, reciting an inventory that made some type of sense to him. "The robe is rotting, so it cannot be that. It must be the belt, my dear."

A long thin belt of scarlet leather encircled the man's waist. The belt buckle was a large elaborate affair of chased silver, styled as a winged serpent eating its own tail. The serpent's wings fit over and under the circle, locking the belt into place. "The belt," repeated Kid firmly.

"Shall I cut it off him?" Ivy slid her sword out of its scabbard.

"No, no, my dear." Kid grasped her arm and pulled the blade back. "You might damage the magic if you cut it. Unlock the buckle, instead. The wings should move."

Ivy had to stand on tiptoe to get a firm grip on the belt buckle. She waggled the wings left and then right.

"Gently, gently, my dear." Kid was hopping from one hoof to the other, sending little pebbles rolling down the rubble pile with his fidgeting.

"I'm trying," Ivy grunted. The smell of dust, mold, and rot filled her nose, much more noticeable now that they had been hauling on the corpse. With her nose that much closer to the body, Ivy could easily smell the must of a corpse long, long past its prime. The belt buckle was uncommonly stiff and seemed permanently locked in position. She stretched up her left hand, candlelight winking on the harper's token on her glove, and twisted the whole serpent while she hung onto its wings with her right hand. With a snap, the two wings folded back. The belt and the corpse came crashing down on top of her, knocking her back on the pile of rubble.

Kid dragged the body off her and helped her to sit up. Ivy gasped a few times until her breath came back. She was not afraid of dead things, not in her line of work, but still. There was something extremely unpleasant about being felled by a rotting corpse.

"He was heavier than he looked," she finally gasped, hunching forward to ease the pressure on her thrice-bruised belly.

The belt hung limply in her grasp. Ivy shook it. The belt still hung straight down. "So, you figured how to get it down. Do you know how to make it go up again?"

"I think so, my dear." Kid ran his clever little fingers round and round the buckle. "This was wrought in imitation of the belts that the ancient ones used to fly to their floating cities. This man must have been one like Toram, who sought to imitate the great wizards of Netheril. Or perhaps he hoped to fly to one of the lost cities and plunder it. But such ambitions are treacherous."

"And you know this because . . ."

"I was Toram's godsight goat." Kid repeated Archlis's earlier words with a bitter, harsh tone quite unlike his normal fluting voice. "When Toram owned me, he trained me to know such magic as this, artifacts that he found in old tombs and crypts. To sniff such objects out for him. I told you Toram was a great grave robber. And all his magic he stole from others, as Archlis stole his power from him. Toram once said that I had a demon's knack for stealing old magic."

"And here I thought that you would have made a better thief without the horns and hooves," Ivy said, but she reached out a hand and ruffled his curls gently as a mute apology.

"After I ran away, my looks did betray me often, my dear," said Kid with a peculiar sound, halfway between a sigh and a laugh. "People drove me out of their towns with curses. I had no home until I met you."

Ivy remembered how she had almost broken Kid's hand the first time that they met (the hand had been cutting away her purse, and she had grabbed it and jerked without thinking). As an apology for her actions, she had chucked Kid over her shoulder and carried him back home for a hot meal. Kid had seemed a little surprised by her actions. But, as she told Mumchance later, it was the bad example that the dwarf set—dragging home all those stray dogs—that had made her drag home the cloven-hoofed thief.

"Well," Mumchance had said at the time, looking Kid over from his horns to his hooves. "You know the rules, Ivy. You made them. If you bring it home, you're responsible for it." But the dwarf, for all his casual airs, grew as bad as the rest of them, sneaking food onto Kid's plate when he wasn't looking and muttering about how he was too thin.

Ivy had always meant to ask Kid about his past. Perhaps sitting on a pile of rubble with a corpse was not the best time. But the sheer obsessive curiosity that she had inherited from both of her parents loosened her lips. "So how did you end up being owned by this Toram?"

Kid kept his eyes on the belt, waggling the wings left and right on the buckle, and then running the leather through his hands. He no longer wore his normal, pleasant expression—a slight smile and mildly sinister tilt of the eyebrow. Instead, his face was blank as though he were working harder than usual to hide his emotions from Ivy.

"When I was so small that I have no earlier memories, the Red Wizards kept me locked in a stone room. Toram came to their temple. He worked as a spy for them from time to time in return for glimpses of their scrolls and magic books. How he learned of me, I do not know, but one night he broke the lock and took me away bundled under his cloak."

"Red Wizards? You mean he stole you from Thay?" The legendary wrath and sheer terror evoked by even a whisper of Thay meant that the wizard Toram had to be exceptionally brave or, more likely, completely insane. Nobody stole from Thay if they wanted to keep their body intact and their soul out of eternal suffering. Even Ivy's mother, that reckless bard who regarded sea serpents as exceptionally annoying large fish, had warned her daughter specifically against encounters with anyone who even smelled like they might wear the scarlet robes. When she asked her father about Thay, he had simply rolled back his sleeves to show the horrible scars on his forearms left by one chance encounter with those terrible wizards.

"Toram wished to find the ancient magic," explained Kid. "He said my kind had a greater sensitivity than others to such artifacts, both beneficial and destructive—especially the destructive kind. As I said, he taught me ways to feel out such objects, to know their history and how they work."

"Godsight?"

"That is what he and Archlis called it." Kid gave another twist of the silver serpent's wings and clicked his tongue when the wings did not move as he expected. "They were partners once."

"You did not mention that you knew Fottergrim's favorite spellcaster when we took the job."

"Archlis used another name when he worked with Toram. Besides, all humans look a bit alike to me. I did not recognize him until I saw Toram's Ankh in his hands and sniffed his scent. Then I realized how he had been throwing so many fireballs off the walls of Tsurlagol."

"What exactly did Archlis do to Toram?"

"He struck him down and left him to die in Anauroch." Kid's entire skin shivered, rather like a horse that had an unpleasant bug walk across its hide. "Archlis thought then that I would serve him as I had served Toram."

"But you didn't stay with him."

"I bit his hand to the bone. You can still see the scar if you look close," said Kid with grim satisfaction. "When he dropped me, I ran away as quickly as I could go."

Ivy remembered when she caught Kid picking her pockets.

"I guess I'm lucky that you didn't try biting off my hand."

"Oh no, my dear," said Kid in his usual gentle voice. He glanced at her, the stony look on his face softening. "I would never hurt you or the others. I told you, I have a great sensitivity to that which is destructive and that which is not. It is like this light." He passed one hand through the candle flame without flinching. "A warmth and comfort shone from you. It has never dimmed, but only grown stronger over the years."

Ivy did not know how to respond, and Kid seemed to expect no reply. With a nod of satisfaction, he pulled the wings apart repeatedly and then snapped them back together again. The belt floated toward the ceiling. Ivy grabbed it and pulled it back down again. Kid twisted the wings, and the belt lay still in their grasp.

"Pull the wings open three times and then shut," instructed Kid as he looped the belt around her waist and fastened the buckle. "And the belt flies. Twist twice to the right and then open to cease the spell."

"Maybe you should wear it." Magical items always made her a little nervous. Such objects rarely worked as she expected.

"No, my dear, it would better for you to have it. Archlis watches me closely, but he ignores you."

"So much for my pride."

"It is because he is a magelord, which means he is even more arrogant than the ordinary wizard," said Kid. "He sees only those who have mastered his brand of magic as a threat. All others are nothing to him. He knows that I knew some of Toram's secrets, but he only sees you as a fighter—someone of no value because they have no magic at all. He is a very foolish man, my dear."

"So, should we see if this works on a live body?"

"Open three times and then shut," Kid repeated, laying his hands over Ivy's gloved fingers to teach her the move.

Suddenly, her feet were no longer in contact with the floor. Ivy was pulled into a horizontal position, face down to the pile of rubble. She bobbed up in the air so quickly that she smacked the back of her head against the ceiling. The force of that blow bounced her back toward the floor. Kid jumped up and hooked one hand through the belt. Now both of them dangled off the ground, but not quite so high. Kid wiggled, and they bobbed up and down a little. Ivy could not feel her own weight or his. For the first time in her life, she was completely unable to tell where the ground was. Usually the earth was pressed against some part of her anatomy, such as the soles of her feet. She stared down. It was there and she was above it, but she could not sense it. If she closed her eyes, she doubted she could tell which direction was up and which was down. She felt like a cloud, just floating along, but without any wind to move her to the next spot.

Ivy bent her chin against her chest to peer cross-eyed at Kid hanging off her belt. "Now what do we do?"

"Try flying, my dear."

"How? Flap my arms?"

"Most probably."

"Of all the foolishness!" Ivy flapped her arms up and down. She kicked her legs. She stroked arm over shoulder like she was trying to swim through a river. Nothing worked. They just hung there, wobbling a bit, but making no noticeable progress in any one direction.

"There may be some other trick to it," said Kid, letting go of the belt and landing lightly on his feet next to the corpse. Without Kid's extra weight hanging off the belt, Ivy floated up to the ceiling. But this time she tucked her head and legs under so the only part that smacked the stone ceiling was her rump. She straightened out and looked down at Kid and the sharp rubble littering the floor.

"Twist twice to the right and then open to cease the spell," Kid reminded her.

"I'm going to fall hard on that pile of rocks. For the second time today," Ivy observed.

Above her, she could hear the scraping of stone upon stone. A tickle of air hit the back of her neck.

"They are prying open the trapdoor, my dear," Kid said. "Quick, or they will see you."

"The gods must truly despise me," Ivy said as she squeezed her eyes closed. "All right. Step back so I don't flatten you."

Tucking her head down on her chest and throwing one arm over her face, she twisted the wings twice to the right with her free hand and squeezed the buckle open. The earth became very evident and very hard as she banged with a teeth-rattling bump into the rubble and rolled across sharp-edged pebbles and potshards.

Above her, she could hear Mumchance calling, Wiggles yapping, and Kid replying, "We are here, dear sir, well enough and safe."

"Speak for yourself," mumbled Ivy, making sure that the scarlet belt was secure and tucked down under her weapons belt. "Next time we get to town, remind me to get some extra protection from falling spells."

"That is it!" said Kid, turning away from the rope that Mumchance had thrown down.

"What's it?" Ivy brushed the dust and less pleasant debris from her gloves.

"The purpose of the belt. It keeps you from falling or sends you falling upward."

"Upward falling?" Ivy turned that phrase over in her brain and decided it just made her head hurt. "How about we just say it makes you float in the air."

"And anyone else grasping it! The belt must have been made

to hold up more than one man—or maybe a very fat man."

"We'll talk about it later," Ivy hushed him. She strode under the trapdoor and looked up at Mumchance.

"Couldn't bear to leave me behind?" she called to the dwarf in a mocking tone.

"Wasn't you," replied the dwarf in a much drier tone, his scarred face wrinkled up in a worried frown. "Archlis wants Kid. But he said we could pull you out too if we were quick about it."

"In that case, I'm going first, and Kid can follow." She grabbed the rope with both hands and shimmied out of the hole. Not surprisingly, as she came out of the hole, she saw that Zuzzara had the other end of the rope tied around her waist and was standing there like a stone pillar, unruffled by the tug of Ivy's weight.

Sanval reached out and helped steady her as she stepped out of the hole. "You are well? Is that another scrape on your face?"

"I fell through a hole and landed on rock rubble. Mildly uncomfortable. Not dead yet," she replied. He started to say something but stopped and just gave her a small bow. She nodded back at him. Stuck underground, surrounded by enemies, his formality never stopped. It must be that gleaming armor that keeps him so stiff and proper, she thought.

"Anything down there?" asked Gunderal, watching her sister lean over the hole and haul Kid up on the rope, like a fish through an ice hole.

"Just rubble and an old dead body. Nothing exciting," said Ivy. "What about up here?"

"Archlis says we have to walk very quietly now," said Zuzzara. "And not talk too loudly."

"At least he didn't ask the impossible, like no talking at all."

"No, Ivy, he said that doesn't matter. They will hear us just by our footfalls on the stone when we get close enough," Gunderal sounded even more worried than usual.

"Who would they be?" Ivy was certain that she would not like the answer.

"He says that we have to see to understand," said Gunderal. "But, Ivy, whatever it is, I can tell that it troubles him. What could frighten a magelord with as much magic as Archlis has?"

CHAPTER FIFTEEN

Sanval fell behind the Siegebreakers. Though relieved to see Ivy back with them, he also felt a familiar frustration. Why could he not have said anything sensible or even interesting when he helped her out of the hole? Instead, he had just babbled the usual Procampur phrases—completely impersonal, if courteous. He watched Ivy walk ahead of him, her head bent to catch some remark of Kid's. Since the first day he had seen her, striding through the dust of the camp, he had thought that she walked through the world as if she had no cares. No, he corrected himself, not quite that. Rather, she walked as if the world did not own her. Laws, traditions, even the gods themselves, seemed to be unable to constrain that cocky stride and the intelligent, mocking gleam in her eyes. And, Sanval was honest enough to admit to himself, he envied that freedom more than anything else.

Of course, Ivy was nothing like the perfumed ladies of Procampur, the silver-tile court intriguers who whispered secrets behind feather fans, or the red-roof girls who swayed their hips as they sashayed down the street. If there were a contest for the most grubby mercenary, Ivy would probably win. Once, when he had been very young, too young for tutors, he had eluded his nurse and gone out to the stableyard. It had been raining, and the yard was a wonderful, slippery mess of mud, perfect for sliding. Sanval still remembered the pain in his ear as his nurse dragged him upright and held him dangling before her, dripping mud upon her clean white apron. "You are the muckiest kid," she had scolded, slipping into the blue-roof dialect of her sailor father at that moment. "Dirtiest boy that I have ever seen!" Mucky was, he felt, a rather apt description of Ivy. Except, and again he had to be honest with himself as he tried to be with others, her collecting of dirt was that same friendly, joyful, defiant roll in the mud that he had enjoyed so much that day. She did it deliberately, he felt, just to tweak the more proper nose of those Procampur officers who were foolish enough to sneer at her as she swaggered up the hill to the Thultyrl's tent.

Those officers—and he had a couple of satisfying duels scheduled with the most discourteous—did not know how very beautiful and courageous and clever Ivy was. She was much finer than any noble lady born under the silver roofs.

Sanval sighed, remembering how Ivy had looked two nights ago. She had just come from the canvas bathhouse used by the mercenaries and was joking with the others as Gunderal braided Ivy's hair. As he stood there, outside of that circle of warmth and laughter, she turned and looked directly at him. "Hey, Sanval, how do you like me clean?" she yelled. "Come and join us. We're more fun than anyone sitting up on the top of that hill." He almost did it—sat down, had a drink, and shared a joke. But the message from the Thultyrl had been urgent, and he needed to return with an answer immediately. So he had said something polite—stupid and dull, but polite—and gone away again. He had never regretted any action so much.

Now he still had a duty to the Thultyrl. He could not let Archlis succeed in his plans. If he could keep Archlis from returning to Fottergrim, it would give Procampur's army an enormous advantage, perhaps even greater than toppling the western wall. Sanval was convinced Archlis would eventually return to Tsurlagol. He knew that Ivy thought she could safely follow Archlis, but she was wrong. As soon as Fottergrim's troops saw her, they would turn against her and her friends. Even her clever tongue would not be able to talk them out of a quick execution, unless Sanval could come up with a way to keep her safe from Archlis and Fottergrim.

Without intending to, Sanval dropped back until he was walking in step with the two bugbears trailing the group. The larger one growled at him and pointed at his armor.

"Your breastplate is very fine," said the big bugbear in Common. The creature wore no metal armor at all, just well-worn leather over his torn breeches and a few clanking chains looped over his shoulders. "A little small for me. But I could wear it. I can trade for it. I have good things, some of Hackermic's things. Poor Hackermic, poor Hackermic." The bugbear sighed deeply, a rumble in the center of his chest.

Sanval nodded, not to agree but to show his interest in the conversation. The creature seemed surprisingly friendly and he thought he could turn that to his advantage.

"Or I could hit you on the head," the bugbear continued more cheerfully, "if you do not give me the breastplate."

Sanval raised one eyebrow but kept silent.

The other smaller bugbear growled some incomprehensible words.

"His name is Norimgic, and I am Osteroric," said Osteroric, gesturing at his companion. "And he says that Archlis does not want you hit on the head. Not yet. I am not afraid of the magelord's anger, not like this one."

Norimgic snarled, showing off his big yellow fangs. "You are afraid of Archlis," said Osteroric to Norimgic, apparently not too impressed by the display. "Or you would have eaten him when he made us leave Lorie behind. Lorie was Norimgic's friend, his particular female friend. But something ate her," he explained to Sanval.

"Where was Lorie eaten?" asked Sanval, although he thought he knew.

"When we first came into these tunnels, something that we could not see bit off her head and an arm. It was very sad," said Osteroric, "because she was Norimgic's first love. This is the problem of being with a fighting female—they get killed so often. Of course, all our females fight. Which means that we males are often heartbroken. Our lives are tragic."

Sanval had never contemplated the romantic disasters of bugbears and decided after a few moments of reflection that he would rather not learn more. Still, he could understand the problem presented by fighting females and offered his own observations, made over the last few turbulent days of his life. "Fighting females," he said, keeping his voice down and hoping Ivy would not overhear him, "can be a very plague upon the heart, making dreams troubled and honorable thoughts difficult."

"You are poet, like us." Osteroric thumped Sanval on the shoulder, a friendly thump not much more staggering that the recent pats that he had received from Zuzzara. "We three brothers (Norimgic is my younger brother, and poor Hackermic was my elder) are all poets. That is why we left our tribe to roam the world. Because in our pack, they did not like poets. Especially after Hackermic broke the chief's jaw when he criticized Hackermic's five-lined verses with the clever triple and double rhymes. The chief thought we should only make verses in the old forms, and Hackermic should not recite his type of verses, especially before his elders," explained Osteroric. "Also, the chief did not approve of Norimgic's poetry—it is all love songs, because he wants to attract the females. Myself, I make the war chant, the kind that makes bugbears bang their heads with clubs or other bugbears. You know, the kind of chant that rouses the blood."

"It sounds very exciting," Sanval said.

"A good *thump-thump* beat is necessary," Osteroric said. "But Norimgic's songs move the blood as well. With passion of a different sort."

Norimgic, who must have understood the Common tongue even if he did not speak it, coughed to clear his throat and then broke into a long, drawn-out caterwaul that caused Archlis to glance over his shoulder. The magelord fingered one of the charms on his cloak, and Norimgic shut his mouth with a snap.

"That man has no appreciation for the songs of adoration." Osteroric sighed. "That song begins 'love is a nightmare, a thousand sword cuts can never sting so much; a hard heart makes for hard times.' In Fottergrim's camp, they often call for Norimgic to sing another someone-betrayed-someone love song."

Sanval was now positive that he wanted to know nothing more about the love lives of bugbears, but, always polite, he replied, "I regret that I do not speak any of the dialects that Norimgic uses for his love songs and thus cannot not fully appreciate his poetry." Like most gentlemen of Procampur, Sanval's tutor had tried to drum a little literature into his head between training in the sword and horseback riding. "I remember something from my lessons about a fashionable form of poetry, very popular with courting gentlemen and ladies, that consisted of one eight-line verse and an answering six-line verse."

Osteroric said that sounded fascinating although he continued to argue in favor of Hackermic's style of a five-line verse using rhythms created by two short syllables followed by one long one.

Now that friendly conversation had been established, Sanval began to consider how he might be able to sway the bugbears to his side. With great courtesy, he turned down Osteroric's offer of a bent knife for his breastplate, pointing out that his armor had been most excellently made by the best smiths in Procampur. Such armor had not only the natural strengths of the steel plate to keep its owner safe, but also came with certain standard magical protections against arrows laid into it. Such protection was hard to come by, especially underground, and Sanval would prefer to wear it himself—or so he told Osteroric.

"You can keep the chain mail," said Osteroric. "It is too small for me."

"Still, I would not trade my armor for something of lesser value," said Sanval, in as reasonable a tone as possible, because Osteroric was at least a head taller than him and bulging with muscles clearly visible under his furry skin. Remembering one former tutor's advice to know one's enemy, he added, "Why would so powerful a being as yourself need more armor?"

"You will see," said Osteroric with a shiver. Norimgic gave a snarl that almost ended with a whimper. The big bugbear patted his brother on the arm. Norimgic began to chide Osteroric in a series of snarls and growls.

"He thinks that I am too friendly to humans," translated Osteroric. "Blind trust in the honor of soft-skinned bipeds is what got us here in the first place, he says. By that he means that we should never have listened to Archlis when he promised to fill our bellies with more meat than we had ever tasted. Still, it was better than what Fottergrim offered us. He threatened to take off our heads and stuff them down our throats if we lost Archlis in the ruins one more time."

They turned another corner. Twitching at each footstep, Osteroric slowed his pace. Beneath his helmet, his fuzzy ears were tilted flat back against his skull. Before them, a small round chamber revealed numerous entrances to other tunnels, radiating out from the chamber like spokes on a wheel. Around the arched and empty doorways, hundreds of symbols had been carved: some were elaborately detailed, and others hastily scratched. In the light of his torch, Sanval could pick out one small sentence scratched in Common. "Here I fought, and here I die. Remember . . ." but the name was obliterated by another symbol written over it, in another style. It was as if every treasure hunter and adventurer who had dared the ruins of Tsurlagol had passed through this point and been compelled to try to leave some record of their passage.

"Better plug your ears," Osteroric growled. Wondering what would worry a bugbear that much, Sanval felt the ground beneath his feet begin to shake. Suddenly a terrible sound, like some giant millstone grinding through his brain, echoed through the chamber.

Archlis handed his Ankh to Osteroric, and Sanval observed Ivy watch the transfer with hungry eyes. She looked ready to lunge for the Ankh, but Gunderal plucked her sleeve and whispered in her ear. Ivy glanced up to meet Sanval's gaze. She shook her head just slightly. Warning him off? Wanting him to look away? Disapproving of his presence? Once again, he wished that he had the same unspoken communication with her that she made seem so effortless with her friends. Once or twice, he thought he knew what she wanted—if she had been from Procampur, it would have been easy for him to separate the sincere words from the formal courtesy. Not that Ivy cared all that much about courtesy, considering some of her more outrageous statements in front of such people as the Thultyrl.

"Do not step through the arch," the magelord commanded them.

Making several complicated passes with his hands, Archlis muttered and spat his way through a series of phrases in an ancient tongue. Both Gunderal and Kid winced as the recitation continued, as if the words themselves were scratching across their skin. Archlis finally pulled another charm from his cloak and ground it between his hands, reducing it to dust. He sprinkled the glittering powder in the air. Something shimmered in the air before them.

"Watch," Archlis instructed them, pointing at the empty chamber beyond the invisible barrier. A trio of huge beasts, light brown and dapple-striped in darker brown, shambled into the room. Hairless and hideous, they resembled nothing that Sanval had ever seen before. Two came through arches leading from different tunnels. The third clawed its way through a hole that opened up in the floor. The monsters jostled for space in the tiny chamber, clambering over each other. Their heads turned to the left and right, blindly questing for the source of the noise that had lured them out there just before Archlis had raised his spell.

"They have no eyes," whispered Gunderal.

"But look at the size of their raggedy ears," replied her sister.

"I'm noticing the size of those great long claws, myself," said Mumchance, putting his hand on Wiggles's head and pushing the little dog deeper into his pocket, as if that would protect her from the beasts. "And do you see all that ugly muscle in the tails? Must hit like a battering ram."

"What are they?" asked Ivy, not taking her eyes off the beasts circling in frustration before them. Blind as they were, the great monsters obviously knew that there was prey close.

"Destrachans," said Archlis. "Watch closely."

One of the creatures lifted its round muzzle to the ceiling. Although they could hear nothing on their side of the invisible wall created by Archlis, a deep vibration shook the ground. The other two beasts also lifted their round, toothless mouths, looking much like a malevolent pack of reptilian hounds howling at the moon. The stone of the ceiling changed almost immediately, melting into a cascade of sand that splattered across the destrachans. Balancing up on their powerful tails, first one and then the next of the beasts used their giant claws to pull themselves into the hole created in the ceiling.

Sanval watched Ivy as the last of the creatures disappeared into the hole in the ceiling, a final flick of its big brown tail sending down a small avalanche of pebbles and sand. Ivy chewed on one gloved knuckle—the most obvious sign of nerves that Sanval had seen her display.

"What did you call them?" she asked Archlis, as the magelord retrieved his Ankh from Osteroric.

"Destrachans. They are rare but not entirely unknown in such ruins as these. They probably trailed into the underground passages following a migration of kobolds, a favorite food of the beasts."

"So they are meat-eaters," stated Ivy. "I did notice that they have no teeth."

"That does not matter. They break their food down with waves of sound or pull it apart with those claws. They especially like intelligent food that they can play with before they devour it."

"If you consider kobolds intelligent." Zuzzara snorted, but Gunderal shushed her.

"Why not just hit them with one of those fire spells that you keep threatening us with?"

"Their cries can shatter metal," admitted Archlis, "and dissolve stone. Also, they seem to have incredibly tough hides."

"So you tried fire on them?"

"Not this group. But I have encountered this breed before. They are the bane of deep ruins."

"And you think they will destroy your Ankh before you have time to destroy them." Ivy was back to making statements, as if she were ticking off some mental list of disasters.

"It is a possibility that I would prefer not to consider," Archlis explained. "The problem with destrachans is that they are sensitive to the slightest sound. Any noise near their lair brings them out hunting."

Osteroric whispered to Sanval that was how he lost poor Hackermic, who caught the edge of the destrachan's scream. "His armor became a cloud of . . . what would you call it," he asked Norimgic. The bugbear's companion rolled his eyes and hissed back. "A cloud of scintillating dust," continued Osteroric. "I told you that Norimgic is a great poet. He is very good with words, even if he will not talk to humans. As for Hackermic, what the creatures did next to him was truly awful."

Ivy's discussion with Archlis was growing louder, which caused Osteroric and Norimgic to back farther away. Norimgic grunted something at Osteroric. "If she pitches her voice any higher," said Osteroric, "she will bring the shrieking beasties back. She is a very formidable female, says Norimgic."

"He is right," said Sanval, watching Ivy cock her head forward so she was standing almost nose to nose with Archlis, her gaze locked with the magelord's. It was a deliberate tactic, he realized—one that she had used to equal effect in the camp on the officers in the Thultyrl's Forty and that camel she had punched out of her tent. If she could get Archlis to back down even one step, she would be on top of him in a flash. But Archlis was more resolute than a Procampur officer or a dromedary. He did not budge.

"You must lure the destrachans away from their lair," Archlis said. "I am running out of bugbears, and they do not make good decoys. They are too slow and too easily caught."

"Poor Hackermic." Osteroric sighed.

"Why not just use that fancy spell of yours? Why not just sneak around them?" Ivy demanded.

"That fancy spell, as you call it, ends as soon as we pass through the barrier," Archlis said, waving a hand at the sparkles of light still shimmering in the air.

Gunderal gave a little sniff and whispered to her sister, "And he doesn't have any more charms like the one he just crushed. Have you noticed all his spells use other objects—no magic coming just from him."

Archlis frowned but ignored the sisters. "We are still far from where I need to be, yet the sounds that we just made drew the destrachans immediately."

"They are what forced you back the first time, not Fottergrim's hobgoblins," guessed Ivy.

"I retreated a strategic distance to consider my options," Archlis said in dignified tones, looking down his long nose at Ivy.

"Ran like a hare," said Mumchance to Kid, not trying to be quiet. Archlis ignored him too.

"Why us?" Ivy pressed the point.

"I have no more silence charms," Archlis admitted in a disgruntled tone.

Gunderal poked her sister in the ribs. Zuzzara patted her on the head in acknowledgment of her cleverness. Swatting her sister's hands away, Gunderal pushed her topknot straight and fluffed up her side curls.

"So I need a distraction—something to lure the destrachans away from this tunnel," said Archlis to Ivy. "You seem more intelligent than those hopeless hobgoblins or my bugbears. Destrachans like to play with their food. If you make the chase interesting, you can lead them a long way from here."

"Which helps you and doesn't help us. I fight for who pays me. Not for who is sure to get me killed. Same for all of us. Offer me something better than what he has." To Sanval's surprise, she pointed straight at him. He knew red-roof mercenaries sold their loyalty to the highest bidder, but still he had not expected so blatant an offering of betrayal from Ivy.

"If you can get the destrachans away from their lair and destroy them while I retrieve my treasure, then I will lead you out of the ruins," promised Archlis. "Which is more than that gentleman can do." Not seeing too much enthusiasm on their faces, the magelord added, "And a reasonable fee. Gems or gold. Whichever you wish. But only if I retrieve my treasure."

Ivy pointed out that the odds of their success were not great, but she did not question whether Archlis would keep his promise. Sanval wondered at her ability to trust the skinny magelord's word. Perhaps Ivy had lied to him earlier, and she or one of the other Siegebreakers did have some magic concealed about her person that would protect her friends and defeat the creatures. After all, everyone knew that red-roof adventurers had all sorts of fantastic abilities, and maybe she was just intending to run away from the magelord as soon as she and the other Siegebreakers were out of sight.

But Archlis could not succeed in his mission and return to the walls of Tsurlagol. Sanval knew that it was his duty to stop Archlis, even if it took him away from Ivy. Besides being the right thing to do, it might also be the best way to help Ivy and her friends. If he fought Archlis, the rest could escape. He just had to pick the right time for his ambush.

"So," said Sanval to Osteroric. "You might have something worth trading for."

Osteroric bent closer to Sanval to listen to his whispered instructions. The bugbear pushed back his battered helmet and scratched his fuzzy head. He puckered his lips and blew out a long and stinking breath. "Hsssh," whistled Osteroric. "This could be big trouble for me. Bigger trouble for you. I wonder what Hackermic would have done. . . . He was even smarter than Norimgic."

"Does that matter?" asked Sanval, loosening the straps on his breastplate.

"Not really," agreed Osteroric. "Hackermic is dead. We are not."

"Then we trade," said Sanval.

"Then we trade," said Osteroric. "But I think that you will end up the same as poor Hackermic."

CHAPTER SIXTEEN

"You have no choice," stated Archlis. "You're running out of time. Or didn't you notice the water tricking along the floor there?"

With some dismay, Ivy saw that Archlis was right. The telltale silver streaks of water caught the light of the torches. Right now, only little puddles formed along the crack between the wall and floor; but she knew there was more coming.

"Eventually the river will flood out these ruins," Archlis complained. "There must have been some storm in the mountains to bring this much water into the ruins so late in the summer."

Ivy decided not to enlighten Archlis about the true cause of the river's sudden rising. It probably would not improve their relationship. "So," she said. "Any last suggestions on how to draw those beasts out?"

"Walk forward until you are on the other side of my spell wall," Archlis said to Ivy. "Then start running. The destrachans will follow you. If you survive, follow us down that tunnel." He pointed to an arched and shadowed entrance. "And if you try to follow us now, I'll burn you where you stand."

"We will do what you asked. But you must keep your part of the bargain as well."

Archlis did not respond to her last comment. Instead, he suddenly grabbed Kid by one skinny arm. "The goat-boy stays with me," said Archlis. "I need his skills."

"That was not part of our bargain," Ivy said. She lunged for Kid, but Archlis pulled him out of her way. Zuzzara swung her shovel at the magelord, intent on breaking his hold on Kid. Rather than hitting Archlis, the shovel twisted in her hands and bounced back, striking her on the top of her head. Zuzzara sat down abruptly. Gunderal immediately raced to her sister's side, standing above the dazed half-orc, and raised her hands, her own injury forgotten.

"Do not even try, little genasi," said Archlis. "My charms make me immune to any and all magical attacks."

"At least my magic comes from me," snapped Gunderal. "It isn't stolen charms and looted trinkets."

Eyes narrowing at the insult, Archlis began to raise the Ankh. Ivy stepped between them. Chin out, gaze steady, she challenged Archlis, "Hurt her, and we turn back. You can play games with the destrachans on your own."

"An idle threat," returned the magelord, but he lowered the Ankh. "You have no hope of finding the way out. The tunnels will be flooded within the day. Help me, and you help yourselves. Once you have distracted the beasts, return to this chamber. I will come for you here."

"Go, my dears, go," said Kid, wiggling in the magelord's cruel grip. "I will see you again."

"Course you will, stupid," said Zuzzara, climbing shakily to her feet. A trickle of blood ran down her forehead, and she brushed it impatiently aside.

"If you hurt him, I will find a way around your charms. I promise," said Ivy. She could not bear to look at Kid. Stay together—that was the rule of her group, the most basic bond that bound them together, no matter how many tricks that fate played on them. For the last ten years, she had begun every day at the farm hearing the muffled sounds of her friends' voices echoing in her ears—all the little arguments and senseless jokes that old friends told each other. More recently, the click of Kid's hooves had been part of that. She did not know how she could return home and fall asleep each night without the comfort of knowing that they were all safely under one roof.

Whatever Archlis was going to reply was interrupted by a howl from Norimgic. The big bugbear was yelling something in Orcish at Archlis.

"What do you mean he's gone?" snapped the magelord. He glared at the two bugbears. Osteroric was now wearing Sanval's breastplate and sporting a "who me?" expression. "I was just trying it on," said Osteroric about his new armor. "And when I looked up, he wasn't here anymore!"

"So he did not dare stay and face the beasts." Archlis snorted. "You were right. He is not like the other nobles of Procampur. But he is also doomed. There is no way out of these ruins without my help. And to secure that, you must lead those creatures away from here."

Ivy hoped Sanval had a better plan than she did. Right now, the only thing that she could think about was running faster than those destrachans. And losing the big guy in armor was not going to make her life easier, especially if what she suspected were true. But no need to make Archlis nervous. Show a brave face—that was her mother's constant advice. Keep quiet and think—that was her father. Time to remember both those lessons.

"Let's go, then," said Ivy to the others. She plunged through the invisible wall that Archlis had raised between them and the destrachans' sensitive ears. She felt a magical prickle on her skin and then just nothing. The wall was gone. She looked back but could see nothing but the burning of the bugbears' torches behind her. Archlis stood watching, one hand gripping the Ankh tightly, the other hard on Kid's shoulder.

Standing directly under the hole created in the ceiling by the destrachans, Ivy could hear nothing. She could see nothing. But she knew that the monsters were out there, just waiting for them.

"Come on," she said, much quieter than she normally would. "Let's run!"

CHAPTER SEVENTEEN

Ivy doubted that Sanval had fled blindly into the dark. Silly, stupid man—she was sure that he was intent on some plan involving some great heroic deed that would get himself killed but save everyone else in the world. He was that sort. She'd known too many like him. Besides, hadn't he said something earlier about attacking Archlis on his own?

But, she was fairly certain that it just was not in his well-polished, honorable soul to do anything so ignoble as leave them defenseless. He must have thought that she could save the others by herself. He had obviously picked what he decided was the more dangerous target—Archlis—and decided to go it alone. Yes, that would be a Procampur type of reasoning. Ivy's own self-confidence bubbled up when she realized that Sanval's Procampur sense of protocol would not have let him abandon the Siegebreakers if he had thought they needed his protection. In a strange sort of way, he had just paid her a compliment. Now, if only she could pay it back—preferably by finding him later and shaking his head until she rattled some sense into his skull.

Mumchance trotted up beside her, breaking into her thoughts about the future by worrying her about their present situation. The dwarf pointed at the sidewalls of the tunnel. "Narrow. Maybe not wide enough for those monsters? Slow down a moment."

Was it possible that the sightless destrachans would enter a tunnel too narrow for their enormous bodies and wedge themselves into immobility? If Archlis had lied about going in the other direction and actually planned to leave through this tunnel once she had killed the beasts, it was satisfying to think of him stuck behind those monsters, staring at their huge flailing tails, unable to get past them. Then Ivy remembered the way the destrachans had crumbled the ceiling of the chamber with their weird vibration cry. Nice idea, but it was not going to happen that way, she knew.

"I don't think that they can get stuck," she said out loud and then wondered if something besides her own group had heard her. How loud was too loud? "Is there any way that we can hear them before they hear us?"

Mumchance shrugged. "Maybe. They are big and pretty noisy." He placed his hand against the ground.

"Mumchance," said Ivy to her friend, "do you remember why we got into this business?"

Zuzzara answered, because the dwarf had dropped to his knees and then stretched flat on the ground, still trying to hear the approach of the destrachans. He pulled Wiggles out of his pocket and set the little dog down beside him. Wiggles looked ready to take a quick nap, her pointed chin resting on the dwarf's rump. It had been a long day for a small dog—a long day for all of them.

"We got into siegebreaking because we needed money," said Zuzzara, rubbing the bump left on her head by the shovel. "Especially after we flooded out our last rainmaking customer."

"Besides that," Ivy prompted.

"Because we are good at what we do," said Gunderal, looking like a defiant flower as she stepped up to her sister and fingered the bump on Zuzzara's head with gentle hands. "Ivy, I can hold the river back. I could twist my water-calling spell to keep these tunnels from flooding for a while longer. I'm sure of it."

"No," said Ivy very slowly, because she had just had a new idea, but she was not sure how everyone would react. "We don't want to hold the river back. We want to let the river in. Archlis was right. These tunnels are low and going lower. If we let the water in . . ."

"We all drown," pronounced Mumchance standing up and dusting off his knees. Wiggles was staying close by his heels, very quiet, as if the little dog sensed danger was close.

"Unless . . ."

"We get out first."

"But what about the destrachans?" asked Gunderal.

"We hope that they can't swim."

"But what about Kid?" Gunderal asked. "Oh, Ivy, you are not going to leave Kid behind?"

"Of course not. Everyone gets out. Everyone except Archlis. Don't much care about him, do we?"

Zuzzara giggled—one of those deep orc giggles that made people nervous. "Are we going after Archlis, Ivy?"

"That magelord is just another tower waiting to be toppled," said Ivy. "Let's bury him down here and take down the walls of Tsurlagol!" She delivered this rousing speech in a low-pitched tone to avoid attracting destrachans, but it got the same reaction as all of her rousing speeches. Everyone looked like they wanted to disagree—Mumchance even opened his mouth and then closed it—and then everyone gave a reluctant nod. If Ivy was crazy enough to think it might work, then they might be crazy enough to go along with it.

"For once, that idea actually sounds like a plan," said Mumchance finally. "One that isn't completely different from what we discussed before."

"Don't look so surprised."

"No, think about it. The tunnels may be a bit deeper than we intended to dig," said the dwarf, "but we can use them just the same. They all run toward the current city as far as I can tell, or the current city was built up on a corner of these ruins, which is more likely. We have been twisting around a lot, following that magelord, but I think we are pretty close to that southwest corner. If Gunderal could force the water toward the city, we could just wash the walls away. Or"—as Mumchance became more enthusiastic about the idea, he also became a stickler for precise details describing underhanded ways of engineering destruction—"we can at least take down that weak corner that we found earlier. The spot where you told the Thultyrl that the wall would fall down."

"That would be good," agreed Ivy as they continued to explore the current tunnel. "Make us look like we know what we are doing. That is so rare."

"I'm serious, Ivy." The dwarf stuck out his lower lip and blew a heavy breath. Ivy recognized his don't-sidetrack-me-when-I-am-thinking sigh. "Look at the cracks running through the walls," said Mumchance, pointing left and right. "I bet those shrieking beasts did that. If they hunt here often, the ground will already be weak above us as well as below. Tsurlagol could end up with a pretty lake on its west side."

"That leaves the problem of how we avoid being crushed," said Ivy. "Or drowned. Or eaten."

"You will figure something out," said Mumchance. "You always do."

"I do, don't I?" said Ivy with just a little more bounce in her step as she walked down the tunnel. "Well then, let's speed up the water coming into these tunnels, and let us hope those creatures can't float or swim."

Gunderal spread out her pale fingers and made a gesture resembling raindrops falling down. Drops of water trickled off her fingers and spattered into the dust at her feet. "I'm feeling much better," she said.

"Knew you could do it," said Zuzzara, "but don't push your magic too hard. What if you can't do what you want when you want to?"

"Sister, I do not even understand that last sentence," giggled Gunderal. A small smile brightened her delicate features. A few long ringlets had come loose from her topknot, and she looped one long strand around her finger very slowly. "Stopping a river is rather boring, but calling one! So much more fun."

"Do you think you can?" her sister asked.

Gunderal's violet eyes gleamed in a way that would be called a glare in a less beautiful woman. "You never think I can do anything."

"I am only asking."

"Zuzzara, I may not be as strong as you or as clever as Mimeri, but I can cast spells!"

"I only said . . ."

Gunderal stood in the shadow of her half-orc sister and stared up at her. "Well, don't, Zuzzara. Don't say another word! I know a thing or two about water magic."

"Unless you know how to kill destrachans, keep your voices down," Ivy finally intervened. "We need to think of some place that we could ambush the creatures."

"Those creatures hunt by sound more than anything else," Zuzzara said, peering through one archway into the chamber beyond.

"According to Archlis, they are blind," Ivy agreed. "And you saw the size of those ears."

"So what if we make a lot of noise and draw them into a narrow place like this," Zuzzara suggested. "Someplace where we could get above them. That might help."

They followed Zuzzara into a circular chamber with stairs running in spirals along the walls to higher openings. In the center of the room stood a small fountain with a trickle of water coming out of its cracked marble spouts. The water was very cold to the touch.

"There's our river," said Gunderal with satisfaction. "Or a branch of it at least."

"Forcing its way in through the old pipes first," said Mumchance. "The dwarves built well when they built this city, every time that they built this city."

"Strange place," said Ivy, looking around the tower of ancient Tsurlagol.

Gunderal ran up a few stairs and rested her hand against the wall. "It is some kind of watchtower, sunk by that weird earth magic that I've been feeling throughout the ruins. Remember the mosaic back in the bathhouse?"

"Odd or not, Zuzzara is right," said Mumchance. "It's a good place for a trap."

Zuzzara shrugged. "I may be ugly, but I'm not dumb."

The old joke made them all laugh a little, and then glance uneasily over their shoulders as the laughs bounced around the room.

Mumchance climbed up the stairs after Gunderal, peering here and there through the openings, swinging his lantern before him. Wiggles stopped before one doorway and let out one small sharp bark. Mumchance took a look and then called back down the stairs. "There's another tunnel. Looks like it runs straight back the way that we came, just higher up."

"Higher is good," said Ivy, watching the ancient fountain that bubbled in the center of the room.

"Now we need to attract the destrachans lower down," said Mumchance. "So the water covers them before it covers us."

"That was what I was thinking," Ivy said.

"Do you want me to use my eye?" The dwarf fingered his fake eye as if he were going to pop it out of his head. "An explosion should bring the beasts quick enough."

"Save that eye. We may need it later. I have a better idea," said Ivy with a wicked grin. "Everyone needs to get to higher ground first. Gunderal, go up to that platform where Mumchance is. Get as close to the exit as you can; you may need to run quickly."

Gunderal climbed to the ledge where Mumchance stood.

"Maybe you should call from inside that tunnel," Ivy suggested. The sound carried perfectly up to Gunderal on the ledge, but she shook her head.

"I need to see the water, Ivy, just to keep my spell anchored in this room."

"All right. Zuzzara, do you have that rope we found earlier?"

"Wound around my waist," the half-orc affirmed. "Do you need it?"

"Tie one end to my belt and get ready to haul me up when I yell. Now I am going to wait for the beasts to get here." Ivy cut off their anticipated arguments. "No, I stay on the floor here. I'm the bait. I'm going to keep them down here, and Gunderal is going to get that river to rise faster, so it's over their heads before they know what is happening."

"But what about you?" worried Zuzzara.

"I've got a few tricks," said Ivy, straightening the red leather belt around her waist so she could easily reach the silver buckle. "And if my tricks don't work, you are going to haul me up like a fish on line. As fast as you can."

"All right," said Zuzzara.

"And how are you going to get the beasts to come to you?" queried Mumchance.

"I am going to sing!"

"Oh, Ivy." Gunderal shuddered, and even Mumchance winced once they realized what she was intending to do. Both of them were fairly musical. Zuzzara, who had inherited her orc mother's taste for music (which consisted of exactly no opinion at all), just bobbed her head in a quick nod of agreement and began unwinding the rope around her waist. She started to thread one end through Ivy's belt.

"Don't tie the rope to that skinny red belt," Ivy instructed her. "Around my weapons belt. I don't want to pull the other one off." Zuzzara tied the knot where Ivy had pointed.

"Ivy, are you sure about this?" Gunderal asked, leaning perilously out so she could see her friend.

"Absolutely. Kid and I found a little extra magic back in the tunnels that is going to help." Ivy pulled off her gloves and secured them in her weapons belt. She placed her bare fingers on the winged serpent clasp of the magic belt that she had retrieved from the floating corpse. If it worked as it had before, she should be able to float right out of the creatures' reach.

"Wait one moment," Gunderal said, leaving the ledge and coming down the stairs with a quick patter of little feet across the stone steps. "Does anyone have a candle?"

"I don't need a candle," Ivy said, who had a lit torch in one hand and her sword in the other.

"But I do. Zuzzara, light this for me." Gunderal pulled one of the candles that they had looted from the bugbear out of her robes and handed it to her sister.

After Zuzzara had lit the candle, Gunderal held her hand beneath its drips until her fingertip was covered with wax. She reached out, touched Ivy, and said, "That should do."

"What's that for?" Ivy asked.

"We know the destrachans hunt by sound, but how can we know if they have a sense of smell? Perhaps not, but still, I think you will be safer without any smell."

"I have heard of wizards removing odor from smelly beasts and dead bodies, but come on, Gunderal, I don't stink that bad!" Ivy objected.

"Most beasts can pick up any scent, no matter how small, and now you have none at all."

Ivy grinned. "Great! I'll never have to bathe again!"

Gunderal said sadly, "It's a weak spell, Ivy. It will only last a short while."

Ivy shrugged. "I plan to finish those monsters quickly."

"Well, if you're actually going to sing, that should drive them mad," said Mumchance. The dwarf scooped up Wiggles and put the little dog in his pocket. He tugged on Gunderal's hand. "Come on, girl, you need to call that river."

As they climbed higher on the stairs, Zuzzara followed them, paying out rope as she went.

"Oh, how I am going to sing!" Ivy said to her friends' retreating backs. "I am going to sing every red-roof ballad that I've learned this summer. If those beasts are as sensitive to sound as Archlis said, they should come rushing to devour me before I get to the first chorus!"

Above Ivy, Gunderal began chanting, her call to the river echoing around the room The smell of water filled the air. Ivy waited until the river began to bubble faster through the broken spouts of the fountain, filling the basin and frothing over her boots. Then she stood with elbows out and fists on her waist, tilted her head back, took a deep breath, and started to sing.

"Procampur men are deadly dull, but Procampur girls are fancy loves." Ivy had never quite figured out all the more obscure slang in the chorus—a rousing ditty about ladies who switched their roof tiles to suit their loves—but Sanval had blanched the first time that he had heard her sing it and muttered something about "duels are being fought for lesser insults." Now Ivy pitched her voice loud and strong, to send the echoes clashing through the carved rock of the chamber. The sound reverberated even better than singing at the top of her lungs in the bathhouse back at the farm (a favorite trick for keeping the place all to herself and avoiding certain people fussing about whether or not she was rinsing her hair out properly).

Gunderal continued to call upon the river to rise. She stood on the ledge above Ivy, her hands held out. Thin glittering strands of light bounced around the chamber, shimmering across her blue-black cloud of hair. Her violet eyes shone in her delicate face. As her gentle genasi mother had taught her so long ago, Gunderal sang the song of water. The lightning scent of the storm became interwoven with the cool, sweet smell of rain falling from the sky to the dusty earth below, the darker tang of an old river carrying that same rain through the heart of a mountain, and—not too far away—the pull of the sharp salt scent of the sea. She sang about how the sea's rich perfume could lure the river out of its old meandering ways and send it hunting, like an elderly blundering hound trailing a fox's scent, into the tunnels and ruins of ancient Tsurlagol.

The water poured faster out of the fountain, washing against the tops of Ivy's boots, and the bard's tone-deaf daughter continued to shout-sing her way through the many verses of the Procampur song, describing the lovers preferred under each roof. Ivy had sung all the way to the third verse when the floor of the chamber began to shake.

Parts of the wall that she was facing began to dissolve into dust as a raggedy-eared, nasty-looking, blind head came pushing through the newly formed hole, a head that was nothing more than an enormous open circle of mouth. There were no teeth, no eyes, and mere breathing slits where the nose should be, with no sort of bone structure to its face that could be bashed with a well-aimed blow. The only large feature on the head, besides the wide-open maw, were the ears. They were shaped a bit like winter-dead tree leaves, folding into three sections with deep indentations and sharp points all around their edges. Each ear twitched wildly in opposite directions.

A second head shoved into the hole above the first one, and a third popped up through a newly formed crack in the floor.

The first beast clawed at its own ears as Ivy continued to bellow. The echoes in the chamber made it sound like more than a dozen singers were caterwauling in different corners of the room, all completely out of tune, and a beat or two behind each other. The creatures butted and banged against each other as they squeezed into the room.

The destrachans had found her, and they seemed killing mad about her singing, as Mumchance had predicted.

CHAPTER EIGHTEEN

As the destrachans came shrieking into the room, the river continued to rise. Each creature was anyone's worst nightmare, almost as large as the hen house at the farm. Worse still were the weird reverberating screams being given by the monsters—howls so ugly that each cry echoed in Ivy's head, making her back teeth ache.

The lead monster moved in a crouch, its back legs bent, and its front legs reaching out. Muscles rippled from its jaw to its humped back and down past the powerful haunches to its heavy pointed tail. Its thick hide looked waterproof, and Ivy wondered again if destrachans could swim. Or float. That would mess up her plans rather badly. The creature's talons curved out from its feet like blades. That it was blind in no way lessened its powers, and there was no way at all of knowing how sensitive it was to movement. Certainly it was aware of her singing, turning its blind head from side to side as it tried to pinpoint where she was standing. Luckily, its fellows kept bumping into it, and it would break off from its hunting to swipe a talon or tail at the other two.

Obviously, Ivy thought, there was some disagreement going on about who would get to eat her first.

Above her, Gunderal's chanting was adding to the confusion. Her light, high song of the river overlaid Ivy's deeper rough voice booming out her ribald love song. With all that sound swirling through the room and the destrachans' own cries adding to the confusion, the monsters tucked down their flapped ears, flat against their heads, rather like a man might squeeze his eyelids closed against a too-bright light. The beasts fanned out, wildly swinging their talons in the space around Ivy and screeching in a way that made her eardrums ache. Bits of stone shattered as the destrachans' oscillating cries nearly deafened Ivy and the watchers on the stairs above.

At least Archlis had been truthful about the creatures' senses. It seemed that they were primarily limited to using their hearing to locate her. If the breathing slits gave them an ability to smell, Gunderal's spell should hide her from that betrayal of her location. Now, if only the river would rise faster. The water was barely up to the small of the creatures' backs.

"Come on," Ivy sang, weaving her worries into the lyrics of her song, "if you find me too quickly, that won't be any fun for you. And ladies of Procampur know blue-roof sailor boys want to roll, roll, roll with the tide!"

The tower was small with three destrachans crashing around its base. Ivy hopped up a few stairs to avoid the heavy bodies blundering in the center. When the destrachans collided with each other, little shrieks would come out of their mouths. The biggest one shrieked loudest, and the other two would back off for a bit, and then start hunting for her again. One of the beasts stumbled into the fountain and got its big foot stuck in the basin. It pointed its mouth toward the marble and let out a moaning cry. As the stone turned to dust, a wider hole formed where the fountain had been, and the river rushed faster into the room.

"Ready?" Zuzzara called down to her.

"Let the water rise a bit," Ivy called, staggering as a wave caused by a destrachan's thrashing tail rushed past her. Gasping, Ivy spit water out of her mouth, blinked, and tried to push her wet hair out of her eyes. It stuck to the dust and mud that already caked her face. "I don't want them to turn back and escape."

One of the ears twitched on the nearest destrachans, and it swung its head up, pointing toward Zuzzara. Ivy immediately broke into a new song, an old favorite of her mother. "In this world is naught but trouble and sorrow, but why walk in shadow, why run in the night, when you can fly, fly, fly away!"

"Ivy, what do you want me to do?" Zuzzara called.

"Time to fly, time to fly away, time to soar," she bellowed in reply, keeping to the rhythm of the song. Gods knew her singing was awful, but it did seem to keep the destrachans from hunting the others. Ivy grasped the winged serpent belt buckle beneath her fingers. "Pull the wings open three times and then shut," Kid had said, and she did. Nothing happened. "There's nothing but trouble, trouble and sorrow," she sang as she grappled with the belt, "when magic belts won't save you."

"Hey," yelled Zuzzara from above. "That doesn't sound right. I think you have the words wrong."

The beasts circled Ivy, bouncing their cries off the crumbling walls of the chamber, tilting their ears to catch the echoes. Now they were circling together around the base of the tower, each step bringing them closer to where Ivy stood on the first step of the stone staircase. A taloned foot shot out, flashing in front of Ivy's eyes. Its claw was so close to her that she felt the movement of air against her face. She clamped her mouth shut, hoping the sudden silence would confuse the creatures.

The three mud-colored destrachans prowled, then stopped and raised their wide mouths toward the ceiling of the chamber. Even their ears became motionless. Were they sens-ing her movements? Could they feel her breathe?

Suddenly all the ears twitched at the same time, and the creatures tilted their heads toward Gunderal, high above them—a frail figure, but calm and concentrated. The creatures let out a hideous howl. Gunderal gracefully placed her fingers in her ears and continued to chant.

"Run with me, sad screamers, walk in shadow, run in sorrow," Ivy sang, and her voice echoed from all the walls. Ivy opened her mouth to sing another verse, and her mind went blank. The words of all the hundreds of songs that she knew tangled in her head and bottled up in her throat. But it was enough. The destrachans had turned toward her again and away from her friends. And the river was over the first step of the stair and rising rapidly. She backed up the spiral a little higher.

"Pull the wings open three times and then shut," she howled at the beasts sloshing toward her, their talons extended like cats looking to play with mice. Her fingers plucked again at the silver buckle. "One, two, three, shut! Surprise! The magic is busted!"

Even where she stood on the staircase, the water was up to her waist and sloshing now around the shoulders of the destra-chans. She thought about yelling at Zuzzara to haul her up, but being dragged on a rope against the rough stones would hurt. Instead she began to move more quickly up the stairs, her boots echoing on the stone steps.

One of the destrachans stretched out its neck and directed a wave of sound from its tubular mouth. Behind her, the lower stairs began to crumble. Ivy looked back and saw the smooth slabs of stone treads crash into the water, leaving jagged mounds. Waves shot up beside her, sloshing on the outer side of the stairs and breaking over her legs.

"Run!" Mumchance shouted from above.

"Blast," Ivy cried, leaping up the stairs, just ahead of the cracking rock. It was a long staircase, circling the full chamber. Behind her, the biggest beast howled and wallowed in the water, tumbled over, and righted itself. Its neck stretched out. Again it let out a burst of sound.

"Keep running! Don't look!" Zuzzara screamed.

She didn't have to look. She felt the stair tread fall away under her back foot. She dragged on her gauntlets as she ran, throwing her weight forward. She sprawled on the upper steps, both feet on a solid stair. Her gloved hands scraped over the stone stair treads, caught, and held. She had collected a whole new set of bruises across her ribs and stomach, but she was safe.

"Shall I pull now?" Zuzzara shouted.

Ivy knew how that would go, her body *bump-bump-bumping* up stone stairs. Which would be worse: face down with her nose scraped raw against the stone, or on her back with every bang on her armor adding more bruises to her much abused body? "No! Not yet!"

Scrambling to her feet, Ivy continued up the stairs, her feet pounding. The sound and vibrations attracted the beasts, but she knew of no way to run up stone stairs silently. Ivy glanced down at the red belt encircling her waist. Magic! It was never trustworthy—not for her. Balancing herself with one hand against the wall, she caught the wings of the little silver serpent buckle in her left hand.

"Pull the wings open three times and then shut," she sputtered, her gloved fingers clumsy against the buckle's delicate mechanism. "One, two, three, shut! Oh!"

She blinked in surprise as her body drifted upward.

"How about that?" she yelled as she floated off the stairs. The section of staircase just below her rising feet now broke apart in another blast of powdered stone, leaving wide gaps. She looked up and saw the chamber's ceiling. There were interesting reflections from the water on it. It was much too close and approaching fast.

"Now, Zuzzara, now! Pull!"

A tug on her other belt kept her from zooming up to the ceiling. Twisting around and peering through her dangling feet, Ivy could see Zuzzara braced in the upper doorway, hauling her down like a kite being retrieved on a windy day. Ivy continued to sing loudly, choosing a song about lovers and yellow-roof maids, because no one had yelled at her to shut up yet. Besides, it did seem to distract the destrachans enough to keep them away from Gunderal.

Far below, the beasts were still circling in the center of the room, trying to find her and ignoring the water that was now halfway up their long necks.

"I love a good audience," said Ivy as her boots scraped against the stone stairway. She twisted the winged serpent so the spell shut off and nearly dropped straight back into the chamber as gravity gripped her. Zuzzara's strong hand on her belt hauled her back to safety on the ledge. Ivy grinned at the half-orc.

With the water now lapping around their ears, the destrachans fell silent. The work of their terrible cries, however, continued. The stairs crumbled away, treads disappearing in showers of powdered stone, and cracks appeared in the walls around them, sending showers of little pebbles splashing in the water below. The destrachans set up a new keening, one that seemed to vibrate into the very bones of the Siegebreakers.

With hand signals, Ivy tried to indicate that they should fall back into the tunnel. Mumchance shook his head and pointed at Gunderal, waving his hands. Ivy could not tell what he was trying to communicate. Seeing her puzzled face, Zuzzara leaned close to her ear and screamed over the beasts wailing below, "She has to finish the spell or the water stops."

Dismayed, Ivy peered over the staircase to check on the location of the destrachans.

The roar of one beast below was changing again, into some type of weird high-pitched cry that seemed to hum through the metal in her armor. Blind as it was, the biggest and most persistent destrachan seemed to have a better fix on them than the others. Now that she had seen it shatter stone with its cry, she preferred not to learn first hand what it could do to people. It started forward, wading through the water and clambering up on the back of one of the smaller beasts, pushing it completely under the water. The big creature clawed its way onto the broken staircase, its heavy talons actually sinking into the stone as it heaved itself out of the water.

"You are supposed to stay down there and drown," Ivy screamed at it. Her cries bounced around the chamber walls, and the destrachan paused. Then it lurched across a broken gap in the stairs and pulled itself higher.

Cursing her luck and wondering why the thing could not stay confused a little longer, Ivy drew her sword and ran down the uneven stairs, hopping over gaps and hoping the remaining stones would hold for a few minutes longer. She continued down until she was only a step or two above the climber. The monster's new howl was causing the blade to hum in her hand. She guessed the metal could only take so much stress before it shattered. Positioning herself on the center of a crumbling stair above the beast, she angled the blade down, gripping the hilt with two hands. Then, with a little promise to find a temple soon and make some type of offering, Ivy flung the sword into the round, upturned mouth of the beast trying to claw its way up the crumbling stairs.

She knew, even as she flung it with both hands, that it would take unbelievable luck to do any damage to a creature who ignored the stones raining down on its hide as the room disintegrated around it. But light glinted on the little harper's token sewn on her glove, and most incredibly, her luck held. The sword point slid straight into the monster's mouth, and the surprised beast swallowed it with a choking sound. "Blast, I truly liked that sword," Ivy complained.

A talon whipped across the toe of her boot, slashing it open. Ivy glanced down, wondering if she could charge a new pair of boots to the Thultyrl. Then the pain hit her. Blood welled through the cut in the boot.

"Choke, you misery, choke and die," she shrieked at the beast.

The sword-swallowing destrachan clawed at its own mouth, obviously trying to dislodge the sharp object in its throat. The attempt caused the creature to wobble on the stairs and then lose its balance. It scrabbled and tried to cling to the staircase, its big claws cutting through the stones, then breaking loose. Again and again the destrachan scratched, caught a claw, heaved itself upright.

"Go on, fall already," Ivy shouted, and her voice bounced around the walls of the circular chamber.

The beast swung his head around, pointing his open mouth toward the ceiling. Some pale pink spit dribbled down from the edge of its toothless maw. It screeched—not its aimed sonic sound but rather a thin cry of pain—and it fell sideways, landing solidly on the heads of the other two below. The impact of the falling destrachan forced all the beasts under the water.

A huge wave rose up, shooting out and showering water over the stairs and the Siegebreakers.

"Let's get out of here!" screamed Ivy. When she turned to race back up the stairs, she nearly knocked Mumchance off.

He had come down to stand behind her, holding his fake eye ready to throw in one hand. When the destrachan plunged down into the water, the dwarf gave a grunt of satisfaction and popped his gem bomb back into his empty eye socket.

The destrachans' heads reappeared above the water, but the monsters' weird cries sounded sluggish and hoarse. "Persistent critters!" screamed Ivy as she put her hands in front of her to shove Mumchance faster up the stairs toward a worried-looking Zuzzara. The half-orc was still standing guard over her chanting sister, but she leaned down and offered one arm to grab the dwarf and swing him up onto the landing.

The stress of their flight proved too much for the remaining steps; the stone turned into glittering dust as the staircase below the ledge literally dissolved. "Good crystal content in these stones," yelled Mumchance as Ivy leaped the last few steps to land winded beside Zuzzara.

"Why won't the lousy shriekers drown?" Ignoring her throbbing foot, Ivy leaned over the landing to check on the location of the destrachans.

The dust and rock that had once been the winding staircase avalanched down into the chamber, becoming mud as it mixed with the water. The destrachans were trapped in the thick goop. It began to fill their ears and mouths. The waters rose over the creatures' heads. They stretched their unseeing faces upward, their ears twitching, their mouths open. Their cries continued to loosen the stones above them, but less now—a mere rain of chips that drifted down into the churning mess of water and stone dust. The soupy gray waters rose above the open mouths, filling them, then covering them. The cries of the monsters ended in gurgles.

The room was finally silent except for the last three notes of Gunderal's sweet chant, echoing above the lapping sound of the river filling the chamber below them. The wizard removed her fingers from her ears and with a pretty smile peered down into the water now steadily rising up the walls.

"I told you I could call the river," Gunderal pronounced with immense satisfaction.

"Yes, but I told you this chamber would be a good place to trap the beasts," Zuzzara said.

"But you could not have done it, sister mine, without my help," said Gunderal, her smile quavering into a lovely but distinct lower lip pout that always signaled an argument. "I'm the only one who can raise rivers."

"Of course your magic was important, but so was using it in the right place," replied Zuzzara, ready to stand still and debate with her younger sister about strategy.

"Ladies, ladies," said Mumchance, peering into what was left of the chamber below and watching the water rise faster up the wall. "We might want to discuss this later." The dwarf called for his dog, and Wiggles's bark echoed out of the tunnel opening off the landing. "Sounds like Wiggles has found a way out."

"You sisters can argue about who is the cleverest later," said Ivy, through the throbbing of her torn toes and the aching of the new bruises on her knees and shins where she had fallen heavily against the landing. "But we'd better leave before the water is over our heads."

They raced along the tunnel in the direction that Archlis had gone. They hit another branch of the tunnel where another stair led down into the tunnels below. Wiggles stood at the top of those stairs, giving out a worried whine. Grabbing the lantern from Mumchance, Ivy peered down those stairs. At the very edge of the light, she saw the glimmer of water. The floor of the tunnel below was already damp, which meant the river was beginning to fill the ruins. "I am truly sick of being wet," she said.

"That's tunnels for you," the dwarf said. "Great conduits for water!" Ivy didn't thank him for the information.

A pair of snakes, thankfully quite small, whipped up the stairs and raced away in front of them.

"Oh, dear," said Mumchance, "I had not thought of that."

"What?"

"Anything else living in these tunnels is going to need to flee too. Or be drowned."

Ivy glanced around. Nothing else appeared to shadow them. "Maybe the destrachans ate everything else living in this part of the ruins?"

"Hope so," said the dwarf, but he whistled to Wiggles, commanding the small dog to heel close to him.

Zuzzara let out a cry. Her sharp eyes had spotted a hoof-shaped footprint in the mud of the floor, overlaid by the mark of a Procampur officer's boot.

"Sanval is ahead of us. Looks like he is following the magelord and Kid."

Ivy spotted a light shining ahead of them, and sped up to the faintly illuminated doorway that opened off the ledge. She found another staircase leading down, but this one seemed dry at the bottom. At least no reflective gleam of water showed in the lantern light. On the top step, the stub of a tallow candle flickered. Ivy remembered looting the dead bugbear and pressing some of the candles into Sanval's reluctant hands. She had told him then that he would need the light. Had he used the candle to leave them a marker? Or was it one of Archlis's tricks?

CHAPTER NINETEEN

The stone stairs spiraled away into the darkness. As Ivy stepped forward, her damp boots squelched even louder than before. She looked down. Water was starting to drip down the sides of the walls and cover the floor of the tunnel where they were standing. Some water began dripping down the stairs. It was just a thin film of water, but she knew that the river was pushing behind it, seeking them out just as the destrachans had hunted them through the black tunnels.

"How can the river be above us now and not below?" worried Ivy.

"It is filling up the old canals first," answered Gunderal. "And following the old wells and sewers. But it will spill over into the other tunnels soon enough."

"Don't suppose you could slow it down a little now?"

Gunderal sighed. "I wish I could, Ivy, but I have only one spell left for today. And that will make more water, not less."

"Save it then. We may need it later."

"Ivy," said Mumchance, "we don't want to go down."

"Water flows downhill," added Gunderal—an unnecessary remark in Ivy's opinion.

"This stair looks dry," Ivy said.

"There may be some solid rock between the river and that tunnel, but it won't hold back the river forever."

Ivy stared down into the blackness of the stairwell. "We have no choice. Archlis must have gone this way. We're not leaving Kid behind. We are not leaving Sanval behind either, and I know he's down there too," she said. "I'm not letting Archlis walk out of these ruins with whatever treasure is down there. I'll swim with destrachans if I have to, but we're going down."

Ivy started to draw her sword and then realized her scabbard was empty. With a shrug, she started down the staircase. For a moment, there was only silence behind her. Then she heard the tap of Gunderal's heels as she entered the spiral behind her, followed by Zuzzara's heavy footsteps and the clump of Mumchance's boots.

"Told you that she was sweet on him," hissed Zuzzara in what she imagined was a whisper.

"Hush," said Gunderal to her sister.

Ivy's shoulders dropped an inch as she relaxed her rigid back—of course, she had never doubted that they would follow her; they always followed her. But every now and then, she did wonder if she'd just been too foolish to follow. As for Zuzzara and Gunderal's whispering, which she could hear perfectly well, she decided to ignore the blush that was creeping past her cheeks and turning her ears red. She was going after Kid, because the little thief had followed her into this mess. She would rather be cursed by every god in the Realms before she let that cloven-hoofed piece of mischief be fried by some crazy magelord. Or more likely, considering where they were, drowned in a hole.

And if her friends tromping behind her thought she was going after a certain captain from the silver-roof district of Procampur, well she certainly wasn't making any comments.

Let them snicker all they want. She knew her duty just as well as Sanval did. And if the gods wanted to snatch away any of her friends, they were going to have to put up with her hanging on with both hands, pulling in the opposite direction, and screaming the whole time. So, even if she had to drag him out by the scruff of his neck, she was set upon getting a certain man safe and sound back to the tents of Procampur. She had quite enough pain going for her, from knees to shins to toes, without adding the troublesome kind of ache that was not physical at all.

Now she was twisting down into a place that would soon become a well to catch a magelord who liked to play with fire. If she were lucky, she would get Kid, Sanval, and the rest of them out of this mess before the tunnels collapsed, bringing the ruins of Tsurlagol on top of them. *I am so sick of being underground,* thought Ivy, *but I know what I need to do.*

"We are going to rescue Kid and anyone else who needs rescuing," she told the others over her shoulder.

"Mind telling us how?" asked Mumchance.

"We'll do like we always do. We'll make one plan as we go along," Ivy replied. "And have a spare plan hidden in our back pockets, just in case something goes wrong."

◆━━━━◆◆◆━━━━◆

Ahead of them, Kid pondered the best way to murder a magelord. He knew that humans regarded him as a child and was often amused by their assumption that anything small must be young and harmless. Actually he was quite capable of defending himself and, prior to meeting Ivy, usually found the most lethal response as the easiest and quickest way to get what he wanted. It was the same with thieving. If you desired something, take it, because no one would ever just hand it to you—that he had learned long ago from the red wizards and the magelords.

But then he had met the Siegebreakers, who gave all the time—food to strays, protection to anyone who asked. They might moan and groan about how they would be bankrupt within days, or bluster about how they were heartless mercenaries only out for profit, but it never stopped them from defending a bunch of hardscrabble pig farmers against a wizard bent on stealing their land and hogs. And collecting no more payment than a few smoked hams.

"They are all children, dear sir," Kid had once told Mumchance, who was the only person on the farm even close to his own age and experience. "So open with their hearts, so naive."

"Of course, they have only lived a couple of decades, not centuries as you and I," said the dwarf. "Their earliest dreams are still fresh in their heads. That is the most terrifying feature of all those with human blood in their veins. They are capable of so much, simply because they believe that they can accomplish their dreams. Both good and bad. Of course, that is also their most attractive quality—one that can seduce even a centuries-wise dwarf and a cunning thief into believing the same dreams." Kid bowed before the old dwarf that day, realizing that Mumchance was right.

In his earliest decades spent in the dungeons of Thay, Kid had never known that the dreams of humans could be anything other than nightmares. Later, as the slave of Toram, Kid had survived by cringing before the grave-robbing magelord and pretending to be the child that he appeared. But the first flash of joy that he had ever known was the day that he sank his teeth into Archlis's hand and escaped from slavery. Now, Archlis thought he could take Toram's place as his master; but not for long, resolved Kid. He would never be a slave again. He had a home to go to, a barn roof to fix, and an odd assortment of a female fighter, a family of half-humans, and one ancient dwarf to protect. Without his cunning, who knew what trouble the Siegebreakers would encounter?

Kid fingered the knives hidden under the collar of his tunic and surreptitiously checked the multitude of charms hanging from Archlis's tabard—he recognized one or two that had formerly belonged to Toram. Such charms protected the magelord from most edged weapons. Still, if he could cut off the charm and then strike with the dagger, he stood a good chance. The bugbears he dismissed with contempt. He knew that he was faster and cleverer than they were.

Kid's ears swiveled back and forth as he considered the quickest way to kill Archlis. But what of Ivy and the others? Behind him, Kid could hear the river rising. Perhaps he should wait to kill the magelord—wait until he knew the way out and could lead the others. After all, they would need rescuing, and it was his duty (an odd word for him, and one that he had never used out loud) to save them.

Perhaps he should wait until the magelord had retrieved his prize. The Siegebreakers needed money, and Archlis would not be in this place unless he sought a very great treasure. Kid remembered the magelord's greed was considerable, but so was the mage's cunning. Archlis would not risk losing Fottergrim's patronage for a mere trifle.

So, wait until the magelord had what he sought in hand and then kill him, Kid decided, glancing up at the long-nosed wizard striding beside him. As Ivy would say, it was a plan. Then Kid's sharp hearing caught another sound coming from behind them—the sound that a pair of well-made bootheels make when their owner thinks he is being stealthy. Kid's eyes slid sideways as he checked the bugbears. They were busy with one of their growling arguments about poetry—love poetry in particular.

"One could say that a past love drives all chance of other loves out of the heart," said Norimgic in a bitter tone.

"Yet, one could still express desire for the nearest female, even long for her," answered Osteroric.

"True. And how much more moving that would be," mused Norimgic. "I want, I need, but I cannot love."

"Two emotions but never the third."

"Yes, but how to express this, my brother?"

"It needs a good strong rhythm, such a love poem."

Clearly the bugbears were paying no attention at all to anything but their own concerns. Archlis also was concentrated on the way before them, checking the corridor's turns against a page in the spellbook that he had stolen from the unlamented Toram.

Kid's right ear twitched back. Yes, that was definitely a pair of proper Procampur boots following them. Which meant a proper Procampur gentleman who believed that such things as duty and loyalty were as real as the crystals studding the walls. Once Kid would have called such a man foolish, but that was before he had met the Siegebreakers. Now he was just pleased that another mad dreamer was following them. Sanval would take care of the bugbears nicely, while Kid found a way around the charms that Archlis wore and slit his throat. Or maybe the charms only worked on metal, Kid suddenly thought, and a good solid rock right to the base of the skull would work.

A pair of golden doors blocked their way.

"Open this!" commanded the magelord.

"Certainly, certainly," said Kid, scurrying to where the magelord pointed. He kept his head down so Archlis could not see the malice in his eyes. The door locks were easy to pick and easy to leave open, all the better for any followers who might be coming after them.

And once they found the magelord's treasure, Archlis would be distracted and so much easier to kill. It seemed like an excellent plan to Kid.

———————◆•◆•◆———————

Once down the stairs, a quick glance showed Sanval that the crystals lining the corridor generated a magical light, a twilight glow that seemed almost bright after nearly a day of tramping through dark tunnels. It made it easy to see the long scratch on the wall, left by the rake of a bugbear's claws. Osteroric was holding to his bargain, and marking the way for Sanval to follow. Of course, Osteroric thought Sanval was just following them to find a way out. The bugbear wasn't going to be too pleased when Sanval ambushed them, and that worried Sanval a bit. Was it honorable to turn on an ally, even if the ally was essentially helping you for a bright piece of armor and was also a creature not particularly known for its social graces? Sanval tapped his helmet to make sure it was straight and decided to deal with events as they happened.

Moving back up the stairs rapidly and as silently as he could, Sanval left his last candle burning on the top step. He remembered what Ivy had said about the keen eyesight of the dwarf and the others. Surely they would spot that light and understand that he meant them to follow him. Certainly the Siegebreakers would have destroyed the destrachans. If they had not . . . Sanval refused to consider that possibility. The beasts were just animals, and Sanval knew that Ivy, Mumchance, Gunderal, and Zuzzara were far cleverer than any animal.

Besides, as much as Gunderal did not fit Sanval's concept of a wizard (he tended to think of all wizards as strange, old, white-bearded men, never mind that the Pearl was the most powerful wizard in Procampur), he had seen her perform magic. Like most of those educated in Procampur—where wizardry was strictly regulated by the Pearl and largely discouraged altogether—Sanval believed that magic could give anyone an overwhelming, and rather unfair advantage in a fight. Which, of course, was why he needed to stop Archlis before the magelord returned to the walls of Tsurlagol and hurled his devastating fireballs against Procampur's troops. And there was that poor little chap, Ivy's friend Kid, who was probably terrified by the magelord. He could not leave a child in the grasp of someone so evil.

So, all he had to do was ambush Archlis and overpower the magelord. Once the fellow was captured or dead (captured would be preferable and more legal, but one did what one could in times such as these), Sanval knew that they would be able to find a way out. The magelord was obviously carrying maps. And with Kid's truly extraordinary tracking ability, they could also find Ivy and the others (assuming they had not seen his signal at the top of the stairs and followed them).

It was a plan, Sanval decided, and then he heard an odd scuttling noise. Something was hunting for him. The shadows filled with sounds of scratching, as though an army of insects skittered within the walls. Sanval stopped, stood motionless on the bottom stair, and moved his eyes from side to side then up and down in case a few thousand spiders were dropping toward his head. Nothing there.

He considered flattening himself against the wall and slipping noiselessly along the corridor, except Sanval was honest enough to admit to himself that sneaking in metal armor and sturdy leather boots might be beyond him. Soundless was not a choice. The crystals studding the stone walls brilliantly lit the corridor stretching before him; so he would be easily spotted if he got too close too quickly. Luckily, he could track Archlis by sound alone. The bugbears were arguing so loudly in their growling language that he could follow them easily.

Sanval tapped the top of his helmet to straighten it properly on his head, squared his shoulders, and stepped from the shadow of the stairwell out into the tunnel. Then he heard the sound again. It was just behind him.

Glancing back at the stairs, he saw a crack running up the wall, thick enough at the bottom for a slender man to crawl through. Water oozed out of the crack along the floor. Sanval wondered if the water was making the odd noise, but then he saw long threads, a bit like feather tips, protrude through the crack, vibrating, reaching, touching the stones, shivering away. He leaned closer, trying to see what they were. The two threads reached out, withdrew, disappeared, then shot out, whipping feathery ropes of an odd brown color and a couple of feet long. They quivered as though they were sniffing. Sniffing? Sniffing feathers? The Procampur captain's hand went to his sword hilt.

Quietly, he started to slide the sword out of its scabbard, trying not to make any noise that would attract the attention of Archlis. He was torn. If he delayed too long, the magelord might slip out of his grasp. On the other hand, if this was some type of trap set by the magelord, some type of feathery magical rope, then Ivy and the others might be attacked by it if they followed him down this stair. He could not leave such a danger behind him to threaten them.

Sanval crouched down on his boot heels and squinted at the crack in the wall, but beyond the opening was heavy darkness, and he could make out nothing in the way of shape or size. Then, looking like something out of the horrific tales that his nurse once told to keep him in bed at night, a head poked out. It was reddish brown with bug eyes; in fact, the whole head was insect shaped. Yes, it was exactly like the giant bug that his nurse claimed ate little boys who were foolish enough to go wandering outside in their nightshirts.

The long, twitching, fuzzy things started below the bug's eyes and arched out, moving like feelers, turning and doing that sniffing thing. One shot out toward Sanval. Antennae! A giant bug head with antennae! Sanval fell backward off his heels and sat down hard on the floor, so fast that he gasped with surprise and his armor rattled.

The antennae swiped in front of him, almost touching him but missing him by inches. They stopped, quivered, and the bug's eyes blinked.

While Sanval sat open-mouthed and watched, the creature wiggled slowly through the opening in the wall, scratching along the stones. Sanval kept thinking that must be all, but the thing kept oozing out, a humped body covered with rust-colored lumps that looked a bit like a giant turtle's shell, and peculiarly hinged legs. It was almost as large as a small bear. Trailing behind it was a long tail covered in armadillo-type plates and ending in a prong.

Don't get much uglier than that, Sanval thought and again started to unsheathe his sword.

One of the antennae whipped forward, catching him by surprise, and slithered rapidly across his metal shoulder guard. Annoyed, thinking the creature had probably trailed some goop that would mar his armor, Sanval scooted back on the floor and then turned his head to look at his shoulder.

He leaped to his feet and darted to the far corner. The guard wasn't scratched and wasn't covered in goop, but it was rusting as he watched, little flecks of rust dropping onto the floor. The creature's antennae scraped along the stones and caught the loose bits of rust, drew them back to its mouth, and it chewed.

"Hey, there, that's my armor!" Sanval howled.

The creature rolled its bug eyes upward and stared at him.

"How fast can you run?" Sanval asked it politely. Its yellow eyes blinked. "That fast, my friend?" Sanval glanced down at his sword and knew that pulling it out of its leather scabbard would be the same as handing it to the monster for lunch. He left his sword where it was.

The yellow eyes rolled upward to stare at the top of Sanval's head, and Sanval could imagine the thing thinking, "Aaah, a beautifully burnished helmet, how delicious!" Oddly, in his imagination, the creature spoke in the exact fussy tones of a former tutor who used to warn him about the dangers of the Vast and the folly of leaving an ordered life lived under the silver tiles of his district.

He tried to think of a plan, because surely a noble of Procampur, even one who had not traveled nearly as much as he wished, should be able to outwit a bug-brained monster. While Sanval considered his options, the monster's antennae made another attack. It snapped toward his helmet, which Sanval had expected. He pivoted and dived away. The antennae hit his elbow, slithered across the metal elbow guard, then whipped back. Sanval reached across with his opposite gloved hand and touched his elbow just in time to feel the guard crumble, crack, and fall to the floor in a pile of rusting metal. The monster lurched forward at surprising speed.

Sanval dashed past it to the opposite wall. The monster ignored him, arching its curved back and going at the rusting pieces on the floor. It bent its legs so that the joints stuck out, and hunched itself over the rusting metal and lowered its ugly little mouth. The *scrunch scrunch* of Sanval's elbow guard being devoured like a hard-crusted loaf was more than annoying.

What he needed was a wooden pole, he thought, and scanned the tunnel. But there was nothing, not a crossbeam, not a door that could be dismantled, nothing. And the monster effectively blocked the staircase. If he dashed down the corridor, would the thing follow? Would Archlis hear him coming?

What if he ran into one of the magelord's firespells? Sanval glanced down at his scorched boot—his manservant would be in tears when he saw what had happened earlier. Sanval's gleaming boots were the envy of the camp, and his manservant Godolfin made a fair amount taking bribes for his polish recipe (of course, Sanval paid him even more to keep the true recipe off the feet of his rivals). So, rust or fire? Which would be worse? Both would be hard on the outfit that he had left.

"I was trained to meet worthy adversaries," he complained, "fighters with swords. Even a bugbear has a sword. Or at least a glaive." He glanced down at the front of his chest. "Just as well I gave Osteroric my breastplate. I suppose if you had it to rust off me, you'd keep right on chewing through my body."

The monster tilted its head and looked up at Sanval.

"Please forget that I suggested such a thing," he muttered. He looked again at the crystals studding the wall. Some were as big as a man's head. He reached up and grasped the one that protruded out the most. By swinging his entire weight off the crystal, he was able to force it out of the wall. He hefted it in one hand, then jumped back as an antennae whipped toward him. The gem was heavy for its size. Sanval clutched it, bent his arm back, and aimed the stone at the monster. It bounced off the lumpy back but certainly did no damage. The monster eyed him, then took a step closer.

"Very well, you disliked that but took no harm from it. Another approach is needed here," Sanval said. Was there a weapon he could put together from his gear that did not contain metal? He glanced at his arms, with metal shields still in place on one shoulder and elbow. His gauntlets featured metal cuffs and guards. His body armor lacked the breastplate, but there was still a fair collection of chain mail and smaller plates, with a few bits of banded armor protecting his thighs and knees. All good for nothing except a meal for the monster.

And last, there were his beautiful leather boots. He had never liked armored footwear, finding it impossibly clumsy; also when he had tried it, he had been rewarded with blisters. Now, as he considered ways to destroy the creature, he was doubly glad that he had chosen leather boots. Walking out of these ruins in his stockings would be less than dignified.

The monster shot out its antennae again, and Sanval dodged again, but how long could he keep this up? Furious at the unfairness of a beast that would not fight with proper weapons, the Procampur ripped off one gauntlet and tossed it into a far corner. The creature swung around, caught it with an antennae, rusted it on impact, and—like any other wild animal—hunched over the nice new addition to its meal.

With the monster busy with its lunch, Sanval pulled off a shiny leather boot. He pried a couple of fist-sized crystals out of the wall, dropped them in, and grabbed another.

The beast made a disgusting gulping noise and swung toward him. Sanval unbuckled his other elbow guard and tossed it in a high arch. The creature raised its head to watch, tracking the guard's path until it clattered into the far corner. *Slither, snap,* into rust, *crunch, crunch.*

"No sense of a fair fight, and no table manners, either," Sanval complained as he grabbed up handfuls of smaller stones and dirt dislodged by his digging of the crystals. He jammed everything into his boot. With foreboding, he pulled off his remaining gauntlet and tucked it into his belt. He had to trust that the creature went for metal before attacking flesh. But what if that were wrong?

By the time the creature had eaten his elbow guard, Sanval was ready. He had undone the remaining shoulder guard and held it in his hand. As the bug-head swung toward him, Sanval did another arched toss, and the bug-head did another follow-it-with-the-eyes turn. The guard crashed into the corner and was rust almost before it landed—a large pile of rust: a feast for the beast. The rust monster curved its humped back, crouched as close to the floor as possible, and let its wicked tail sag as it chomped away.

The back was leathery, the tail was hard-as-shell plates, which only left the head and legs. Clutching his boot closed by its cuff, Sanval leaped forward and landed on his stocking-clad foot. The silk of his stocking made his landing a little slippery, but he managed to stay upright. Sanval swung the stone-filled boot down on top of the creature's head while kicking his booted foot at a jutting joint of its back leg. The joint cracked. The monster's head swiveled so that the bug's eyes stared up at him. Sanval saw an antennae quiver, ducked, and was hit by the other one. It slapped across his banded shin guard. Rust flew. He didn't bother to watch it crumble; he could feel the weight dropping away. He stomped down on the beast's front leg with all his weight and held fast while bending over the monster to beat on its head with the stone-filled boot.

Although pinned to the floor by his weight, the creature flipped its head to glare up at Sanval. Even as he brought the boot down toward its face, an antennae slithered up, way up, straight to the brim of his beautiful helmet. That helmet had been carefully designed for him. It carried family crests as well as military insignias in its elaborate, etched ornamentation, and he loved it almost as much as he loved his sword. He did not feel the tap, but he felt the disintegration. With the helmet pressed around his ears, he could hear the rust eat through—a sound much like the monster's chomping, *crunch, crunch*—and the rattle of falling pieces.

Sanval thought of himself as a rational man, possessed of self-control as well as courtesy, but even as he tried to remember this he heard himself screaming, "Do you know how much my armor cost? And how long I had to wait to get a perfect fit? And how much time it takes poor Godolfin to polish each piece? And how much I have to pay him to do that?"

With each scream he beat at the monster's head, hitting its eyes until they rolled shut, smacking at the antennae until they shriveled and curled away from him, and finally catching a soft spot between the skull and the first protective plate at the top of its spine. He heard something crack, and the beast gave a horrible gurgle. Sanval continued whacking away until the rust monster slid flat to the floor, its legs stretched out, its tail twitching but unable to lift the fanned tip of spikes. The antennae collapsed, their tips touching the wall in front of the monster's head, then sliding slowly down the stones until they, too, were stretched lifeless across the floor.

"Very dramatic. You died with style," Sanval said to the carcass, trying to regain his self-control. He stepped away from the beast and looked down at it. It was not the sort of battle to go home and brag about—not like besting a dragon or a famous orc warrior. The creature might have been destructive to his gear, yes, but dead it simply looked pathetic.

Shaking his head at the pile of rusted armor under the monster, Sanval assessed his remaining equipment. He emptied the crystals and stones from his boot, pounded it to knock loose any small bits, then pulled the tail of his silk undershirt out at his waist, and used it to try to rub his boot clean. Would his boots ever be bright again? Could he even ask Godolfin to polish them? And wasn't that the way it always went—he had used the boot that was not scorched across the toe. Now it, too, was thoroughly scuffed from beating it against the monster.

At least he had been wearing a linen shirt, padded vest, and leather pants under his armor. He shuddered to think what Ivy would have said if he had been left just standing in his silk underwear. She probably would have made up some song that would never, ever die in the red-roof quarter.

Sanval pulled on his leather boot, then brushed stone dust from what little was left of his armor. He finger-combed his dark curls, brushing back damp tendrils from his forehead. He looked in dismay at his hands, now covered with stone dust and rust. Deciding that was the best he could do, he started to march on down the tunnel.

And stopped and hopped and cursed as he pulled off his boot again. He muttered words that he would never say if anyone else were present. He had missed a very sharp bit of stone when he had shaken out his boot.

With his boot and his dignity restored, Sanval paused and listened. He could not hear the bugbears arguing. Had they gotten too far ahead? As quickly and as quietly as he could, Sanval hurried down the corridor. At least he knew that his sword would work just fine against bugbears. As for Archlis, if he put up any resistance, well, Sanval would just brain him with his own Ankh. In his present murderous mood, a full-frontal attack seemed like the most sensible plan that he had ever had.

CHAPTER TWENTY

Ivy emerged from the staircase and blinked as she went from the darkness of the shadowy stair into the glowing corridor.

Behind her, Mumchance let out that soft half-sigh, half-whistle that can only mean one thing coming from a dwarf—that there was a fortune in raw gems surrounding them. He set down his sputtering lantern to better examine the strange corridor where they found themselves. Obviously others had come before them, as various crystals had been pried loose from the walls and littered the floor.

"Oooh, that is so ugly!" Gunderal squealed. The dainty wizard had just tripped over a large dead creature, sprawled over a rusty pile of armor.

"We better hurry, Ivy," said Mumchance. "The ground is getting unstable here."

"How do you know that?"

The dwarf pointed at the dead monster. A number of large crystals and smaller stones were scattered around the body. "Those must have fallen out of the wall and brained the creature while it was eating," said the dwarf.

"Lucky for us. One less thing for us to fight," said Zuzzara.

"Hey, doesn't that look like Procampur armor?"

"It's too rusty," said Gunderal. "Can you imagine anyone from Procampur letting their armor get into such a state!"

"Let's move," commanded Ivy. "That creature may have had friends, and we don't need any more trouble. Let's find Kid and get out of here."

"And what about Sanval?" Gunderal hopped neatly over the pile of rusted armor and gave Ivy a teasing look.

"Oh, him too."

"So there is still treasure in the ruins of Tsurlagol," said Mumchance, still checking the crystals studding the wall as he walked besides Ivy.

"Apparently. Funny that nobody ever looted this part."

"I think we are in the oldest bit," said Mumchance. "The most buried bit."

"What do you mean?" Ivy asked, picking her way carefully along the corridor. Besides the gems studding the walls and ceiling, more were poking up through the floor. It made the way rough, and tripping was a distinct possibility. Worse yet, there weren't enough clear flat bits to show any good tracks. Kid might have been able to see something, but Ivy didn't have his clever eyes and cleverer nose.

"Look at these tunnels, straight, narrow, and slanting down. This bit isn't some part of the city that sunk below ground. Someone chiseled this bit out of solid stone."

"Why?"

"Well, if they had bothered to take the rocks out of the walls, I would have said it was a mine shaft. But, as it is, and seeing what is in front of us, I think this is a tomb shaft," Mumchance said, halting before a pair of golden doors, emblazoned with the type of funeral scenes that they had seen earlier in the old city bath and in the ossuary. Only these scenes were much more finely wrought and studded with colored gems.

Above the funeral procession, the walls of a long-lost Tsurlagol tumbled down before a solitary figure with upraised arms. Again, the pictures showed a fantastic gem clutched in the man's hand, radiating out lines indicating some type of magical force. And above that were the runes for earth, sky, water, and emptiness that had decorated the floor of that odd trapped room. "I'd bet that this was the first time they made those pictures," said Mumchance, looking up at the doors, "and all the others in the ruins were just copies—what people remembered about these pictures."

"How about warnings?" suggested Ivy, still staring at the huge doors. She had never seen that much gold in one place. One door could probably buy an entire mansion in Procampur.

"Could be," said Mumchance, who also looked a little stunned by the sheer amount of gold that somebody had thought made an excellent door.

"Don't suppose they are just gold foil over wood," said Zuzzara, also blinking at the wealth on display. Gunderal was just tilting her head from one side to the other, seeing how her reflection looked in the polished gold panels.

"It's solid," said the dwarf, rapping the door with a heavy fist. "And too heavy for us to carry out."

At Mumchance's knock, the doors before them creaked half open, the lock neatly sprung. Wiggles jumped forward, squirming through the open doors ahead of the rest of them. "Charmed and mechanical," said Mumchance, stopping to peer at the lock in front of his nose. "But somebody went through it quick and clean. Must be Kid's work."

"That's why Archlis took him," Ivy said. "He needed Kid's talents to get through this door and any other locks he might encounter."

"Because he has no talents of his own." Gunderal sniffed.

"Told you that it was all stolen magic and Kid's just another token to him."

"Still," said Ivy. "If Archlis needs Kid's talents, he should keep Kid alive until we can retrieve him." She looked back the way that they had come. Even with her human nose, she could smell river water.

"Ivy," said Gunderal, confirming her fears. "The river is coming closer. It will be in these tunnels soon."

"Then we go forward," Ivy said.

"And close the doors behind us," added Mumchance, clicking his fingers at Wiggles to bring the dog to heel. "Solid metal, dwarf-made, these should seal tight. That should keep the water out of this section for a while."

"But we can't go back." Even as Ivy voiced this objection, she realized that the doors were the least of their problems. With the river filling up the tunnels behind them, returning the way that they had taken into the treasure trove would soon be impossible.

More gems gleamed on the other side of the door. With Ivy's help, Zuzzara was able to drag the heavy golden doors closed again. With a firm click, the doors locked into place.

"So now we hope that Archlis has another way out," said Gunderal.

"I'm sure that he always did," said Ivy. "He just wanted to get here, and he couldn't with those destrachans in the way. When we drew them off, he came straight here and straight through. He is moving fast, hunting for one particular treasure, or he'd be chipping out part of these walls, wouldn't he?"

"They are good crystals," admitted Mumchance, trailing his fingers along the wall. "Useful for spells—the sort of thing most wizards would want. If it had been me, I'd have slowed down and taken a few with me. Maybe tried to shave a bit of gold off those doors."

"So he's blind to all of this, and set on getting some other treasure out of these ruins," Ivy said.

"Must be. And there's something odd about these walls. Has been since we came down those stairs."

"What?" Ivy asked.

"These crystals shouldn't be here at all. Wrong type of rock for such gems. These come from lower down probably. And they weren't set here by somebody. Not like dwarves studded the walls, if you see what I mean. More like the gems just pushed themselves out of the dirt here."

"There's more earth magic here," agreed Gunderal. "Very strong and very close now."

"I just wish I had not lost my sword back there," Ivy said, pulling the long knife from her belt. It would work for close fighting, but she most certainly regretted feeding her sword to the destrachan. The corridors still blazed with an internal light, and for the first time since she had fallen into the river, Ivy could see clearly ahead of her—no shadows, no darkness, nothing hiding in front of her. It made her exceedingly nervous. Remembering the phantom fungus, she had the queer feeling that whatever you couldn't see might turn out to be worse than what you could.

Zuzzara and Gunderal seemed equally anxious, starting at their own footfalls as they passed through the crystal-studded tunnel. Obviously, they too thought this was just too easy.

Only Mumchance seemed carefree. He was too intrigued by the gems surrounding them on all sides to notice much else. Turning slowly, his real eye gleamed with appreciation of the stones arrayed in front of him, and even the fake eye appeared to sparkle in the light of the corridor. "I'm sure that these crystals were pushed straight out of the earth, called out of it as it were. This was done by magic. Then somebody came along later and made those doors and sealed the place off. And who seals off a terrific source of wealth like this?"

"Somebody who is afraid of the magic down here," said Gunderal with a shudder. "Whatever is here is what buried Tsurlagol before."

"What was it?" Ivy asked. Whatever it was, this had to be what Archlis was hunting—an artifact so powerful that he had led Fottergrim to Tsurlagol and plunged an entire city into war just so he could roam around these ruins.

"Something was hidden here a long time ago," Gunderal said. She pushed her dark hair back from her face and closed her eyes, a small worry line marking a perfect crescent between her eyebrows. She waved both hands with palms upturned, like a seer trying to draw scented incense toward her face. Gunderal swayed twice, and Zuzzara stepped forward to steady her sister. Ivy gestured her back. Gunderal sighed and then opened her eyes. "An object of great power. A gem that calls to other gems and rules the earth beneath it."

"Is it evil?"

Gunderal shrugged. "No more than any other jewel. It is how it is used that has caused both trouble and sorrow. And fear. It was fear that caused them to build the golden doors and lock this treasure away."

"She is more sensible than she looks sometimes," said Mumchance. "Treasure is never evil. But the spending of it—that can cause great wickedness."

"Well, then," said Ivy, "it would probably be best to keep this treasure away from Archlis. Because I feel that he would be a very careless spender of wealth."

The tunnel branched in two directions ahead of them. Both ways curved off into shadows; neither showed a clear path. There were no boot prints on the gem-studded floor, and no visible archways or flickering lights beyond the branching.

Better still, Ivy noted with some relief, no trail of blood or beastly fluids.

"Right or left?" queried Zuzzara.

"Don't see which way." Ivy missed Kid more than ever. "What do you hear, Zuzzara?"

The half-orc cupped her hands around her ears. "Metal striking metal. Somebody in a fight, but no yelling or screaming. Not like a normal fight."

Ivy grinned with relief. "Sounds perfectly normal for a man from Procampur who thinks it is uncivilized to insult his opponents. Which direction?"

"Left," Zuzzara said.

Ivy pivoted on her heel and started down the tunnel that Zuzzara indicated. Her fingers tightened around the handle of her dagger. "Come on, Sanval is down there," she said.

Whipping around a corner, Ivy barreled into the melee. Sanval and the magelord's two bugbears were whirling in the middle of the corridor, stuck in an odd three-way fight with each other. The bugbears were snarling softly, but Sanval, as expected, was fighting with his usual silent expertise.

Ivy was surprised to spot a new foe—two skeletal arms appeared to be floating through the air and spinning around the other fighters, wielding a rusty sword. There was nothing but empty space between the arms where a body and shoulders should have been. Still, when any of them moved, the upper arms drew slightly toward each other, the elbows shot out, and the hands tightened on the sword hilt, exactly as though the arms were attached to an invisible body. Each arm was polished white bone, from shoulder to elbow to wrist to the ivory hands that clutched the rusty sword. This was a creature created by magic, and one that the Siegebreakers knew, and there was something rather comforting and welcome about facing a danger that you understood, rather than one like the destrachans.

"Oh dear," said Gunderal behind Ivy. "More undead."

"A dread!" said Mumchance. "Lousy, lousy dread. I hate dead things that don't stay dead!" Wiggles's ears pricked up, and she gave a happy bark as she spotted the flying bones.

"A skeleton without a head, a head without a skeleton, and now arms without a body. Another undead guardian," Ivy agreed. "Somebody liked to play with bones in old Tsurlagol."

The dread seemed to be guarding a doorway. Each time Sanval or one of the bugbears got too close, the arms would swing the sword. If they backed away, the arms stayed floating in front of the entrance.

"So where are Archlis and Kid?" asked Ivy. "Why didn't that bony thing attack them?"

Gunderal gave a little sniff. She twitched her nose a couple of times to be sure. "No sword on Archlis."

"Lacking a sword is an advantage? So I can march right past it?" Ivy asked. When Gunderal did not reply, and continued to stand with her head tilted back, nostrils flared, Ivy added, "How do you know Archlis doesn't have a sword?"

"Keen sense of smell," Gunderal said.

"You can smell that?" said Zuzzara. "You are kidding, little sister."

"Of course not. I'm that good. I keep telling you that I can smell magic."

Zuzzara gave Gunderal a "big sister" look. "You can smell a missing sword on someone who isn't here?" the half-orc asked.

Gunderal giggled and then admitted, "I can smell an old command spell in this space, and I can see that Archlis and Kid shed their blades." She pointed across the floor. Just outside the doorway lay the magelord's slender sword and Kid's three stilettos. "Kid probably told him how to get around the dread—most likely it has a command on it to attack anyone bearing edged weapons. Kid's good at guessing such things. Remember the dreads that we found under the wizard's tower—the ones that were commanded to attack only dwarves? Besides, watch the arms. Anytime Sanval or the bugbears get near it, it attacks their weapons. It's there as a barrier, but one that would be easy to pass for anyone who knew what its commands were."

"I hate those things," muttered Mumchance, who still had a few scars from his previous encounter with the dwarf-activated dread.

"They're mindless, at least," said Gunderal. "They'll only fight what they are told to fight. Sort of like you, big sister."

"Ha-ha. So what about those three? Do we rescue Sanval first? Or get rid of the dread?" asked Zuzzara.

"We really can't afford to lose any more weapons," Ivy said. "Fairly soon, we'll be down to chucking stones. I would rather dismantle the bones than shed any blades that we have left." She gave the fight ahead of them a cool look. "Sanval's doing all right. Let's get rid of the dread first. It's upsetting those bugbears—look at them snarl and whine. And a frightened, upset bugbear is a big, hairy problem."

A dread always cast an aura of fear. As Ivy had learned in previous encounters, that fear could be ignored if you knew what was causing it. But if you didn't know what was causing it, that creeping feeling of terror could shake your confidence. The bugbears obviously didn't know why they were feeling so panicked, and that was making them fight all that much harder. Their huge ragged ears twitched, their tiny eyes narrowed to pinpoints, and their bear noses quivered. One of the bugbears had clenched his jaw so tightly he had thrust a pointed fang through his own lip, and a fine line of blood trailed down his chin and dripped over his matted chest. He brushed at it where it fell onto his shiny breastplate, dulling the gleam, and let out a low growl of frustration. In one clawed hand he clutched a glaive, and with the other he pulled his dagger from its scabbard. He hunched forward and swung wildly at the dread with the knife.

The dread lifted its arms and made a quick downward slice that missed the bugbear's sword but clipped against the loose chains hanging from the bugbear's shoulders. The blow did no harm other than rattle the chains and clang loudly. The bugbear let out a howl of anger; or was that fear? He jerked in a clumsy turn on his clawed feet, and the chains spun out around him, banging against the wall but missing the dread. It floated up and away, then paused beyond the bugbear's reach.

"Suggestions?" said Ivy.

"Break the dread's hold on its sword," said Gunderal. "That should weaken the spell. Might even dispel it."

Ivy looked at the arm bones floating in front of her. They were very skinny. A slow, wicked grin crept across her face. "Hey, Wiggles, come on, come on. Let's play fetch!" Ivy shed her knife, the only edged weapon that she had left, and skipped toward the arm bones, waving the little dog on.

"Ivy!" shouted the dwarf as his dog went racing after her, attracted by Ivy's whistle and "come hither" gestures.

Wiggles danced on her back paws, her fluffy white tail beating back and forth in an eager wag. As neither the dog nor the woman carried any type of edged blade, the dread ignored them. Ivy lunged for the bones and grabbed the nearest forearm. She punched down on the slender bones with her mailed gloves. As with most dreads, the thing was too tough to break, but she forced it near to the ground. Wiggles immediately leaped forward and clamped her sharp little teeth around the nearest wrist bone. She growled, backing away and dragging the dread after her. With no command laid upon it regarding small dogs with sharp teeth, the dread just went bumping after Wiggles, its sword still scraping behind it.

Ignoring the tough old bones, Ivy jumped directly on the rusted blade, landing hard on her boot heels. Unlike the bones, the blade was not magically immune to breakage. It cracked and crumbled under her feet. She stomped a few more times. The bony hand now held only the remnants of a rusted handle, a weapon that posed no danger to anyone. Wiggles still growled and tugged at the bones. She had hooked one paw over the hand bones in an attempt to hold them down for better chewing. With her sharp little teeth, she finally worried free a thumb bone. As soon as it snapped off, the entire dread broke into a shattered pile of bones. Ivy shuffled through the pile, scraping her soles along the floor, and quickly scattered the pieces as far apart as possible. She glared at the bones for a moment, but they remained only broken bits on the floor with no flicker of magic trying to paste them together.

With the dread no longer attacking him, the largest bugbear, Osteroric, whipped around and tried to brain Sanval with his glaive. Ivy shouted for her knife. Zuzzara grabbed it and flipped it blade over handle to her. Ivy caught it with one mailed hand. She took a running jump and flung herself at the bugbear, kicking with both feet at the creature's knee.

The impact sent a shock of pain through her injured toe, and Ivy screamed in a mix of anger and aggravation. More startled by the scream than injured by her kick, the bugbear tripped and rolled with Ivy on top of him. She dropped her knife and wrestled the glaive out of his hands. She used the long pole to swing herself upright, turning it again to swing the iron ball hard against Osteroric's chest. The ball rang against the shiny breastplate that Osteroric wore and knocked him flat. The bugbear waved his furry hands in a gesture of surrender.

"Peace and parley, peace and parley. Don't dent my new breastplate," he wheezed. "Pull your friend off Norimgic before he harms him."

"Sanval!" Ivy shouted. He ignored her, matching dueling sword against glaive with the snarling Norimgic. "Hey, Sanval, stop!"

When Sanval ignored her commands and continued to battle Norimgic, Ivy realized the spell of the dread was still upon them, terror driving them to fight with mindless fury. She thrust the glaive between Sanval's legs, tripping him and sending him rolling off to one side. Norimgic tried to follow, but she shoved the glaive's blade against his throat. "Back off," she said, pricking the bugbear's skin enough to draw blood. "He's mine to kill, if I want to."

Norimgic turned his head and looked at the blood pooling in the hair on his shoulder, blinked his tiny eyes, flattened his ears against his skull, and whined in the same tone that Wiggles used when she knew that she had been a bad dog. Ivy eased off on the pressure of the blade balanced against his throat.

"Fighting females," said Osteroric, scrambling upright and dusting off his breastplate with gentle, concerned strokes. "You should never argue with them."

Ivy reached past the bugbear, grabbed Sanval by the back of his neck, pulled him upright, and shook him until his feet were firmly planted under him. Then she glared at him. She noticed his dark hair was amazingly mussed—the black curls were dusty, streaked with rust, and sticking up in all directions. She looked him over more carefully and frowned. "Aren't you missing something? Shiny stuff?"

Sanval managed a growl.

Ivy felt like she could stand there all day hanging on to Sanval, but she really had other things to do. She settled on a way to keep him out of trouble until she could get them above ground. She shoved him into the arms of a bugbear.

"Hang onto him. Tight," Ivy instructed Osteroric. "Now, where's Archlis? I want to get out of here."

A little cowed by her tone, Osteroric gestured to the archway in front of them. "He went into the crypt. He took the other one with him."

Turning to Sanval, the bugbear held the Procampur captain at arm's length, stared at him, and said, "You have nothing much left to trade, you know that?"

Sanval's growl deepened.

"Good thing I got that breastplate when I did. Did you lose your other stuff? I would not have thought of you as careless."

Sanval pulled his lips back from his clenched teeth and hissed. The bugbear gave him a wary look and stopped talking.

Ivy strode through the archway formerly guarded by the dread and entered the crypt. Its walls shone with the reflected glitter of countless gems, and patterns of light danced across the arched ceiling. Ivy stopped, turned slowly, and stared at her surroundings. It was like being inside a treasure chest. But that wasn't why she was here, she remembered, and she forced her attention back to her job.

"Never hesitate when going to confront a magelord with a lethal command over fire" was going to be her new motto. Just stroll on in like you expect to be paid, and see if you can bluff your way out of this mess, she told herself.

Of course, she was a little startled to find herself wading through gems that rolled underfoot like pebbles on a beach.

"Oooh," moaned Mumchance when he spotted the piles of gems that rose higher than his head in some corners of the room. "Rubies, emeralds, diamonds. Oh, look, puppy, look.

It is all our favorite friends." Wiggles trotted proudly beside him, tail still wagging and the dread's thumb bone clenched in her jaws.

Norimgic went down on his furry knees, grabbing gems and stuffing them into his pockets. He might have been a bugbear poet, but he was bright enough to recognize portable wealth when he saw it. Osteroric kept one hand clamped tightly around Sanval's wrists and used the other big hand to scoop up jewels and stuff them behind his breastplate. "I can buy many beautiful new chains with these. Maybe even some fine black leather vests for my brother and I. Females always like that look. You should try that. It is better than that rust you wear in your hair," the bugbear said in friendly tones to his prisoner.

The prisoner's eyes gleamed darkly, and the sound of grinding teeth could be heard, but Sanval remained silent.

Kid was on his knees, kneeling on what looked like a pile of black sapphires. The carved chest before him was remarkable for its very plainness after the golden doors and the crystal corridor. It was a sarcophagus carved from gray stone, with a number of strange symbols etched into its side. From the stone box an ululation rose, a moaning cry rather like a wailing kitten trapped in a box. Kid's face was wrinkled in concentration, and he apparently did not notice the tip of the magelord's Ankh pressed into the back of his neck. Ivy, however, was very conscious of the grim and greedy expression on the face of Archlis. His eyes had narrowed to yellow slits; frown lines creased down the sides of his long nose and past his scowl to his jaws. His hand tightened around the shaft of the Ankh. If he leaned forward over Kid or stumbled at all, the Ankh would crack the little thief's neck bones.

Ivy hand-signaled for quiet. She did not want to startle Archlis into a sudden attack. Behind her, she could hear the clicking noise of gems being trickled into pockets. She hoped it was just the bugbears and the rest of her friends were paying attention.

Kneeling in front of the gray stone box, Kid pointed a finger at the etched markings on its surface. He did not turn his head to look up at the magelord and seemed completely unaware of the threat looming over him. But Kid was clever, and for now she would have to trust his instincts to save himself. He wasn't one to make some rash move, unlike a certain captain from Procampur who was ready to risk his life for a chance to kill Archlis. At least she did not have to worry about that sort of foolishness from Kid. He who saves himself first lives to save the rest of us, she thought, and decided to add it to her growing list of mottos. The list that started with "The only good day is one where we all walk away" and Mumchance's old favorite: "If the wall is falling down, don't stand under it."

"So, my lord, so," said Kid to Archlis. "We press in the pattern of the name. Three times and then three times more. A little tricky, but no great barrier."

As he had with the silver buckle that made the belt float, Kid's quick fingers danced in the perfect rhythm needed to trace the secret code and unlock the chest. He kept his head down, his fingers moving, and played the lock as though it were a musical instrument. Once, twice, *tap tap tap*. The lid popped open.

"Mine! Mine at last!" cried Archlis. He threw his arms up toward the ceiling, the force pulling his tall body to its full height. His sleeves flapped, his stringy blond hair bobbed on his shoulders, and the Ankh lifted off of Kid's neck.

The shouts of the magelord were drowned beneath a sobbing wave of noise that reminded Ivy of funeral mourners. It crested into a terrible moaning sound, and it issued from the stone sarcophagus.

Behind her, Ivy heard Gunderal cry out, her genasi nature sensitive to any spells or curses near her. Even Ivy could feel the chill prickle of the magic that issued from the granite coffin.

CHAPTER TWENTY-ONE

Archlis lowered his Ankh to his side as he knelt to peer into the stone chest. "I have my treasure now," he said. He paused, his long fingers suspended, as though he feared that what he reached for would burn him. Ivy took a step forward, to see for herself what he coveted. Before she could lean over his shoulder to see, Archlis drew out a large diamond from the chest. He held it up in an outstretched hand, and the gem shot out beams of light that glittered off of every bright surface. It was as close to being a living thing as a crystal could be, pulsing with brilliance. From the diamond issued the weird moaning sound that had been evident even when the sarcophagus was closed.

Kid backed away from Archlis. Paying no attention at all to Ivy, who was hissing at him to move behind her, Kid stooped and picked up a very large ruby. Rather than dropping it into his pouch, as Ivy expected, Kid drew out a leather slingshot from a hidden pocket. He stared intently at the back of the magelord's head.

Just as Kid dropped the ruby into the slingshot, a cry echoed through the room, a shriek that went higher and became more shrill as the cry went on. "Thief, thief! There you are! Thief!"

Ivy spun around to confront a flameskull rocketing through the door. "Oh blast, I thought we'd broken that thing!"

"Thief! Give me back my tooth!" The flameskull darted at a startled Kid, who tumbled out of the way, dropping his slingshot as he dodged. The flameskull's eyes shot sparks; its mane of green flame swirled and flashed with its fury. Ivy grabbed for her sword and then realized her scabbard was still empty. She snatched at her belt. Her dagger was gone too, dropped when she was fighting with Osteroric. But she still had the glaive. She swung at the flameskull, which made a jeering noise and whizzed out of reach.

Mumchance gave a shout behind her, and Ivy ducked at the dwarf's warning. He had scooped up a handful of rubies and flung the jewels at the flameskull to distract it from Kid. The gems ricocheted off the flying skull, rattling away into the corners. The flameskull spat a ball of fizzing green sparks at them, but it was turning toward Kid even as the spell left its mouth. Both Ivy and the dwarf rolled out of the way of the spell, which fizzled harmlessly in a pile of loose diamonds.

"You have my tooth!" screamed the flameskull. "You stole my tooth!" Kid looked around the room.

"Get rid of that tooth!" shouted Ivy to Kid. "Give it to me." She was wearing the most armor, and if all the thing could do was spit sparks, she stood the best chance of surviving its attack.

Kid shook his head and jumped sideways, clutching at the pouch where he had stashed the flameskull's molar, and drawing the flameskull away from Ivy. The flameskull let out a howl and dived toward him, scorching past Mumchance and almost setting the dwarf's beard alight. Mumchance hopped from foot to foot, cursing undead creatures that wouldn't stay dead. He stooped and gathered another handful of gems, throwing emeralds, sapphires, and one enormous blood red garnet at the flameskull. Each stone hit the bony pate and bounced away. The flameskull barely even glanced at the dwarf before it began to follow Kid around the room again.

"Give me back my tooth!" it screamed as it dived after the little thief. Kid wisely decided to shelter behind the stone sarcophagus, curling his body into a small target—head down, hands and hooves tucked neatly beneath himself. The flameskull zipped after him, almost striking Archlis. The astounded magelord, clutching the diamond to his chest with one hand, swiped at the flameskull with his Ankh. The metal staff rang with a clang against the skull but had no other effect.

"Get it away from me!" Archlis shouted at Kid.

"Give me my tooth!" sobbed the skull and hovered above Kid.

Kid whipped out from behind the sarcophagus, the flameskull in hot pursuit behind him.

"That's it! I've had it with you!" Ivy was still wearing her armored gloves. When the flameskull went whizzing by her, she reached out both hands and snagged it through the empty eye sockets and jawbone. The green flame licked harmlessly at her heavy gauntlets. The skull was a simple catch for anyone who had grabbed a dread or the head of a floating corpse and felt the nose rot off into her hand. Some things just got easier with practice.

"Wwwarghts!" The skull let out a muffled shriek, unable to speak any words with Ivy's left hand wrapped tightly around its jawbone. It tried to tug out of her hands, continuing to make strange gargling noises.

"Careful, Ivy," Gunderal warned. "It's trying to cast a spell."

"Shut up!" Ivy yelled at the flameskull. She held it in front of her and stared into its flickering eye sockets, confronting it with her jutting chin almost touching its naked jawbone.

The flameskull gave an involuntary tremble. Ivy smiled—and it was not a nice smile—and slung the flameskull into the stone box in front of her. Before the magical creature could recover, she slammed the lid of the sarcophagus down. "And stay there!"

Muffled bumps and bangs echoed from inside the box. A puff of smoke came out of the crack between the lid and box. Ivy ignored it. She swaggered up to Archlis, grabbing a stunned Kid by the shoulder and pulled him behind her. The little guy was obviously feeling murderous, but attacking Archlis at this moment might not be the best plan. She thought that she had a better idea.

"Admirable style, my dear," Kid whispered.

"Thank you," Ivy whispered back. "Now stop trying to play hero. If I tell you to throw me a moldering molar, throw it."

"Yes, Captain." Kid sketched a quick bow in her direction. She ignored it, swiveling toward the magelord.

"You!" Ivy said, jabbing a finger at Archlis.

The magelord blinked.

"All right, we have saved you. Destrachans drowned. Flameskull boxed up. Can't ask for more than that from any mercenary," Ivy announced loudly. "So pay up and lead us out of the ruins."

Archlis blinked and slowly turned his head toward her. When he did not reply, she snapped her fingers to be sure she had his attention. Not a flicker. His gaze dropped back to the Moaning Diamond. It was as if the gem were speaking to him, distracting him from more normal concerns and cares.

"Hurry up," Ivy said, pressing Archlis to make his decision—there was a creaking sound coming from the corridor behind them. "Those golden doors behind us won't hold the water out forever. We need to get out of here before the river breaks into this room."

"The river is no problem." Archlis sneered. "Not while I hold this treasure." He fondled the Moaning Diamond in his hands.

"It's pretty," said Ivy. What was the matter with the man? He was like a child with a new toy, aware of nothing else. She wanted to wave both of her hands in front of his eyes to determine if he could see anything besides that stupid diamond. Fighting to keep control, she said, "But there are bigger ones lying all around here."

"Those are just gems. This artifact toppled the walls of Tsurlagol. Even muffled in that stone box, it called the other gems out of the depths of the earth."

"Knew this stuff didn't come here naturally," muttered the dwarf behind Ivy.

"Now I can use its power to unearth all the hidden treasures of the world!" Archlis started forward, hurrying, paying little attention to where he stepped. His feet caused a small avalanche of gems, and he stumbled and shot out an arm. To Ivy's regret, he managed to stay upright. She started to reach a hand toward his Ankh, but Mumchance whispered a warning behind her. Archlis had recovered his balance and was glaring at them, the fingers of one hand white around the Ankh's handle. Ivy did not dare to set him off; they had nothing to protect them from his fire spells. With an oath, Archlis strode past her, kicking at the rolling gems.

"Watch what the Moaning Diamond can do!" Archlis raised the Moaning Diamond in one hand, holding it high above his head. The magelord began to cry out the words of some spell, using the same grating language that he had used with his charms earlier. The ululations from the gem grew louder with each of his shouts.

On the edge of her vision, Ivy saw the wall changing. Without turning her head away from Archlis, she slid her eyes to the side to better see what was happening. A part of the wall at one end of the room began to melt away. It did not crumble with roaring dust clouds, as had the stone chamber walls when the destrachans had attacked them. Instead, the material of the wall seemed to evaporate, as though it were no firmer than mist. Within the widening opening she saw a hidden staircase spiraling upwards.

The smell of clean air was immediately evident to the keener noses in the group.

"It is headed outside," whispered Zuzzara to Ivy.

"What is?" Ivy hissed.

"The diamond. It wants out," Zuzzara answered. "Look! It has found a way out. That staircase leads outside."

"Fresh air," explained Gunderal.

"Even I smell that," her sister elaborated.

With a sweep of his arm, Archlis motioned them all forward to the staircase. His head still bent down to stare into the depths of the Moaning Diamond. The Siegebreakers looked at each other, their eyebrows rising in question. Ivy shrugged and then gave a slight nod. The group silently began the climb upward to daylight. Archlis came behind them, the Moaning Diamond gripped in one hand and the Ankh in the other.

"I thought we were deeper in the tunnels," Zuzzara whispered.

"Wrong again," Gunderal murmured as she drifted ahead of her large half-sister. "I could tell that we were near the surface."

"So what do you smell now?" Zuzzara asked.

With a quick glance over her shoulder, Gunderal whispered, "Trouble, bloodshed, full-scale, all-out warfare."

"Oh good. All stuff we can handle."

Ivy reached out a hand and touched Kid's shoulder. She

leaned close to his ear to say softly, "Whatever happens, stay on the far side of me, away from Archlis."

"I can take care of myself, my dear."

To Mumchance, climbing the stairs in front of her, she said, "Get your eye ready." She saw the back of his head nod.

And as she passed Sanval, still held between the two bugbears, she whispered, "Stay alert."

His lips stiff, his face expressionless, he whispered back, "I am always alert."

CHAPTER TWENTY-TWO

The stairway twisted up, one endless turn after another. They climbed and climbed and continued climbing. The air was no better here, still close and musty; the one whiff of clean air had dissolved into dust. Ivy had hoped for a fresh breeze to indicate that they neared the surface and an escape from the ruins of old Tsurlagol.

"I guess we were deeper than I thought," said Gunderal.

"Or we're going higher than we should," said Mumchance. "We should be level with the city streets by now."

"Or our knees are so tired we think we've climbed more steps than we have," Zuzzara muttered.

"Quiet!" whispered Archlis behind them. He was still leaning over the Moaning Diamond in his hands as if the gem were speaking to him in some occult tongue.

"Look how the stone of the stairs has changed," observed the dwarf, ignoring the magelord's command. "Ivy, I think we are inside the city walls."

"How can we be in the walls?" Ivy asked.

"Don't know. But the stair is forming inside the wall. Look. It's the same stone as the outside of the southwest corner. The stuff we surveyed earlier." Mumchance trailed his hand over the stone as they passed. Cracks ran up the walls surrounding the staircase. "It's being shifted from the inside by Archlis. This was all filled with rubble or mortared closed, and he's forcing it open—changing the stones of the wall to make the stair. And I don't think the wall wants to be opened here." The stones of the stair creaked and groaned around them.

"So what does that mean?" Ivy was not sure that she wanted the answer.

"Lots of stress on the stone. Stress on stones is good if you want to break a wall." Mumchance was talking very softly, almost speaking to himself. Wiggles ran up the stair ahead of him, but the little dog was uncharacteristically silent. Not a yap or yip or whine.

Ivy stared at the stocky dwarf climbing in front of her. "Not so good if you happen to be inside the breaking wall."

Mumchance squinted over his shoulder at her. His one good eye looked very worried. "I was thinking the same thing."

Ahead of them, Zuzzara gave a surprised grunt. Ivy peered past Mumchance's shoulders to see the dazzle of daylight silhouetting the half-orc's head.

"Hey, we are going outside." Even with a crazed magelord, the Moaning Diamond, and a couple of bugbears behind her, Ivy could not help feeling pleased by the sight of sun shining ahead of her.

"Ivy," Zuzzara said sounding unusually worried. Her large frame blocked the exit, a hole in the wall where the stairs ended. It was neither doorway nor arch, but rather a jagged entrance that looked as though some force of magic had blasted away a section of the rock. Zuzzara spread her large hands on either side of the hole and leaned forward. "I don't think we want to be here."

"Oh dear," said Gunderal, peering around her big sister. "I think she's right."

The press of Siegebreakers pushed behind them, and one of the bugbears hissed out an inquiry, starting to lower his glaive to prod the reluctant half-orc in the back. Sanval stumbled against him and knocked the glaive's blade into the wall with a harsh scraping sound. Zuzzara looked back over her shoulder at them, and her brows drew together in distress, unwillingness clear in her expression. Then she shrugged and stepped through the hole, and Gunderal followed her large sister out into the open. Ivy popped through the hole in the wall to sidestep around Gunderal and Zuzzara, swinging by them on her long legs so that she stood in front of them. If there was an enemy here, she preferred to be in the lead.

Ivy found herself standing on the top of one of Tsurlagol's city walls, a flat pathway of stone built to be used by patrolling guards. The view of the fields beyond the wall was magnificent—clear sky, brilliant sunlight, and fresh air best of all. She could see the line and cornering of the wall, the tumble of city buildings on one side, and the slope of hill on the other, falling away to the patchwork of fields trampled into dust by the summer-long siege. If she squinted, she could even make out the dark outline of the forest that the Thultyrl had wanted to use to shield his troops before their charge of the western wall.

But far closer than the forest were the other troops who occupied the besieged Tsurlagol. Ivy found herself sharing the top of the city wall with a full complement of orcs and hobgoblins, all looking quite stunned to see her and the other Siegebreakers suddenly pop out of a magically appearing hole in their fortifications.

Ivy never could decide which she disliked fighting the most, hobgoblins or orcs. Today she thought the orcs were the bigger problem. The hobgoblins were larger, better equipped, and smarter, but there were only four of them.

On the other hand, there were a lot of orcs on the wall. Short, ugly creatures covered with tufts of stiff black hair, their little red eyes glittered in their mottled gray faces, and sharp tusks protruded from their lower gums. And there were taller ones too—mountain orcs by the look of them, with big pig snouts and even redder, madder eyes than their gray kin. Fottergrim's troops wore armor that was a hodgepodge of stolen bits, which Ivy could not fault as her own gear fell into that category. But at least she cleaned off the dried blood and rust whenever she could. They wore the blood and rust proudly, and added bright orange and purple rags of clothing. They moved in a crouched stance, and those who lacked helmets blinked rapidly, reminding her that bright light bothered the eyes of most orcs. It was one of those facts that might never be useful but was worth noting. In battle, who knew what information was or wasn't useful? She didn't underestimate the orcs. They might not be the smartest fighters, but these orcs carried enormous weapons, and all she had was one empty scabbard.

Both type of orcs were snarling at each other. But none snarled at the four hobgoblins forming an honor guard around the big orc commander who barreled through them. That puzzled Ivy. Hobgoblin mercenaries usually controlled orcs, not the other way around, but here the hobgoblins pushed back the smaller orcs to allow this one large orc to march toward them.

Ivy expected them to rush her. She planted her feet in a wide stance, her arms spread in front of her company so that the line building behind her on the walkway was less visible. Let them think she led an army that snaked down the steps and would emerge in great numbers—at least until she could determine their strength.

"What is this? What is *this!*" An enormous orc was pushing to the front of the troops, shoving past his hobgoblin guards.

"What are you doing here?" the orc continued. His high forehead slanted beneath his helmet, and his face seemed all big pig snout and enormous jaw. He was almost as tall as the mountain breed but with clearer silver skin. Wiry tufts of chestnut hair sprouted between his lupine ears. Ivy wondered what type of orcs his parents had been—the clever kind or the stupid kind? Because as all the gods knew, there were both in the breed, as Zuzzara always said. Ivy rather hoped that this orc descended from an exceptionally stupid and slow family, because all she had at the moment was a fast tongue and a heart full of regret for her lost sword and missing dagger.

Ivy drew herself to her full height, then cheated a little, rising up on her toes so that her eye level was as close to his as possible. With her fists jammed into her waist, she turned her body slightly to the side so that he could not immediately see that she had lost her sword. She jutted her chin forward and challenged the big leader confronting her as belligerently as she could. "Looking for Fottergrim, sir! Have an important mission! Need to go past immediately, sir!" She barked out her sentences in a fine loud herald's voice, hoping the troops would part and let the Siegebreakers advance to wherever Fottergrim was encamped in Tsurlagol. With good luck, Fottergrim's headquarters would be a long, long walk from their present location—a long enough walk to allow them time to ambush Archlis, disarm two bugbears, and make a dash for freedom.

It was, Ivy would have been the first to admit, a fairly shaky plan, but maybe with enough shouting she could bully her way past this big and hopefully stupid orc. What she was going to do about being on the completely wrong side of the besieged city's walls—well, she would figure that out later, gods willing. Right now, she just needed to get past the troops all goggling at her like she had said something extraordinarily surprising.

"Need to report to Fottergrim, sir!" Ivy repeated. "Immediately, sir! Let us pass!"

The silver orc stared at her in bewilderment. "I am Fottergrim! What is this?"

"Oh dear," whispered Gunderal behind Ivy.

Ivy did not even blink. "Reporting for duty, sir. Glad to find you so quickly. New troops. Returning your magelord as you commanded."

"What!"

Ivy reached behind her and grabbed the magelord as he emerged into the sunlight and blinked. Her strong fingers balled the front of his robe into a knot that just happened to pull the cloth tight around his neck. Archlis sputtered, caught off balance and unable to catch his breath. If he had not kept such a desperate hold on his Ankh with one hand and the Moaning Diamond with the other, he might have been more difficult to handle. Grabbing his shoulder with her other hand, Ivy swung him in front of herself. She pushed him, hard, at Fottergrim. "Here's Archlis, sir. Just where you wanted him!"

Upon seeing Archlis, Fottergrim let out a bellow of rage. His boarlike tusks curved from his lower gums over the outer corners of his upper lip. "Traitor! Where have you been?"

Osteroric, seeing the supreme commander of the orcs confronting his master, gave a surprised squeak, sounding like a terrified mouse. The bugbear dropped his hold on Sanval and grabbed his brother, whispering something in Norimgic's ear. The two started backing away from Archlis.

"I bring you victory!" yelled the magelord, holding up the Moaning Diamond.

"Some little gem! You abandoned me for that! Look, look! We are under attack!" Fottergrim pointed to the fields clearly visible from the wall. The silk banners of the Thultyrl's army snapped in the breeze, and the beat of the cavalry drums could be heard on the wind. With a howl of rage, Fottergrim slapped Archlis, sending the Moaning Diamond rolling out of his hand, and screamed, "Use your magic. Set them on fire! Or I'll toss you down on the first man to reach the wall."

With a howl almost as loud as Fottergrim's, Archlis dived after his Moaning Diamond, snatched it up, and safely stowed it in his shirt. "You stupid orc!" he cried. "I almost lost it! Fire, fire, fire . . . Do you think that is all that I am capable of! Well, enjoy my talent!" He raised the Ankh and shouted a word of command. The bouncing sphere of fire that he had used so effectively against the hobgoblins suddenly appeared, spinning toward Fottergrim. The orc obviously knew the trick, because he picked up one of his lieutenants and used the frightened orc to knock the sphere over the edge of the wall. Tossing away his cringing minion, Fottergrim charged at Archlis with a great shout of rage. He grappled with the magelord, trying to tear the Ankh from his grasp.

Seeing Archlis and Fottergrim locked in each other's grasp, Ivy spun on her heel and ordered the Siegebreakers to run. As she passed Sanval, standing alone and free of the bugbear's clutches, she shouted, "Pick up your feet, man!"

She led them at full speed toward a round tower that anchored one end of the wall. Such towers usually had stairs leading to the guards' rooms and, with a little luck, a door to the outside.

"Come on," Ivy called. "We'll take this way out!"

She skittered to a halt. Out of the tower's doorway boiled fresh troops—big mean orcs with enormous double-bladed swords and huge warhammers. The orcs drove a troop of orange goblins before them. They were small, quick creatures, half the height of a human. Their bodies were twisted and gnarled, their limbs thin and powerful, and their fingers taloned. Their small faces were all features: wide mouths, huge slanted eyes, and wide flat noses. Large pointed ears grew up through their stiff tufts of hair. The goblins' armor was little more than torn bits of leather strapped together.

Ivy knew better than to underestimate these fighters who stood only waist high. They were small, yes, but cunning, and as pesky as wasps. Most were carrying modified goblin sticks, nicely sharpened to poke into any soft spot presented to them. A few were whirling rawhide whips to pull down their opponents and make it easier for the small fighters to overrun them. Or perhaps they just meant to use those long lariats on anyone storming over the walls. Such tactics often proved most effective in toppling siege ladders. However, once the orange goblins spotted Ivy and the Siegebreakers, they burst into squeals of their own language. Behind them the orcs screamed, urging the little fiends to fight.

"Oh blast," said Ivy, frantically waving behind her back at the others to retreat.

"Hey, lads, look what we found." Mumchance shifted in front of Ivy and called out to the orcs who led the charge. From both his hands dripped diamonds, rubies, emeralds, and other jewels that he had picked up in the crypt below. A few gems slipped between his blunt fingers and rattled on the stones. The orcs stared at the treasure in the same way that they would eye fresh meat. Beneath the overhang of their helmets, their little pig eyes blinked against the sparkling light of the jewels in the sun, and their mouths widened into ugly grins.

The orange goblins hung back, darting glances at Mumchance, at the gems, and at the orcs. Obviously, they would love to grab the riches, but they knew that the bigger orcs would quickly overrun them and snatch any treasure away. Fear of their masters warred with greed, and they set up a series of grunting cries, obviously arguing within their own group.

"A reward for Fottergrim's loyal troops," roared the dwarf, throwing the jewels at the feet of the largest orcs. Some even dropped their weapons to free their hands and extended their claws.

As the orcs grabbed for the jewels, Mumchance shouted the word that ignited the gem bomb that he had concealed among the hoard. It exploded, shooting out sparks and force. The orcs squealed and screamed, blown off their feet. They stumbled into each other, knocking a few off the wall. Their weapons and armor clattered as they crashed onto the walkway and tried to grab at any ledge and at each other. Those who managed to stay on the wall scrambled to their feet, howling their fury and snatching up their weapons.

Sparks flamed overhead. The orcs stopped, looked up, and bellowed. The explosion had set the wooden roof above the walkway on fire. The orcs turned and raced away, knocking each other over. Behind them, a group of hobgoblins coming out of the tower automatically raised their shields, and the orcs rushed into them, catching their outflung arms on the spikes. Blood and curses flew.

The small goblins leaped to the edge of the walkway, then pulled themselves up easily onto the roof. With one last *phhtt* of outstretched tongues at their former masters, the goblins dashed through the sparks, cutting back and forth, until they reached the stone corner tower. Silently they dropped down to the far walkway beyond the flames and fighting.

"I am going to miss that eye," Mumchance declared, rubbing his empty eyesocket with his fist.

"Best time to use it. Could not have done it better," Ivy congratulated him, slapping him on the back. "Buy you another one out of the Thultyrl's payment!" Looking at the pile up of orcs and hobgoblins fighting in the doorway of the watchtower, Ivy swung around.

"Back, back," she yelled at the group.

Once again, going full speed, she passed Sanval, who looked slightly confused but was doggedly guarding the rear of their group. He spun around to follow her, now becoming the frontguard instead of the rearguard.

"Ivy, the roof is on fire!" Gunderal screamed a warning. Ivy looked up. The fire was keeping pace with them. The crude wooden roof was built to shelter archers from stones flung by siege engines. The wood had dried out under the hot summer sun and now burned beautifully. Big roof timbers were starting to sag, and the smaller boards were burning right through and dropping down on the walkway, with an occasional thud as the wood hit the helmet of some hobgoblin or orc below.

"That's the problem with crude holdings like this," Mumchance observed as he trotted at Ivy's side. He sidestepped to the left to avoid a couple of embers dropping from above. "Too easy to set on fire. A couple of well-placed flame arrows, or a nice little gem bomb, and, *whoosh*, your defenses go up in smoke."

"Let's discuss defensive strategy later," suggested Ivy. "Gunderal, can you put it out?"

The little wizard scanned the skies above them. A lone white cloud floated harmlessly overhead. "It won't be much," Gunderal said, "but I think I can wring a short burst of rain out of it."

"Well, do it, Sister, do it!" said Zuzzara, dodging a falling beam and leaping over the body of a stunned orc trapped beneath it.

Gunderal concentrated, giving out a series of complicated commands that almost sounded like bird calls. The cloud turned from white to black. There was a rumble of thunder somewhere far overhead.

"Nothing fancy, no lighting," yelled Mumchance. "This roof won't protect us."

Gunderal nodded, and the cadence of her call changed. It began to rain. Heavy drops sizzled on the burning roof and formed enormous puddles on the walkway. Ivy watched with satisfaction as one of the orcs charging them with raised sword and spiked shield stepped in the water, slipped, skidded on the wet stones, and bounced over the edge of the wall. The creature tumbled into space, its weapons flying. Its mouth opened with a furious howl, then it disappeared into silence far below them.

The rain slowed to a dull pattering and then stopped. The roof smoldered above them, letting off damp puffs of black smoke.

"We won't be barbecued today," Ivy said.

"That's it," said Gunderal as the last drop fell gently on her blue-black curls. "And that is my last spell of the day. I need to rest before I can do any more." She paled and swayed.

"It's enough, little sister. It's more than enough," said Zuzzara as she hugged Gunderal, almost lifting her off her feet. Ivy eyed the smoke-smudged Siegebreakers. Sanval was fighting in shirt sleeves, but at least he had a sword, and it had already been bloodied on the wall. Zuzzara still had her shovel—it was a bit dented, but that iron was hard. Kid had grabbed a discarded goblin stick, and he had a wicked gleam in his eye. Mumchance was best protected—his sturdy summer armor had survived their day underground basically intact. For once he had remembered to draw his short sword instead of his hammer.

"You and you, flank me," said Ivy, pointing at Kid and Sanval. "Mumchance, stay with the sisters and keep anything you can off their backs."

"What are we going to do?" asked the dwarf, dropping back to the rear as she had commanded.

"Hit them hard," shouted Ivy as she picked up speed again.

Sanval and Kid kept a nice half stride behind her; they formed a perfect flying wedge heading toward the battling Archlis and Fottergrim.

"Hit them low," screamed Ivy, not bothering to look back over her shoulder. The Siegebreakers were tight on her heels, and she could hear thuds and screams as they overran any leftover orcs still littering the walkway. She raced along the top of the wall—head down, braid swinging, fists tight, forehead lined, and eyes narrowed—as she tried to turn herself into an one-woman battering ram. Nothing like flying into a fight with an empty scabbard, she thought.

Ivy barreled into the magelord and the orc, breaking the two apart. A joyously barking Wiggles dashed through her feet. Ivy teetered. Sanval grabbed her waist and steadied her upright as he twisted her out of danger and skewered one of Fottergrim's startled hobgoblin bodyguards. Ivy leaned around him and caught an answering slash of a sword on her forearm armor.

"Thank you," said Sanval, following her earlier advice and dropping low to slash at the knees of another bodyguard who was trying to scramble out of their way.

"It was nothing," panted Ivy, hoping that the blow had only bruised her arm and not broken anything. "Where did the dog go?"

Ahead of them, Wiggles zigzagged around a raging Fottergrim, heading straight for Archlis. The little white dog bit the magelord, hard, and her sharp white teeth cut through his suede boots. Like the dread before him, the magelord had obviously not placed a protection against small white dogs among his many clanking, clinking charms. Archlis screamed and tried to hop away, clinging to the Moaning Diamond, then doubled over to slap at the dog with his other hand. The edge of the Ankh hit the rock wall, and he lost his hold on it and dropped it. Wiggles dashed off, scampering toward Mumchance. Fottergrim picked up the magelord's Ankh and retreated up the walkway. The big orc shook it as if he expected it to launch a fireball directly at Archlis. Nothing happened, much to his surprise.

"You fool," screamed Archlis. "I could have made you a king!"

"Traitor! Human!" the orc screamed insults back at him.

With another cry of rage, Archlis glared at Fottergrim, raised his hand, and twisted a rusted iron ring on his finger. The bony magelord transformed into an enormous hairy demon, so unlike his narrow-shouldered, skeletal self that for the blink of a moment, no one understood what had happened. Then they all stopped whatever they were doing and stared. The transformed Archlis was so huge that his furry shoulders and giant boar-tusked head broke through the charred, soggy wooden roof above him. Bits of timber rained down on both sides of the wall. Orcs unfortunate enough to be standing near Archlis were pushed over the edge of the wall by his sheer bulk.

"What is it?" Ivy asked, staring up at monster.

"Huge and ugly," Zuzzara called. It was certainly that—a beast three times the height of the magelord, covered in fat, muscle and scruffy fur, with taloned fingers that hung on apelike arms, and hands that almost touched the ground. Its ears were wide and notched, its face a scrunched up horror, its body an expanded grotesque imitation of an ape. On its shoulders were black feathery wings, completely out of proportion, appearing much too small to lift that enormous weight.

Kid called softly, "It is a nalfeshnee, my dear, a demon from the Abyss."

"Thanks for the lesson," said Ivy. "How do we kill it?"

"We may not have to, my dear," said Kid, pulling her back

from the crumbling edge of the wall. "Wait and watch."

"Hey, sister, why don't you have a ring like that?" shouted Zuzzara over the screams of crushed orcs, caught between the nalfeshnee's bulk and the stone walkway.

"And turn myself into something that hideous? Never!" yelled Gunderal.

Ivy stuck out her foot and tripped up a fleeing hobgoblin who tried to dash past her. It threw out its arms to maintain its balance, and its halberd—with its axelike head and long handle—cartwheeled into the air. Stretching out a long arm, Ivy caught the halberd, then spun away and let the hobgoblin rush past. The hobgoblin paused for half a step, glanced back at the giant demon, shook his shield at Ivy, but continued running.

"Look at the magelord," crowed Kid. "He went too large. The nalfeshnee cannot fight on top of this wobbling wall."

"Kid is right," Mumchance shouted. "Look at that wall. It is cracking."

Bits of the stone crenellations snapped off as Archlis tried to steady himself. The sheer size of his backside, in the beast's form, forced the stones off the wall, following the roof timbers and squashed bodies to the ground below.

"We need to get out of here now," commanded Ivy.

Sanval thrust with his sword at an attacking orc. With one swift move, he skewered the creature. It doubled up, its weapons flying out of its hands. Sanval pivoted, the orc still caught on his blade's point. When he twisted his wrists to free the blade, he managed to fling the orc off the wall. While he wiped the blade clean on a fallen orc, he said, "I knew following you would get us out of the ruins. I know you will find a way out now."

"Thanks," shouted Ivy, touched by his confidence in her abilities. She ducked under the blow of another pig-snouted fighter, using her stolen halberd to ram the surprised orc between the legs and send it sprawling. Stepping hard on the orc's stomach once it was prone, she retrieved the halberd and jumped to Sanval's side. "All part of the job, rescuing our friends!"

"I thought you did not believe in heroics." Sanval slicked his tumbled curls out of his eyes as he skewered another orc one-handed.

"I lied," Ivy admitted. "Heroics are fine." She grinned at Sanval as she reached around him to smack the backside of a startled archer who had wandered into this section of the wall seeking his friends. The barbarian fled with a yell for reinforcements.

"Watch out!" Sanval dived past Ivy, ramming another screaming orc over the wall before the trooper could brain Gunderal with his warhammer. The pretty wizard gave Sanval a sparkling smile as she ducked around her big sister to help trip up two orcs attacking Zuzzara.

Swinging his blade at another orc, Sanval sliced it below the knees. The creature lost its balance and toppled into space. Sanval and Ivy pivoted around each other to strike more attacking orcs.

"Ask me what mercenaries and red-roof girls have in common," she said, reaching past him with her stolen halberd to crack an orc across the side of his head.

"Nothing at all," Sanval exclaimed, glancing at her with a most peculiar smile that lit up his dark eyes. He jabbed away at an oncoming hobgoblin.

"Do too," she laughed. "Both always figuring out every move. Both more fun than an entire room full of proper Procampur ladies. Don't for a moment think that I did not have a plan in my back pocket for everything that happened in the ruins."

"There goes Archlis," Zuzzara said, pointing with her shovel. She gave a formidable whack on the top of the head to a poor little goblin sneaking around them, obviously a stray still seeking an escape route off the creaking, groaning wall. Fottergrim had retreated even farther back, so he stood in the doorway of the farthest watchtower, screaming some type of order over his shoulders.

"Look! He really can fly!" said Gunderal.

Incredibly for a creature of its bulk, the tiny wings lifted the demon Archlis off the wall. His feet hung no more than a half a man's height above the surface. As he lifted off the wall, Norimgic and Osteroric took one look at the orcs bearing down on them and then leaped after Archlis, each grabbing a long arm. Archlis gave a roar and shook his hands, but the screaming bugbears held tight. Bobbing and weaving, Archlis began a ponderous flight off the wall. The bugbears dangled off his arms, both paddling their big flat feet like swimmers, as though hoping to keep themselves afloat.

"It would appear that flight is a good choice, with perhaps a touch of magic?" Kid tugged at her waist, and Ivy realized that rather than pulling her out of the way, he was trying to get her attention by dragging the red magic belt out from where it was tucked down behind her weapons belt.

"That's a good idea," observed Ivy, thrusting the halberd's tip through the breastplate of an orc. She bent her knee and pressed the sole of her boot against the orc's armor to pull the halberd free from the dead creature. With a grunt, she stated, "Let's follow him down."

"I am pleased that Osteroric escaped," said Sanval, close on her heels as she headed for the edge. "He and his brother were rather civilized for bugbears."

"And their pockets are still stuffed with jewels, which is more than what we got," mourned Mumchance.

"We'll just add it to the Thultyrl's invoice," declared Ivy. "Come on, we need to get out of here."

Ivy jumped up on the edge of the wall. Looking straight down, she had a clear view of the ground, a long, long way below her. Piles of dead orcs with twisted limbs and shattered heads and bodies testified to the height. Ivy stood on the ledge, teetered forward, then stepped back and beckoned her crew. "Grab my belt!" she yelled.

"I don't understand," Sanval began.

"Trust me," she said, looking down at Sanval. Despite all the dust and rust and assorted grime that they had picked up that day, his upturned face just shone with honesty, bravery, and all those other fine Procampur qualities. The man did not need highly polished armor to dazzle her. Sanval smiled up at her.

"Ivy!" Zuzzara and Mumchance and Kid shouted together, with Kid adding a gentle, "My dear."

Startled, she swung around to look at them, then completed the turn to look in the direction they all pointed.

Archlis as the demon Nalfeshnee beat his wings frantically, trying to distance himself from the battlements. But he was sinking. The huge creature looked like some six-legged, three-headed bat that could not fly very well. The bugbears, dangling from the giant monster's arms, their legs churning, weren't helping. Tossing their considerable weight in their terror, and swinging their weapons and occasionally pricking the demon's hairy body, they howled and screamed and blubbered. The bugbear brothers had been brave fighters when grounded, but flying was not something any bugbear ever yearned to do.

"We need to get out of here!" Mumchance had finally caught Wiggles. Tucking the little dog firmly into his pocket, the dwarf nimbly avoided one of the falling orcs who had just been brained by Zuzzara's wildly swinging shovel.

"Got a plan!" screamed Ivy. "Everyone to me! To me!"

"Coming, my dear," said Kid, as he leaped up and drummed another orc on its snout with his sharp hooves. The creature let out a howl and clapped both hairy hands over its injured proboscis.

"What are you going to do?" Sanval asked, backhanding an orc trying to detain him as he climbed up on the edge of the wall next to her. Ivy was holding herself steady by wrapping one arm around a wooden pillar supporting the burned-out roof.

"Grab my belt!" Ivy screamed at him over the noise of the fight behind them. There was such confusion that Fottergrim's gray orcs and mountain orcs were busy trying to brain each other—each group was convinced that the others had started the fight that now engulfed the top of the wall. The battered Fottergrim was howling orders at all of them, but nobody could hear him over the general hubbub. The hobgoblins who had come late to the fight, following the orange goblins into the fray, jabbed with their spiked shields. The orcs crouched below them, red eyes gleaming, and thrashed their halberds like scythes. The hobgoblins shouted to each other, closing ranks, occasionally saving each other with a sword thrust, and occasionally overreaching and stabbing one of their own kind.

"My belt!" Ivy yelled at Sanval. All the other Siegebreakers had figured it out, but he had not been there for the fight with the destrachans. She could feel Zuzzara's big hand firmly anchored in her weapons belt. The big half-orc had snatched up her little sister and tucked Gunderal under her other arm. Mumchance and Kid each had their hands locked on her legs. Ivy let go of the wooden post and grabbed the silver buckle of the narrow red belt that she wore loosely below her heavy weapons belt. "Pull the wings open three times and then shut," she whispered to herself as her fingers caught the small silver wings. She twisted them and prayed to whatever gods might be listening that the belt's magic would hold them all up. It had worked well underground, lifting her out of the reach of the destrachans, but she had been the only weight to lift. Now there was a lot more weight hanging off her, and she prayed that her weapons belt would hold and that her pants would stay up. That would be all that she needed—to plunge to her death baring her ass to the fighting orcs and screaming hobgoblins behind her. Then again, it wasn't that bad of a final fate, she decided. It would be a way to leave the world with a certain ragged style.

Either way, Ivy just had to trust that her luck (and her belt) would hold.

"Jump!" she screamed at Sanval as she snagged his collar with her free hand and pulled him off balance. His booted feet shot out and up, his arms flew up, his fist tightened around his sword hilt, and his dark curls blew every which way.

Ivy plunged off the wall.

Chapter Twenty-Three

The belt's magic was strained, but not broken. Rather than shooting toward the sky, they dropped, jerked level, and then started to gently descend to the ground.

Sanval hung straight down from his collar, where Ivy held him in a tight grip, his body rigid, his arms and legs pointing hopefully toward the earth, his face a frozen blank. He made a slight choking sound, and Ivy tried to shift her grip so she would not strangle him before they hit the ground.

Zuzzara had let out a single huge bellow when they leaped off the wall. Ivy looked down at the half-orc, dangling from her white-knuckled grip on Ivy's heavy weapons belt. Beads of perspiration popped out on the half-orc's forehead. Zuzzara was as pale as Ivy had ever seen her. Suspended with Zuzzara's arm around her waist, Gunderal looked like some pretty bird, her body perpendicular to the ground, her arms stretched out like wings, her hair and skirts fluttering around her. She seemed to be shaking with soft laughter.

Ivy looked past them to the two hanging on her legs. Mumchance was staring at the ground, or was that his good eye that he had squeezed closed? Wiggles was a lump in his pocket, not even an ear sticking up over the edge. Kid clung to her other leg, and it did not surprise Ivy to see him look up at her, wink, then grin at the floating Gunderal.

They sank slowly, spiraling down in an odd zigzag pattern, and then they all hit the ground in a tumble of legs and arms.

"Oooh," Gunderal moaned, flattened beneath her big sister.

"Sorry," Zuzzara said, rolling off her onto all fours. She pushed herself upright and pulled her little sister into a standing position.

"It's all right," said Gunderal. She smoothed down the front of her skirt and ran her fingers through her hair, pushing it back from her face. Her blue-black curls fluffed obediently into perfect ringlets, with highlighted streaks of blue and aquamarine framing her pearly features. "Good fighting up there, big sister."

Zuzzara shrugged. "It's what I do best!" Imitating Gunderal, she straightened her waistcoat and shook her head so that her many braids swung out, the iron beads clattered, and the braids fell neatly into place. She smiled weakly and wiped the perspiration from her face with her hand. "Give me a hundred hobgoblins every day, as long as I never have to fly."

"No, it was wonderful," Gunderal said with a little laugh. "I must get a new spellbook—one with flying spells in it."

"How could you like that? You are water genasi, not air genasi!" said a surprised Zuzzara.

"Oh, you remember daddy. He always leaped before he looked. I must have inherited a love of flying from him," replied the little sister.

"Shut up and grab me!" Ivy shouted, as everyone released his or her hold. What was the stupid spell to make the belt stop, she wondered, as she once more began to drift skyward.

"Twist twice to the right and then open it, my dear," Kid called, grabbing at her leg as she started to float up. A heavy, solid, most welcome weight of steady Procampur hands fell on her shoulders, pushing her back down until her feet touched ground. Ivy glanced around quickly while her fingers worked at the belt buckle.

Mumchance had been right about their location. They had landed at the southwest juncture of Tsurlagol's walls—the very point that the Siegebreakers had originally identified as a weak spot. Above them Fottergrim was screaming at a bunch of barbarian archers, driving them into place along the shattered edge of the wall. Across a field were Procampur's forces, obviously readying themselves for a charge against the same wall.

"I know it hasn't been two days," grumbled Ivy as she twisted the clasp of the belt. "Twice to the right, then open. Twice to the right, then open. Ah, blast. If I wanted to be a bird, I would have grown wings."

Only Sanval's strong grip on her shoulder and Kid's firm clasp on her thigh were keeping her on the ground. The stupid belt was tugging her toward the sky again. She fumbled the buckle and wondered exactly how high she would go without a ceiling to stop her, if their grip slipped.

"Breathe," whispered Sanval in her ear. "You have won. You have saved us all. Do not panic now."

She rather suspected he used the same murmuring voice to calm his horses, but it worked. Her heart rate slowed, her own hands stopped fumbling at the clasp. She grasped the belt buckle ornament firmly, her fingers tightening on the little silver wings of the serpent, and the ancient metal crumbled under her hand. The narrow red belt slipped from around her waist and shot up into the clouds with a little whistling noise, rather like a child's jeer at adult authority.

The barbarian archers on the wall saw it, their heads turning and tilting back in unison to track the red whip of belt. They all knelt to a firing position, one knee down, and lifted their crossbows. Their arms snapped back to grab bolts from the quivers strapped between their shoulder blades, and with the speed of a blink, they filled the sky with bolts. Perhaps they thought the belt was some wily mercenary trick, meant to magically bring down the wall. The archers followed the belt's path with flying bolts until it rose beyond their reach and disappeared into the sky.

"Good riddance," panted Ivy, who could feel a whole new set of bruises around her waist where the pull of the belt had crushed her chain mail against her. The cavalry across the field was obviously getting into formation. Banners were raised, snapping in the wind. She could hear the faint echoes of the big war drums being pounded, so the various leaders of the horse-mounted troops would know their position. "What is Enguerrand trying to do? He can't be charging the gate on this side. That won't work. I told him that wouldn't work."

She glared at Sanval, as though expecting an explanation. He stared at the Procampur cavalry through narrowed eyes. "I do not think that he has an extra plan in his back pocket," worried Sanval.

"Look," Kid whispered, and Ivy felt his hand brush her elbow. Turning to see where Kid pointed, she saw the giant Nalfeshnee do a crash landing, its wings beating. It rolled in a furry tumble with the two bugbears.

"Any moment now, my dear," Kid added.

While they watched, the giant demon disappeared. There was no puff of smoke, no shooting sparks, just all at once gone.

"What happened?" Ivy asked.

"Very short term spell, my dear," Kid said. "Another few moments and he would have changed while still in the air."

"Let me guess. Another artifact that he stole from Toram."

"Oh yes," said Kid. "I rather hoped that he would crash."

"But we all would have missed him so much. He kept our day so exciting," Ivy said, looking at the magelord running around the field, gathering up his fallen belongings. "All right, come on. We'd better see what he's up to."

Back in his human form—a tall bony creature with dirty yellow hair sticking to his neck, his robes torn and pulled askew—the magelord strode toward the wall, then stood a short distance away from it. He hunched his shoulders, and Ivy could see him raise his arms, hands together. The high-pitched crying began again.

"Thought we'd heard the last of that," Zuzzara complained.

"You wish," her sister said.

The Moaning Diamond cradled in Archlis's hands increased its eerie noise. It attracted the attention of Fottergrim's archers on the wall above them. A multitude of faces turned from scanning the skies after the belt's surprising flight to searching the ground below. They lowered their bows and held their hands above their eyes to shade them as they looked down and tried to locate the source of the sound.

A cry of "Archlis! Archlis!" went up. It was not a happy sound, more like the scream of a cage full of enraged tigers. A bloody and bruised Fottergrim could clearly be seen peering down.

"Traitor," screamed Fottergrim, waving the Ankh in impotent fury at Archlis. The orc commander obviously did not know how to use it, or there would have been nothing but black ash in front of the walls of Tsurlagol. "Kill the traitor!"

Archlis appeared to have completely forgotten the Siegebreakers. A tall disheveled figure, the narrow features of his face hard with concentration, his blue eyes blazing, his whole attention was focused now on Fottergrim. He raised the Moaning Diamond in his hand as though it were an offering to a god and began screaming out the activation spell.

Ivy commanded her group: "Run!"

They all stared at her for a moment, then she saw understanding widen their eyes as they remembered the disappearing wall in the tunnel—no warning, no fading, just gone.

Ivy grabbed Sanval's hand and pulled him after her. Mumchance dropped Wiggles out of his pocket. "Run, run!" he cried, stretching his own short legs as he followed her. Cracks opened up in the ground, but the little dog swerved and swerved again, each time avoiding places where the ground was collapsing.

Ivy cursed when she saw Kid dart away toward Archlis, but she could not turn back to grab him. If she stopped, all of the Siegebreakers would stop. She opened her mouth to shout his name, then thought better of it. Either he knew what he was doing, or he didn't, but she had to trust that he did not want to be noticed by Archlis, and screaming at him wouldn't help.

Sanval started to go after Kid. She tightened her grip on his hand and tugged. He could have twisted loose but didn't.

"You know what you're doing," Sanval said.

"He's the fastest," she yelled and kept running. "He can catch up." Sanval continued at her side, his long strides matching hers.

Archlis shook the Moaning Diamond at Fottergrim. His shouts were even louder than the weird cries of the gem. At the base of the wall, great fissures appeared in the stone. They widened as they spread upward, like some vine twisting up a tree trunk. Rock and dirt and fill and small pebbles popped out of the wall at increasing speed.

Ivy yelled, "The ground is breaking up!" Everyone picked up their feet and ran faster. Only Kid ignored her, running toward Archlis. Kid reached around the magelord's waist and plucked the purse from his belt. Kid's small horns gleamed in the sunlight where they poked up through his dark hair. Then

Kid aimed a deliberate and very hard kick at the magelord's knee. As his sharp little hoof connected, Archlis howled and stumbled forward.

"I can't believe this," Ivy muttered. She was still running as fast as possible away from the wall, but she watched Kid's brazen thievery over her shoulder. Sanval also twisted around to look and nearly tripped over a stone in the field. She caught him and steadied him.

"I think Kid wants to be a hero," Sanval explained as she pulled him upright.

"But now? When the world is falling on us?" Ivy panted.

"Keep moving!" Mumchance shouted over the rumbling of the earth beneath their feet. "Come on, Kid. Run, you little goat, run!"

Kid sprinted toward them.

"Told you," said Ivy. "He's fast."

Dust was spilling out of cracks in the wall, running down the stone in threads of gray like streams before a flood. The ground before Archlis was also starting to crack and cave in. The magelord had fallen to his knees, but he was still howling out his spell and waving the Moaning Diamond over his head.

Kid raced back toward the Siegebreakers, leaping lightly on his small hooves over the widening fissures in the ground, zipping around holes, holding the magelord's purse over his head and waving it.

As he neared them, he dug into the purse, pulled out a thick object, and held it overhead, laughing and waving his arms. When he reached Ivy's side, Kid waved the object at. It was Toram's spellbook.

"Don't stop," shouted the dwarf again. "Keep moving!"

Kid raced along at Ivy's side, his upturned face one wide grin.

"A book? You went back for a book?" Zuzzara thundered. The half-orc reached out, grabbed her sister's wrist, and rushed away. Gunderal's feet barely touched the ground. Her hair whipped around her head and across her face, enamel pins dropping like rain behind her.

"Let me go," she shrieked, "I want to see what Archlis is doing."

Zuzzara shouted, "He's bringing down that wall. Want to watch while it falls on you?"

The group was almost halfway across the field when Mumchance called a halt.

They stopped, bumping into each other, then turned around. The two bugbears were racing away in the opposite direction, Norimgic obviously limping from the recent landing in the field. The sun glittered on Sanval's former breastplate as Osteroric followed his brother away from the magelord.

"Look at that!" exclaimed Mumchance.

The wall was twisting now, and the goblins, orcs, hob-goblins, and barbarian archers were falling forward—a rain of timbers and screaming soldiers. A deep note sounded, the voice of stone twisted out of the earth, smothering even the ululations of the Moaning Diamond.

The ground completely crumbled beneath Archlis as the wall tilted out and rained stones and a shrieking Fottergrim down upon the screaming magelord. Archlis tried to roll out of the way, throwing one arm over his head. His other hand, extended and clinging to the Moaning Diamond, held the gem up as though he thought it would protect him.

Archlis dropped down through the widening hole in the ground, down to the twisting tunnels and the flooded levels of the ancient city. His robes whipping around him, and the last they saw of him was his sleeves fluttering above his upraised hands, and a quick flash of light. They heard a shrill scream that could have been Archlis or could have been the Moaning Diamond returning to its underground crypt.

A great roar shook the watchers as the ground in front of the wall caved in. The entire fortifications collapsed on the magelord. An enormous cloud of dust belched out of the fissure, a spiral of smoke twisted up to the sky, and then silence. Then there was another distinct popping sound, and a huge jet of water plumed into the sky and fell back to earth.

For a moment the Siegebreakers stood speechless, staring in shock. The water cascaded in high arches, like jets in a splendid castle fountain, then ran in spreading circles and grew from a pond into a lake.

"Not quite how I'd planned to bring that wall down," Ivy muttered.

"Shh," said Sanval, holding a finger to his lips. "I would not tell anyone that. It might make it harder to collect your fee." Then he smiled at her.

"Good plan," said Ivy with an answering smile.

"Told you that we would get a small lake on that side," said Mumchance with satisfaction. Gunderal smiled and nodded. Then she turned to look at her sister, lifting one delicate eyebrow in inquiry.

With a belly-deep orc laugh, Zuzzara shouted, "You're the best magic show in town, little sister!"

A shout sounded from the line of Procampur's army on the wooded hillside. Now the rumble of hooves shook the ground as Enguerrand's cavalry swept past them. More men went running after them, lines of mercenaries yelling as they swept over the rubble of the western wall and plunged into Tsurlagol.

Ivy shaded her eyes from the midday sun and looked toward Enguerrand's troops. She could see rubble and cavalry and foot soldiers, and in the swirl of dust she glimpsed goblins and the surviving barbarian archers disappearing between the ruins beyond the wall. They were running low, obviously hoping to hide before Enguerrand found them. As quickly as they had appeared, they were gone, and if she knew anything at all, she knew Enguerrand would never find them. But it was not her problem. Somebody had to lose. But today, it was not her.

The Siegebreakers looked at each other, very pleased. They had accomplished their mission.

"Just let the Thultyrl try to wiggle out of paying," said Ivy. Something like a contented purr underlaid her hoarse voice.

As the army of Procampur thundered past them to drive Fottergrim's troops out of Tsurlagol, Sanval looked after them longingly.

"You don't have a horse. And you're missing most of your armor," Ivy chided him, but she did it very gently. He appeared so very forlorn standing there in a torn, smoke-smudged shirt, rust-smeared breeches, and indescribably dirty boots, watching someone else ride off to glorious battle. Even his hair was standing up in every which way, dust and rust streaking his dark curls. Of course, Ivy thought he looked wonderful. After all, he was breathing, and he wasn't bleeding. And that was worth paying a temple a visit and giving thanks to any gods who wanted to listen. However, right now she needed to convince Sanval that this was a very good day for them all. "Look, you are with us," she said. "And when the dust clears, we are going to be the biggest heroes around here. After all, we tumbled the walls of Tsurlagol."

"Actually, it was Archlis who—" started Zuzzara.

"He didn't have a contract with the Thultyrl. And he was on the losing side," Ivy reminded her.

"And we are the winners," said Zuzzara. Gunderal giggled at her sister and patted her lovingly on the back.

"Oh yes," said Ivy, looking around and realizing that despite all the odds against it, they were all there, even Wiggles. "It has been a good day . . ."

Mumchance chimed in, "We were not standing under that wall . . ."

"When it fell down!" finished the others with a happy shout.

Then Ivy remembered a promise that she had made to herself, down in the dark. "And now I am going to find the handsomest healer that I can."

"But we must report to the Thultyrl," said Sanval. "And there are certain prayers and sacrifices that I should make at my family shrine. To give thanks to the gods." He gave a deep, gut-wrenching sigh. "And then I am going to have to go back to my tent and explain to Godolfin about my boots." He brightened up a little. "And get a clean shirt, and a bath."

"Good ideas," said Ivy. "And I have a couple more ideas that I may want to discuss with you later. Tell me. The gods attached to Procampur—are they fussy about attendance to proper times of worship and all that? Or are they just pleased to see you whenever you happen to stop by?"

"We have many gods and goddesses beneath the black-roof tiles," said Sanval, looking a little puzzled. "Some for a household, some for an occupation, some for the protection of a district. There are appropriate and inappropriate days to enter the temples, if that is what you are asking."

"And every black-roof Procampur temple probably has long lists of rules and regulations about what else is appropriate and inappropriate," guessed Ivy.

"Certainly. There is a proper order to such things, after all."

"Hmm. I may need to find some place a little less organized. Maybe over there," she said, glancing back over her shoulder at the fighters swarming over the broken wall of Tsurlagol.

The side with the shiniest armor looked like they were cutting through the remnants of Fottergrim's orcs with the ease of a hot knife through sealing wax.

"I don't understand," Sanval said.

"Wait until we meet with the Thultyrl. I don't suppose he'll have much interest in over there."

"Over there where?"

Ivy shrugged and pointed over her shoulder with her thumb. "There. What's left of Tsurlagol and what's left underneath. Might even find you better armor."

Sanval stared down at himself, noting sadly the bits of badly dented leg guards that were all that was left of his once-fine equipment. "Almost any armor would be better than this."

"Uh-huh. Digging rights, I'm thinking," Ivy said.

Sanval still looked confused, but asked no more questions.

The Thultyrl was going to be pleased, generous even. Ivy knew it. And his steward, that officious Beriall, would never notice one more little expense tucked into their bill. After all, she had so very many expenses to put down.

"Going to go find the best-looking healer in the camp," repeated Ivy, striding across the fields to the tents of Procampur. Every bone and muscle in her body ached. She had bruises on top of bruises. She did not care. She walked as if the world did not own her—better than that, she strode as if the world owed her one very large payment for a job well done.

CHAPTER TWENTY-FOUR

Tsurlagol was once again a free city, and Ivy stood before the Thultyrl in clean boots. Actually, extremely well-polished boots. While a terrifically handsome cleric soothed and mended all her aches and pains, the oddest little man by the name of Godolfin had arrived to confiscate all her clothing. He had returned with every item clean, brushed, mended, and polished to a bright gleam where possible. Then he had hustled her off to a private bath (really, it was amazing what Procampur nobles managed to drag to war with them), full of hot water and scented oils, so she felt personally polished. Her blonde hair was a bright golden banner, floating free from a high crest drawn up to the top of her head. And there wasn't a bruise anywhere on her body. The healing that she had gotten from the Procampur cleric with the lovely, lovely hands was worth every single coin that she had donated to his temple. And he had promised to say a couple of prayers for her too, just a few little thanks that she felt she owed the gods.

The rest of the Siegebreakers were looking equally well-scrubbed, she noticed when she met them outside the Thultyrl's pavilion. Even Wiggles looked like she had been washed and brushed. Sanval, of course, was beautifully turned out in a pure white linen shirt, well-fitted cloth breeches, and a different but gorgeously polished pair of boots. His hair had been combed down into a gleaming mass of black curls, but Ivy was pleased to note that one curl was still defiantly going in the opposite direction of its fellows.

Flanked by an honor guard drawn from the Forty, Ivy was led before the Thultyrl, who immediately chided her for not letting him know sooner about her plans to bring down the western wall of Tsurlagol.

She told him that they had been a bit busy that day or they would have sent him a message.

"So everything happened exactly as you planned?" questioned the Thultyrl.

"Certainly it did," Ivy said. If her plans had swerved off course a bit, what did that matter, and who needed to know? All ended at the desired outcome.

"Lady, we are most pleased," said the Thultyrl.

"And we are pleased that the Thultyrl is pleased," answered Ivy. She was, too. There was enough gold stuffed in the bottom of their bags to pay for a new barn roof and maybe a bit to spare. Still, the farm could use a few more improvements. A bigger kennel for Mumchance's dogs, thought Ivy, set very far from the house. Ivy looked back to the walls of Tsurlagol. The rubble of the western wall formed a ragged gap in the city's defenses. She smiled as she turned to the Thultyrl.

"Sire, can I assume that the treasury of Tsurlagol will cover the rebuilding of the city's defenses? After all, if the wall is left like that, the first wandering band of brigands or underpaid mercenaries . . ."

"Will dance right through the gap and set up camp in the center of the city," said Mumchance.

"And given the treaties that we hold with the city . . ." added Sanval.

The Thultyrl exchanged a fleeting look with his steward Beriall. It was a glance that said "this is going to be expensive." Ivy smiled very sweetly.

"This is what you get when you hire mercenaries," said Beriall, who had been a bit vocally bitter about the amount of gold that Ivy had already collected from him.

"Still, they have been most effective in carrying out your wishes," added the Pearl with an elegant roll of her shoulders that stopped just short of a shrug. She was dressed all in palest blue today, with her namesake jewels stitched into elaborate patterns on her long robe. Long metal guards of enameled silver covered her fingernails and winked in the sunlight when she gestured with one elegant hand.

"Quite so," said the Thultyrl. "Do we understand that you are wall builders as well as wall breakers?"

"Well, it takes a larger crew, but once we bring the harvest in, we could pull more people from our farm," stated Ivy. "We could hire from the city too. After a siege, there are always people needing work. That way you would be giving some of the wealth of Tsurlagol's treasury back to Tsurlagol's people. A popular thing to do, I would think."

"Does a Thultyrl need to be popular?" asked the Thultyrl.

"You already are," answered the Pearl. "But it would be a kindness to give some of Tsurlagol's wealth to those who labor hardest and best with their hands."

The Thultyrl nodded.

"Mimeri would love to travel," suggested Gunderal. "She is so good with stone spells."

Sanval cocked an eyebrow at Ivy, and she hissed back, "Youngest sister. She gets it from her mother's side of the family."

"And her mother was?"

"I'll explain to you later."

"I was thinking of flying buttresses on the west side," continued Mumchance, drawing plans in the dirt with the tip of his sword.

"Ground is too flat," said Kid, scuffing a few lines with an edge of his hoof.

"Good thinking. Dry moat," replied Mumchance. "Maybe two. At an angle. To baffle any stonethrower from coming close to the walls."

"Such tricks will not stop a wizard, dear sir," said Kid.

"A couple of glyphs. Something subtle." One old dwarf and one cloven-hoofed thief bent their heads together to contemplate the designs etched in the dirt, oblivious of the others watching them.

"Fascinating," said the Thultyrl. "Truly fascinating. Lady, you may bring Beriall your plans; we shall leave him as steward of Tsurlagol until the city is ready to govern itself. But we think that there are other matters which must be settled first."

One of those matters was a dripping trophy now prominently displayed before the Thultyrl's chair.

"And what do you want done with that?" sniffed Beriall. One of the Forty had dug out the big orc's body from the wreckage of the wall and hacked the head off, bringing it back as a trophy.

The Thultyrl bent forward, wincing a little from his healing wound, and stared into the dead eyes of the creature that had so disrupted his life. For the first time, the two were close enough to touch—the dead leader of the last remnant of the Black Horde, and the man who had never wanted to go to war. In profile, there was a certain grim resemblance between the two. It was, decided Ivy, the bare-toothed smile. Fottergrim's lips were curled up over his big fangs, as if he were still snarling insults from the top of the walls, and the Thultyrl's upper lip curled in an unconscious imitation of his foe.

"We will display it," declared the Thultyrl, straightening up. His face relaxed into the more charming smile that he typically wore. "A reminder to those who break the peace in Procampur or Tsurlagol."

The Pearl rustled forward. She signaled to a servant to remove the head.

"I will boil it down to the bone," stated the Pearl, as matter of fact as if she were reciting some recipe for stewed chicken, "and have it plated in silver with eyes of crystal. I will set it on a pillar of stone with a warning inscribed to all who doubt the strength of the treaties that tie Procampur and Tsurlagol."

"Oh very good," said the Thultyrl. "Put it on the side of the road exactly halfway between Procampur and Tsurlagol."

"As you wish," she agreed.

"And," he added, his glance sliding across Ivy and her group, "you'd best place some strong charms around it, or the next red-roof adventurer to pass it by is sure to steal it."

"Certainly," said the Pearl.

So it was done. The head of Fottergrim gleamed atop a pillar with a warning written below: "Fottergrim watches in vain for his rescue. So fall all who dare to assault Procampur's allies." Ivy passed the monument many times during her travels, and she always stopped to give the orc's silver skull a proper salute. If she tested the Pearl's charms against theft, she never admitted it to Sanval.

"And now there is the matter of the bugbear," continued the Thultyrl. Sanval groaned, although not very loudly.

"I wonder how a bugbear in the service of the enemy ended up wearing a piece of Procampur armor," said the Thultyrl.

Sanval turned bright red as the captured Osteroric was led forward by the youngest member of the Forty. The oblivious bugbear thanked Sanval for his breastplate, despite Sanval's best efforts to wave him off.

"It stopped an arrow," said Osteroric, displaying the dent. "That helped save my life!"

"Not exactly the use intended for an officer's armor," mused the Thultyrl, who pulled out a scroll from the basket beside his chair. Unrolling it, he hummed a little as he scanned its lines. "According to this section of the Grand Codex of laws," said the Thultyrl, "aiding the enemy is against the law, losing your armor when you are an officer of Procampur's army is against the law, failing to inform your Thultyrl about your plans is most definitely against the law, and so on and so forth."

Ivy stepped forward. After all, somebody needed to defend Sanval. The Thultyrl was having far too good a time teasing him, and she rather considered that particular form of amusement was reserved for her and her alone.

"I believe his actions were a credit to Procampur," she began and heard the others chorus their agreement.

"Still," said the Thultyrl with a slight smile, "his appearance when he returned to the camp was far less presentable than is considered proper for an officer of Procampur. Astoundingly so, I was told by several who saw him pass."

"Oh, yes, he definitely needs some extra polish, sir. Can't have an officer of Procampur that doesn't actually shine in the sun. Look at him today, not a scrap of shiny armor on him," said Ivy, looking Sanval up and down. "But he's not nearly as scruffy as the mercenaries in the lower camp. Still, I can see that the loss of uniform armor to a bugbear is a grave offense. Yet, he has done us some service, and some service to Procampur; for the defeat of Archlis was very much his doing." She gestured with her hands, a scale tipping up and then down again. "How about we pay his fines for him?" she concluded.

"That would be an acceptable solution and most comforting to have a little gold returned to us," murmured Beriall, who clutched the long list of claims given to him by Ivy. He kept pulling it out of his sleeve and checking it again. It was the most remarkably detailed document. Beriall intended to have it placed in its own niche in the library when he got home, in the section painted red and labeled "Fraud."

"Gold is such a common thing and most certainly not worthy of a discerning ruler like the Thultyrl," said Ivy. She heard Sanval choke behind her at her insolence, and Beriall give a little moan of disappointment. The Thultyrl only looked amused.

Ivy held up the battered spellbook that Kid had stolen from Archlis.

"It is one of a kind," she said. "A rare volume for one of the greatest libraries ever to be built."

Beriall rustled forward and took the book from Ivy's hand. He turned the pages slowly. "There are some interesting runes here," he said slowly. "Most unusual, sire." Pausing, he ran one plump finger down the center of the book. "And some missing pages."

"Well, it may have been slightly damaged dropping off a wall and so on," said Ivy.

"And what do you ask in return?" said the Thultyrl.

"Finely polished and fitted armor is fairly common in your city—the type of thing that every gentleman in Procampur usually has, am I right?"

The Thultyrl said nothing, but he looked suspicious.

"And the book is so very uncommon and thus more costly. And, really, it will have great historical significance in the years to come. Snatched from the villainous magelord, just before the walls fell on him. The sort of thing that bards write ballads about," Ivy reasoned. "Repaying the fine losing common Procampur armor could be seen as a partial payment on such a treasure."

"With the book being so exceptional," murmured Mumchance, not looking up from his design for a new wall for Tsurlagol.

"And gotten with a certain amount of fighting on our part," pointed out Zuzzara.

"And cunning," added Kid.

"It is a tome of magical mysteries," added Gunderal.

"Very old and truly unusual, most illustrious liege," finished Ivy, who kept her face serene. She waited. Sometimes, silence was the best bargaining tactic.

"Not another bill," sighed Beriall.

"We doubt that even the Siegebreakers would be so bold," said the Thultyrl with a significant look at the group.

"Of course not, sire," said Ivy, maintaining her poise. "We were just hoping to obtain some digging rights along with a pardon for Captain Sanval's unfortunate loan of armor to a bugbear."

Sanval's eyes widened. Ivy smiled at him and laid her finger casually against her lips for a second.

"Where the wall fell?" the Thultyrl asked.

"Yes, just the west fields would be fine," said Ivy. "We are seeking to recover lost gear, that sort of thing. But you know how it is after the end of the siege. Confusion, lawlessness, looting. We would not like to be accused of illegal looting. Just a nice short and simple legal contract, making anything that we recover legally ours. The law being so important and all."

The Thultyrl still looked suspicious, but he nodded and beckoned a scribe to him. A few quick lines were scribbled on a piece of parchment. Hot wax was applied to the bottom of the document and sealed with the Thultyrl's own stamp.

Ivy glanced at the oblivious Osteroric, another mercenary but one who had landed on the losing side. Sanval was also staring at the bugbear. That Procampur sensibility probably was pricking him, telling him that he had some type of debt of honor there. After all, the creature had let him escape often enough. Sanval glanced at her. She calculated the costs of feeding a bugbear and sighed. "And perhaps we could have a detail of prisoners? Like that one and any bugbear that looks like him. To help with the digging?"

"As you request," said the Thultyrl. "But the expense of their care shall be your responsibility."

"I assumed so." With luck, the stupid creature would run away as soon as they found his brother, but the friendly, eager look on his furry face did not bode well. He looked a lot like Wiggles when she got a new bone.

Beriall took the scroll from the scribe and personally handed it to Ivy. "Some day," he said to her, "I hope that you will come to Procampur and teach our young scholars about proper accounting. I think it might improve our city's wealth in ways that we never dreamed."

"I am flattered," said Ivy. "I am just a simple mercenary who knows how to make three and three add to six."

"Or even seven and eight." Beriall felt the bill tucked safely in his sleeve. It was an astonishing document, most worthy of preservation.

"You have our invitation to come to Procampur some day," said the Thultyrl, signaling forward the next group of petitioners. "Perhaps when you are done with your digging." And, for the first and last time in front of Ivy, he dropped the royal "we" and added in the eager tones of a young man who liked hunting as much as law-writing, "I would be interested in hearing more about your adventures underground."

"You are both generous and kind, sire," said Ivy. Then she gave the Thultyrl the most elaborate court bow that her bard mother had taught her, hand on heart in a sincere gesture of respect. When she straightened up, she saw that even Sanval looked impressed. She didn't know why he should stand there blinking like that. It wasn't as if she'd been raised by orcs in the wilderness; she had told him that she knew how to behave when she had to. Restraining the urge to whistle some startling and scandalous tune just to see if she could make the Procampurs' ears turn red, Ivy gracefully drew back and let the next group of petitioners claim the Thultyrl's attention.

CHAPTER TWENTY-FIVE

Outside the Thultyrl's pavilion, Ivy paused. The others hurried ahead to collect their shovels, sweeping Sanval away with them as they pulled him along in a swirl of amiable bickering stronger than any iron chain. Mumchance and Zuzzara were already arguing with Gunderal and Kid about the best way to dig down to the crypt full of jewels. Ivy just hoped they didn't say the words "Moaning Diamond" or "buckets of gems" too loudly or too often. She didn't want anyone else to get the idea that there was still treasure to be found in the ruins of Tsurlagol. Of course, she did have the only royal permit, signed by the Thultyrl himself, to dig and retain anything that she might find in the fields outside Tsurlagol's western wall.

Ivy watched them go, lit by that little aura of affection that always surrounded them in her view—even silly, fluffy Wiggles happily dancing around their ankles and doing her yippy best to trip them up and send them tumbling down the hill. She reflected with relief that she had gotten away with everything that she wanted. Truly amazing, she decided, and she wondered if she should waste any more coin on a temple tribute. After all, the gods and goddesses had plenty of worshippers and priests and temples stuffed with gifts, and it seemed silly to distract them from truly needy prayers with her minor concerns.

From where she stood, the broken wall of Tsurlagol was clearly visible, as were the swirls of Procampur's army and mixed mercenaries going down the harbor road, out into the wooded hills, and back to Procampur. There would be days of running down what was left of Fottergrim's horde, messages going out to all the little kingdoms in the Vast that another orc threat had been destroyed, and even more messages to dwarf enclaves and human cities that there was once again building work to be done in Tsurlagol.

The sun glinted on the pretty little lake that had spread out from the destruction of the western wall. In less than a day, the water level had already dropped considerably. Gunderal had speculated that the river was returning to its old course, now that her spell was fading away and no longer pulling it into the underground ruins. Ivy hoped that she was right. It would be easier to find the Moaning Diamond and that treasure-filled crypt if they were not underwater.

The Pearl rustled up to her. "You did very well," she said, startling Ivy out of her contemplation of treasure hunting beneath Tsurlagol.

"We took some chances and got lucky."

"Chance is less random than you believe."

"It is odd, you know, that the Thultyrl did not start healing until today," said Ivy, trying to fill the silence, glancing at the Pearl. "There must have been some poison in that wound to keep him so weak. Or maybe it was a spell. I wonder if Fottergrim had Archlis send some curse against the Thultyrl."

The Pearl's face was without expression—a proper face for a Procampur lady—as she watched the hubbub on the plain below. "The Thultyrl was supposed to die in his twenty-sixth year, after a great duel with Fottergrim at the base of that wall. Dead so young and with so much left unaccomplished. What do I care if Gruumsh wanted to raise another warlord to unite the orcs? My Thultyrl will build a great library. His codex will serve as a model for other cities and their lawmakers."

Ivy looked at her own hands, the wounds easily vanished by that handsome cleric in Procampur's hospice tent. Every bruise, every ache, even that odd little kink in her left big toe, dismissed by the strong magic held by Procampur's healers. She knew that even better healers would have been tending the Thultyrl throughout the summer. But the best of them probably could not combat the magic of a woman who had ruled the wizards of Procampur for three generations. Especially if they did not suspect what she was doing. "You kept his wound from healing so he could not take to the field. You changed his destiny."

"I spun his fate as I could," said the Pearl. "I also gave you what luck I could."

Remembering the Pearl's tap on her harper's token when the Pearl handed back her glove, Ivy glanced at the gauntlet tucked so carelessly into her belt. Had the Pearl changed the little silver leaf? Enhanced it with a little more luck than it usually carried? While she had been wearing it, a certain floating corpse had drifted into her grasp, and a sword thrown in desperation had lodged in a monster's throat, among other lucky coincidences.

"I should thank you then?" asked Ivy. "For all my luck?"

"Luck only goes so far," replied the Pearl. "It takes courage and it takes skill to use luck wisely."

Ivy bowed, a sincere acknowledgment of gratitude to a woman whose powers she barely comprehended. As far as she knew, very few could dice with destiny and win. "It takes a great deal of audacity to challenge the gods, even gods like Gruumsh," said Ivy, with real admiration in her voice.

"Oh, I am a red-roof girl," sang the Pearl very softly in her funny deep voice and winked at Ivy with a wicked smile.

"And we red-roof girls do have a soft spot for men from Procampur," said Ivy, startled into a moment of enlightenment that was less than polite.

"It's the armor," admitted the Pearl. "But it is more than that. It is their belief that they should be doing the right thing whenever they can. Their absolute belief in the value of law."

"Of honor."

"Of good," the Pearl concluded. "That is important. To have rulers who believe that good is the natural order of the world. That is what Procampur needs. And I am pledged to Procampur as truly as the Thultyrl."

"Even if good is not the natural order."

"How do you know that?"

Ivy remembered an argument about the Thieves Guilds with Sanval, and she concluded that every citizen of Procampur was just a little bit crazy when it came to topics like law, honor, and general good. It was an insanity that might just be catching. She rather hoped it would, or that at least it caught in places where she wasn't trying to run some scheme or other. If sieges went out of style, she would need to find a new line of work. "I wish him well, your Thultyrl. A long and a happy life writing laws and building his library."

"He will have it," promised the Pearl with the same placid tone that she used to describe how she would boil Fottergrim's head. "Even if I have to twist fate every day into a new pattern."

Sanval was waiting for Ivy when she reached her tent. All of their gear was right where they had left it. No thieves had dared disturb the pack of panting dogs that had distributed themselves on top of their bags and boxes. The whole pack greeted her return with thumping tails. Everyone but Sanval was rummaging through their stuff, gathering up tools and looking for food. The Thultyrl's people had fed them, but everyone was packing extra snacks into their clothing. After all, you never knew when you might drop down a hole and feel a little hungry.

Ivy started into her tent to look for a tin of sweetmeats that she thought she had left there. Sanval caught her arm as she passed and hastily let go when she stopped. The tips of his ears were slightly pink, but he also had that determined air about him. He was going to ask a question even if the answer was guaranteed to embarrass him. She was beginning to feel quite comfortable with those almost expressions of his.

"Why did you speak for me in front of the Thultyrl? Why rescue me so many times below ground? Why trade away that spellbook?"

She could have told him the truth. About how she could no more leave him behind than she could let Wiggles be eaten by a snake. Except, of course, her feelings for Sanval were even more complicated than that, and she needed some time to unravel them in her own mind. Once, when she was fifteen and setting out to be the most terrible and fearsome fighter in the Realms, she swore that she would never become too fond of anyone—she wasn't going to have some tragic love story turn her into a tree like her father. Except somewhere along the way, she had picked up all these odd attachments—more attachments than the Pearl had pearls. Furthermore, Ivy had a suspicion that her fondness for a certain noble character who owned an unbelievable amount of clean linen would be more troublesome than all those other attachments combined. It might even be the kind of feeling that made you put down roots in one way or another.

Still, Sanval had saved her life more than once, and she did owe him an answer. After all, running away had never got her anything but being stuck under a dead horse, as Mumchance pointed out all too often.

"Friends are important," she finally said.

He had a new expression on his face, one she hadn't seen before. Sort of pleased, sort of disappointed.

"It was the right and proper thing to do. You should appreciate that, being from Procampur." Ivy noticed that everyone had stopped hunting through their bags, and they were listening very casually to their conversation. "Anyway, Gunderal could not translate Toram's spellbook—even Kid could not puzzle out what language it was in. Some type of code, we think. Basically worthless to us, except for the maps, and we tore those out before we gave it away." Sanval's expression was shifting further toward the disappointed side. Ivy hurried on, wondering why the others were all rolling their eyes at her. "The Moaning Diamond, on the other hand, would be very useful to us. Certainly it would lower the risk of our trade, seal the deal as Siegebreakers, if you know what I mean. Mumchance is sure that he knows where to dig to recover it. Want to help?"

Of course, she knew that he would refuse. He was too proper a gentleman to go treasure hunting underground.

He startled her by nodding. "Well, why not?"

Zuzzara and Gunderal laughed at Ivy's expression.

"Pay up, pay up," said Zuzzara to Mumchance and Kid. "Told you that he was going to stick around."

"Just remember the rules, Ivy," said Gunderal.

"You brought him back, my dear," said Kid.

"You're responsible for him," added Mumchance.

"If he makes a mess," concluded Zuzzara.

"Him?" said Ivy staring at Sanval. All of his bright shining armor might be missing, and he might be wearing his second-best pair of boots, but he still appeared cleaner and neater than any fighter she had ever met. Procampur men!

Sanval stared back at her, looking carefully at the free-floating ponytail of golden hair waving on the top of her head and her generally well-groomed appearance. "How about I keep her cleaned up and looking like that?" Sanval asked the others.

"Could you?" asked Zuzzara.

"Would you?" asked Gunderal.

"It seems like a very fair trade, my dears," said Kid with his pointed little smile.

"I have to agree," said Mumchance.

"Hey!" said Ivy, because she was their captain, and she occasionally did deserve just a bit more respect (not that she ever got it). Still, she couldn't stop grinning.

Zuzzara, Gunderal, Mumchance, and Kid bent their heads together. There was a buzz of whispers.

"We would appreciate your help in keeping Ivy scrubbed," said Mumchance finally. "There's a spare room at the farm if you want to visit."

"I might," Sanval said directly to Ivy. "If you come to Procampur."

"I might," said Ivy with just the same emphasis. She cocked her head forward, got almost nose to nose, but he did not back down. He just narrowed his eyes and gave her that typical Sanval look of noble composure. It was, she had to admit, a very impressive and rather attractive expression. One of these days, she was going to figure out how to do it herself. After all, she was the daughter of a couple of heroes—a bard and a druid who rattled the world in their own way—and in some places that made her just as much a lady as Sanval was a gentleman. Still, she wondered how stuck he was on Procampur's views about people like herself. "What color are your roof tiles today?"

"I think," said Sanval with a faint but distinct smile, "I think that they should be red."

"Humans! This flirting back and forth is going to take forever. Come on," said Mumchance to the others. The dwarf whistled for Wiggles and the rest of his dogs. "Let's go for a run, puppies! We have some digging to do."

THE KNIGHTS
OF MYTH DRANNOR

A brand new trilogy by master storyteller

ED GREENWOOD

Join the creator of the FORGOTTEN REALMS® world as he explores
the early adventures of his original and most celebrated
characters from the moment they earn the name "Swords of
Eveningstar" to the day they prove themselves worthy of it.

BOOK I
SWORDS OF EVENINGSTAR

Florin Falconhand has always dreamed of adventure. When he saves the life of
the king of Cormyr, his dream comes true and he earns an adventuring charter for
himself and his friends. Unfortunately for Florin, he has also earned the enmity of
several nobles and the attention of some of Cormyr's most dangerous denizens.
Now available in paperback!

BOOK II
SWORDS OF DRAGONFIRE

Victory never comes without sacrifice. Florin Falconhand and the Swords of
Eveningstar have lost friends in their adventures, but in true heroic fashion, they
press on. Unfortunately, there are those who would see the Swords of Eveningstar
pay for lives lost and damage wrecked, regardless of where the true blame lies.

August 2007

BOOK III
THE SWORD NEVER SLEEPS

Fame has found the Swords of Eveningstar, but with fame comes danger. Nefarious
forces have dark designs on these adventurers who seem to overturn the most clever
of plots. And if the Swords will not be made into their tools, they will be destroyed.

August 2008

FORGOTTEN REALMS, WIZARDS OF THE COAST, and their respective logos are
trademarks of Wizards of the Coast, Inc. in the U.S.A. and other countries.
©2007 Wizards.

PAUL S. KEMP

"I would rank Kemp among WotC's most talented authors, past and present, such as R. A. Salvatore, Elaine Cunningham, and Troy Denning."
—Fantasy Hotlist

The *New York Times* best-selling author of *Resurrection* and The Erevis Cale Trilogy plunges ever deeper into the shadows that surround the FORGOTTEN REALMS® world in this Realms-shaking new trilogy.

THE TWILIGHT WAR

BOOK I
SHADOWBRED
It takes a shade to know a shade, but will take more than a shade to stand against the Twelve Princes of Shade Enclave. All of the realm of Sembia may not be enough.

BOOK II
SHADOWSTORM
Civil war rends Sembia, and the ancient archwizards of Shade offer to help. But with friends like these . . .
September 2007

BOOK III
SHADOWREALM
No longer content to stay within the bounds of their magnificent floating city, the Shadovar promise a new era, and a new empire, for the future of Faerûn.
May 2008

anthology
REALMS OF WAR
A collection of all new stories by your favorite FORGOTTEN REALMS authors digs deep into the bloody history of Faerûn.
January 2008

 FORGOTTEN REALMS, WIZARDS OF THE COAST, and their respective logos are trademarks of Wizards of the Coast, Inc. in the U.S.A. and other countries. ©2007 Wizards.

JEAN RABE

THE STONETELLERS

"Jean Rabe is adept at weaving a web of deceit and lies, mixed with adventure, magic, and mystery."
—sffworld.com on *Betrayal*

Jean Rabe returns to the DRAGONLANCE® world with a tale of slavery, rebellion, and the struggle for freedom.

VOLUME ONE
THE REBELLION

After decades of service, nature has dealt the goblins a stroke of luck. Earthquakes strike the Dark Knights' camp and mines, crippling the Knights and giving the goblins their best chance to escape. But their freedom will not be easy to win.

August 2007

VOLUME TWO
DEATH MARCH

The escaped slaves—led by the hobgoblin Direfang—embark on a journey fraught with danger as they leave Neraka to cross the ocean and enter the Qualinesti Forest, where they believe themselves free. . . .

August 2008

VOLUME THREE
GOBLIN NATION

A goblin nation rises in the old forest, building fortresses and fighting to hold onto their new homeland, while the sorcerers among them search for powerful magic cradled far beneath the trees.

August 2009

DRAGONLANCE, WIZARDS OF THE COAST, and their respective logos are trademarks of Wizards of the Coast, Inc. in the U.S.A. and other countries. ©2007 Wizards.